VALLEY OF THE FIREFLIES

EMMA FRASER

Storm
PUBLISHING

Ebook ISBN: 978-1-83700-374-7
Paperback ISBN: 978-1-83700-375-4

Cover design: Eileen Carey
Cover images: iStock

Published by Storm Publishing.
For further information, visit:
www.stormpublishing.co

ALSO BY EMMA FRASER

Writing as Morag Pringle

Rachel McKenzie Mystery Series

The Liar's Bones

The Highland Dead

The Final Truth

Dedicated to my friend Martha and the people of the Casentino Valley

But still I dream that somewhere there must be
The spirit of a child that waits for me.
The Poet's Journal: Third Evening – Bayard Taylor

In the middle of the journey of our life I found myself within dark woods
where the straight way was lost.
Inferno – Dante

PROLOGUE

The boy was woken by the low rumble of trucks. Excited, he slipped out of the bed he shared with his nonna and little sister, his bare feet hitting the cold floor. He waited for his eyes to adjust to the darkness before yanking on a jumper and shorts over his vest and pants.

Judging by the whine of the engines, the trucks were getting closer and there must be lots of them. No one in his village even owned a car. Maybe they'd let him clamber over their vehicles, sit up next to the driver perhaps! Maybe his friend from next door would join him.

Mama had lit an oil lamp and was standing in a pool of light by the window, her loose hair tumbling over her shoulders. He hurried over to stand next to her. Her hand reached down and grasped his.

Vehicle doors banged in the road above the village, and voices shouted orders to each other. The clatter of hobnail boots on stone almost drowned out the throb of idling engines.

Mama's sharp intake of breath made his heart thump painfully in his chest. 'Don't let it be!' she cried, making the sign of the cross on her chest.

It was the first time he'd heard fear in his mother's voice, and he didn't like it one bit. 'Wake your nonna. Your sister too,' she whispered urgently.

But the commotion had woken them already.

'What's happening? What's going on?' his nonna asked, shambling over to them, his half-asleep sister following close behind.

Mama gave a small shake of her head. 'We must get dressed,' she said.

Nonna nodded and retreated with his sister in tow.

Mama hunkered down in front of him and cupped his face between the palms of her hands.

'I need you and your sister to be safe, *figlio mio* – there are bad men outside. You have to hide in the flour chest where we keep the chestnuts now. Burrow as deep as you can. Stay there until I let you know it is safe to come out. Do you understand?'

His lower lip quivered. 'No, Mama, no. I don't want to! I want to stay with you.' His legs began to shake, and no matter how hard he tried he couldn't control the tremor in his voice.

She straightened. 'You're the man of the house now, and so you have to be brave and strong like your father was. For my sake and for your sister's.'

He didn't feel brave, and he wasn't very strong. Not really. Hot tears stung his lids.

'Please, Mama. I want to stay with you.'

Bang! Bang! Bang! His heart jerked with each thump of a fist on a neighbour's door. 'Get up and come out!' men's voices shouted in bad Italian.

'Do not argue with me!' his mother snapped. She'd never used that tone with him before. 'There's no time,' she continued, her voice faltering. She knelt before him again until their eyes were almost level. 'Oh, my boy, my beloved child.' She wiped away the tear rolling down his cheek with the pad of her thumb. 'Don't cry. Have courage!' A scream ripped through the air followed by a rat-a-tat-tat. There were more shouts and a long, drawn-out wail that made him shiver and his mother flinch. She exchanged a look with Nonna, who had dressed and fixed her hair in an unusually untidy bun at the back of her head. It made him feel even more afraid.

Mama pressed something hard into his palm. 'This is yours now,' she said, curling his fingers over it. 'My promise I'll always be with you. If they take me away, I won't rest until I find you. Keep it safe for me until then.'

Before he could ask what she meant, she straightened, gripped him by the shoulders, twirled him around and gave him a push. 'Take your sister! Now!'

When he went to grab his sister's hand, she pressed her face into Nonna's legs and clung to her. Nonna tried to prise her away, but it was no use.

'Let her stay with me,' Nonna said. 'They won't hurt an old woman and a little girl.'

The footsteps were getting closer. His mama's shoulders sagged. She shoved him towards the wooden chest. 'In you go. Hurry!'

He tried to burrow under the chestnuts as his mama lowered the lid, but it was too hard. He closed his eyes and clamped his fists over his ears, the object his mother had given him cutting in to his palm, his heart banging in his chest.

But nothing could block out the noises of gunfire, of doors being broken down, of men and women protesting, crying and screaming, of children wailing, and of more gunfire. The horrible sounds coming from outside seemed to go on forever. Eventually it grew quiet. Then the door of his house crashed against the wall, and boots clattered on the wooden floor. He heard wardrobe doors being flung open, and the trapdoor to the cellar being lifted and slammed shut. He held his breath as the footsteps came to a stop right beside his hiding place.

A shout from outside, and the steps receded. The trucks started up, the vibrations running through his body. Another silence. He started to cry and pressed his hands over his mouth in an attempt to smother his sobs. Was it safe to come out? No. Better to wait until his mother came to find him.

Then, terrifyingly, he heard returning footsteps. Someone was in his house again.

The footsteps stopped in front of his hiding place. He was too scared to breathe.

Whoever it was stood in silence until, slowly, the lid of the chest began to open.

ONE

AMELIA

All the reports said that Italy was cooler than usual this March, but by the time Amelia arrived at the castello she'd sweated so much during the terrifying ninety-minute drive from Florence that her hands were slippery on the steering wheel, her muscles taut with tension.

A wave of exhaustion swept over her. But she'd made it. Over the last ten months she'd hardly budged from her father's sofa, and right now she would have given anything to be back there. Reminding herself why she had to leave, she blinked the grit from her eyes and stepped out of the car. The sunshine was blinding. Back in Scotland it was the tail end of winter, with short, overcast days. Stretching the kinks from her back, she shielded her eyes with her hand and took in her first sight of Castello di Porciano – her home for the next few weeks. It was certainly impressive – not unlike the watchtowers or keeps of Scotland, but considerably larger and higher and topped with crenelated ramparts.

She'd grabbed the offer of a job – to help establish a museum in the castello – like a lifeline. The pay wasn't much, but it included board and lodging.

A breeze rustled the leaves of a chestnut tree, and her skin prickled. All of a sudden, she had the weirdest sense that she'd been here before. As if she'd stood on this very spot, looking up at exactly what was in front of her. She gave herself a mental shake. It was, of course, complete and utter nonsense.

A woman emerged from the shadow cast by the castello and hurried towards her. 'Hello, there! You must be Amelia.' She came to a panting halt and thrust out her hand. 'Welcome to Porciano. I am Beatrice.' She pronounced each syllable separately and with emphasis. *Beh-a tree-che.*

The contessa was not what Amelia had expected. Her grey hair was pulled into a knot at the back of her head, and she was wearing a pair of trousers and a simple blouse. Until now Amelia hadn't realised that, throughout their email exchange, she'd imagined a woman bejewelled, tall and slim with a haughty expression.

'It's good to be here,' Amelia replied, more from habitual politeness than honesty. Yet, she surprised herself by finding it was almost true. There was no pity in Beatrice's cool blue-grey eyes, only curiosity and anxiety.

'I am so sorry, Amelia. I've been trying to get you on your mobile all morning but either I couldn't get a signal – it's hopeless around here – or then when I did manage to get one your phone went to voicemail.'

Amelia's sleep-deprived brain struggled to make sense of what she was saying. What had been so important that the contessa had been trying to contact her? Knowing she needed all her concentration to cope with the drive through the mountains, she'd switched off her phone.

'Is there a problem?' Had one look at Amelia been enough to change the contessa's mind about employing her? Before Amelia had left Scotland, she'd decided that if she were to start her life anew she might as well look different too. More than anything she wanted to leave the old Amelia behind – cast her off like a snake shedding its skin. But if she'd thought cropped hair and the dark screw-you red she'd dyed it would make her appear fearless instead of shattered, she'd been wrong. Given she'd taken the scissors to her hair herself, and that the dye had come out of a packet, she looked more like a little girl lost than she had before.

'I have to go to America,' the contessa rushed on. 'My daughter has just had a baby. She wasn't due for another four weeks, but there was a problem with her blood pressure, so they delivered her early by caesarean section.' That explained the anxiety. 'She's fine,' she added, as if Amelia had expressed alarm or distress, 'but I promised I'd be there when the baby was born. She needs help with the other children. I'm so sorry. I hadn't expected to go until after your work here was finished.'

A familiar ache blossomed behind Amelia's ribs, and she felt saturated with sadness. Mothers and daughters.

'Of course, you should be with her. When do you go?' she asked.

'This evening. It was the first flight I could get.'

'And you hoped to contact me to tell me not to come?'

'I hoped we could delay your arrival until I returned, yes.'

Anxiety clawed at Amelia's chest. It had taken a superhuman effort to get here, and she desperately wanted to stay. She needed this job. She couldn't – wouldn't – move back in with Dad. It would destroy him. She couldn't return to Cove either, but that left her with nowhere else to go. Besides, the very thought of being on her own with nothing to occupy her filled her with horror. She dipped her hand under the collar of her T-shirt and touched the pendant her father had given her before she'd left, and took a steadying breath.

'I could make a start while you're gone?' she suggested.

Beatrice hesitated, apparently sizing her up and giving the offer some thought. 'Almost everything you need to know about the castello and its history is in the emails I sent you. I was counting on having the museum open for the start of the tourist season, and you *are* perfect for the role,' she said, reaching a decision. 'Your previous employers gave you a glowing reference. And of course there is the family connection.'

The family connection was pretty tenuous, but, if it satisfied the contessa, who was Amelia to disagree?

'But will you be all right here on your own?' Beatrice continued, a frown puckering her brow.

'Absolutely. I'm used to my own company.'

'If you're sure,' she said, looking relieved. She glanced at her watch again. 'There's just enough time before I have to leave to give you a quick tour.'

The contessa ushered Amelia up a short flight of stone steps and through an enormous wooden door – gouged and cracked as if by swords or axes – and into a room. Only a trickle of daylight came in through two high, narrow windows.

Beatrice flicked a switch, and a single bulb glowed with barely enough light to make a difference. She waited for their eyes to become accustomed to the gloom before she spoke again. 'This is the ground floor. It's mainly used as a basement for storage' – she gave Amelia a quick smile – 'although in the past it would have held a prisoner or two. Once, it was the first line of protection for the castello. That's why the windows are narrow. Archers could shoot arrows but attackers couldn't get in.'

In the middle of the room was an iron cart, an anvil and, along one wall, several rows of boxes, piled three high. A rusty spade was propped in a corner beside a stepladder. Amelia jumped as a figure materialised out of the murky light. Shorter than either Beatrice or herself, whoever it was stood stock-still, observing them.

Following Amelia's gaze, the contessa laughed. 'It's a suit of armour that was found in the rubble years ago. I keep him here as an informal guard. I call him Piero, after Piero the Gouty, Lorenzo de' Medici's father. Not very respectful I know, but it makes him seem less scary. He used to terrify me as a child.' She nodded towards an old-fashioned lift. 'My parents had this installed when they renovated. They were worried that as they got older they wouldn't be able to climb the stairs to their living quarters. It's a bit temperamental and goes off when the power does – which happens not infrequently, particularly when there's a storm. Come on, let me show you the rest.'

The contessa hustled her up a flight of stone steps and into a light-filled room.

Three large glass display cases stood in the centre of the room, each filled with various objects.

'Those artefacts were found during the renovations,' the contessa said, gesturing towards the cases. 'My mother offered the best pieces to the Uffizi, but they already had more than they knew what to do with. A few years ago, I had the idea to create a little museum in the castello. We don't use this floor, and it makes the loveliest setting, don't you think?'

'It does,' Amelia replied honestly. Without the distraction of modern furniture, the fine carving on the arches and stonework was accentuated, the connection with the past emphasised.

Amelia had barely enough time to draw breath, before Beatrice led her over to the other side of the room, up another flight of stone steps and into another spacious room.

'This is the original grand hall, where previous generations would have lived their public lives and where Dante might well have written some of his most famous work. He stayed here when he was in exile. Did you know that? We call it Dante's Hall in his honour.'

Amelia did. She'd done her research. A frisson of delight coursed through her at the realisation she might well be standing where the famous thirteenth-century writer had stood.

'Dante's association with the Castello di Porciano is one of the reasons it has to be saved for future generations,' Beatrice continued.

Behind Amelia, and close to the rafters of the hall, was a wooden gallery, above which was another window with a stone seat set into its recess. As far as Amelia could see, there was no way of accessing the gallery. She turned back to Beatrice and raised an enquiring eyebrow.

'We think it was once a musicians' balcony and that there must have been a flight of steps leading to it,' Beatrice said. 'One day I'll look at reinstating them.'

Amelia's head filled with images of musicians holding flutes, playing to a room of aristocratic Italian women in long velvet dresses tied beneath their breasts with belts of silver, their sleeves swooping towards the ground, their hair braided with gold. In a separate group, men lounged against the wall, swords sheathed at their waists. It was as if the ghosts of the castle had steeped into its very stones and gathered around her. She smiled inwardly; her mother had always said Amelia had a vivid imagination. Imagination or not, once again Amelia had the strange sensation that she knew this place, that she was meant to be here.

'I have some ideas on how we can attract visitors,' Amelia said, dragging her attention back to Beatrice. 'We could do a board with a large transverse drawing of the castello, each floor peopled by figures of the period, showing how they were dressed and how the rooms were used.' She could see it all in her mind's eye. 'And perhaps another board on the opposite wall, in Italian as well as English, explaining the key people and moments in the castello's history while referring to the broader history of the Casentino region, putting the castello in context. Maybe have another one entirely dedicated to Dante. I could also draft a brochure to send out to tourist information.'

'Excellent suggestions.' Beatrice smiled, then frowned again. 'Are you sure about staying alone? The castello can seem... a little empty, spooky even, when one is here on one's own.' She gave a little laugh. 'Once I thought I heard snoring coming from outside my bedroom door. Thought Piero the Gouty had come for a visit. Turns out a barn owl had got in through a window.'

Amelia managed a smile. 'I'm not easily frightened.' What could possibly scare her now?

The next flight of stone stairs took them to what could only be the contessa's private living quarters, judging by the personal touches. Similar in size and proportion to the room below, it was furnished with comfortable armchairs and sofas arranged around a fireplace identical to the one in Dante's Hall, but clearly recently used. A dark wood table took up most of one side of the warm, welcoming space.

To Amelia's right was an open, full-length window. She stepped over to it and looked out to a cluster of houses beyond the ruined wall of the castello. Only a hip-high railing stood between the window and the ground. Suddenly she was gripped by a powerful sense of danger, undercut with overwhelming sadness and fury. Her head spun, and she clutched at the railings, convinced that if she didn't she was going to tumble over and down to the ground.

'That's the village of Porciano you are looking at,' Beatrice's voice cut through the noise in Amelia's head – no doubt caused by lack of sleep. She'd been awake since four, and tiredness – along with the effort of getting here – was taking its toll. Moreover, she'd barely eaten in the last twenty-four hours.

She breathed deeply, and focussed on the rows of small topsy-turvy houses with the typical terracotta roofs and ochre walls of the region, until slowly the dizziness passed.

'The village is almost as old as the castello,' Beatrice continued, and came to stand next to Amelia. 'It was built to house the servants and farmers that served the conti. A few locals still live there all year round, mostly the older generation. The rest of the houses are now used as second homes by Florentines in the summer when their owners wish to escape the heat of the city.'

An arch opened up from the main living area to a small kitchen with a balcony – large enough for two people to stand on at a push – with a view of the densely forested hills behind the castello.

'The kitchen has everything you might need,' Beatrice said, opening and closing the cabinet doors. 'There's enough food to keep you going for a day or so. Anything else you need you'll find in Stia.' Given the job was expected to take anywhere between four and six weeks, Amelia imagined several trips to town would be required.

Yet another flight of stairs took them past a mezzanine level lined with floor-to-ceiling bookcases and up one more, even narrower, set of steps. At the end of a corridor, the contessa opened a door with a flourish. 'I thought this could be your bedroom.' She stepped aside to let Amelia enter first.

The room was pleasantly and simply furnished, the single bed made up with blankets rather than a duvet, a small table on either side of the bed, and a chair and desk by an arched window. Despite its monastic simplicity, it had everything Amelia could possibly need, and she liked it.

'We call this the Warrior Abbess's room.'

Beatrice walked over to a heavy mahogany bureau and rearranged the box of tissues on top.

'We think it was her favourite place to sleep.'

'Warrior Abbess? Not two words I'd normally put together. She sounds interesting.'

'She was. Very. She even had a children's book written about her. There's a copy somewhere in the castello.'

'In which case,' Amelia said, 'she must be included in the display and brochure.'

'I'll leave you to explore the ramparts on your own,' Beatrice said with an apologetic smile. 'I wish I had more time to spend with you. There is so much more of the history you should know. There's always the internet, I suppose, although you'll have to go down to Stia or Pratovecchio to get online.'

Her impatience to be on her way was evident. But before Beatrice left, Amelia had a couple of questions of her own.

'I'm curious to know how your mother knew my grandmother,' Amelia asked, as they retraced their steps to the sitting room.

'I believe they were old friends. In the thirties many Brits made their homes in Florence. We called them the Anglo-Fiorentini. Most of them left when war broke out but stayed in touch with their Italian friends and continued to do so all their lives.' She gave Amelia a puzzled look. 'But doesn't your father know how they were connected?'

'No. I only found out recently that he was adopted from Italy just after the war. Apparently, his adoptive parents never liked to speak of the time before they took him in, and it seems neither did he.' It had been a shock to Amelia. Although her father spoke fluent Italian, even taught it at university until he'd retired, she'd assumed he'd learned it as a second language. Learning more about her father's childhood had been an added incentive to take this job. Amelia took out a photograph of her grandparents and father from her handbag and held it out to the contessa. 'This is them. My dad must've been about five when this was taken.'

Beatrice took the photograph, studied it, and shook her head. 'I'm sorry, I don't recognise them.' She handed the photo back. 'My parents and their friends were part of the war generation. You must have been born when he was – er – what is the correct expression? Getting on?'

'Forty-five. He's seventy-five now. My mother was his second wife and more than fifteen years younger.'

Beatrice nodded, as if something that had been bothering her now made sense. She sighed. 'The war destroyed so many homes and left many orphans. Most were taken in by their extended families – if they could be traced. But too many lived out their childhoods in orphanages. Some were adopted – and not always by Italians – as your father must have been. Things were chaotic in those days. People wanted to help care for children who had no one, and unless anyone objected' – she gave another elegant shrug of her shoulders – 'better surely than being brought up in a children's home? His life seems to have turned out well. He became a professor after all. Quite an achievement.'

'He wasn't related to your family in any way then?'

The contessa's eyebrows shot up. 'As far as I know, the only connection was the friendship between his adoptive parents and mine. I'm an only child, as was my mother.'

Amelia undid the pendant her father had given her before she'd left, and passed it to Beatrice. It was made of battered silver, and at one point had been sheared roughly in two, so was really, oddly, only half a pendant.

'The only memory my father has of his past is this. He remembers a woman giving it to him and saying it was a promise she'd come back for him. She never did. Does it mean anything to you?'

The contessa considered it for a moment, turning the pendant over between her fingers. 'All I can tell you is that, in medieval times, mothers used to take the babies they couldn't afford to feed to the Ospedale degli Innocenti in Florence. They'd leave them on a stone turntable, placed in the wall for exactly that purpose, along with half a coin or other trinket. When they were able to care for their child, they'd bring the half they'd kept to the priests, who would compare it to the half left with their child. If it matched exactly, they'd release the child back to the mother's care.'

Was it possible the woman her father vaguely remembered had been his birth mother? Perhaps she'd intended to come back for him but had been prevented from doing so? In which case, why? It had been a long shot, but Amelia had hoped the contessa would have known.

'I believe that's St Francis of Assisi on the engraved half,' Beatrice continued. 'The monastery where he lived out his days is a couple of hours' drive north. You should go and see it if you get a chance.'

She passed the pendant back to Amelia who refastened it around her neck. 'Do you think my father's birth mother might have links to Tuscany?'

'I really couldn't say,' Beatrice replied. 'During the war, orphans came here from all over – especially Rome and Milan, which endured the worst of the bombing. I'm sorry I can't be more helpful.' Beatrice clearly sensed Amelia's disappointment. 'It's important to know who your family is.' She lifted a photograph from the sideboard and looked at it for a moment, a soft smile on her face, before holding it out to Amelia. 'My parents,' she said. The photo was of an American officer in uniform, holding the arm of a woman in a wedding dress.

The newlyweds' heads were turned towards each other, the bride's smile adoring and the groom looking at her as if he couldn't believe his luck. It brought memories of Amelia's own wedding day flooding back. She swallowed the lump in her throat and passed the photograph back. 'They were a very good-looking couple.'

But it was the photograph next to the one of Beatrice's parents that caught Amelia's attention and held it. The woman in it was even more striking than Beatrice's mother. They had the same fine-boned features – although this woman's mouth was larger, and there was a definite imperious tilt to her chin. Dressed in a long evening gown caught up at the side of her waist with a large bow, she stared directly, almost defiantly, into the camera. Even frozen in time there was an energy about her that made it seem as if she were about to step out of the photograph and talk to Amelia. Yet there was a wistfulness in her expression that made Amelia think she wasn't happy.

'Who is the woman in the other photograph?' Amelia asked. 'The one in the evening dress?'

'That's Flavia. Her parents died when she was a child, so she came to live with my mother and my grandparents.'

Beatrice was quiet for a while, apparently lost in her memories. 'Some of Flavia's belongings are still here in a trunk. Mainly clothes, I think. My mother could never bring herself to go through them.' She looked hopefully at Amelia. 'I don't suppose you would care to do it for me? I know it's not really part of your remit, but...'

'I'm happy to. I'd rather be kept busy.' The busier the better. Amelia couldn't remember the last time she thought about something apart from her own pain for more than a few minutes.

'The trunk is in a corner of the basement. It has her initials on the lid. "FC". She took my parents' last name when she came to live with them.'

'What would you like me to do with the contents?'

'There will be dresses from the thirties and forties: evening gowns, furs, perhaps some costume jewellery. If any of the clothes are still in reasonable condition perhaps I could give them to a second-hand shop.'

Amelia had an idea. 'If any of the dresses are in a decent condition, why don't we make them part of the display in the museum? I think visitors would like that. They would give a sense of more recent history.'

Beatrice's eyes lit up. 'That's an excellent proposal. I don't know why it didn't occur to me. Some of them are probably made by well-known designers.'

'I'm not sure I'd recognise a designer dress if I saw one,' Amelia admitted.

But the contessa had the bit between her teeth. 'If you find any that look as if they might be one-offs, you could take them to the costume museum at the Pitti Palace in Florence. I know the woman in charge. Signora Fiorini.' She rummaged in her handbag for a small address book, flicked through the pages, scribbled on a piece of paper and handed it to Amelia. 'This is her email address. If you do come across a gown that's in decent condition, email Signora Fiorini and let her know I suggested the two of you meet. She'll be able to tell you if they are by someone well known and, if so, who the designer was.' She was clearly delighted to have something different to add to her museum. She looked at her watch again, frowned and lifted her bag and keys from the table. 'Forgive me, but I really must be on my way. If I leave any later, I'll get caught up in the traffic and it'll take me twice as long to get home to Florence. I still have packing to do. I did mention that we tend to use the castello mainly as a weekend retreat? I love Porciano, but it is a little out of the way. My husband and I are still very involved with our lives in Florence.' Anxiety puckered her brow. 'I really am sorry to abandon you like this.'

'I shall be perfectly all right.' Amelia realised that, unconsciously, she'd been mimicking Beatrice's precise way of speaking. 'It's not as if I won't be safe in a castle!' She attempted a laugh that even to her own ears sounded a little forced.

'If you need anything, email me. I only use my phone for emergencies when I'm abroad. Speaking of which, it's almost impossible to get a signal inside the castello because of the thickness of the walls, but if you go up to the ramparts, or outside, you can usually get some sort of connection. If for any reason you can't get hold of me, I have a tenant in one of the cottages in the village – Kelly – who'll be able to help you. She divides her time between here and Florence. She's there now, but I'll phone her when I get home to ask her to come over and introduce herself when she returns.'

As they descended into the gloom of the lower floor, Beatrice gestured towards the boxes piled up against the wall. 'These contain the books I'd like you to catalogue, many of which are very old. Those with illustrations, or any you believe to be first editions, even if you aren't sure, set to one side. I have someone who will make a further study of those. My friend Benedetto has some expertise in these matters. There are too many for him to go through individually though, and he'll only be interested in any that might be of significance.' Another glance at her watch.

They stepped out into the bright sunshine, and Beatrice handed Amelia an old-fashioned key, almost the size of her palm. 'This is for the front door. Please keep it locked at all times even when you are inside. Also be very careful not to lose it. It's the original, and there isn't a copy. Oh, and Benedetto might call to see how you're getting on.'

Amelia hoped neither he nor Kelly would drop by any time soon. As distracting as the last hour had been, pretending to be normal had taken every ounce of her energy.

Beatrice gave Amelia a final anxious look, opened her mouth as if she were going to say something, but instead waved and, with a crunch of gravel, drove away.

Amelia removed her small suitcase from the boot of her rental and went back inside. Without the contessa's larger-than-life presence the castello felt empty. Far, far too big for one person.

Amelia took the lift back to the living area and dumped her suitcase in the sitting room. She checked her phone for messages. None. At least not that had been downloaded. She could go onto the ramparts to check, but even the thought exhausted her. Her eyes still felt gritty, her head as if it were filled with cotton wool. Everything would have to wait until she'd had some sleep.

TWO

When Amelia woke up, for a blissful minute she didn't have a clue where she was. Then memory slammed into her. Where she was, and why.

As grief threatened to engulf her, her fingers sought out the pendant her father had given her. She wouldn't be here if it hadn't been for him. She'd moved in with her father when he'd found her teetering on the edge of the cliff outside her home in Cove, and she had more or less taken up residence on his sofa, hardly budging, sometimes not even to take a shower or get dressed. So when the letter had come from the contessa, asking him if he knew anyone who was both fluent in Italian and a professional researcher, it felt like the Fates were intervening. She mustn't waste this opportunity. She flung the bedcover aside.

She had to have been asleep for a couple of hours at least. Her throat was as dry as a camel's hoof, and she badly needed caffeine to dispel the thickness in her head.

Downstairs she put coffee on to brew. While she was waiting for the water to boil, she picked up the book of Dante's *Inferno* and turned the pages, pausing at one with the illustration of the journey through hell. In his epic poem, Dante treks through the nine levels of hell over the course of three days – from Good Friday to Easter Sunday – before finally emerging on the other side. It is a poem filled with ranting, weeping and tormented figures, of demons and fighting lovers, of traitors eating the brains of their victims. Had he really written part of it within this very castello? Had he been tormented by loss too?

Her eyes came to rest on a figure trapped from the waist down in a sea of ice – unable to move forward or backwards – stuck in the lower levels of hell for all eternity. That's where she'd been these last ten months. Trapped in hell. She closed the book and set it back down on the table.

Coffee in one hand and a biscotto in the other, she headed for the ramparts, crossing the mezzanine and climbing a spiral of stone steps, so narrow her shoulders bumped against the walls, passing the floor of bedrooms tucked into the eaves, and up yet another flight to a heavy oak door. Intriguingly, the door was locked with an old-fashioned key, similar to the one for the front door, and Amelia was only able to turn it with difficulty. She wondered why the contessa felt the need to keep it locked from the inside. Surely she wasn't worried anyone could enter the castello from above? There were no outdoor steps – at least not that Amelia had noticed – to the top of the tower. Habit, perhaps. Taking one more short flight of stone stairs, she emerged on the ramparts.

It was a breathtaking view. Miles of rolling Tuscan hills, dotted with villas partly shaded by cypress trees, stretched into the distance. There was an almost unearthly quiet – apart from bird-song, tinkling bells in the distance and the occasional muted rumble of a car.

Further off, Amelia could see Stia and Pratovecchio: once two distinct towns, but recently merged into one.

A road wound its way down in a series of hairpin bends until disappearing out of sight. As she sipped her coffee, a truck pulled over and a man got out and surveyed a field, hands on hips, before climbing back into his vehicle. Silence fell as he drove away. In the far distance another tower, similar to this one, stood on top of a hill. Having studied a map of the area, Amelia surmised it was the Castello di Poppi, which, along with the castelli at Porciano and Romena, had been owned by Beatrice's ancestors.

Once more Amelia's head was filled with images. This time it was of a soldier dressed in armour. He was standing close to her, scanning the fields and valleys, checking for unwelcome visitors. Amelia could almost hear the clash of steel, the blowing and stamping of horses, the light voices of women as they went about their work, the whisper of silk on silk. Just then the breeze lifted, and she felt a sensation like a breath on the back of her neck – almost as if someone had been standing behind her whispering into her ear, lightly touching her shoulder as they did so. The hairs on her arms stood up, but as the wind died down the weird sensation disappeared with it. Just her overactive imagination again. A brief smile crossed her lips. Perhaps a medieval castle wasn't the best place for a woman haunted by her own ghosts?

She sent a quick text to her father, letting him know she'd arrived safely, but keeping the fact she was alone in the castello to herself. He would only worry if he knew.

She used the creaking lift to get to the basement. The sight of the boxes – so many of them – was overwhelming. Spotting a trunk – the sort often seen in old films being taken onto ocean liners, and with the initials 'FC' embossed in gold leaf on the lid – Amelia turned her attention to it instead. Flavia's belongings. Unable to resist, Amelia crouched down and opened it. The reek of mothballs and the faint scent of violets spilled out. The trunk was full of tissue-wrapped clothes, and she carefully lifted each one out.

There were dresses from the thirties, and others, plainer and – judging by their style – from the forties. The evening gowns were made from chiffon and silk, trimmed with beads or lace or ribbon, sometimes all three. Each one was in perfect condition. Beatrice would be pleased. There were also several evening bags: Amelia's favourite was a small black one decorated with feathers. And shoes. One pair in particular, with a cork wedged heel, looked modern. Evidence that fashion always came back around. Amelia tried one on. It was a couple of sizes too big. She held one of the dresses against her. It trailed on the ground. Flavia must have been quite a bit taller than her. She draped it over a box of books.

Near the bottom of the trunk was a heavily patterned velvet coat. Embroidered on the back was a pair of urns or, alternatively, depending how a person looked at it, the profiles of two women facing each other. Even with her limited knowledge of designer fashion, Amelia knew it had to be a one-off. Her last discovery was a gown in deep-blue silk with a bow at the side. Excitement raced along her spine. She was sure this was the one Flavia was wearing in the photograph upstairs.

Amelia held it to her face, the delicate material slithering through her fingers, and breathed in the scent that still clung to the fabric. Immediately she saw Flavia. It was as if she could reach out and touch her and she'd be solid flesh beneath her fingertips. She was swirling around the room, her face alight with happiness. A man was there too, watching Flavia with the same look of possessive delight as Cameron once looked at Amelia. The man reached for Flavia and, as they collapsed onto a sofa, she buried her head in his neck and his arms tightened around her. She peeked out from under his arms, and her eyes and Amelia's met. She even had the uncanny feeling she could talk to Flavia and she would answer.

Amelia blinked and the image vanished. But she couldn't shake the feeling that Flavia had been right there in the room with her. And not only that, but that Flavia was in danger. *It's only your imagination*, she told herself. *She's not real. This has happened to you before. It is all in your head.*

But God, it felt so real. And scary. Was she hallucinating? Becoming unwell again? She gasped for air, her heart beating so hard and fast it felt as if it was going to explode. *Please, no. Not a panic attack.* She'd had several in the weeks after the accident, but none over the last couple of months. She forced herself to take deep breaths until the horrible feeling she was having a heart attack passed.

When her breathing – and heart rate – was under control again, Amelia began to fold the dress with the intention of returning it to the trunk. But before she could, she noticed a small leather pull at the base. When she tugged, it lifted easily, revealing a number of leather-bound notebooks. Next to them were two boxes: one of tin; the other larger and made from walnut, inlaid with pieces of coloured glass or semi-precious stones; and a roll of papers.

She lifted the notebooks out one by one. Like the trunk, they were monogrammed with the initials 'FC'. Leaving them aside for the time being, Amelia turned her attention to the tin. Inside there were several black-and-white photographs of balls and dinners, evenings around a piano, as well as several taken in the countryside of picnics or walks by a river. Amelia recognised Flavia in some, Beatrice's mother in others; several had both women.

She needed more light. Recalling a standard lamp and chair she'd noticed on the mezzanine, she used the lift to bring them down to this floor. Easier, she thought, than dragging everything upstairs.

When everything was arranged to her satisfaction, Amelia turned back to the trunk and removed the walnut box. She hesitated, pretty sure this wasn't what Beatrice had in mind when she asked her to go through Flavia's belongings. But curiosity got the better of her, and she tried the lid. To her frustration it was locked, and a quick, futile rummage through the trunk suggested the key had either been lost or put somewhere else for safekeeping. Instead she unrolled the papers. They were drawings, mainly in charcoal, sometimes in pencil, all with the initials 'FC' in the corner. The first few were sketches of statues – Michelangelo's *David* among them – the others were replications of famous paintings Amelia recognised from the Uffizi. They weren't bad, but unformed, as if the artist was unsure, in the process of learning her craft. As Amelia looked through them, the sketches turned to more everyday scenes. One was of a group of women in a large, open hall or gallery, their backs towards the artist as they themselves worked at easels. Others were of village life: a girl lying in a field of poppies, her arms tucked behind her head as she grinned up at the artist; men working in a field, a horse and cart in the background. There were city scenes too: a man polishing the shoes of another as he sat perched on a throne-like chair, reading a paper; a grey-haired nonna selling posies of flowers; smartly dressed women strolling arm in arm; people riding bikes; a man, his posture stooped in defeat or boredom, holding a pail and looking with resignation at a piece of rubbish thrown to the ground by a passer-by.

With the more personal subjects the artist appeared to be finding her stride – developing both her technique and her confidence. However, as Amelia progressed through the sketches, the subject matter became darker. Women in fur coats, suitcases at their feet, held the hands of gaunt-faced children who stared out at Amelia with desperate, pleading eyes. There were others of soldiers in uniform, machine guns slung across their shoulders, or pointing at men and women who stood with their arms raised. Amelia could almost feel their fear. Flavia had clearly witnessed some grim events in her life.

Rolling the sketches back up, Amelia picked up the notebooks. There were five. They appeared to be diaries. She opened each one in turn. Several pages had doodles in the margin. Not every day had an account, but almost all were filled, the writing becoming smaller and neater over time. The last entry was dated 15th October 1943, and intriguingly the pages after that had clearly been ripped out.

Inscribed on the first page of the first diary was a dedication. *2nd May 1938. To darling Flavia on the occasion of her 16th birthday – with love from Sophia.*

Amelia hesitated again. The diaries were personal. She had no right to read them. But she already knew nothing would stop her. She yawned. Despite her nap she was still shattered. Time for bed. Checking the downstairs door was locked, she made her way back upstairs. The wind had risen again, and the castello creaked and groaned around her. Realising she'd had nothing since the biscotto with her coffee, she grabbed a banana from the kitchen and forced it down. Selecting the earliest diary, Amelia left the rest on the coffee table and took it to her bedroom. After washing her face and brushing her teeth in the chilly bathroom she changed into pyjamas, slipped into bed and, pulling the blanket up to her chin, began to read.

THREE

FLAVIA

Florence, 12 May 1938

Chewing on her lower lip, Flavia Corsi stood in the Uffizi Gallery in front of the series of Virtues, wondering which one she would be. Most likely Prudence, given that Prudence was the closest thing to boring one could get. She'd thought as soon as she'd turned sixteen she'd feel different, grown up, fully formed. She couldn't have been more mistaken. Nothing had changed.

She spun round to confront Botticelli's *Birth of Venus*. Now that's what real women looked like! If it wasn't for Flavia's hair which fell to her waist when it was loose, anyone would be forgiven for thinking she was a boy. The woman in the painting had breasts like small melons. Flavia's had yet to sprout, although there were two hard lumps under each nipple. Was that normal? It wasn't the sort of thing she could ask her godmother – lovely though she was. Italian women of their class simply did not have such conversations. Flavia sighed. Courage was a Virtue she clearly *didn't* have. Nor Wisdom. She continued to scrutinize Venus. She was so beautiful with her frothy mass of auburn hair framing a face you never wanted to stop looking at. Narrow-waisted and full-hipped, *her* body wasn't straight up and down with legs like two sticks and too long for her body so that she kept tripping over her feet. For that matter, if Grace were a Virtue Flavia could remove it too. (Chastity and Temperance could remain: it wasn't as if she could do anything about them.)

She glanced over to the other side of the gallery where her godmother was admiring the *Primavera* in splendid solitude, the other visitors keeping their distance as if they could tell she was a contessa just by looking at her. Was gratitude a virtue? If so, she could strike that one too. She was perfectly aware she had much to be grateful for: the affection of her godparents and Sophia their daughter, and an easy life filled with wonderful things. It was quite, quite wrong of her not to be thoroughly grateful. And she *was* content, in the way she imagined a goat chomping on grass was content, but she wanted – yearned – for more. Was that ingratitude?

'Flavia! Girl!' Lady Lansdowne's peremptory tones rang across the room, causing everyone's eyes to swivel in her direction.

Lady Lansdowne was one of the Scorpioni, a group of elderly English ladies who had made Florence their home and were part of the Anglo-Fiorentini: British men and women who had come to visit Italy and fallen so much in love with it that they had to stay. The Scorpioni were comical in many ways, stiff as boards in their manners, wearing so many clothes even in the heat that they were constantly red-faced and perspiring. Yet they were also supremely confident and entitled. If they decided they wanted to put up their easels and paint in the middle of one of the most famous galleries, then they would! They even brought tea and sandwiches with them.

Flavia adored them.

Her godmother had been bringing Flavia on regular visits to study the art of Florence since shortly after she'd come to live with them over ten years ago. At first Flavia had hated these trips – hours spent in half-empty galleries, moving from painting to painting. She simply couldn't see the point when all the artists were dead, their subject matter in the past. But her godparents wouldn't be dissuaded. The study of great works of art was only part of her education. They insisted no one could truly understand or appreciate art unless they understood the context in which great paintings or sculptures were created. So Aunt Lucrezia, as her godmother preferred Flavia to call her, would segue effortlessly between the art and history. Eventually Flavia had started to *see*. Art was about joy and sorrow, rage and pain – a celebration of the past as well as a promise of a future. It was something everyone could share. A person didn't have to be able to read or be educated to enjoy a painting.

Once she'd begun to understand that, she'd started to enjoy the excursions. Then, on a visit, she'd seen a group of Englishwomen sketching in one of the rooms. She'd been fourteen when her curiosity had got the better of her. She'd stood behind the would-be artists and peered as discreetly as she could over their shoulders. Some achieved reasonable likenesses, but on the whole their work bore little resemblance to the original. But the women didn't let that put them off. They would simply put the canvases aside and start again. Flavia admired their determination. It occurred to her that she too could do better, so she'd asked her aunt for a sketch pad and pencils.

Now the Scorpioni asked Flavia for *her* opinion. A situation that required a great deal of tact. She hurried over to Lady Lansdowne. It didn't do to keep her waiting.

Lady Lansdowne tapped the painting on her easel with the end of her paintbrush. 'Well, girl, what do you think?'

Flavia could tell that the painting was of Botticelli's *Venus*, but only because of the cloud of red hair that threatened to envelop the figure in the centre of the painting, ensuring her naked breasts were completely hidden from sight. Lady Lansdowne had made the hand placed modestly between Venus's thighs over-large to ensure the goddess's private bits couldn't possibly be seen from any direction. Flavia swallowed a giggle. Lady Lansdowne would have been better attempting a landscape.

Flavia became aware that an answer was required. How to frame it without causing offence?

'I think you capture her, erm, essence very well.' Flavia wasn't sure what she meant by that, but she thought it sounded positive. After all, the point wasn't to copy a painting exactly but rather to develop one's own style.

'Do you really think so?' Mrs Cosgrove harrumphed from across the room. The English ladies were always competing with each other.

'Ready, Flavia?' Her godmother, with her perfect sense of timing, appeared at her elbow, saving her from having to answer.

Relieved not to be drawn into taking sides, Flavia bade the women goodbye and tucked her arm into her godmother's.

Emerging into the Piazza della Signoria, they passed by the statues in the loggia, and Flavia was again struck by how many of the paintings and sculptures in Florence depicted violent scenes; a permanent, insistent reminder of the imminence of death. As if Flavia needed reminding.

In the piazza a man in his sixties, polishing the shoes of a gentleman sitting on a chair, caught her eye. Like most working men he wore a coarse cotton shirt with the sleeves rolled up. She must have passed him a hundred times before without seeing him. There was something about the set of his mouth, the way his shoulders bunched, the concentration on his face, the shape of his mouth, that fascinated her. It was as if she knew his history, could read his past from the landscape of his body and face. He'd lived in the country, been married once; his children, unable to make a living off the land, discontented and wanting more, had left home, so he had come to the city to be near them. She didn't know if any of that were true, but she felt it could be. A sense of purpose surged through Flavia. She would draw him when she got home. Why attempt to replicate the greats? Why not sketch *actual* people as they went about their daily tasks? The thought excited her. It felt right. It was like putting on a pair of gloves and finding they fitted perfectly.

'I have something I'd like to talk to you about,' Aunt Lucrezia said. 'Shall we have a drink at the Caffè Rivoire?'

They were silent as they dodged their way between cars and bicycles. As Flavia breathed in the delicious smells of apple fritters and *bomboloni* she realised she was starving. Again. She was always hungry. *That* was most certainly greed.

She and her aunt were shown to their seats in the Caffè Rivoire by a waiter dressed in a black suit, crisp white shirt and bow tie. Aunt Lucrezia ordered two hot chocolates and a slice of cake. The contessa wouldn't dream of ordering tea – it was no longer patriotic after the way the British had imposed sanctions on Italy for invading Ethiopia. Neither would her aunt drink *orzo*, the concoction made from roasted barley that passed for coffee in Italy these days.

'We are going to spend the summer in the Casentino,' her aunt said as soon as they'd given the waiter their order, 'so your uncle and I can oversee the renovations of the castello.'

Her godparents had spoken for years of the need to repair their castello in Porciano. It appeared that they were finally getting down to it.

The contessa sighed. 'It's not much more than a ruin at the moment. It's been years since anyone has lived there. But it will fall to the ground if we don't act now to save it.'

Flavia knew that the Castello di Porciano had been built sometime during the second half of the twelfth century by the Modigliana branch of the Guidi family, which at that time were at the height of its power, and that one of her godmother's ancestors – Abbot Count Giuseppe Goretti de Flamini – had inherited it in the eighteenth century.

The waiter arrived with a tray. While he fussed with their hot chocolate and Flavia's cake, Flavia stared out across the piazza where almost every window or balcony was festooned with a banner proclaiming one of Il Duce's slogans.

Aunt Lucrezia waited until they were alone again before continuing. 'We will have to stay in one of the houses in Porciano until the castello can be made liveable. Perhaps by next summer.' She fanned herself with a menu. 'It will be nice to have a permanent summer home in the mountains to retire to when we want to escape the heat of Florence. It will be so much more pleasant than always being a guest. Friends do make one welcome, but so much nicer to stay in one's own home.'

'How long will we go for?'

'Two months.'

'Two months! What will I do there for two months?'

'You can sketch and study there just as easily as here. There are two towns close by to explore. The churches have their own artworks for us to view and discuss. We will visit Castello di Poppi and Castello di Romena, both once owned by my family, you know, and the monastery in La Verna where St Francis of Assisi lived. There will be plenty to occupy us, mia cara.'

Excited though she was to see the castello, Flavia couldn't imagine leaving Florence. Apart from the visits to the churches, galleries and museums, there was tennis at Le Cascine, which she was getting rather good at, and Sophia, the conte and contessa's only child, had promised Flavia could sign up this summer, if she liked, at the Circolo dei Canottieri, a rowing club just below the Uffizi at the foot of the Ponte Vecchio. As yet, she was too young to attend the dances at the Naval Academy of Livorno on the coast where, according to Sophia, there were always throngs of good-looking men who trained in the National Aviation Corps. That didn't matter. Flavia wasn't at all interested in the male sex. Even if she were, none would notice her.

Nevertheless, there were plenty of other diversions in Florence. Ever since she was little she'd had the belief that she would do something important, something to make her mark in the world, whatever that might be. If she planned to be ready for whatever was coming her way she had a great deal to learn – not least how to comport herself – and surely that could only happen here?

She glanced out of the window. The *fiaccherai* stood next to their horse-drawn carriages, smoking cigarettes and gossiping as they waited for fares; the shoe polisher had a new customer; the *spazzino* was taking a rest on a *banco* below a banner proclaiming *Mussolini is always right*. *This* was where all of life was happening.

'Couldn't I stay in Florence? With Sophia? I'll be no trouble. I promise.' Sophia was six years older than Flavia. Old enough to chaperone Flavia if that's what her godmother was concerned about.

'Quite out of the question. You are only just sixteen. Sophia can't be expected to keep an eye on you. She has her own life to lead.' Her aunt leaned across and squeezed her hand. 'I promised your dear mama and papa I would take care of you as if you were my own, and I don't intend to break that promise.'

'But—' Flavia started to protest that she would have no need to trouble Sophia. Cook and Bruna would take care of the cooking, shopping and cleaning as usual, and Flavia could easily look after herself.

'I have no more to say on the matter, Flavia,' her godmother interrupted, stirring her hot chocolate, thick as mud, with a tiny spoon. Aunt Lucrezia's tone said it all. Her godmother always treated her kindly, but Flavia knew that once she'd made up her mind nothing could change it.

It appeared, like it or not, she was going to Porciano.

FOUR

The Casentino, two weeks later

Flavia Corsi stood at the foot of the castello and looked up in dismay. Her godmother hadn't exaggerated when she'd said their ancestral home wasn't much more than a ruin! Piles of stone and building equipment were strewn everywhere. Yes, it had four walls, all of which were covered with scaffolding, but Flavia, even craning her neck, was still unable to tell if it had a roof. Thankfully there was no plan for them to camp out there. For this summer at least, they were staying in one of the houses nestled close to the foot of the tower.

Once more, she wondered what on earth she was going to do here for the whole summer, *hours* from Florence in the middle of nowhere. How was she to fill the days? In Florence she had her visits to the museums and art galleries, her sketching, and tennis. It might not be an exciting life but it kept her busy. Here she would have nothing to distract her from the distinct feeling life was something that happened to other people.

Yet there was no denying the castello's presence. It might take years to renovate, but when it was finally finished it would be an impressive home. And there was no shortage of people employed to make it so. Workers, their sleeves rolled up, shouting and joking with each other as they raised buckets on ropes or clambered up and down the scaffolding, lapsed into respectful silence when they noticed the conte and contessa.

'Let's see what progress has been made,' the conte said to his wife as a villager lifted their luggage out of the boot of their car.

They approached the castello tentatively, picking their way through the rubble and building equipment. Flavia was acutely, embarrassingly, aware of the workmen's surreptitious glances in her direction. She tried her best to appear dignified – which was difficult to do when she had to clamber over stones, tripping in the process. Cheeks burning, she lifted her chin, ignored the stares, and followed her aunt and uncle inside.

It took a few moments for her eyes to adjust to the darkness after the bright sunshine outside. It appeared the renovations were further advanced than she'd realised. The roof *was* on, and temporary staircases had been fashioned from wood to fill the gaps between the floors to allow access until the stone stairs could be rebuilt. There were five floors, six if you included the lowest floor: the castello's first defence against invaders and originally used as a cellar and dungeon, it only had two high narrow windows that let in little light, and therefore would remain a storage space. Flavia shivered. She couldn't stop herself imagining some poor soul shackled in irons, chained to the wall and left in complete darkness.

Leaving the conte to consult with the foreman, Flavia and her aunt went to inspect the house that was to be their summer home until the castello was renovated sufficiently for them to live in.

The village of Porciano lay just outside what was once the tower's protective wall – although most of that had crumbled. Cobbled lanes, too narrow for a motorcar, threaded between the houses which were crammed together. Each one had either a pergola and tiny patio where the occupants had placed tubs of brightly coloured hydrangeas, or a small piece of planted garden. The house that was to be theirs for the summer was the largest in the village, set slightly apart from its neighbours and with an uninterrupted view of the valley. While it was nowhere near as spacious or as fashionable as their home in Florence, at least it had four walls and a roof. And some privacy.

Nevertheless, it was difficult not to be aware of the proximity of the villagers; the shrieks and happy shouts of children as they played, the laughter rolling out from the cool depths of the houses, the scent of cigarette smoke mingling with the rich scent of cooking. Not for the first time, Flavia wished she was part of a loud, noisy family with a sibling near her age. Her godparents were kind but always so busy; they were grateful when Flavia entertained herself. Sophia, at twenty-two years of age, had her own life.

Flavia left her aunt and one of the local women to unpack while she explored the village. It didn't take long. Everyone smiled and greeted her respectfully as she passed, but otherwise paid her little attention – immediately turning back to their chores and conversations. Disappointingly, as far as she could tell there was no one her age. It was a good thing she had brought several books to read and her sketching pad and pencils. Otherwise, she'd go out of her mind with boredom.

A few days later, searching for something to do, she followed a farm track upwards, passing a few houses on her way, and plunged into the forest. It was darker than she'd expected, and when she heard the snap of a branch and a sudden swish in the undergrowth she froze. What had made the noise? A snake? A wild boar? Her godfather had warned her to be careful around them, particularly if they had young.

She was berating herself for her lack of courage when a figure appeared from the forest as if from nowhere. Flavia and the apparition both let out little shrieks.

They stared at each other in silence. Flavia had seen this girl in the distance once or twice since she'd arrived. She was around the same age as Flavia and on the small side, with large brown eyes and thick dark hair, mostly hidden under a scarf. She wore a skirt and a faded but clean blouse a size too big. Even so, there was no disguising her curves. No one would mistake *her* for a boy.

Flavia was the first to recover. 'Good day. My name is Flavia Corsi.' She nodded over her shoulder in the direction of the tower. 'I'm staying in Porciano while my aunt and uncle are renovating their castello.'

The girl was halfway through a curtsey before she stopped herself. At the same time, Flavia had reached out a hand. 'You mustn't...'

The girl flushed bright red and looked down at her feet which, Flavia couldn't help but notice, were shoeless. Flavia's hand was still suspended in mid-air, so she stuck it back in her pocket. 'I was hoping to meet someone my age,' she continued into the awkward silence.

The girl looked up and regarded Flavia with unwavering brown eyes, her head tipped slightly to the side. It was clear to Flavia that she was being appraised.

'Who might wish to be my friend,' Flavia went on doggedly. The girl seemed incapable of speech. 'The village seems to be full' – Flavia lowered her voice and glanced around as if there was the remotest possibility of being overheard – 'of old people.'

An enormous smile spread across the girl's face, and she gave a bark of laughter. 'That is mostly true, but there are some of us who are not so old. I am Margherita Rossi. I live on a farm with my mama and my two brothers and little sister. I've been collecting mushrooms for supper.' She indicated the basket she was holding with another tip of her head, after which she pointed away from the forest and towards a copse of trees. 'That's our farm there. We own it,' she added proudly. She grinned at Flavia. 'I can see the top of the castello from my bedroom. We watched you arrive. I thought you were beautiful, with your blonde hair and pale skin. Just like a princess.'

Flavia checked to see if she was teasing, but she seemed perfectly serious – although her dark eyes sparkled. More, it was as if her whole person glowed. Flavia decided she liked this girl. It wasn't because Margherita thought her beautiful – unfortunately that simply wasn't true – that made Flavia like her, but that she'd said it. Especially when *she* was the pretty one. Now *she* could have modelled for Botticelli! Flavia's fingers itched to sketch her.

Margherita stepped forward and held her arm against Flavia's. 'Your skin is the colour of goat's milk.' She shook her head despairingly. 'Mine is the colour of nuts.'

Tanning was all the fashion among a certain set, but Flavia never sat in the sun. Her skin only burnt if she did. Next to Margherita she felt pale, almost insipid, certainly overdressed in her fashionable frock and sun hat.

'What is that you're holding?' Margherita said, pointing to Flavia's drawing pad.

'Oh, nothing really. I sketch a little, that's all.'

'Show me,' Margherita demanded, handing Flavia her basket to hold.

Somewhat taken aback, Flavia relinquished her sketchbook. The girl flicked through the pad, a little smile on her face. She stopped at a page and turned it towards Flavia. It was one of the sketches Flavia had made of the comical figures in the church in Stia. She'd imagined the gargoyles coming out to play as soon as the parishioners had left the church, and had given them all their own distinct personalities, drawing them gambolling and playing across the page, getting up to all sorts of nonsense. It was one of her more fanciful drawings.

'I like your little monsters,' Margherita said. 'You have quite an imagination!'

'Oh, those monsters don't come from inside my head. They're carvings on top of the pillars of the Church of Santa Maria

Assunta in Stia. I've just tried to imagine how they would behave if they were alive.'

Taking the pad back she carefully tore out the page and offered it to Margherita. 'Would you like it?'

'Oh, thank you. I have never noticed these funny figures.'

'Then I will show you one day. If you like?'

Margherita nodded. 'Very much.'

As if it were the most natural thing in the world, they fell in step together, heading back down the hill. It seemed Margherita was in no more of a hurry to part from Flavia than Flavia was from her.

They chatted as they walked. Flavia learned Margherita was fifteen – a whole year younger than herself, which surprised her as she seemed so self-assured – and that she helped her mother on the farm, milking the sheep and making cheese to sell, as well as all the other usual household chores. She had two older brothers: Luca, nineteen, and Roberto, who was seventeen and was serving with the Italian army in Spain although he was home on leave for a few days. She also had a much younger sister, Rosina. It seemed now she'd found her tongue she had plenty to say.

In return Flavia found herself telling Margherita that the conte and contessa weren't really her aunt and uncle but that she'd been taken in by them after her parents had died in a car accident in Rome.

Margherita's eyes filled. 'That is so sad!'

'I'm used to it.' It wasn't true, but it seemed kinder to Margherita to say so. The truth was she both was, and wasn't, used to it. She had a few memories of her parents, but most were mere fleeting impressions, like bubbles that would burst if she tried to hold onto them too tightly. But she did have some: of her father, smelling of wool and pipe smoke, the way his voice rumbled through her whole body when he held her; of her mother, who smelled of flowers, whose red lips were always smiling, whose golden hair slid through Flavia's fingers like silk; of a house filled with laughter and warmth and love. Some days she missed them with an intensity that stole her breath.

'My father is also dead,' Margherita said. 'But only last year. Luca takes care of the farm now.'

'Oh, I'm so sorry.'

Was that the reason Flavia felt drawn to this girl? Despite the happiness that emanated from her, Flavia had sensed a reciprocal underlying sadness.

'I am so happy you are here,' Margherita said, tucking her arm into Flavia's. 'We thought it was just the conte and contessa who were coming. Everyone was so pleased when we heard that the castello was to be renovated and that people were going to be living there again.' Margherita stuck out her lower lip. 'Everyone except my brother Luca, that is. He thinks people shouldn't own castles. When he saw you, he said you would be like a princess in a tower – looking down on everyone.'

Flavia was stung. 'Your brother has no right to make assumptions about someone he's never met. My godparents along with many other landowners voluntarily gave up large tranches of their land, possibly even the bit of land your farm is on. And that was fair. But there is little point in giving away a castello, especially when it is a ruin, and it will take a small fortune and a lot of love and patience to repair it. He should not be so quick to judge others, particularly the conte and contessa.'

Margherita's eyes flashed. 'Are they above being judged? Especially by people like us. Is that what you are saying?'

The air seemed to throb around them. Flavia could have kicked herself. She'd offended her new friend, and Margherita had done nothing to deserve it. It was the brother Flavia was annoyed with.

'I'm sorry. I shouldn't have said that. Aunt Lucrezia is always reminding me to think before I speak. It is the result of spending too much time in my own company and in my own head.'

The apology was enough to make Margherita smile again. She took Flavia by the hand. 'You must come and meet my family. My horrible brothers included.'

'I couldn't intrude.' Flavia tried to tug her hand away, but Margherita was having none of it.

'Basta!' Margherita said. 'Come and say hello to Mama. You would be very welcome.' And as she started running, pulling Flavia behind her, it seemed that Flavia had no choice but to do what her new friend demanded.

The farmhouse kitchen was almost the size of the Corsis' drawing room in their apartment in Florence, and that was saying something. An enormous fire blazed in a fireplace that took up most of one wall. It was hardly surprising the temperature inside was even hotter than outside. A bubbling pot, suspended over the flames, filled the room with the pungent smell of garlic and tomatoes. The Corsis' cook in Florence never used garlic, claiming it was much too strong for their palates. Strings of dried herbs and onions, and haunches of pork marbled with fat, hung from the ceiling next to flypapers – which had been doing their work and were almost hidden under their unsuspecting victims. The walls were painted a traditional soothing blue. Strands of rolled-out pasta lay on the table. Margherita's mother, a small dark-haired woman with bright eyes just like her daughter's, and flour up to her elbows, was in the process of laying a damp tea towel over them. Flavia took in the scene in a moment, already planning how she would sketch it.

'Where have you been, Margherita? You know what time we have lunch,' Margherita's mother scolded.

'Sorry, Mama. I lost track of the time. Look! I brought someone to meet you. This is Flavia Corsi. She's from the castello.'

Signora Rossi couldn't have looked more taken aback if Margherita had brought one of the sheep into her kitchen. She started to whip off her apron, then retied it as if she couldn't make up her mind what was appropriate. 'You are welcome in my home,' she said finally. 'I understand the conte and contessa are staying in the house next to the church while the castello is being renovated?'

As Margherita handed her a glass of water, Flavia nodded. She would have been very surprised if there was anything about the contessa and her domestic arrangements the villagers didn't know.

'Please sit down, Signorina,' Signora Rossi said, removing a bundle of knitting from a chair. 'Margherita, set the table. Rosina, you must fetch your brothers if they aren't here by the time she's finished.' Margherita's mother put some water on to boil.

Flavia hadn't noticed the little girl. She was only three or four and clung to her mother's skirts, peeping out at Flavia every now and again.

'You will stay for lunch, Signorina?' Signora Rossi asked.

'It is very kind of you to invite me, Signora, but no thank you. The contessa is expecting me at home.'

At that moment two men walked into the kitchen. Flavia had the distinct impression they'd been arguing, not only from the stormy expression in the taller one's eyes and the ferocious frown on the shorter one's forehead but also from the waves of discord they brought into the room with them.

'My brothers' – Margherita introduced them with a sweep of her hand – 'Luca and Roberto.'

Luca had thick, wavy hair that was so black it was almost blue and was fashionably cut, longer at the front and shorter at the back. Looking taken aback to find Flavia in his home, he scowled and muttered under his breath about the princess in the tower coming to see how the peasants lived. Flavia was certain he meant her to hear. She gave him what she hoped was a withering look, which he ignored. As she'd anticipated, she didn't care for him one bit.

The other brother was shorter and plumper and had protruding eyes. At least he'd smiled at her.

'Anyone who was a true Italian would wish to fight for the Spanish Nationalists. You are a coward not to,' Roberto addressed his brother, clearly continuing an argument that had started outside. He picked up Rosina, tweaked her cheek and kissed the top of her head. 'People are fighting to give those they love a better life,' he continued. 'What's wrong with that?'

'I have no wish to fight for another country!' Luca responded, drying his hands on a towel. 'Particularly for a cause I don't believe in. But if I did go to Spain I would fight against Franco – not for him.'

Roberto put Rosina back on her feet. 'Then you'd be a traitor! Against your country and the Pope! Doesn't it matter to you that the Republicans murdered hundreds of innocent priests and nuns?'

Luca lifted a disbelieving eyebrow. 'How do you know that is true? Each side will say anything to make its point. Perhaps you should be asking why Il Duce' – there was a definite sneer in his voice – 'is so keen to have Italians fight someone else's war.'

Flavia listened in disbelief. Priests and nuns murdered! That was horrible. It couldn't possibly be true. But if it were, surely it was a good thing Italians were helping to do something to stop it. As for the contempt in Luca's voice when he talked of Mussolini! She'd never heard anybody speak of Italy's leader except with love and awe.

'How dare you criticise Il Duce?' Roberto snarled. 'He is the only leader ever to think about the people who are the backbone of this country. Did you ever hear of another politician delivering blankets and baskets of food to the poor? I would die for Il Duce and you should be prepared to do no less!'

'Enough, boys,' Signora Rossi snapped with a pointed look in Flavia's direction. 'I will not have this sort of discussion, and certainly not when we have a guest.'

Luca's glance flicked towards Flavia. He looked startled, as if he'd completely forgotten she was there.

Although she longed to stay in that delicious-smelling, comforting and *intriguing* kitchen, it was time to go. She suspected that Signora Rossi was waiting until after she left to serve her family lunch.

'Thank you for the water, Signora Rossi,' she said, getting to her feet. 'Let me leave you to your meal.' She nodded to the two brothers. Luca didn't even acknowledge the gesture. Roberto just gaped at her and blushed. Really, the male sex was a different species – one best not thought about.

Margherita walked Flavia to the door.

'When can we meet again?' Flavia asked.

'Tomorrow? After lunch? Unless you'll be taking a rest? I never do.'

Flavia smiled. It might not be quite as boring in the Casentino as she'd imagined.

FIVE

AMELIA

Amelia woke to a pillow drenched with tears. She'd been dreaming of Cameron and Fiona. They'd been down in the harbour, building sandcastles and laughing, when an enormous wave had roared in and swept them both out to sea. Amelia tried to swim towards them, but she couldn't; the waves kept tossing her back ashore. Try as she might, she couldn't get to them.

Throwing the covers aside, she forced herself out of bed, her bare foot encountering something unexpectedly hard on the carpet. Flavia's diary. Amelia must have fallen asleep reading it last night and knocked it to the floor. As she reached down to pick it up, she realised a photograph had slipped out from between its pages. It was of a group of people – two women, a child and a man. Amelia recognised Flavia immediately. She was wearing the flower-sprigged dress, or one very similar to the one in the trunk, and was sitting on a low wall next to a dark-haired woman. They were holding hands and laughing, clearly friends. Could the brunette be Margherita? She was wearing a skirt and blouse, simple in design, with a scarf covering her hair and stout boots on her feet. Her clothes contrasted with Flavia's elegant heels, extravagant straw hat and well-fitting summer dress. Slightly to the right, looking shy and uncomfortable, was a little dark-haired girl. The other woman's child perhaps? Or Rosina? Behind Flavia and the dark-haired woman, a man, arms folded, leaned against a building – house, barn, store? He too was smiling into the camera, although Amelia detected a hint of impatience in the curve of his mouth – almost as if he were about to say something or was getting ready to push himself away from the wall. He was wearing twill trousers and an open-necked shirt, the top two buttons undone, and the sleeves rolled up to the elbows.

Off to the left of the photograph was a plough and cart, and in the background the tower of the castello rose in the distance. Wherever this photo had been taken must be nearby. Amelia studied the castello, counting the windows. It was the west wall, so the farm, if it still existed, was to the west and only a short walk away.

She replaced the photograph between the pages of the diary. It was time to get on with the day.

She pulled on a T-shirt and a pair of leggings and trainers. She'd read somewhere that exercise was at least as effective as medication for treating depression. She'd never been a fan of working out, and had always flatly dismissed jogging as a form of exercise. But unless there was a gym in Stia, which she doubted, she didn't have a lot of choice.

She swilled her mouth out with water straight from the kitchen tap, ran downstairs and let herself out into the fierce, clear morning light, locking the door behind her.

She considered what to do with the key. It was too large and awkward to carry. Spotting a pot planted with blood-red geraniums by the front door, she dug a little hollow in the soil and buried it.

Outside, the sky was an endless dome of blue, the sun a bright orb. Amelia followed a track that led towards the forest and started to run. The road climbed steeply, and within minutes her lungs were bursting, her legs feeling as if they weighed a hundred pounds each. She slowed to a walk. The new exercise regime wasn't starting well. She gave herself thirty seconds to catch her breath and started running again.

There was something improbably wonderful about the agony that came from forcing her reluctant lungs and legs to keep pumping. Even better, she could think of nothing except putting one foot in front of the other. In a sequence of jogging and walking, her fingers crossed no one was watching, she reached the top of the hill. From there the road narrowed to a path leading into a forest. Amelia staggered to a stop, hands on knees, and gasped for breath. The feel of the cool breeze rippling across her skin transported her back to the day the three of them had gone out in Cameron's boat a few days before the accident – the sun warm on their skin, Fiona grinning from ear to ear as she stood next to her father, bracing herself against his legs as she gripped the miniature fishing rod he'd made for her. Amelia winced as pain sliced through her. She shoved the memory away. She couldn't allow herself to think of them – otherwise the fragile bubble she'd built around her in order to function would shatter.

Amelia turned away from the forest and the direction her thoughts were taking, and looked towards the castello. Between the fields of swaying grass and the hills in the distance, there was a series of forked roads marked 'private', leading off to homes partly hidden by trees. The village of Porciano below was more distinct from this position than from the castello. From here she could see that the village had been built in three tiers with narrow, cobbled lanes threading their way between the houses, and a broader street, almost a mini piazza, in front. Two women sat at a table on their tiny veranda doing something Amelia couldn't make out. Otherwise, there was little sign of activity. In front of the compact village square was a church with a bell tower, and another larger house on its right. Was that the one Flavia had stayed in when she'd come to Porciano as a girl?

Amelia hobbled back towards the castello, her aching muscles beginning to stiffen. Mid-morning and she hadn't even started on the job she'd been employed to do. However, immediately outside the crumbling walls, she noticed a small graveyard and was irresistibly drawn to it. Inside the crypt, she found the gravestones of

Beatrice's mother and father. Outside the crypt, but still contained within what was clearly a private family cemetery, were seven other graves. She read the names, only realising when she failed to find it that she'd been searching for Flavia's. Was it possible she was still alive? Or was she buried elsewhere, next to a husband perhaps?

Back inside the castello, she showered and had some yoghurt with a squirt of honey and a handful of nuts sprinkled on top, before going down to the lower floor. The sight of the boxes, the sheer bloody number of books they must contain, stopped her in her tracks. It would take several days, if not weeks, to go through them all and record each one.

Suddenly, she was overwhelmed by the task in front of her. Since the accident she hadn't been able to concentrate long enough to write a shopping list – let alone do this.

Small steps, she told herself. She opened her laptop and wrote a list of what she needed to do. Lists were good. Lists were manageable.

Empty all boxes.
Create a database to record the books.
Put aside any book that might be of particular interest.
Write an outline for the brochure to go along with the exhibits.
Research the Warrior Abbess.

Resisting the impulse to crawl upstairs and into bed, she opened Excel and set about creating a database. It took several attempts and a great deal of concentration. But she managed. Turning back to the boxes, she pulled on a pair of cotton gloves she'd brought with her and lifted the first book out. Its spine was cracked. Very gently she placed it on her lap and opened it at its first page. As she did so, the musty smell of old books and leather escaped. In the first column of her database she entered the publisher, in the next the date of the edition, and so on until all the columns were filled. She did the same with the next book, and soon she was in a groove.

She worked steadily until her grumbling stomach reminded her she should eat again. She was surprised. Hunger wasn't something she'd experienced for a while. Back upstairs, she made herself a salad of tomatoes, olives and feta, adding a toasted chunk of once-crusty Tuscan bread. She was almost out of fresh food. She needed to go to the village to stock up soon.

Knowing she should work some more but unable to resist, she selected the next diary from the pile on the coffee table, curled up in the window seat and continued to read.

SIX

FLAVIA

July 1938

Margherita and Flavia met almost every day that summer, usually after lunch when everyone else was indoors staying out of the heat. They would walk in the forest above Porciano or lie under the shade of a chestnut tree with the tinkling of goat bells the only sound apart from their voices, and talk.

Flavia usually had her sketch pad with her, and sometimes she'd draw Margherita or Rosina while they chatted. Once Flavia found herself absent-mindedly sketching Luca and had hidden the page quickly before Margherita saw it.

Rosina followed them everywhere like a lamb trailing after its mother. Although Flavia thought her sweet, with her big brown eyes and engaging, toothy smile, she and Margherita couldn't talk so openly or roam as far when the little girl followed them, so they gave the child the slip whenever they could. It wasn't as often as they would have liked, as the little girl kept a close eye on her sister.

If it became too hot even in the shade, they would return to the relative cool of the farmhouse veranda to drink cold lemonade or to snack on figs picked straight from the tree. Sometimes Margherita would stuff the fruit with ricotta made on the farm – there were always enormous cauldrons of goat's milk simmering over the fire for this purpose – before roasting them in the oven until they were sticky and delicious. When Margherita realised Flavia couldn't cook, she was horrified and insisted on teaching her. She showed her how to make pasta, how to shape tortellini, how to make tomato sauce and how to bottle it.

Flavia tried her best, but her pasta always broke into pieces when she rolled it out, and her tortellini ended up looking more like lumps of clay than edible mouthfuls of deliciousness. Her friend would shake her head and laugh at Flavia's incompetence.

Whenever Roberto discovered them in the kitchen, he'd hang about, making cow's eyes at Flavia. Luca, on the other hand, continued to ignore her. Which was fine. She had no interest in him either.

The brothers were rarely together before Roberto returned to his unit in Spain, but on the few occasions they were the tension Flavia had felt between them the first time was always present. She couldn't understand it. If she had brothers and sisters, she'd be overjoyed. One day, when she and Margherita were alone in the kitchen, she asked her friend why Luca and Roberto seemed to dislike each other. Was it just their different political beliefs?

'Roberto is jealous of Luca. Poor Roberto is not very handsome, and girls don't look at him the way they look at Luca. *He* can have anyone he wants. Girls from the other villages are always mooning around the farm, pretending they have come for cheese, but we all know it is to see Luca.' Despite the shake of her head, she was smiling. 'He rarely spends more than a week or two with each one. He gets bored quickly.' Margherita stuck her finger in a vat of cheese and licked it. Satisfied it was ready to have the first curd skimmed off the top, she carted the pot over to the kitchen table. 'Roberto would be content to get a tiny bit of the attention that Luca gets. Sometimes I think that's the only reason he volunteered to go to Spain. I suspect he thought it would make girls like him better. Some chance! I think he regrets it now but can't say so.'

Flavia preferred not to think about Luca's love affairs. A few days ago, when she was on her way to meet Margherita, she'd seen him emerge from the double doors of the Rossis' barn. Luca was shirtless, wearing only a vest that accentuated the muscles of his arms and shoulders. Her heart had somersaulted in her chest. He *was* very handsome. She was just lifting her hand to wave to him when a woman, her hair all mussed up, appeared behind him, tucking her blouse into her skirt. Flavia let her hand drop. It was clear they had been involved in some sort of tryst. The woman sidled up to Luca, who gave her a quick peck on the cheek, a slap on the rear and sent her off as if she were a pack horse.

'It seems to me there is more to the bad feeling between them than that,' Flavia said.

Margherita sighed. She'd finished skimming the curd and lifted the pot back on the fire. 'They disagree about everything too, particularly politics.' She turned her attention to a pan of sauce and stirred it, releasing more delicious aromas into the room. 'Roberto is always going on at Luca to enlist and fight in Spain too. Luca just laughs at him when he says that. Says Roberto is a fool to want to throw his life away for another country – another man's war.' She frowned. 'Sometimes I think Roberto would kill Luca if he thought he could get away with it.'

'You can't mean that!' Flavia exclaimed, horrified.

Margherita sighed. 'Oh, of course not. I'm just being dramatic as usual.' She turned back to the fire, preventing Flavia from reading her expression. It was time to change the conversation. Talk of wars in other countries and fights between brothers wasn't what they preferred to discuss.

Mostly they chatted about Florence. Margherita had never been to the city and wanted to know everything about it: the grand shops where a person could buy anything they wanted, the parks, the people, the palazzos, the tennis club where Flavia played, what fashionable people wore and when. Margherita hung on every word, and Flavia had to admit she found being the centre of someone's attention intoxicating. Often, she'd ham up her life in Florence simply to make her friend laugh.

Sometimes they walked down to Stia to get shopping for Margherita's mother and, while they waited for the shops to open, they'd sit in the cool of the church. They'd always say a prayer while there, but afterwards, as long as there was no one else worshipping in the church, they'd whisper to one another or make up stories about the strange, impish figures carved into the tops of the piers.

Flavia tried to explain the paintings and the famous Della Robbia family terracottas to Margherita, but her friend soon lost interest and, inevitably, their conversation returned to Flavia's life in Florence.

Most evenings after the workmen had finished for the day and before supper, Flavia would go with her aunt and uncle to the castello's basement, which was the best-preserved part of the building and in which any treasures from the past might still be unearthed with careful excavation. Much of what they'd found had been damaged by falling rock, but some of the vases and jugs remained intact, and the conte and contessa hadn't given up hope of finding something of value preserved in the earthen floor, the sale of which would help finance the ever-increasing costs of rebuilding the castello. As there was very little light even during the day and nothing to sit on except the dirt floor, they brought Tilley lamps and camp chairs with them, although most of the time Flavia sat on an upturned bucket as she worked. Her aunt and uncle had shown her how to carefully brush dirt off anything embedded in the soil.

'Why was the castello abandoned?' Flavia asked, as her delicate brushstrokes revealed part of a pottery vase.

'The Guidis lived in turbulent times. Everyone was choosing and changing sides all the time, and if you picked the wrong side, like the Guidi counts did' – her godfather shrugged – 'it was your bad luck. The victors took your property and land.' He went on to tell her about the Guelphs and Ghibellines, and how Dante had been expelled to Tuscany for having the misfortune to be on the losing side, but that the Conti Guidi had sheltered him in their Casentino castello.

Despite having heard the same stories often, Flavia listened attentively. She loved imagining the battles between the vying Guelphs and Ghibellines; the knights in their armour, the women waiting and watching from the ramparts or the ladies' balcony for their safe return. She tried not to think of the prisoners kept down here, possibly right where she sat now, in pitch darkness for years. It gave her the shivers. A life without light was no life at all. She imagined their despair and horror, their fear seeping into the very walls of the castello. How terrible it must have been for them. She would rather have been killed outright.

Her favourite story was of the Warrior Abbess who, because her brother wasn't much use in a crisis, had taken charge of the dukedom, leading her knights into battle while finding the time to found a convent where she and her nuns could help the sick in Pratovecchio, bringing prosperity and peace to the region. The Abbess sounded so brave, exactly the kind of woman Flavia wished to be one day. If she ever got the chance, *she* would be a warrior!

'Why are all the statues of men?' she asked, a thought occurring to her. 'There should be a statue of the Abbess somewhere.'

'I agree, but at least she's been memorialised. Every Tuscan child grows up knowing about her,' her aunt replied, referring to the children's book based on the Abbess and her feats.

Returning to her careful brushing, Flavia wondered if it had occurred to the people who'd once stayed here all those centuries ago that someone would one day find their belongings, part of them and their lives, frozen in time? Could people ever truly disappear? Especially if they left something of themselves behind like Dante and his work, or the great painters – or the Abbess and her monastery. She liked to think not. Now the castello was on its way to being restored it would shelter several more generations, stretching into a future so far away it was impossible to imagine. Would anyone remember *her* after she'd gone; would someone, one day, long after she was dead, find something belonging to her? A comb or a mirror, even her diaries? She smiled to herself. If they did, and read them, they'd be bored witless.

'Now this is interesting.' Her uncle's voice jarred her from her musings. He'd been sifting through a trunk containing books and papers that had been passed onto his wife through the generations. He squinted at the documents he held in his hand. 'Most of these are badly damaged, but some of them might just be salvageable. At some point I'm going to have to get someone who knows what they're doing to look through them properly.' He turned to Flavia. 'If your father had been alive, he would have known exactly what is of value and what isn't.' Flavia's father had been a professor of history.

'Tell me again how Mama and Papa met,' she begged.

Her godparents shared a smile. Flavia asked this often, but they were always happy to oblige.

'As you know, Chiara and I were always good friends,' the contessa said. 'We met as children in Florence. Her family and mine knew each other well, and Chiara and I did everything together. She was the more outgoing of the two of us, certainly the more beautiful with her blonde hair and fine features.' She sighed with more than a hint of sadness in her eyes. 'You look more like her every day.'

Flavia closed her eyes, picturing her mother in a shimmery dress with tassels that swung when she moved, and a multi-coloured scarf tied around her head. Flavia was never sure if it was an actual memory or one she'd made up, but she liked to believe it was real.

'Your mother met your father at a lecture at the British Institute in Florence. He was so reserved – the complete opposite of Chiara. She liked to have fun and rarely took anything seriously, but she was fascinated by what he said. She insisted on cornering him after the talk to give him the benefit of her opinion.' A reluctant smile tugged at the corner of her godmother's mouth. 'Your mother never doubted that anyone might not wish to hear her opinions, which were sometimes a little... let us say, contentious. She wrote a column for a newspaper, mostly about social events; where they were held, who was there, what they were wearing, what food was being served.' Aunt Lucrezia's hands stilled, and she sat back in her chair, seemingly lost in her memories. 'She had a way with words, adored fashion and knew everyone, so she was the perfect person to write it. But what many people didn't realise was that behind her fun-loving demeanour was a sharp brain. Your father recognised that straight away.' Lucrezia reached across and took Flavia's hands in hers. 'You remind me of her in many more ways than looks, you know. Although you are more solemn than she was – you take after your father in that regard – you have the same resolve, the same sharp brain, the same quiet determination.'

Flavia was surprised her godmother thought all these things of her. She doubted she'd ever be as interesting as her mother. 'Do you think Il Duce was right to send troops to Spain?' she blurted. She'd been thinking a lot about the Rossi brothers' conversation since the day she'd met them.

Her godparents shared an uneasy glance. It was her godfather who answered. 'Not everyone agrees with Mussolini – what he did in Abyssinia – or his sending Italian troops to war in Spain. Some think Italy can't afford to be spending so much money on such things. Not when there are Italians who still live hand to mouth – especially in the south.' From the corner of her eye Flavia noticed her godmother give a small shake of her head. Her godfather cleared his throat. 'However, most people agree he has done a great deal of good for the majority of Italians.'

It seemed to Flavia that her godparents weren't being as direct or as open with her as she'd like.

'Why do you ask?' Uncle Francesco continued.

'Margherita's brother, Luca, said he would never fight for Fascism. He said he disagreed with Il Duce sending troops to Spain, and that if he were to fight it would be against Franco, not for him. But Margherita's other brother, Roberto, said that nuns and priests were being murdered, and that's why Italy sent troops. To save them.'

The conte's expression darkened. 'Luca should keep his opinions to himself. People have got into a great deal of trouble for saying much less.'

That was no answer at all! 'What would my papa and mama think?'

Was it Flavia's imagination or did the colour leave her godmother's face?

'We can't say what they thought,' her godfather said shortly.

'Can't, or won't?' Flavia was on his words quick as a flash. 'Didn't you just say that my mother liked to let everyone know her opinion?'

'Enough!' her godfather thundered. 'It is wrong for us to be even discussing such matters.'

Wrong? How could discussing important matters be wrong?

'I'm sixteen!' Flavia protested. 'No longer a child, even if you don't see it. You have always insisted I should learn to think for myself. What is the point of education otherwise?' It was the first time she'd ever challenged her godparents, the first time her godfather had ever raised his voice to her, and it made her feel a little shaky.

The anger drained from her uncle as quickly as it had arrived. 'You are certainly your parents' child. They too liked to debate everything.'

'But—'

'Basta, Flavia! No more. You must learn to keep these thoughts to yourself. Do not discuss them with anyone, even – *especially* – your new friends. Sharing opinions in the current political climate can be dangerous. As far as we are all concerned, Mussolini is our prime minister and above reproach.'

None of it made sense to Flavia. Why should a person keep their thoughts and opinions to themself? Why not debate important matters? How could keeping things secret, unsaid, be good?

The conte stood and tousled her hair as if she *were* still a child. 'Life is not as straightforward as any of us would like it to be, my dear. It is rarely black and white. You should leave such matters to those who understand the finer points of policy and not trouble yourself.' He picked out a dirt-encrusted piece of metal and held it out. 'Look at this, carissime. What do you think this might be?'

That evening Flavia was at her dressing table brushing her hair when she overheard her godparents talking. They were sitting in the garden right outside her window, so although they were speaking in hushed voices Flavia could make out almost every word.

'Perhaps we should stop Flavia visiting the farm,' the conte said.

Flavia held her breath.

'That would be a shame. It's good she has made a friend here.'

'It's the brother I'm concerned about. If someone reports what he says, he could bring trouble on his family and, through association, ours. We know better than most that Mussolini is a dangerous man, Lucrezia, and still has his spies everywhere. We must never forget how dangerous.'

Spies! What on earth was her godfather going on about? And saying things like that outside – where he might be overheard! Hadn't he warned her to keep her thoughts to herself?

'He will take us into another war – another one we have no chance of winning,' her godfather continued. 'What he did in Abyssinia was not worthy of the Italian people. What was done in our name makes me ashamed to be Italian.'

'He says he has no intention of taking us into another war.'

'That's what he says publicly – privately, it's a different matter. He and that Hitler fellow between them. Can't you see? Il Duce worships that overbearing, jumped-up peasant. I fear and detest what is happening in Germany. The German nationalists are doing the same as the Fascists did in the twenties, arresting – even murdering – those who oppose them. Hitler has plans, big plans – I don't think he'll stop with the annexation of Austria – and he'll drag Mussolini along with him. As for what the German führer is doing to the Jews! Where will it stop?'

'Perhaps it will all blow over...'

'I doubt that, cara. Mussolini gets more pumped up with his own importance every day. He's made himself head of the army and the navy. So much power in the hands of one man – two if you include Hitler – can't be right, or safe.'

Their voices faded as they returned indoors. Would there really be a war? Flavia couldn't imagine it. People killed for disagreeing with the government? She must have misheard. Mussolini wasn't a dictator. People had elected him. She thought back to what Luca had said – about not wanting to fight for Fascism. It was odd that the son of a farmer and her uncle seemed to share some of the same thoughts.

Who or what to believe? She needed to find out more. Her godparents had made it clear they weren't prepared to discuss these sorts of matters with her, in which case she would find a way of getting to the truth herself.

However, right now, more worrying was the prospect of being forbidden to spend time at the farm. That mustn't be allowed to happen. She'd need to keep all thoughts and questions about politics to herself from now on.

SEVEN

AMELIA

Over the next few days Amelia developed a routine. Each morning she made coffee and took it up to the ramparts, sipping it as she watched the early morning mist lift from the valley.

Then she'd go for a run. For the remainder of the day, she'd work solidly, relieved the effort of concentrating stopped her from thinking too much. In the evenings she'd curl up on one of the window seats she'd piled with cushions and blankets and listen to an audiobook or podcast, or read Flavia's diaries until she felt she could sleep. It didn't stop her dreams being plagued by nightmares, but at least she was just about functioning.

She'd been in Porciano for the best part of a week when, returning from her morning run – if it could be called that – she saw a woman she didn't recognise outside one of the cottages. Middle-aged, tall and wiry, her grey hair was cut short emphasising strong features. She was wearing loose grey trousers and a long grey cardigan over a bright red shirt.

'Now, guys,' the woman drawled in an accent Amelia identified as from the American South, 'wait your turn. You know you'll get more than your fair share.'

She had to be Kelly – the tenant Beatrice told her about.

She was too preoccupied with feeding the cats winding

between her legs to notice Amelia. For a moment Amelia was tempted to slip past. Even a casual encounter might result in questions she couldn't bear to answer.

Too late. The crunch of her trainers on gravel alerted the woman to her presence, and she swung round, clutching her hand to her chest. 'My goodness! Where did you spring from?'

Amelia wiped her sweaty palms on her leggings and held out a hand. 'I'm Amelia Simpson.' She nodded towards the tower. 'I'm staying at the castello, helping the contessa out with a project.'

The woman grinned and pumped Amelia's hand enthusiastically. 'Of course you are. I'm Kelly, if you haven't already guessed. I was going to come over and see you later. It's wonderful to have some company around here.' She lowered her voice. 'The villagers are all very dandy and all that, but while I can read Italian, they speak much too fast for me to follow their conversation. So much easier to communicate in your own language, don't you think? Hey, I don't suppose you have time for a coffee? I was just about to make some. I just need to finish feeding my boys and gals.'

It took Amelia a moment to realise Kelly was referring to the cats. She counted five. Although it seemed, as a tabby appeared from the undergrowth to rub itself against Amelia's leg, there were more. She resisted the impulse to bend down to stroke it. Despite liking cats, she was allergic to them. 'Are they all yours?' she asked.

Kelly, whose cardigan Amelia noticed was covered in cat hair, looked at them with affection. 'They are now. The strays all make their way to me eventually.' She picked up the empty tins of cat food and placed them in a plastic bag.

Amelia sneezed.

'I'm sorry, I have to say no to coffee,' Amelia said. 'I'm just about out of food, so I need to go to Stia to stock up.' She hadn't got around to making the trip to the shops but couldn't live on pasta with grated parmesan forever. 'Another time perhaps?'

If Kelly was keen on socialising, she should add antihistamines to the shopping list.

'If you're going to Stia, could I come with you?' Kelly asked, tying a knot in the bag and placing it in the bin. 'The walk is way better when there's folk to chat to. However,' she continued with a hopeful look, 'if you're intending to drive that's even better. I don't have a vehicle' – she pronounced the word as if it were made up of three syllables, vee-hic-ul – 'even though it's pretty impossible here without one.'

'How do you manage then?' Amelia asked.

'With a great deal of difficulty.' Kelly gave Amelia a rueful smile. 'It's my own fault. I could hire a car – buy one even. But I loathe driving in Italy, especially on the road from Stia to the castello. It's so narrow. And all those hairpin bends! I'm terrified I'll go over the edge and that would be the last of me.' She picked up one of the cats and rubbed behind its ears. 'Anyway, when I'm in Florence – I spend around half of my time there, I don't know if Beatrice said – a car would be a positive hindrance, and when I travel between Porciano and Florence the bus is fine. But here, unless I can beg a lift from Beatrice whenever she's around, I have to use my two pins. However, as you have a vee-hic-ul' – she looked at Amelia expectantly with a touch of mischief in her eyes – 'life is going to be so much easier. I can hitch lifts with you to the shops. We could even go on trips together!'

Amelia's heart sank. It appeared Kelly took it for granted they were going to spend significant chunks of time together. She seemed pleasant, fun even, but Amelia was barely holding it together right now. Any prodding, or difficult questions, and she suspected she might fly apart. But if Kelly noticed Amelia's dismay, she gave no sign.

'If we are going to Stia,' Kelly hurried on, 'we should go now. The shops close between one and four. The Italians like to take their time over their meals you know.' She flashed Amelia another beaming smile. 'We could have lunch after we finish our shopping. To be honest it gets a bit lonely here. It would be cool to have someone to speak English to.'

Amelia couldn't see a way to say no without sounding rude.

'Sure. That would be nice. I need to shower first though.' The sun was beating down on Amelia's already-overheated skin. 'Meet you here in twenty minutes?'

'Make it thirty and you're on.'

EIGHT

Despite the cooling effect of her shower and the breeze coming in the open car windows, within minutes of setting off for Stia Amelia's skin was slick with sweat.

'I don't mind walking down to the town,' Kelly grumbled good-naturedly, 'but coming back up the hill kills me. Especially when it's this hot and I have shopping to carry. So, this is great.'

Given Kelly's lithe figure, she appeared to Amelia as someone who would beetle back up the hill without having to draw breath.

'What on earth possesses you to run uphill?' Kelly continued, as if reading her thoughts. 'I saw you yesterday when I was feeding my cats and thought you might be having a heart attack.'

Amelia smiled. 'I felt as if I was having a heart attack. And that was only after a couple of minutes.'

'You should run by the river,' Kelly continued. 'It's just at the end of this road. It's flat there and shaded by trees. So much easier than running uphill, I would have thought. And you can have a dip if you need to cool down.'

'I might just do that. I might manage five minutes without collapsing that way.'

Kelly shot Amelia a disapproving look. 'Don't know why you

bother. You don't look as if you need to lose weight. Quite the contrary. You're painfully skinny.'

Trust an American not to mince her words. However, Amelia couldn't find it in her to take offence. Kelly was far too... *nice* was the word that came to mind.

'Are you married?' Kelly asked. 'No, of course you couldn't be, otherwise he'd be here with you.'

Pain surged through Amelia. Probing questions were the reason she didn't want to become friendly with anyone. Life was hard enough without them. 'I was. Not anymore.'

Kelly waited for her to elaborate, but Amelia remained silent, pretending to concentrate on negotiating a tight bend.

'What about you?' Amelia asked, aware she'd been abrupt. 'Did you ever marry?'

'Yes. Divorced him several years ago after he found a younger version. Bastard.'

Amelia surprised herself by laughing. She couldn't remember the last time she had.

'Children?'

'No,' Kelly replied flatly. It seemed she too had stuff she didn't care to discuss.

'How do you know Beatrice?' Amelia asked, moving to safer ground. She pulled over to allow a car that had been hugging her rear bumper to pass. The driver, a dark-haired woman around her age, smiled and waved a greeting.

'I met Bee just over a year ago. I don't know if you know, but she has an apartment in Florence she lets out too. I'd been travelling for several months and was getting tired of living out of a suitcase, so when I saw her advert I immediately thought – why not stay the winter in Florence? What better place to hunker down? Then I came up here one day with Bee and fell in love with Porciano. Bee owns a couple of the houses in the village and was happy to rent me the one I'm in. Now I spend my time between Florence and Porciano, depending on my mood and the time of year. That way I have the best of both worlds.' She gave a rueful shake of her head. 'It's a funny old life sometimes, isn't it? I only came to Italy for a week or two, yet here I still am. I like it that life can still throw the odd curveball.'

Amelia winced and took one of the bends a little too fast. The movement caused Kelly to sway towards her.

'How are you getting on in the castello, anyway? Isn't it an amazing building?' Kelly continued, righting herself and thankfully changing the subject.

'It's beautiful. I feel privileged to be staying there.'

'Do you know, I've never seen it properly? I've been over for drinks once or twice but never had a good look around. Bee and her husband only spend the odd weekend at the castello, although I assume they'll stay more often once the museum is up and running.' There was a pause as she waited for Amelia to invite her, but Amelia couldn't bring herself to – it was bound to result in reciprocal offers. Lovely as Kelly seemed, Amelia wasn't up to the effort being her friend would demand.

'Do you work from Porciano?' Amelia asked into the awkward silence. She wanted to keep Kelly talking about herself so she wouldn't ask about her. To Amelia's relief, she seemed content to do so.

'Took early retirement a couple of years ago. Given I'd got rid of The Bastard and have no kids I thought I might as well chuck it all in and travel the world. Managed to see a bunch of Greece and Turkey before I washed up here. Can't seem to tear myself away.' She flashed Amelia a smile. 'Maybe after next summer – or the summer after that. There's no rush. As long as the body stays healthy, time isn't an issue. I had to tell myself that at first, but now...' She shrugged. 'I find I like taking time out. I couldn't be more different to the person I was when I was working. You know the deal: up at six, work twelve hours a day, eat out, roll into bed and start all over again. At least that's the way it was for me. What about you?'

'For most of my career, I was an archivist. Latterly, I worked from home, mostly. Translating Italian into English. The work was steady, not overwhelming.' That had been the way Amelia liked it. She'd had plenty of time to spend with Fiona that way. Her throat constricted. All that felt as if it belonged to another life, a different person. 'What was it you did?' she asked. Much better to concentrate on Kelly.

'Worked for Big Tech.'

'Don't you miss America? You must have family and friends there?' Amelia asked, genuinely curious. Kelly struck her as someone who enjoyed company.

'Hell no! The pace of life in California just got too much. Anyway, you'd be surprised how many people want to come and visit when you have an apartment in the centre of Florence and another in rural Tuscany. Although, to be honest, mostly they prefer to come to Florence. A couple of days in the Casentino is usually enough for most people, unless they are keen walkers or lovers of Italian churches and history – or Dante groupies. You know he's supposed to have spent part of his exile in the castello?'

Amelia smiled. 'So I understand.'

Kelly grinned. 'I'm a bit of a Dante nut myself. People are really proud of his connection with the area. Makes a change from everything centring around Florence. I assume Bee told you about the family legend?'

'What legend?'

Kelly raised an eyebrow. 'Only that a family member along the line found something written by Dante – a letter or poem, perhaps even part of the original *Inferno*! Rumour has it that it was hidden again, but no one so far has been able to find it. So keep your eyes peeled, you hear.'

Amelia laughed. 'Will do. But don't hold your breath.'

After parking the car on the outskirts of Stia, they took a steep, cobbled lane into the main piazza. The heart of the town was much the same as it must have been for decades, if not centuries. In the middle was a fountain, at the centre of which was a bronze lion with a snake emerging from its mouth, almost as if it were being regurgitated by the lion. On each side of the street were green-shuttered homes, most with the ubiquitous terracotta roofs, interspersed with the odd trattoria, bar and restaurant. Kelly and Amelia appeared to be the only tourists, which was not to say they were the only people around. On the contrary, the little town was buzzing: men huddled on plastic chairs playing cards or dominos; women sat on benches gossiping; mothers walked with children, clearly intent on doing their shopping but without the urgency you'd find in Britain. Everyone seemed to be making the most of the beautiful day, enjoying the outing as much as the purpose.

'What would you like to do first?' Kelly asked. 'I'd offer to show you around, but there's not much to see. The church is quaint, and there's a mill over there that sells jackets made to a traditional design.'

'I'm afraid my priority has to be stocking the fridge.'

'That's easy. I'll show you the best places to shop. When you're done, I'll take you to this darling place for lunch.'

It seemed there was little chance Amelia was going to be able to avoid spending time with her new neighbour.

They took a left up another narrow lane and crossed a bridge before reaching a clutch of shops: butcher's, baker's, greengrocer's, one selling only hats and another wool coats made in the local mill. When both of them had bought what they needed Kelly told Amelia she wanted to go to the Coop, the sole supermarket a little further along the main road, for cat food. Having had enough of shops, Amelia suggested Kelly went without her.

Her thoughts returning to Flavia, she wandered over to the church. It wasn't much to look at from the outside, with a rather plain facade. A plaque identified it as the Pieve di Santa Maria Assunta and dated it to the eleventh century. Amelia felt a fizz of excitement in the pit of her stomach. Definitely the one Flavia wrote about in her diary.

Amelia slipped into the welcoming coolness and paused as her eyes adjusted to gloom. A handwritten notice directed her to a light switch on her left.

As the lights flickered on, the first thing Amelia noticed were the tops of the pillars. Much like those in Rosslyn Chapel, they were adorned with several intricate carvings of odd, cipher-like shapes and tiny ugly gargoyles. Exactly as Flavia described, and which occasionally appeared as doodles in the margins of her diary. To Amelia's right, in an alcove, was a triptych of the Annunciation. The alcove was poorly lit, and Amelia stepped closer to get a better look. The Madonna looked thoughtful, perhaps a little stunned. As she might well have been. Unexpected pregnancies could do that to a woman. At its base – or the predella, to give it its correct name – a single lion rampant stood with its front legs against a shield. Amelia knew from the research she'd done before leaving Scotland it was the Guidi emblem. A small noticeboard informed whoever cared to read it that the triptych had been painted by Bicci di Lorenzo in 1414 and, as she'd already gleaned, had been commissioned by a Guidi – more specifically, the Count of Porciano. Amelia was delighted. This church was directly connected to the Guidis and should be mentioned in the brochure.

To the left of the chancel was a terracotta statue of the Madonna and child. Amelia instantly recognised it as the work of Andrea della Robbia. Both the painting and the terracotta had to be worth a small fortune, yet anyone could just walk out with a piece of priceless art under their arm.

It was only when Amelia was about to leave that she saw the sign warning visitors not to step within a metre of the art as it was alarmed. Given that she'd practically had her nose pressed up to the triptych, it seemed someone had forgotten to switch it on. If it even existed.

Amelia waited for Kelly on a bench on the main street. A few minutes later she arrived, laden with shopping bags.

'Let's get these bags in your car's trunk and then get lunch.'

Once they'd stashed their shopping, they returned to the town centre. The restaurant Kelly had chosen had tables overlooking a fast-flowing part of the Arno which fed the nearby woollen mill. More importantly, as far as Amelia was concerned, it had free Wi-Fi.

'Right,' Kelly said. 'I need to visit the restroom before I do anything.'

While Kelly was in the bathroom Amelia checked her phone for emails. There was one from her father. The snow had melted, he said, and, in the garden, roses had begun to bud. He was re-reading Milton's *Paradise Lost* and enjoying it very much. But how was *she*? Did she like Porciano? What was Beatrice like in the flesh? She sensed the anxiety in his questions but was pleased he was returning to some of the things he enjoyed.

Amelia immediately emailed him back, describing the castello and Porciano, explaining about the lack of internet or a decent phone connection and telling him not to worry if he didn't hear from her for a few days. Knowing he wouldn't like to think of her on her own, once more Amelia didn't mention that Beatrice had been called away.

She was just finishing another email, this time to the director of the costume museum, when Kelly returned. She took a seat and politely looked out the window while Amelia typed.

'Sorry,' Amelia apologised as soon as she'd pressed send. 'I can't log onto the internet at the castello, so I'm taking advantage of Wi-Fi while I can.'

'You can always use mine if you need to. It works fine.'

'I'd appreciate that.' Amelia gave up; clearly she and Kelly were going to spend time together whether Amelia liked it or not, and it might be handy to have access to Wi-Fi without having to come to Stia.

While she'd been emailing, the trattoria had filled up with locals; several tables had been taken by women around Amelia's age, the rest by businessmen and – Amelia's heart twisted – mothers lunching with their children. Her fingers instinctively went to her neck, seeking the comfort of the pendant her father had given her. Odd how quickly it had become a self-soother.

Kelly recommended the ricotta-stuffed ravioli with sage and butter, and when Amelia agreed it sounded delicious she ordered for both of them.

'What exactly are you doing for Bee?' Kelly asked.

Amelia gave a brief description, explaining that she had a joint honours degree in Italian and Medieval History.

A buzz from Amelia's phone alerted her to a new email. To her surprise it was a reply from Signora Fiorini. She was about to go on leave, but if Amelia could make this coming Friday afternoon at three she'd be delighted to see her. Signora Fiorini was certainly efficient.

'Good news?' Kelly asked.

'It's from the director of the costume museum of the Pitti Palace.'

'I didn't know there's a costume museum in the Pitti Palace!' Kelly said, as a waiter placed plates of pasta in front of them.

'There are some clothes in a trunk that belonged to a woman who lived with Beatrice's family in the thirties. Some of them are exquisite. Beatrice suggested the director might be able to tell me who designed them.'

'Oh, I'd love to see them,' Kelly said around a mouthful of pasta.

There was another awkward silence as once again Amelia didn't issue an invitation to come and have a look.

'Hey, why don't we go to Florence together? You could stay at my apartment. You'd have to sleep on the sofa, but I'm told it makes a comfortable bed.'

'I wouldn't want to impose.' Pleasant though Kelly was, the thought of spending hours in her company filled Amelia with dismay. She simply wasn't ready to spend a lot of time in *anyone*'s company.

'It would be great to get a lift,' Kelly continued, running a tongue over her lips as if searching for a spare crumb. 'It would be a chance for me to fetch some things I need from my apartment. We could go to the costume museum together and have dinner out afterwards.' She tucked into her pasta again, spearing a piece with her fork and waving it at Amelia. 'It'll be awesome.'

Amelia capitulated to the inevitable with a smile. 'Sounds like a plan. Although I'm not sure about staying over. There's a ton of stuff I'd like to get done before Beatrice gets back.'

Thankfully, talk turned to Kelly's forthcoming holiday on the island of Elba the weekend after next.

Back at the castello, Amelia fully intended to continue working. Instead, needing to decompress from the unexpectedly social day, she found herself on the window seat again, with Flavia's diaries on her lap and a cup of coffee in her hand.

NINE

FLAVIA

August 1938

Shortly after their return to Florence from Porciano, Flavia made her way to a refugee centre she'd read about. She'd spent the remainder of her time in the Casentino mulling over what Luca and her godparents had said. What to believe? Deciding she needed to make up her own mind – not wait to be told what to think – she'd read every newspaper she could get her hands on and listened to the BBC world news on the wireless when no one was about. What she learned troubled her. Apparently, Hitler was making life very difficult for Jews living in Germany and Austria. He'd introduced laws that restricted their right to work, to attend university, even to visit parks or other public spaces! In response, many Jews were fleeing the countries of their birth, seeking sanctuary in countries across Europe including Italy. More concerning, it was whispered Mussolini was considering following in Hitler's footsteps.

Arriving at the refugee centre, Flavia hesitated in the doorway, twisting the straps of her handbag between her fingers, taking everything in, shocked at how busy it was. All these people! Was the situation so very bad in their countries?

Long trestle tables had been set up along three sides of the hall, on top of which were large hot water urns, cups and saucers, enormous cooking pots filled to the brim with sauces, bowls piled high with pasta or salad, still more heaped with fresh tomatoes and fruit. Clearly the women of Florence had no intention of letting anyone go hungry on their watch. Another table was covered with clothes of every size and type: cardigans, dresses, skirts, trousers, shirts, shoes.

Three women sat behind a desk with men and women facing them. Information was clearly being given and received. Flavia recognised Julia, an acquaintance from her tennis club, among the women taking notes and gave her a discreet wave.

But it was the small groups of people who took up most of the middle of the room that drew and held Flavia's attention. The women ranged from the elegantly dressed – wearing fur coats despite the heat, handmade shoes, fashionable hats perched on top of neatly coiffed hair – to those in rough wool coats, their hair wrapped in scarves, ill-fitting boots on their feet. Almost all of the women had children – some of whom had somehow along the way become separated from their footwear – clinging to their hands or supported on hips.

A baby tucked inside his mother's coat peeped out at Flavia with large brown eyes, regarding her as seriously as a general surveying his soldiers. Flavia made a face at him, making him laugh. Despite the number of people in the room, the atmosphere was calm and organised.

Spotting Flavia in the doorway, a dark-haired girl about her age hurried towards her. She was dressed in trousers and blouse, her thick, wavy hair falling to just below her ears. She looked confident and self-assured. 'May I help you?'

'I'm Flavia Corsi. I'd like to help.'

The girl raised an eyebrow and cast a sceptical glance at Flavia. Wanting to impress, Flavia had chosen her outfit with particular care – a linen dress with three-quarter-length sleeves, cinched at the waist with a matching belt, a thin cardigan, T-bar shoes and stockings. She'd completed her ensemble with a little handbag and a cloche hat which she'd set at an angle. Flavia groaned inwardly. She should have worn more practical trousers and a blouse.

'I'm prepared to do anything,' she said quickly. 'Cook' – thank goodness for all those lessons Margherita had given her! – 'offer drinks, whatever is needed. I promise I'm more useful than I look. Anything I can't do, I'll learn.'

The girl broke into a wide smile and stuck out her hand. 'I'm Natalia Montefiore. We always need more volunteers, so you are most welcome.'

Flavia returned the smile, then frowned. 'Are *all* these people refugees?' She kept her voice low, although it was impossible in the hubbub for anyone to overhear.

Natalia followed the line of Flavia's gaze. 'Sad to say, yes. Anyone in need of help finds their way here eventually. Rich, poor, we help them all. The thing they all have in common is that it has become dangerous for them to stay in their own countries.' Natalia pressed her lips together and gave a despairing shake of her head. 'Most are – or should I say *were* – wealthy, certainly wealthy enough to pay extortionate amounts to leave their country of birth. Consequently, they currently have little or no money left, even if they did at one time, and even supposing they were permitted to take it with them. Almost everyone has left their homes and businesses behind, not knowing when they'll be able to return and what will be left when they do. Many have arrived here with only the clothes they are wearing – either because they fled in too much of a hurry to take anything with them, or because their suitcases were stolen or left behind at some station.'

Flavia was appalled. How could the world allow this to happen?

'We collect good-quality clothes to give them. Some need to be altered – it would be marvellous if you can sew?' Natalia raised a hopeful eyebrow.

Sewing wasn't Flavia's forte, but she'd said she could learn anything, so she'd do the best she could. Barely waiting for Flavia to nod, Natalia hurried on. 'The majority are only passing through on their way to Britain, Switzerland or other parts of Europe – some even go to America. Most don't wish to stay here. They are too fearful that what is happening in German-controlled territory could also happen in Italy.'

'You don't think it could? Surely not?' Flavia protested, still unwilling to believe what so many people, including her godparents, clearly feared.

'Jews – me included – don't trust the close relationship between Hitler and Mussolini. In the meantime, in order to continue their journey, they need papers, visas, financial help with their transport. While they are waiting for us to organise all that for them, they need a safe place to rest – a room or apartment for a night or two.' She glanced across at the refugees. 'However, not everyone leaves Italy for a safer country. Some, like friends of my parents, stay.' Natalia's mouth twisted wryly. 'Forgive me if I don't say where.'

If what Natalia was saying was true, matters were worse than Flavia had thought.

Natalia's expression brightened. 'Now if you still want to help, come with me. I'll show you what we do here, and who needs your help most.'

TEN

October 1938

The next few weeks passed in a blur of activity, and Flavia spent every spare hour at the centre. She made soup and pasta and handed out drinks. She took delivery of bags of donated clothes and sorted them by size and gender, refolding them into neat piles and laying them out on one of the trestle tables. In quieter moments she listened to the stories the refugees had to tell. Some had walked for miles on their journeys here, either because they lived too far away from a train station, or were too frightened to buy a ticket in case they were stopped and arrested for not having the right papers. After Hitler made it clear that he was intent on taking back the Sudetenland, representatives from Germany, Italy, France and Britain met in Munich, but instead of standing up to Hitler they conceded to his demands and slunk back to their countries, proclaiming the meeting a success because they'd averted a war that could be more disastrous than the previous one.

As the leaves dropped from the trees and the weather cooled, more refugees flooded into the centre, their stories becoming increasingly shocking and unbelievable. There were accounts of ordinary people being sent to prison camps – allegedly for being 'asocial', but actually for holding different views to Hitler and his regime. There were also accounts of Jews being beaten up and robbed or even disappearing. Flavia's sympathy for the refugees deepened every day. They'd left everything they owned and loved behind: grandparents, grown-up children, sisters and brothers, friends – many of whom refused to see or believe what was happening – as well as their homes and businesses, and their most precious possessions. They had to be convinced it was more dangerous to stay than for them to walk away from it all. It was a shocking discovery.

One family in particular struck a chord. They were from Vienna, and for generations the women had run a successful clothing store beloved by well-to-do Austrians.

The mother, Rebecca, shared their story one day as a group of women, including Flavia, sat at a table altering and repairing clothes.

'When Germany took back Austria, claiming it had always belonged to them, we weren't too alarmed at first,' Rebecca began. 'Some people even went out on the street and cheered, whether they wanted to be part of Germany or not. We didn't think it would affect us too much, but it didn't take long before German soldiers were everywhere. Soon it was no longer unusual to be stopped in the street and asked for our papers.' Rebecca's fingers paused mid-stitch. 'We didn't like it, but we came to accept it. One day, Mother and I were on our way to open our store when we, and many other Jews who were also just going about their everyday business, were stopped by German soldiers. They waited until they had a number of us gathered together, then they pointed their guns at our heads and told us that we'd made the street dirty with our Jewish filth, and we needed to scrub it off and make the streets clean again for respectable Austrians.' Her eyes filled. 'We were outraged, as you can imagine, and we waited for all the people on the street who were watching to be enraged too. For them to protest on our behalf. These were people who frequented our store, people we had dined with, who we sat next to at the opera, people who we thought of as friends, who knew us as well as their own families. But no one said a thing! The more decent hung their heads and hurried on, others stayed to watch as if they were attending a show and we were the act. It was horrible, unbelievable! The soldiers nudged us with their weapons. We had no choice. We dropped to our knees, right there in front of our fellow Austrians, and scrubbed.'

She looked up from her sewing, her eyes swimming with incomprehension. 'How could our friends do nothing?' she whispered. 'We realised then that if they didn't speak up for us at that moment, they never would. That is why we left.'

The more of these stories Flavia heard, the more her uneasiness grew. Crazy things were happening across Europe. In which case, crazy things could happen in Italy too.

As autumn deepened and increasing numbers of bewildered and frightened refugees poured in, Flavia continued to work at the centre in Florence. There were so many people to feed now that the refugees were forced to queue for food and clothes – a process many, understandably, found humiliating.

Most had left in such haste and had stuffed their small suitcases so full that some of their clothes caught in the lid. The sight of a hem of nightgown, the sleeve of a vest or the leg of a trouser brought a lump to Flavia's throat. It had to be the worst thing in the world – having to flee your home, your country, with barely enough time to pack precious possessions in a small suitcase.

There were so many stories, heated discussions too, but what everyone did share was a sense of disbelief and betrayal. One old man from Czechoslovakia had fought alongside the Germans during the Great War, winning the Military Merit Cross in the process, yet he too had been evicted from the country he'd been born in, simply because he was Jewish. It made no sense.

Whenever she wasn't needed to dish out food or clothes, Flavia would draw the refugees, sometimes encircled by several fascinated children who watched every stroke of her pencil intently. At other times she sketched them in play. She'd come to understand that, as long as they were loved, children soon recovered from the shock of suddenly finding themselves homeless. If their parents wished, Flavia gave them the drawings of their children; the sketches she made of the adults' despair and fear she did from memory, in the privacy of her room back in the apartment on Borgo Santa Croce.

Every evening, along with her aunt and uncle, Flavia huddled around the radio tuned to the BBC World Service, which had recently started broadcasting in Italian, trying to make sense of what they were hearing, as if it were all some ghastly mistake. In early November, Jewish homes and businesses were vandalised, many burnt to the ground. The madness only grew as time passed, as Hitler's influence on Mussolini increased antisemitic feeling across Italy.

At the end of November, Flavia, Julia and Natalia arranged to meet for coffee in the Piazza della Repubblica. Working so closely together had made them firm friends, and they often spent time together outside the hours they worked in the centre. The Caffè Giubbe Rosse was one of Flavia's favourite places. It was where the intelligentsia of Florence met. She'd spotted the writer Amalia Guglielminetti there more than once, as well as the artist Anita Pittoni. It was proof, if Flavia needed it, that women could achieve great things in their own right.

Huddled in their fur coats, Julia and Natalia were already waiting for her at an outside table under a canopy. Straight away Flavia noticed Natalia was trembling and white-faced.

'Did you hear?' Natalia demanded, two spots of colour on her cheeks. She threw a copy of the *Corriere della Sera* on the table. 'They've excluded all Italian Jews from attending university. I am not to be allowed to complete my studies. Am I not Italian as well as Jewish? Is this not my country too?'

Flavia picked up the paper and read the article. Her friends waited in silence until she was finished. The newspaper described the Manifesto Razziale. In summary it informed the people of Italy that races were biologically based, and that some were superior to others. The Italian race was pure and Aryan and therefore had a right to rule others, in particular Jews. From now on Italian Jews would be subject to separate rules – among which was the need to register. Most alarmingly, Jews and non-Jews were no longer allowed to socialise together or to marry.

'It's utter nonsense,' Flavia said. 'Dangerous nonsense. I can only think Mussolini is falling more and more under Hitler's spell.'

A disbelieving Natalia shook her head. 'How could he do this? Many Jews, including my parents, have been loyal Fascists all their lives! How can Il Duce say that now there is a pure Italian race! How dare he say that Jewish Italians do not belong to it? Wasn't Mr Sonnino, once our revered prime minister, of the Jewish faith? Would he now be excluded from the cabinet?'

'It *is* nonsense,' Julia agreed, with a quick glance at Flavia. 'And what about Margherita Sarfatti, Il Duce's favourite mistress? Is she to be banished from his bed?'

Natalia remained incensed. 'My grandfather fought for Italy in the Great War. All Italian Jews, whether they are politicians, shop-workers, farmers, or whether poor or rich, are citizens of Italy.'

Her voice had risen to the extent they were attracting attention from the patrons inside the cafe as well as from passing pedestrians.

Before she knew it, Flavia found herself standing on the table. 'Fellow Italians,' she shouted, 'we must protest against these ridiculous, unfair and irrational laws!'

Natalia and Julia stared up at her, mouths inelegantly open.

'We must refuse to obey these laws. Stand up for our fellow citizens!' Flavia continued.

A crowd had gathered to watch. Several laughed, others looked bemused. Flavia squirmed under their scrutiny, knowing her cheeks were burning. Mightn't she have protested just as easily from the pavement?

'What's going on here?' The crowd parted to let a man wearing the uniform of a Blackshirt through. Flavia's heart gave a little kick of fear. Although she'd never actually encountered one, she was aware of their reputation for state-endorsed brutality.

Mussolini's special armed police had always been a law unto themselves, but recently they'd being getting bolder, accosting people in the street, beating them for random, spurious reasons, and Italians were increasingly frightened of them.

'We are making a peaceful protest,' Flavia told him, doing her best to keep her voice steady. The majority of the bystanders slunk away or stepped back inside the cafe. Incredulous, Flavia watched them go. Was nobody going to add their voice to hers? 'My Jewish friend has been informed she may no longer attend university.'

'Is this your Jewish friend?' the Blackshirt asked, pointing to Natalia.

'Yes, she is.'

'In which case, Signorina, I am going to have to arrest you.'

'Arrest me? For having an opinion?' He had to be joking.

'For socialising with a Jew. It is against the law and it's clear you know that. Now get down from that table unless you want me to forcibly remove you.'

Although she was shaking inside, Flavia looked down her nose at the policeman in exactly the same way she'd seen her aunt and Sophia do when they wanted to intimidate someone. 'I intend to stay exactly where I am.'

Finally, Julia was jolted from her paralysis. She stepped forward. 'Captain Lambini, it is too long since we have had the pleasure of your company at our home. My mother often asks my father to invite you for dinner or drinks. Unfortunately, Papa is very forgetful.' Anyone would think they were at a social event, not outside a cafe with one of the guests on a table. Flavia's head spun. Julia knew a Blackshirt – had clearly welcomed him into her home! How was it possible? She'd heard more and more of these people – no more than thugs really – were invited to gatherings, as if people were too scared not to invite them. But Julia's family? How could they? Especially when Julia must have shared the refugees' stories with her parents.

Captain Lambini smirked, clearly delighted to be acknowledged in public by someone of Julia's social standing.

Flavia was about to insist that she had every right to stand where she chose, but a look at Natalia's pale face and the warning in Julia's eyes changed her mind. If Flavia could be arrested what might happen to Natalia?

Flavia used Julia's shoulder to steady herself as she climbed down from the table. 'I will continue to have tea with whoever I wish.' She was acutely aware of how pathetic her protest had been, and her cheeks still burned with mortification.

The captain gave her a long, hard look. 'I won't arrest you this time. But be under no illusions, Signorina – if I catch you breaking the rules again, I will make an example of you.'

Flavia watched as he walked off, unsure of how she felt.

Her act of defiance had been small and feeble and over in a moment, but unlike the friends of the Austrian family made to scrub the streets on their hands and knees, she had protested, and that made her feel as if the Fascists weren't having it all their own way.

ELEVEN

Florence, May 1939

Flavia's heart fluttered as if it were a bird, her chest its cage. Her first proper dance! And she'd only just turned seventeen. The party was being held at Julia's parents' palazzo. Her mother was a friend of Aunt Lucrezia, and Flavia had been included in the invitation. Natalia on the other hand hadn't been. (Flavia was sure it didn't have anything do with Natalia being Jewish. Julia's parents were 'not inclined' to pay much attention to Mussolini's decrees.) Over recent months Jews had been banned from skilled professions – putting lawyers, architects and engineers out of work. They couldn't own radios or enter public buildings, parks or vacation spots. As the laws grew more outrageous, some Jews chose to leave Italy, but many stayed, refusing to believe that what was happening in Austria and Germany could ever happen in Italy. Natalia was one of those who refused to leave, partly because her frail mother had come to stay with her, partly because she had nowhere else to go.

Flavia shook the gloomy thoughts away. For tonight, at least, she was going to forget what was going on in the world and enjoy herself.

Studying herself in the mirror, twisting her head this way and that as her godmother put the final touches to her hair, she could hardly believe that the face staring back at her was hers. At some point over the last few months she'd developed cheekbones, and with her hair up her eyes looked bigger. Her mouth was still too wide and her nose too long, but that couldn't be helped.

'You look beautiful,' Aunt Lucrezia murmured from behind her, an ache in her voice. 'So like your dear mother at the same age.'

Flavia stood and whirled for her aunt. The dress she was wearing – a deep blue silk with a plunging back and a fishtail hem – clung to her hips, swirling around her ankles.

'Your mama loved dressing up,' her godmother continued with a wistful smile. 'It seems you're no different.'

'Who wouldn't love to wear a gown like this?' Flavia said, running her fingers across the silky fabric. One of her godmother's friends was a famous dress designer and had given Flavia the dress. It had been last worn on the catwalk and had a tiny stain that was almost invisible but prevented it from being sold. According to Signora Schiaparelli, Flavia's figure was exactly what the gown needed to show it off. Although Flavia knew she was still far too skinny, the dress gave her the appearance of having a half-decent figure. Even her breasts looked normal, if on the small side. Finally, she was growing into her body, even if her legs still felt too long for her torso, and her limbs sometimes still behaved as if they didn't belong to her. She prayed she wouldn't trip over her feet or spill her drink or do something equally clumsy at the party. That would be mortifying.

Her godmother stood on tiptoe to kiss Flavia's forehead. 'Your parents would be very proud of the young woman you have become.'

The palazzo where the private party was to be held was one of the grandest in Florence. It was lit up, the street on either side nose to tail with cars depositing the guests. Anyone who was anyone in

Florence would be here. The invitations were the most sought-after in the city.

Flavia stepped inside and, as she paused to have her coat taken, she caught sight of herself again in a huge gilded mirror. She still couldn't believe the woman reflected in it was actually her.

It was difficult to move in the crush of guests. The conte and contessa were immediately swallowed up by the mass of bodies, and Sophia spotted a friend and disappeared too, leaving Flavia on her own. Waiters threaded their way through the crowd, holding trays of drinks and *aperitivi* aloft, and Flavia accepted a glass gratefully. She'd never drunk champagne before, and it tasted much better than she'd imagined. She particularly liked the way the bubbles tickled her nose, making her want to giggle. A few sips later she was feeling much more relaxed. Despite the fug of cigar smoke, the light cast by the many chandeliers sparkled off the jewels at the women's throats and wrists. Beautiful floor-length gowns, many with swooping backs and cinched-in waists, clung to slender and not-so-slender frames. The women were of all shapes and sizes, but what they all had in common was confidence. Flavia lifted her chin and let a small – and, she hoped, mysterious – smile play around her lips, praying she was disguising her anxiety. A braying came from the middle of the room followed by a loud voice.

At that moment the crowd parted to reveal a circle of men and women. The British and Americans. The Forestieri. The Excelsior and the Grand Hotel were always bustling with foreign visitors, who were sought-after guests at any party. Many Italians adored the British in particular, and all Italians longed for and treasured an invitation to the American and British consulates on the Arno, which were where the Forestieri congregated and where the best parties were held. Anyone would think that they had as much right to Florence as the Italians. They had their own churches, the British their own cemetery – the Cimitero degli Inglesi. And if all that wasn't enough, they had their own newspaper for both local and international news and even their own grocery store so they wouldn't be forced to do without their favourite treats. It was as if they were determined to enjoy the best of Florence but keep a foot in their own countries at the same time.

She didn't see why some Italian women thought British men were so marvellous. In her opinion they were too pale, too foppish, too boastful. And now, astonishingly, there was talk of war between their two countries.

'We're leaving tomorrow,' one of the Englishmen was saying. 'We've done Florence.'

Flavia's English wasn't quite fluent enough to understand everything that was said but sufficiently good to follow most of it. Done Florence! How did one *do* Florence? What did that even mean? She'd seen the way these young men and women visited the churches and museums. Grasping their Baedekers in their hands, they rushed from one masterpiece to the next, barely glancing at each one before moving on. That was how they did Florence! 'We're off to Venice tomorrow,' the same man said, 'then Rome and Naples.' He counted off each city on his fingers as if he were a child counting his numbers. 'Then we're sailing to Greece.'

Didn't he know there could be a war? Many Forestieri had already left for their own countries.

Flavia hooked another glass of champagne from a passing waiter and sipped it greedily. Why had she never tried champagne before? Across the other side of the room, she spotted Julia. Her friend waved and pushed her way towards her.

'Flavia!' Julia kissed her on both cheeks. 'You look absolutely gorgeous. You make me feel positively dowdy. My goodness! Is that a Schiaparelli you're wearing? It looks stunning on you.' Julia's frank admiration brought heat rushing to Flavia's cheeks. 'I can't spend too long talking as I must circulate, but I hope to see you soon,' she continued. Before Flavia had a chance to reply, Julia kissed her again and rushed off to speak to another guest.

'We meet again, Signorina Corsi!' a voice came from behind Flavia. She whirled around to find the odious Blackshirt from the day she'd stood on the table last year in front of her. Everything inside her recoiled. Following the scene at the cafe, she'd quizzed Julia about the Blackshirt, and her friend had explained that Captain Lambini had been an employee at her father's law firm and therefore someone who he had no choice but to invite to social occasions. 'Papa says it is better to keep your enemies close,' Julia had whispered to Flavia. 'That way you know what mischief they might be about to get up to.'

'Allow me to introduce myself. I am Centurione Vincenzo Lambini.' His accent gave him away. This man would never be part of Florence society if he wasn't a Blackshirt. Not that she cared about that. What bothered her was that he was part of that group who bullied and intimidated those who dare not reciprocate.

To Flavia's relief someone attracted his attention, so she was able to move away. She found Sophia and was drawn into her conversation. Waiters kept offering champagne, and Flavia kept taking it until her head was spinning. It was no longer making her light-headed in a pleasant way.

She excused herself and hoping – but not at all sure – she was walking in a straight line, headed for the garden and fresh air. Across the lush lawns, hundreds of lanterns had been hung from the branches of trees. Finding a stone bench set apart from the guests and hidden in the shadows, she sat down and slipped off her shoes. She wasn't used to wearing high heels for any length of time. Taking hold of her right foot, she massaged it between her fingers. The sound of laughter, some high pitched, some a low rumble, drifted across the honey-scented air. Suppressed giggles came from the darkness.

She smelt the smoke of his cigarette before she saw him.

'So here you are! I was wondering where you went.'

She looked up to find Captain Lambini in front of her. She groaned inwardly.

'I was just about to go back inside.' She shoved her feet back into her shoes and stood. Happily, with his arrival, the dizzy sensation had passed. 'If you would excuse me?'

'Do you know, I think you are the most beautiful woman I have ever seen.'

Did the man imagine she wanted his compliments? Not only was she *not* flattered but he made her uneasy. Judging by his corpulent frame, his soft belly straining against his belt and his jowly cheeks giving him a clownish air, he was clearly a man who enjoyed his food. But it was the way he looked at her, his protuberant lower jaw jutting out as if he were a dog at the table begging for scraps, that revolted her most.

She went to move past him, but to her surprise and irritation he stepped in front of her, barring her way.

'Would you have dinner with me one evening?' he asked.

She thought about making an excuse, but he would see past it. Besides, why should she bother?

'I'm very sorry. That won't be possible.'

'Lunch then?'

'I'm afraid not.' Not even if he were the last man on earth.

The oily smile vanished as if it had never been. 'Too good for me. Is that it?' he spat, his voice vibrating with anger. 'You think you are out of my reach because of who your godparents are?' He jutted his chin at her. 'Life has been easy for you. You have never had to fight for your place in life, so don't you dare patronise me. What gives you the right to look down on me? It's not as if you're a member of the aristocracy—'

'How do you know anything about me?' She refused to let the venom in his voice shake her. 'We have barely exchanged more than a few words.'

His piggy eyes bored into hers. 'I made it my business to find out. I learnt a great deal about you, Signorina Corsi. For example, I know what your guardians, the conte and contessa, say in private when they think they are among friends. They should be more careful about who they trust – especially given their association with you.' His fleshy lips stretched in a sneer. 'They should have thought twice before taking in the daughter of two of Il Duce's enemies.'

Flavia's blood ran cold. 'What is that supposed to mean?' What on earth was he implying?

It was his turn to look surprised. He thought for a moment, then narrowed his eyes. A smile crossed his fleshy lips. 'They haven't told you, have they?'

Despite the warmth of the evening, a chill swept across her skin. 'Told me what?'

'That your parents – your father in particular – was no friend of Il Duce. And your mother wasn't much better. They should have been more careful about what they said.'

'I can't imagine what you think you know,' she said, suppressing a shiver. 'Your sources are mistaken. Now would you excuse me?'

She stepped forward, determined to move past him again, but he grabbed her wrist and squeezed it painfully. 'It's always a good idea to have friends in the right places. Even better not to get on the wrong side of them.'

How dare he touch her! She wrenched her arm from his grasp. 'All I know is that people like you use that uniform to hide behind. You think wearing it gives you the right to stop innocent people in the street and beat them.' She drew herself to her full height. In her heels she was a good few inches taller than him. 'If I don't go out with you, would you beat me too?'

A look of such fury crossed his face that for a terrifying moment she thought he would do just that. She would never know for certain, for at that moment the familiar figure of Sophia appeared behind him.

'Flavia! I wondered where you'd disappeared to. I was beginning to think you'd left and gone home.' Sophia turned a steely gaze on Captain Lambini, looking down her aristocratic nose. She was her mother's daughter to her very fingertips. 'And who is this? I don't believe we've met.' She gave Flavia another sharp glance.

'This is... I'm sorry, but I don't recall your name.' Flavia did, her memory was excellent, but she wanted him to know how little attention he merited from her.

'Centurione Vincenzo Lambini,' he said, through gritted teeth.

'Then, cara, let us leave Centurione Lambini in peace to finish his cigarette.' Sophia gripped Flavia's elbow and steered her back across the lawn. Flavia glanced behind her. The captain had remained where he was but continued to stare in their direction. 'Why on earth did you accuse him of being a bully?' Sophia said, keeping her voice low. 'It's bad enough to have said it to anyone – but to a Blackshirt! Are you mad? Rattling a man like that's ego is like poking a nest of snakes. What if it gets to Mussolini's ears?'

'I hardly think Il Duce would be interested in anything I had to say.'

'It's how it reflects on Mama and Papa. It is not just what *you* say – you fool. It is also who you are connected to!'

Flavia was immediately aghast. She'd spoken without thinking. She hadn't thought about the effect her behaviour might have on anyone else. If she caused trouble for the conte and contessa, after everything they'd done for her, she'd never forgive herself. It must have been the champagne that had made her so reckless, as well as his hints about her parents.

'He said something about Mama and Papa.' Flavia swallowed. 'He said they'd been enemies of the state.'

Sophia stopped at the foot of the steps and looked around. She couldn't have appeared more furtive if she tried. 'Keep your voice down,' she hissed, although by this time they were too far away from Captain Lambini to be overheard. Nevertheless, Sophia tugged her into the shadows. 'You should speak to my parents,' she said gently. 'But wait until we get home.'

'Why? What do you know? Tell me!'

Sophia shook her head. Even in the half-light Flavia could see the sympathy in her eyes. 'I'm sorry, cara. Whatever you need to know has to come from them.'

TWELVE

Flavia and her godparents left the party shortly afterwards. Although Flavia was burning to ask them what Captain Lambini had meant, she bit back the torrent of questions lest the driver overhear. Inside their apartment Flavia turned to face them. 'I would like to speak to you about something.'

She waited until they were seated in the drawing room, her godfather with a cognac in hand, her godmother with a small sherry. Flavia had never seen either of them look so ill at ease. She suspected Sophia had warned them that she had questions for them.

'What happened to my parents?' she launched straight in. 'Did they really die in a car accident?'

It was what she'd been told, and as a five-year-old she'd had no reason to doubt it. But had anyone actually said how the accident had happened? All she remembered from that time was her parents heading out for an evening and not coming back, and everyone crying, and being told that they had gone to heaven and that her mother's friend was coming to look after her.

A look passed between the conte and contessa. Flavia's godmother was pale, and there was a slight tremor at the corner of her eye – the only sign she ever gave when she was uncomfortable about something. When the conte lit a cigarette with hands that weren't quite steady, Flavia's unease grew. Nothing ever rattled him.

Her godmother leaned forward and took Flavia's hands in hers. 'We always meant to talk to you about it. We were going to tell you on your tenth birthday, then your eleventh, but every year we decided to leave it just a little longer. You were such a sad little girl for such a long time, and when you finally began to smile again we couldn't bring ourselves to do anything that might take that smile away.'

'Please tell me now.'

The contessa kept hold of her hands. 'As you know, Chiara and I were the firmest of friends – although we were very different. She was the more outgoing of the two of us, certainly the more beautiful with her blonde hair and fine features.' She took a shaky breath. 'As I said earlier, you remind me of her more and more every day.'

This was all very interesting, flattering even, but it didn't answer Flavia's question.

'We told you that she wrote for a newspaper.' This time it was her godfather who spoke. 'Both your mother and father hated what Mussolini was doing, and they spoke up about it – your father in the lectures he gave to his students and wherever he was invited to speak. And your mother in little digs in her newspaper articles – digs that didn't escape notice either. That was the problem.' He sighed deeply. 'Your parents thought they were untouchable. They weren't.'

Flavia's stomach somersaulted. She wasn't sure she could bear to hear what her godfather had to say.

'You asked about Il Duce when we were in Porciano last summer,' the conte continued. 'At first most people believed in what the Fascists were trying to do. But your parents saw the writing on the wall and saw that the Fascists meant to become dictators. They were correct. In 1926 all opposition parties were banned, and the Fascists took control of the press, persuading newspaper owners to sack anyone with anti-Fascist views. I told you your mother mainly wrote articles about what dances were happening and so on, but over time her articles became increasingly political. To her fury your mother was one of those let go. However, she didn't let that stop her from saying what she thought. She simply would not keep her opinions to herself. Neither would your father. Over that time the police had been given much greater powers, and a secret police force, the Opera di Vigilanza e Repressione dell'Antifascismo, was formed.'

He paused to take a long swallow of his cognac. 'They tried to make all the university professors sign allegiance to the Fascist party. Many did, and who can blame them? But your father refused.' He sighed. 'He and your mother were as stubborn as each other.'

At that moment a memory edged its way into Flavia's head. It was of her dressed in her smartest hat and dress – picked out by her nanny – for some parade in Mussolini's honour. All the children were taking part, and Flavia had been almost beside herself with excitement. But just as they were getting ready to leave, her father arrived home and said she couldn't go. No amount of crying and pleading had persuaded him to change his mind. For the first time it occurred to Flavia that she'd never wondered why. In every other respect her father never denied her anything.

'We don't know for certain what happened to them – they were just two among the thousands that "disappeared" in the purges by the Fascists.'

'The government took them?' Flavia was struggling to understand how this could be. 'Are you certain they're dead?' Hope surged. 'Maybe they're still alive!'

'I am so sorry, my dear,' Lucrezia said gently. 'You must not think there is any hope.' She glanced at her husband again. 'My father – he was still alive then – used his position and connections to try and find out what had happened to your parents. The Fascists eventually showed him photographs of their bodies. Claimed they had died in a crash when their car had careered off the road. From the appearance of their bodies my father knew it couldn't be true. He was in no doubt that they had been killed – murdered – but also in no doubt that it could never be proven.'

Flavia felt as if she might be sick. Thoughts, images and questions tumbled through her head. How had her parents been killed? Placed against a wall and shot? Hanged by their necks?

She knew now why her father had forbidden her to take part in the parade. Her insides churned. Her parents had been murdered! By their own government. Simply for protesting. And no one had told her – not even her godparents. How could these two people she cared about, and who she thought cared about her, who she looked upon as her family, have kept something this big from her? What else had they not told her? She'd asked them about her parents a year ago, given them the opportunity to talk to her as an adult, and they'd palmed her off. How could she trust them again? They'd allowed her to grow up believing that the world was essentially a safe place, with the government, whatever its mistakes, having the good of its citizens at heart. What a fool she'd been to believe them. She should have known there was evil in Mussolini when he brought out laws against Jews, when he sided with a man who was even more evil. It was as if the earth had shifted under her, the innocent, trusting child – yes, child! – she'd been only a few hours ago gone as surely as a cobweb by a duster.

She hauled herself out of the chair onto jelly legs.

When Aunt Lucrezia put out a hand to steady her, Flavia pulled away.

'I would like to go to my room,' she said stiffly, 'if you'll excuse me.'

'Don't you have other questions? We'll answer any you might have.'

'Later perhaps, but right at this moment I need to be alone.' She headed to the door. She had to reach the sanctuary of her room before she fell apart.

'Before you go, Flavia,' her uncle called after her. 'You must never repeat any of what we have told you to anyone – no one at all. It is not a good thing that Captain Lambini knows so much about you and also appears to have us in his sights. You must promise us that you will not do or say anything that will bring more unwelcome attention.'

She didn't answer. She would do her best not to bring trouble on the conte and contessa, but she was her parents' daughter and fully intended to make them proud. Like them, she would never stand by and do nothing in the face of injustice. That was the only promise she was prepared to make.

THIRTEEN

AMELIA

Amelia got up before dawn to get ready for the trip to Florence. She and Kelly had agreed to leave at seven. The night before, she'd selected two dresses to take to Signora Fiorini, one of which was the dark blue silk with the bow, the other a red velvet. She'd also decided to take the coat with the pattern, along with a pair of cork-heeled shoes. She wanted to see what Signora Fiorini had to say before she showed her the rest.

A sleepy-eyed Kelly was waiting next to the car, shivering in the cool mountain air. The roads were quiet and, as Amelia was less tense than she'd been on the drive up, she was better able to appreciate the scenery she'd missed, despite the fact she kept sneezing. Crap – she'd forgotten to buy antihistamines in Stia. Tuscany was exactly as depicted in the travel brochures, with its rolling hills, cypress trees and forests and, as they approached Florence, olive trees and vineyards with their first buds. Kelly dozed most of the way, and Amelia's thoughts kept straying back to Flavia's diary. How shocking to find out that your parents had been murdered by your own government. That was bound to change a person. No wonder she felt a bond with Flavia. They'd both lost people they'd loved in horrible circumstances. Her godparents had clearly treated Flavia with kindness, but nothing could compensate for growing up without two loving parents. Amelia had been an only child too and had often felt lonely.

Her thoughts turned to her father. Was his inability to show affection to those he loved due to feeling abandoned by his family? She wished he'd told her years ago that he was adopted. Italians weren't known for having only one child. Wouldn't there have been grandparents, aunts and uncles? In which case why hadn't they taken him? Was there a way of finding out? It was almost a relief to have other stuff to obsess over besides her grief – even if she never found the answers. She intended to visit the Innocenti Museum while she was in Florence.

As they entered Florence, Kelly woke up and directed Amelia to a parking space outside her apartment on the Via Maragliano. They parted after agreeing to meet at the main entrance of the Pitti Palace at quarter to three. It was only ten o'clock, so Amelia had several hours to fill before then.

It was a short walk into the centre, and after being in the car Amelia was happy to stretch her legs and reacquaint herself with the city. The first time she came to Florence it felt like she'd landed in a Hollywood film set. Everything was just as she'd imagined – but bigger, better and more beautiful. As she approached the Piazza della Repubblica she was bombarded with noise – scooters, horns, snippets of conversation in several languages, delighted exclamations – and people, at least twice as many as when she'd been here last, and there had been hordes of them then. She jumped out of the way as a cyclist almost ran into her and immediately had to make another side step to avoid a group of tourists, their guide holding a small placard aloft, crying for the group to follow – their phones perched on selfie sticks, more interested in taking photos than looking. The familiar smells of garlic, pizza, rich coffee and cigarettes, as well as the less pleasant, drifting, putrid smell of the sewers, assaulted her senses. The shop windows displaying cakes and gelati of every flavour were equally familiar, as were the scores of outdoor cafes and restaurants.

Apart from the masses of tourists, Florence was essentially the same as it had been for centuries, the same city Flavia described in her diaries; the market stalls bursting with flowers, shoes, handbags, vases – everything a person could possibly want – the carts selling tripe and *bomboloni* – all still there. Amelia imagined Flavia striding beside her, her face alight with joy and pleasure, and her mood lifted. It was as if she could sense Flavia's approval, and she couldn't shake the fanciful notion that she wanted to show Amelia her Florence. Amelia walked to the Palace of the Innocents and spent an hour in its museum, reading about its past and examining the little drawers with the relics and the stories of the orphans once raised there. She wondered again about the significance, if any, of her own half pendant.

Afterwards she drifted into San Marco and eventually found herself outside the Chiesa dei Santi Apostoli, the small church in the Piazza del Limbo where Beatrice's mother married her American. Who but Italians would build a church in a piazza reminding people of the need to always be ready for death? Needing no such reminder, Amelia turned away.

Late morning, she stopped for thick hot chocolate at the Caffè Rivoire in the Piazza della Signoria, which appeared to have changed not a bit since it first opened; she imagined she was sitting at the same table Flavia sat laughing at with friends or perhaps sketching passers-by with her sketch pad.

She paid her bill, trying not to wince at the price of her drink, and went to the Uffizi. Kelly had given Amelia her annual pass, so she didn't have to queue. To her delight she found most of the paintings Flavia had sketched. She could have stayed for hours, but a glance at her watch told her she needed to hurry if she wasn't to miss her appointment with Signora Fiorini. First though, she needed to retrieve the bag with the clothes from the car.

By the time she reached the Ponte Vecchio the tourists were out in force. She crossed the bridge, thinking of the Medicis who ruled Florence, and who used the corridor above the bridge to travel between the Uffizi and the Pitti Palace. She was struck again by how people lived, loved and died over the centuries, yet the world continued to spin on its axis even when it seemed impossible – shocking – that it should.

Kelly was waiting for her at the entrance of the Pitti Palace. Amelia explained to one of the attendants about having an appointment with Signora Fiorini, and she led them up several flights of stairs and along corridors festooned with artworks and frescoes, whizzing past masterpieces as if they were mass-produced prints, before eventually reaching the costume museum. At the desk, the woman in charge of issuing tickets made a call and a few minutes later the director of the museum appeared. Signora Fiorini was small and slim, dressed in a two-piece business suit, her glossy dark hair twisted into a neat chignon. She looked as if she had stepped out of a magazine or, in another time, a couture house. She shook their hands and asked about Beatrice before leading them through another series of corridors and into a back room. Amelia unpacked the clothes from their layers of tissue and laid them on the table.

Signora Fiorini gasped at the red velvet gown and, pulling on a pair of cotton gloves, ran her hands reverentially across the material.

'Why, this is from Chez Madeleine Vionnet, one of the most popular and expensive designers of the time.' She studied the coat with equal excitement. 'And this is by Elsa Schiaparelli. See how the embroidered design on the back can either be faces or urns? And the blue silk gown is by her too. The shoes are by Ferragamo, the shoemaker to the stars. They are beautiful pieces. If you were interested in loaning any of these to us, we would be delighted.'

Amelia explained that the contessa hoped to display them in her little museum. 'But I'll mention you are keen to borrow them when they are not on show at the castello.'

'Please. We have many fine examples of both Schiaparelli's and Vionnet's work, but these are exceptional.'

She spread the coat on the table and ran her hand over it as if it were made of fragile glass. She paused. 'There is something in the pocket.'

The three of them stared at it as if they had X-ray vision.

'What do you think it is?' Kelly asked.

'It feels like paper. Shall I take it out?'

Amelia nodded. She could tell by the look on Kelly's face that she was just as curious as Amelia to see whatever it was.

With the finesse of a surgeon, Signora Fiorini removed a piece of paper that had been folded into a thin strip and handed it to Amelia. Amelia carefully opened the single sheet of paper.

It was a letter written in Italian in a large, expansive hand.

My dearest Flavia,

I trust this finds you safe and well. You know how your godfather and I wish we could be with you. I hope it isn't too long before this wretched war is over and we can be together again.
Bella, I am writing this to implore you to be careful. Do not tell anyone what you have discovered, no matter how much you believe you can trust them. You must keep it hidden. We are living in difficult times and cannot be sure who is a friend and who an enemy. We cannot even be certain that those who pretend to be our friends are what they seem.
This wretched war will be over soon, and we can decide then, together, what is to be done. In the meantime, keep your counsel.
If you are still writing your diaries, my child, as I am almost certain you will be, and have written any of what you've told me in them, then destroy them – immediately. I know how much this will grieve you, but it is for the best. You must do whatever you can to keep yourself safe.

Until then,
L

Amelia blew out a breath. Kelly had been reading the letter over her shoulder. Signora Fiorini had discreetly turned away, pretending to be absorbed in the contents of a drawer. Amelia read the letter again.

There was no date on it, no address. When was it written, and where had Flavia been when she received it? What discovery was her aunt referring to? As for the diaries, was whatever information her aunt was alluding to in the pages that had been torn out?

Although her eyes were bright with curiosity, Signora Fiorini didn't ask about the contents of the note. Instead, she reluctantly refolded the clothes and handed them back to Amelia. 'I'll be in touch with the contessa when I get back from my holiday,' she said, 'but thank you for bringing these to show me.'

Kelly was a different matter. She could barely suppress her excitement. 'Who is Flavia?'

Instead of answering Kelly, Amelia slipped the note into the side pocket of her handbag. After thanking Signora Fiorini for her time, she and Kelly left by the side door and emerged into the Boboli Gardens, blinking as their eyes adjusted to the blinding sunlight. The heat was more intense than ever, and there was a mixture of locals and tourists making use of the gardens to escape the frenetic squash of the city.

'So, what do you think?' Kelly asked as they walked towards the exit.

'About the letter?'

'What else?' Kelly looked at Amelia as if she were bonkers. 'Do you know who Flavia was?'

'She was raised by Beatrice's grandparents after her parents were killed – or more accurately murdered – apparently because they were anti-Fascist. I think the "L" in the letter is Lucrezia, her godmother.' She didn't mention the diaries, knowing damn well she shouldn't be reading them without asking Beatrice's permission.

'What do you think she found – the thing Lucrezia asked her to hide?'

'I haven't the faintest idea. It doesn't have to be an object though. It might be information. Some secret about someone or something.'

'I don't understand why you aren't more excited! Remember what I told you about the family legend? The rumours about the lost Dante work? Don't you see? This could be evidence it does exist. This Flavia girl could have found it!'

'In which case, she would have told Beatrice's mother, Sophia, who would have told Beatrice, and the world would know about it!'

'What are you going to do?' Kelly continued. 'At least tell me you're going to ask Beatrice about the letter.'

'Of course,' Amelia said, suddenly feeling drained. She gave Kelly an apologetic smile. 'I'm sorry but would you mind if we skip dinner? I'd really just like to get back to Porciano.'

'So you can start looking?' Kelly's eyes were bright, almost feral.

'So I can get back to work,' Amelia replied firmly.

Kelly linked her arm in Amelia's. 'In that case I'll come back with you.'

'There's no need. I'll be fine.'

'I don't think so. You're tired. If you want to survive the journey, you're going to need me as your wing man.'

'I thought you were going to stay the night at your apartment?'

'Easily done another time.'

Once more Amelia had no choice but to give in.

On the return trip Kelly tried to bring up the subject of the letter again, but when Amelia said she needed all her concentration just to keep the pair of them in one piece she lapsed into silence, only rousing herself to point out a car on the wrong side of the road, or the turnoff they needed to take.

By the time they arrived back in Porciano every muscle in Amelia's body ached with fatigue. Kelly invited her to supper at her place, but Amelia refused, claiming she'd only enough energy left to shower and go to bed. That wasn't entirely true. During the drive back she hadn't been able to stop thinking about the letter. What if there was something in the trunk Beatrice didn't know about? Hadn't she said it hadn't been opened in years?

Amelia went through it again, taking each item out, until reaching the bottom she found the walnut box inlaid with mother-of-pearl. What if whatever Flavia had found was inside? Although she knew it was extremely unlikely, she had to know for sure.

Without the key, the only way to open the locked box was to prise it open. Which was out of the question. Not only might it damage the lock irreparably, but then there would be no disguising that someone had recently tampered with it. There was still a chance Amelia might be able to explain why she'd been reading Flavia's diaries, but there would be absolutely no excusing her behaviour if she attempted to force open a locked box.

She looked through each one of the handbags. They were all empty. Next, she checked the pockets of all the dresses. Nada. She had given up and was refolding the fur coat when she felt something small and hard in the collar that shouldn't be there.

Too impatient to take the lift she ran upstairs, fetched her nail scissors from her toilet bag in the bathroom and, on her return to the basement, carefully snipped away at the stitches of the collar. Within minutes she was holding a small brass key in the palm of her hand. She hesitated. What the hell was she doing? She had no right to be undoing the stitching of an expensive coat that wasn't hers, no right to open a locked box that *definitely* did not belong to her. Beatrice had asked her to look through the trunk to discover whether there was anything to display – not to snoop. She couldn't justify her actions, not even to herself. Nevertheless, as if on automatic pilot, she inserted the key into the lock. It was stiff, the mechanism rusted with age, but – after a little wriggling – it caught and turned.

Inside, there was a plain gold ring and a rolled-up piece of paper. Amelia's fingers shook as she unravelled it. To her intense disappointment it was neither a document nor pages ripped from a diary, but a sketch of a man lying on a bed of rumpled sheets, his hands tucked behind his head. Looking at the artist through half-closed eyes, he was bare chested, perhaps even naked – she couldn't be sure as a sheet covered his lower half. Whoever he was, Amelia was certain that the artist, Flavia, adored him. She was equally certain that Flavia had just left the bed he lay in.

Good on you, Flavia. But why go to such lengths to hide this sketch? On the other hand, it was such an intimate portrait it was probably never meant for other eyes. As for the ring – why hide that?

There was something else right at the bottom of the box. Amelia lifted out a package and carefully unfolded the brown paper wrapping to reveal a long silk-embroidered christening gown. It was old, possibly passed down from generation to generation. Was this the gown Flavia was christened in? If so, it seemed to be the only memento of her childhood she'd kept. Poor, orphaned Flavia. Amelia raised the tiny gown to her face and breathed deeply, searching out the familiar scents of babyhood but detecting only the faint smell of mothballs. Yet it was enough to undo her.

The day Fiona was born was the happiest and scariest of her life. Although her body ached in places she didn't even know existed, the joy she felt as she cradled Fiona in her arms took her breath away. Cameron looked at Amelia as if she'd just climbed Everest (and to be honest her body thought it had), or had single-handedly discovered a cure for cancer. Amelia, on the other hand, was terrified she wouldn't know what to do with a baby. For the first time in years, she longed for her mother.

It had been Cameron's wish to have Fiona christened, and Amelia had been happy to go along with whatever he wanted, just as he always said it was his mission in life to make Amelia happy. He said if he didn't make her laugh every day he'd have failed. The way he held their daughter, enveloped in her christening gown as if she were fragile glass, had brought a lump to Amelia's throat. She guessed most fathers were awed by and proud of their children, but they'd been trying for more than four years, and Amelia had had two early miscarriages during that time. When Amelia had sunk into depression, Cameron had barely left her side. He'd taken time off work, coaxed her out of the house with trips in his boat, hikes in the Pentland hills, concerts and shows in Edinburgh, promising her that – although he wanted to have a child with her – she was enough for him, would always be enough. She couldn't believe they'd finally managed to make this perfect child. In front of the small audience of family and friends, they'd promised to guide, love and protect her.

She'd loved her child, so very much, but she'd failed to protect her. And so had Cameron.

FOURTEEN

Amelia wasn't sure what wrenched her from sleep, only that every nerve in her body was thrumming. She strained to hear in the darkness, trying to work out where she was. Slowly it came back to her. She was in Italy. In the castello, in her bed in the Warrior Abbess's room, the sheets tangled around her. Last night had been the worst since she'd arrived in Italy. She could barely remember going to bed, only that she'd cried herself to sleep.

The wind wailed through the window, making the curtain flap viciously. Still disoriented, she got out of bed to close it. As she reached towards it, the room was illuminated by a flash of light, followed seconds later by a growl of thunder. She checked the time on her phone. Three o'clock. Much too early to get up. However, she was wide awake now. She and Cameron had loved storms. When a storm blew in, they'd watch the waves crash against the Cove harbour walls, spewing foam into the sky. If the gale woke Fiona, they'd hold her close, promising that the wind couldn't hurt her – that they'd never let anything hurt her. She'd truly believed they could save her from anything and everything. Fuck. No. Amelia thrust the memory away. She could not – would not – go there again.

She slipped a sweater over her head and headed towards the

ramparts, pausing in the passage to put on the light. Nothing happened. As Beatrice had warned, the storm had disrupted the electricity. Amelia reminded herself to avoid the lift.

Using the light from her phone to guide her way, she climbed the narrow stairs, trying to ignore how pitch black the floor above her bedroom was in its depths. Carrying on up she let herself out and onto the roof, into another brilliant flash of light. She leant over the chest-high ramparts to check whether the power was off in the village too. All the houses were in darkness, although that could be because everyone was in bed. She crossed to the other side of the ramparts. The streetlights in Stia and Pratovecchio were also out. It seemed the power cut was affecting the whole valley. Gusts of wind dived and weaved through the trees, shaking them as if with a giant hand, causing branches to spiral to the ground. Amelia revelled in the disorder the storm was causing: the discordant sound of a tin rolling across gravel; the plaintive moaning of the wind. It suited her mood. Another flash of lightning, then seconds later a crash of thunder; rain began to fall in sheets. Amelia remained where she was, letting it wash over her.

Lightning split the sky again, illuminating the ground below as well as the village, and for a fraction of a moment Amelia saw a figure. Darkness fell again so quickly she didn't have time to make out whether it was a man or woman, but she was certain whoever it was was looking up at her. Instinctively, she hunkered down behind the ramparts, her pulse thrumming in her temples. She stayed there until, aware she was behaving like a twit, she stood. Thunder rumbled and then, hard on its heels, another flash of sheet lightning. Amelia peered down between the crenelations, at the place where the person had stood, but there was no longer anyone there. Weird. Visitors to the area sometimes hiked up to look at the castello. Yet who would come in a thunderstorm? Particularly in the middle of the night. Could it have been someone from the village? A shepherd looking for a lost sheep? Or someone else who couldn't sleep, walking their dog? Or – Amelia suppressed a giggle that verged on hysteria –

Piero the Gouty, the armoured resident in the ground floor, out for a walk?

The rain was falling harder now, bouncing off the ground, and she realised she was drenched, her clothes clinging to her like a second skin. Teeth chattering, she returned to her room and dried off. Too on edge to go back to sleep, she dressed in a pair of leggings and a long-sleeved T-shirt. She'd make some hot milk and hope the power came back on soon.

She padded down to the kitchen, trying each light switch as she went, just in case the electricity had come back on. The gaps between the thunder and lightning were getting longer, the torrent of rain slowing to a drizzle – the storm was moving away. Still using the torch on her phone, she poured milk into a small pan and lit the gas stove before returning the bottle to the fridge. As she turned round, she saw movement on the other side of the kitchen balcony door. Her blood froze. For a long moment she stared at the glass door, completely unable to move. Questions tumbled through her mind. Who was it? How did they get up there? What did they want? More importantly, was the balcony door locked? She couldn't remember. At that moment the lights came back on. Amelia blinked and the figure disappeared.

Amelia had thought nothing could spook her. She'd been mistaken. Her pulse was racing, her heart banging so loudly she was surprised she couldn't hear it. Her fingers automatically sought her father's pendant, hoping to draw courage from it. She reached out and tried the door to the balcony. It was locked. From the inside. She hadn't been out there since she arrived. She pressed her face to the glass and, shielding her eyes from the light, peered into the darkness. Lightning flashed, making her jump again, completely illuminating the small balcony. There was no one there. Taking her courage in both hands she stepped out onto the balcony. Of course, there was no one there. Nevertheless, her heart continued its ceaseless hammering.

It was only when the milk boiled over that she was able to turn away from the door. She poured the scalding milk into a mug, her hands shaking so much she spilled a good bit of it on the worktop. She took deep breaths in and out, in an attempt to steady her heart rate. She was letting the atmosphere of the castello get to her. All she'd seen was her own reflection. No different to looking out of a train window when it was dark outside and seeing your blurry reflection staring back – as if there were another you in the darkness. She'd been in a state of high alert, spooked by what she saw – *thought* she saw – from the ramparts.

Feeling reassured and taking her milk with her, she went down to the basement and catalogued books until grey light seeped through the narrow windows. She stood and stretched stiff muscles, pleased with the progress she'd made. There was only one box of books left to catalogue. It was time to start on the brochure and the boards depicting the history of the castello. Perhaps with the Warrior Abbess. Later she would go to the cafe in Stia, access the internet and start her research. Or maybe visit one of the other Guidi castellos.

She continued to work for a few more hours until her stomach reminded her it was almost lunchtime.

Up in the kitchen she took tomatoes and cheese from the fridge and was about to crack eggs for an omelette when she heard the crunch of tyres on gravel. She crossed to the other side of the room and looked out of the long window. A car had pulled up outside, and the driver's door was opening. Her heart lurched. Could it be? When he stepped out of the car, it only took her a few moments to realise he was a stranger. The crushing disappointment she felt took her by surprise. The man looked up at her. He was tall, in his late forties or early fifties. Judging by the way he was dressed (tailored fawn trousers and a collared shirt with highly polished slip-on shoes with tassels, no socks; a look no British man could – or should – attempt to carry off), he was Italian. He paused for a moment before striding towards the door. With a jolt Amelia realised Flavia's belongings were spread out downstairs, pretty much as she had left them the night before. In a jumbled heap.

Dashing down the stairs to where she'd left them, she re-folded the coat and the christening gown and returned them along with the box to the bottom of the trunk, placing the dresses on top of everything. She slammed the lid and had only enough time to take a deep breath before the door opened and, without knocking, the man stepped into the room.

He looked almost as startled to find Amelia in the basement as she was to see him.

He collected himself quickly. 'I'm sorry,' he said in perfect, only slightly accented English. 'Did I disturb you?' He held out his hand. 'You must be Signora Simpson. The contessa told me you'd come to help her. She suggested I call on you if I were in the area.'

'How did you get in?' Amelia demanded, reverting to Italian. The door was locked. She was sure it was. Or was she? She thought back to her movements when she and Kelly had arrived back from Florence. She'd been excited, eager to look in the trunk. Then she'd found the christening gown, and it had got all blurry from there.

'The door was unlocked. I knocked, but when I didn't get an answer I let myself in.'

She hadn't heard him knock, although the heavy wood might have muffled the sound. But how could she have forgotten to lock the door? How could she have been so careless? Anyone could have come in and helped themselves to any of the items in the castello. She'd promised the contessa she would take good care of her home and its possessions.

Annoyed with herself, Amelia only just refrained from telling him that usually people waited to be invited in before they entered. It was hardly his fault she'd left the door unlocked. Instead, not wanting to draw his attention to her carelessness, she shook his outstretched hand.

'I didn't catch your name,' she said.

'Me?' He smiled and shook his head. 'Forgive me, I should have introduced myself. Benedetto Fabini. An old friend of the contessa.'

So, this was the family friend Beatrice mentioned.

'She asked me to look in on you,' he continued. 'She wanted to know you had everything you need.'

'Yes. Thank you. Everything's wonderful.' So, Beatrice hadn't been completely reassured about leaving her there. 'I'm pleased to meet you,' she said. 'Please tell Beatrice I'm fine when you next speak to her. The work is going well, and I'm managing to feed myself.' *Shut up, Amelia!* She attempted a smile, aware she was babbling like a child caught out in some misdemeanour.

He flashed over-white teeth at her. 'The contessa asked me to remind you I'm available to look at anything you might find. She knows how much I like searching for evidence of the past.'

Although Amelia couldn't imagine anyone who looked less like a man obsessed with the past, she also knew people were rarely what they seemed on the surface. Take Cameron. On the outside he looked exactly how one would expect a fisherman to look: broad shouldered, stocky, his weather-beaten face often covered in stubble. No one would ever have guessed that he was once a banker in London. She prodded the ache that thinking about him brought, like someone testing a sore tooth. Her thoughts shied away. *Mustn't think, mustn't remember...*

'Have you found anything interesting?' Benedetto continued.

For a split second Amelia wondered if he was referring to the letter – or the diaries. How would he know about either? It was on the tip of her tongue to tell him, but something stopped her. Beatrice did say she should show him anything of interest, yet inexplicably she was reluctant to do so. She told herself it was because a) she felt guilty about reading them in the first place, and b) she hadn't actually found anything of historical value. At least not yet.

Conscious he was waiting for a response, she shook her head. 'I've catalogued most of the books. So far I haven't come across any that strike me of being of particular value, but you're welcome to take a look at the list of the ones I've catalogued. There are some articles of clothing that would make a good display, but I can't imagine they'd be of interest to you.'

He looked disappointed – or relieved; Amelia didn't know him well enough to decipher his expression. 'You're correct there. I wouldn't know a Dior from a Chanel. Clothes – at least women's clothes – don't interest me. Unless I'm taking them off.' He made no attempt to disguise the gleam in his eye when he looked at Amelia.

Oh, pu-leeze. Now she saw him close up, she realised she'd underestimated his age. He had to be in his mid- to late fifties, at least twenty years older than her. His comment was entirely inappropriate.

Recognising she wasn't impressed, Benedetto shot Amelia a rueful smile. 'Anyway, the eleventh to fifteenth century is really my period.'

'Mine too! But I *do* love fashion.' They were words that the old Amelia might have thought and uttered. Once, particularly before Fiona had come along, she'd spent hours scouring charity and second-hand shops for unusual outfits. She winced inside. *That* Amelia bore no resemblance to the woman who was wearing baggy leggings and a T-shirt that had clearly seen better days.

'Could I take you to lunch?' Benedetto asked.

'I was just about to have mine,' she said, more abruptly than she intended. There was something about him that she found unsettling. And not in a good way.

'Join me. Please. I hate to eat alone. And I must reassure Beatrice that I've taken care of her guest. There's a place in Pratovecchio that serves excellent local delicacies as well as a very decent house wine from a local vineyard.'

She hadn't had a drink since the night her father had found her teetering on the edge of the cliffs at Cove. But there was something of the little boy lost about Benedetto which, although Amelia suspected was put on, made her soften towards him. Moreover, the contessa clearly intended for them to work together – or at least communicate – so she couldn't really refuse.

'Very well,' she replied and, as his eyebrows rose at her ungracious tone, she quickly added, 'That would be lovely. Although I don't want to be away too long.'

'Shall we go then? Or...' he hesitated, 'do you wish to – how do you British say? – do your face first?'

Heat rose to her cheeks. How rude. It wasn't her who suggested they have lunch. Nevertheless, she raked her hand through her hair, trying to discreetly unravel some of the worst tugs at the back. She hadn't even showered.

'Could you give me a few moments?'

'Certainly. I'll wait in the sitting room if that is all right?'

After locking the door (it felt weird locking a stranger in with her, but no way was she ever going to forget to lock it again), they took the lift, standing uncomfortably close in the small space as it creaked and rattled its ponderous way up.

'I'll be quick as I can,' she said.

Benedetto plonked himself down on the sofa and crossed one elegantly shod leg over the other. 'Take as long as you like.'

She ran upstairs, gave herself a quick wipe under the armpits, splashed water on her face, changed into one of the two dresses she'd brought and slipped on a pair of sandals.

She arrived back in the sitting room to find Benedetto holding a book, fanning through the pages.

He looked surprised to see her back so soon. Barely ten minutes had passed.

Back down in the basement she took the key from the hook next to the door and unlocked it. Benedetto stood aside to let her go in front of him. She locked the door behind them, double checking to make sure. She mustn't ever forget to check it was locked again. The castello wasn't alarmed. Perhaps it should be. The contents might not be of interest to the museums in Florence, but that wasn't to say they weren't of value.

Benedetto opened the passenger door of a Lexus and waited until Amelia had settled herself before closing it and walking around to his side. The car was heated from the sun, and Amelia felt as if she were going to spontaneously combust.

Benedetto didn't speak as he navigated his way down the narrow road but waved and smiled broadly as they passed a farmer and his donkey. The farmer grinned back, revealing a mouth missing half its teeth, and lifted a hand in return, touching his cap.

'It's not very difficult to imagine what life must have been like here in medieval times,' Amelia said.

'Not so different to now,' Benedetto agreed. 'The castello would still have been the most prominent building for miles around, the lands farmed by men much like the one we just passed. There would have been many more people living in the area, however.' He opened his window and placed his elbow on the open sill, using two fingers of his other hand to steer. 'What do you know about the history of the castello?'

'Not as much as I'd like. I know it was built in the eleventh century for the Guidis, and that Dante was a visitor.'

'Ah, Dante. You have read *Inferno* then?'

'It was required reading for my Italian degree.'

He flashed a smile. 'I wasn't talking about the *Divine Comedy*. I was talking about Dan Brown's book. *Inferno*.'

Hah, bloody hah. Amelia gave him a brief smile in return.

'Since the film came out, we have even more tourists in Florence.'

'That's where you live?'

'Yes. I also have a small house in Pratovecchio I use mainly at weekends. The rest of the time I spend in my apartment near the Duomo.'

Bit like Kelly. And Beatrice. Flitting between town and country homes seemed to be the norm here.

They drove through Stia and continued on to Pratovecchio where he abandoned – no other word could possibly describe the way he parked – the car, bonnet across the pavement, boot sticking into the traffic.

'The restaurant I like is just round the corner. It makes the most delicious *scottiglia*, the delicacy this area is best known for. Perhaps you will try some?'

Without waiting for a reply, he steered Amelia across the piazza, much larger and busier than the one in Stia, and into a tiny, cramped restaurant where almost every table had already been taken. A bald man of around sixty hurried over, opened his arms and kissed her companion on both cheeks.

'My dear Benedetto. It has been too long. Now, who is this lovely lady you have brought as your guest?'

'This is Signora Simpson, Antonio. She is staying at the Castello di Porciano. She is helping the contessa with some archiving.'

Antonio beamed and kissed Amelia too. 'It is an honour to have a friend of Benedetto or the contessa eat in my little restaurant.' He ushered them over to the only empty table and whisked off a reservation sign. 'They are only tourists. I will explain there has been a mistake in the booking. They will believe it and not mind. Especially when I tell them to come back tonight and have *aperitivi* on the house.'

'*Scottiglia* all right for you?' Benedetto asked. Amelia nodded. She couldn't care less what she ate. Food was simply fuel. Once Antonio had left, Benedetto leant back in his chair. 'So, you studied Italian? I'm not surprised to learn this. You speak it almost like a local.'

'I spent a year in Italy as part of my degree.'

'Ah, that explains it.' He frowned. 'But how is it that the contessa has asked you to go through the books from the castello? It is a job for an expert, surely?'

Amelia bristled. 'I did a joint honours degree. Italian and Medieval History.'

'Having a degree in history as well as Italian would be useful, I can see that. You said your period was medieval and early Renaissance. That fits with the heyday of the castello.' Benedetto appeared pleased, as if he'd solved something that was puzzling him.

'It is helpful to have a good understanding of both,' Amelia agreed. 'Knowledge of the past puts historical documents into context while the forensic skills of a linguist – an awareness of genre, plot and rhetoric – are vital for interrogating historical documents. Knowing for example that Dante was the first to write in what we now understand as the modern Italian language helps us date other documents, while knowing what was happening in history at the time he wrote the *Divine Comedy* helps us understand better what he wanted to say.'

She was quoting almost verbatim from somewhere, though she couldn't remember from where or from whom. But she was glad it had come back to her. It made her sound knowledgeable, if a little pompous and smug.

Benedetto held up his hands in mock surrender, but the look he gave Amelia was sharp-eyed; almost as if he was assessing – or reassessing – her.

'Is that what she has asked you to do? Look for such a document?'

'No,' Amelia admitted reluctantly. Aware she'd deliberately passed over another opportunity to mention the letter or the diaries, she wished she was back at the castello, away from his searching gaze – and questions.

'But to come across such a thing. To find something slipped between the pages of a book. It is possible. No?'

The question appeared casual enough, but he watched her carefully. Did he know more than he was saying?

'If there are undiscovered, historic documents I haven't found any I'm afraid,' she said. However, it was an idea to search through the books. If Flavia had found a document that might be the perfect hiding place.

'What do you do?' she asked before he could question her further.

'I work for my brother mainly. You may have heard of him – Sebastian Fabini?'

Amelia shook her head. The name was familiar, but she couldn't place it.

Benedetto looked both dismayed and a little amused. 'You haven't heard of Sebastian Fabini? Possibly, hopefully, Italy's next Foreign Minister?'

'You have a brother in the Italian government?' Amelia shouldn't be so surprised. The contessa was bound to move in exalted circles. 'What is it you do for him?' A waiter placed a plate of bread and olives in front of them.

'I'm his researcher, among other things. If he needs to know something, about anyone or anything, I get the information for him and put it into a report. A politician is expected to have all the answers at his fingertips. It's my job to see that he does,' he said, looking unbearably pleased with himself. Amelia suppressed a shiver of dislike. She didn't know why she'd taken so against this man. Perhaps guilt was making her tetchy and defensive?

'Tell me what you know about the castello's history,' she asked. 'Anything or anyone I should be particularly interested in?'

'Dante, clearly. But almost any of the Conti Guidi. They were an interesting bunch. Including the Warrior Abbess. You've heard of her?'

Amelia nodded. 'Beatrice mentioned her. I gather she was quite a woman and founded a monastery here in Pratovecchio. I haven't had a chance to research her properly yet.'

'Not everything about the Guidis has been recorded – and there's even less about the Guidi women. The Abbess is an exception to the rule, although what is known about her is surprisingly little, given she was such a remarkable woman.' Benedetto popped an olive into his mouth before continuing. 'Most people only know of her because she appears in a fable in one of Italy's best-known children's books. The tale has her leaping over the walls of Porciano on her horse.'

'Did she leave a record of her life? A journal perhaps?' And if she did, could Amelia find that too? That might be valuable. Interesting at least.

'I doubt many women of the Abbess's generation kept diaries as such. Much of what we know is conjecture. We do know for a fact she founded the Camaldoli monastery. It's very close to here, and she eventually took orders herself. We have reason to believe that she went to war in her brother's place. Hence the name the Warrior Abbess.'

'I'm hoping to include her in the information board for the castello.'

But the Abbess didn't appear to interest Benedetto.

'More famously, it is known that Dante spent some of his exile in the Casentino – perhaps even some of it at the Castello di Porciano,' he continued.

'So people keep telling me. I'm planning to do a board on him also. I gather he stayed all over the place while he was in exile.'

'That's true.' Benedetto put his arms behind his head and leant back in his chair. 'But most of his time away from Florence was spent in this area. The people of the Casentino are very proud of the valley's association with him. You know he wrote the *Divine Comedy* when he was in the Casentino?'

'And at least three of his best-known letters while at the Castello di Porciano.'

A tiny lift of his eyebrows gave away his surprise. Amelia could almost hear the wheels turning as he adjusted his opinion of her again.

He leant forward. 'What if he wrote personal letters there too? It's highly likely, wouldn't you agree? Perhaps he even wrote part of the *Divine Comedy* while a guest at the castello.'

Her heart gave a thump. Could this be the discovery Flavia had mentioned in her letter? In which case she should tell him.

'I understand there's a family legend that he did, and part of the original might still exist,' she probed instead.

The smile vanished. 'Who told you that?'

'Kelly.'

The lines between his brows deepened. 'Ah, Beatrice's American tenant. If I'm obsessed with old documents, I hear she's worse. A real Dante fanatic.'

'You know her?'

'I've met her once or twice. Briefly.'

'Do you think there is any truth in the legend?'

He shrugged. 'Nothing has ever been found, but that doesn't mean that it doesn't exist.'

She really should mention the letter. Otherwise, when he learned of its existence – surely only a matter of time – he would wonder why she hadn't.

'Do you know, there are hundreds of unread and unarchived documents in the library at the Castello di Poppi?' Benedetto went on before she could say anything, and the moment passed. 'I've spent almost all my spare time for the last few years looking through them, hoping to find the gem that will make me rich and famous.'

Amelia felt an unexpected pang of sympathy for him. It couldn't be easy playing second fiddle to a man as successful as his brother.

'Perhaps if you stick at it you'll get lucky.'

He laughed. 'I very much doubt it. Do you have any idea how many people have searched for such a thing? But imagine how tourists would flock here if something were found!'

'If part of the original *Divine Comedy* was ever found it would be stored in a museum far superior to – and more secure than – the one at the castello,' Amelia said.

'Toh, tourists would still come to the Casentino valley in droves,' Benedetto said emphatically.

Antonio returned with a bowl of steaming mixed-meat stew which he placed with a flourish in the centre of the table. The smell made Amelia realise how ravenous she was.

Benedetto picked up his fork and gave her a rueful smile. 'I doubt if you will find anything of interest, but if you do, show it to me first. We don't want to get Beatrice's hopes up unnecessarily.'

For the remainder of the meal they talked about where Benedetto studied (Florence), where he liked to go on holiday (South America and Britain), his brother and his brother's family (two teenage girls and a boy of ten).

'How do you know the contessa?' Amelia asked, after a waiter had cleared their plates.

'We bumped into each other in Florence at a talk about rare books. I knew who she was, of course. The contessa is well known in Florence as well as the Casentino. It turned out her mother and my father moved in the same social circles.'

'Sophia?'

'Yes.'

'What about Flavia?' Amelia asked, her pulse kicking again. 'Did your father know her?'

Benedetto ignored her question. 'Would you like a cognac? Or something else?'

'No thank you.'

Benedetto dabbed at his mouth with his napkin, called a waiter over and ordered a cognac for himself.

'Did your father know Flavia?' Amelia asked again when she had his attention once more.

'I believe he did – although not very well.'

'Is your father still alive? I'd love to speak to someone who actually knew her.'

'No. He died. Quite recently as it happens.' Benedetto looked around as if wondering where his drink had got to.

'I'm sorry for your loss. Did he ever talk about Flavia? Can you remember?'

Benedetto frowned. 'Why are you so interested?'

Amelia shrugged. Good question. 'She was a young aristocrat living in troubled times. What's not to find intriguing?' The truth was everything about Flavia fascinated Amelia. Through the young Italian's diaries, Amelia had come to feel as if she knew her and thought they might have been friends had they lived at the same time. She liked Flavia's sense of humour, her innate kindness, but most of all she admired her guts; she'd lost both her parents but hadn't let that stop her living her life. She wasn't about to confide all that to Benedetto, however.

Benedetto took a sip of the cognac Antonio brought along with the bill.

'Do you know what happened to her?'

Something shifted behind his eyes, and he was silent for a while as if pondering how to reply.

'Didn't Beatrice tell you?' he said finally.

'No. She was in a bit of a hurry the day I arrived.'

Benedetto eyed her speculatively. 'Perhaps she didn't want you to know. It's not something the family like to talk about.'

Amelia leaned forward. 'But *you* know.'

His previous ebullience had gone. He was clearly not happy at the turn the conversation had taken. He smoothed out his napkin, folded it, and placed it with care on the table. 'Her body was found at the foot of the castello. No one knows how she got there, but there are rumours,' he said at last.

Amelia was almost winded by a jolt of shock. It was the last thing she expected to hear.

'What rumours?' she whispered.

'That she threw herself out of the large window on the third floor. The one that used to be a door onto the ladies' balcony before the castello fell into ruin.'

Amelia couldn't believe what she was hearing. Something terrible must have happened to make the vibrant woman who wrote those diaries want to die. Was this why Amelia felt such a strong connection? Had she felt echoes of her own pain in Flavia?

'Could it have been an accident?'

'Perhaps. I'm only repeating what I've heard. You'll have to ask Beatrice if you want to know the details.' Benedetto tossed some euros on the table, scraped his chair back and got to his feet. 'Shall we leave now?'

Benedetto dropped Amelia off at the castello, refusing her automatic but unenthusiastic offer of coffee with a smile and shake of his head.

'I'll be back next week,' he said as she opened the door. 'If you need anything, or if there's anything you want me to look at before then, of course you must phone me straight away. May I have your mobile?'

When Amelia passed it to him, he entered his number into her contacts. Then with a spin of his tyres he was gone.

The coolness inside the castello was a welcome relief. She locked the door behind her and ran upstairs. After a shower and change of clothes, Amelia considered going back to the job she'd been employed to do but thought about Flavia instead. What happened to that carefree woman Amelia had been reading about? She wanted, *needed* to know. She settled herself in the window seat. Maybe she'd find the answer in her diaries.

FIFTEEN

FLAVIA

July 1939

When her godparents invited Flavia to join them in Porciano for a couple of weeks in July, Flavia jumped at the chance. Her anger towards them had faded as she'd absorbed the news about her parents. As they'd said, her godparents' only intention had been to protect her. They'd been wrong to do so, but they had meant well.

Flavia hadn't seen Margherita since the previous summer, although they'd exchanged the occasional letter. Would they still have the bond they once shared? Flavia was a different person now to the one she'd been when they'd first met: less naive, less trusting, more confident. If she'd changed did that mean Margherita had too? What about Luca? Would she see him? She'd thought about him often. She'd even dreamt about him once – a dream that had left her all hot and bothered.

The work on the castello was still not finished. However, the roof was watertight, the floorboards had been replaced in Dante's Hall and the supporting beams were in place. There was a yawning gap where a lift was to be installed, but enough work had been completed on the third floor and the floor above to allow them to stay there, albeit with limited facilities. The electricity hadn't been connected, so they'd have to rely on oil lamps and candles and a two-ring gas stove to cook on. Most of the remaining work was internal and could be finished while they were in residence.

As soon as Flavia had pleased her godparents by showing sufficient interest in the progress, she changed into her favourite high-waisted trousers and a white shirt, and tucked her hair into a bandana. Walking boots replaced her town shoes. Dressed like this she felt freer, more herself. She strode towards the Rossi farm, keeping an eye out for her friend, waving and calling out greetings to the now-familiar faces of neighbours. She breathed in the particular scents of the Casentino, registered the tinkling bells of the goats, and drank in the enormous expanse of blue Tuscan sky. She hadn't realised how much she'd missed it here, how much being back felt like coming home.

She found Margherita milking the sheep in one of the sheds.

Margherita's eyes, always mischievous, were sparkling; her cheeks were flushed, and there was a fullness to her face and figure that hadn't been there before.

'What is it?' Flavia asked after they had kissed hello. 'What's happened?'

Margherita laughed. 'How do you know I have something to tell you?'

'Because,' Flavia said dryly, 'you are as easy to read as a book. Whatever you are thinking or feeling is written all over your face for the world to see.'

'As is yours. At least to me.' Margherita stepped away from Flavia and scrutinised her from top to toe. 'It's not just that you've cut your hair – I like it, it shows your cheekbones off to an unfair advantage. Or your daring trousers – you'll shock the nonnas terribly. You're different somehow. Not just on the outside. You're sadder. Oh, cara, has something happened to *you*?'

'It's all this talk of war.' That was only part of the truth. But Flavia couldn't confide in her friend about her parents. She'd promised her godparents. 'I want to hear all your news first!' she said instead.

Margherita wrapped an arm around Flavia's waist, and they headed for the forest – their favourite place last summer when they wished to remain undiscovered or speak in private. They sat down under the spreading, gnarled branches of a chestnut tree.

'I am to be married!' Margherita said, with a wide smile.

'Married! But you don't even have a beau.' Flavia couldn't quite manage to hide her shock. 'And you are only sixteen!'

'I'll be seventeen in a few months!'

'Why didn't you write to me and tell me?' Flavia said, swallowing her hurt. Margherita should have let her know something as big as this.

Margherita pouted. 'It seems to me the moment you left Porciano and the valley you forgot all about me.'

'I could never forget you!' Flavia protested. It was true she hadn't written very often though. It was that vile secret her godparents had insisted she keep. She'd found it impossible to write to her friend and not pour her heart out. Hadn't their friendship flourished on the understanding they could tell each other anything? Or was that the thinking of a child? 'It's just that I've been busy – volunteering at a centre for refugees.' She went on to give a brief description of what her duties there entailed.

'But enough about me,' she finished. 'Tell me about this man you are to marry. Who is he? Is he handsome? Kind? Did you fall in love immediately? If you are to marry, you must have known for ages it was serious!'

'I didn't know it would get so serious so quickly. Oh, don't look like that, Flavia! You will adore him too when you meet him. Of course, you must be at my wedding and be godmother to my children. Please say you will! Don't say you are too above us to agree!'

'I have never thought myself above you,' Flavia retorted.

Margherita raised an eyebrow. 'Never?'

They laughed, and the tension between them eased. Their friendship might be different – they were young women now, in charge of their own destinies, their lives moving in different directions – but Flavia still felt at ease with Margherita. She hugged her friend. 'Tell me everything. Don't leave a thing out.'

His name was Niccolo. Margherita had met him when he came to collect cheese for his family in Vallucciole. Usually it was his younger brother's chore, but Paolo had hurt his leg so Niccolo had to do it for him. Margherita hadn't thought too much of Niccolo at first – he'd hardly said a word to her – but after a few weeks they began to speak. Apparently, Paolo's leg had healed some time ago, but Niccolo kept coming in his place. Just so he could see her. Margherita told Flavia that he blushed bright red when he told her this.

'We are to marry in two weeks. Please say you'll still be here.' It was Margherita's turn to blush. 'We don't want to waste any time starting a family.'

Flavia hid her dismay. She was happy for her friend. How could she not be? But wasn't she too young to settle down to a life of domesticity? Her life had barely started. However, she couldn't bring herself to say any of this in the face of her friend's joy.

'Of course I'll be at your wedding. I wouldn't miss it for anything. If you're going to marry then we should make plans. What will you wear?'

Margherita's face fell. 'The dress I wear to church, I expect. There's no money for a new one.'

'I have just the thing. One of my gowns. It has the tiniest tear in the hem, and I brought it with me to repair.'

Margherita looked at her askance. It will never fit me! You are too skinny! Almost a bag of bones. No Italian man will look twice at you.' She gave a small shake of her head. 'Mama will feed you up while you are here.'

'I promise you I eat like a horse! It's not my fault I have no curves.' Flavia laughed. 'Just as well that I have become an excellent seamstress in recent weeks, so I can easily alter it to fit you.' Catching Margherita's raised eyebrows, she added, 'Well, maybe not an excellent needle woman, but not bad.' After almost a year sewing and mending at the refugee centre, she'd improved.

'I *would* like to see it,' Margherita said.

'Then let's do that right now.'

Flavia led her wide-eyed friend up through the floors of the castello until they reached the one the family used as a sitting room. The conte was reading his newspaper, and the contessa was flicking through some samples, trying to decide on a fabric for the sofa. They smiled in response to Margherita's shy hello, and the contessa quizzed her for a couple of minutes on the health of her mother and grandmother. Before taking Margherita to her room, Flavia couldn't resist showing her friend the view from the ramparts.

Margherita was suitably impressed. 'You can see everything from here. Even our farm!'

'Isn't it amazing?' Flavia said. 'Come on, let's go look at that gown.'

Back in Flavia's bedroom, the one they had christened the Warrior Abbess's as it was reputed to have been her favourite, Margherita fell upon the contents of Flavia's suitcase. As she rummaged, Flavia told her all about the refugees and their individual stories, and how sad that made her.

'Do you really think they can all be true?' Margherita asked, oohing and aahing over each item of clothing as if they were spun from gold. Flavia bit back the impulse to share what she'd learned about the fate of her parents.

'I have absolutely no doubt.'

Margherita paused, her fingers travelling over a gown of white organza over silk, trimmed with purple velvet on the hem and under the bust. 'Roberto is back from Spain, all pumped up by the Fascists' victory. He talks of nothing now but of Italy joining forces with Germany.' Margherita held the white organza against her, and her face lit up. 'Is this it?'

'Yes! Do you like it?'

'I love it!'

'It will need to be shortened, let out a little, but that should be easy enough.'

'But if we do that you might not be able to wear it again.'

'It's yours to keep. My wedding present to you.'

Margherita squealed with delight and flung her arms around Flavia. 'I am so happy you are back, cara.'

SIXTEEN

Over the next couple of weeks Flavia spent most evenings in the farmhouse kitchen alongside Margherita's mother and nonna, helping to sew Margherita's trousseau. In addition to altering the white organza dress, most of which was done by Margherita's mother and nonna as their fingers were the nimblest, they sewed tablecloths and bedsheets from the finest Tuscan linen supplied by the conte and contessa. They also stitched nightdresses, trimming the neckline and sleeves with lace and using the leftovers to embellish otherwise plain underwear. They made baby clothes too: tiny nightdresses and a christening gown made out of the softest cotton. Margherita's nonna knitted miniature cardigans and blankets until the basket on the floor beside her was heaped with enough to clothe a small army of babies.

As they worked, they either sang or gossiped about the villagers – who was having a baby, whose husband was always getting his ears boxed and who was getting frail and needed help with chores. Flavia relished every moment she spent in the farmhouse; she had a sense of belonging and loved feeling she was part of this large family. How would her life have been had her parents lived? Might she have had brothers and sisters? Would she have her own family one day, she wondered, as she placed another stitch in the christening gown. Wanting to memorialise the tableau of these women to whom she felt so connected, Flavia would set her sewing to the side and sketch them, letting their voices and laughter ripple over her as she drew.

Later, Flavia would come to think of these evenings – the laughter and companionship; the rich smells of tomato sauce and garlic; the pungent smell of sheep's milk as it simmered on the stove; the heat from the fire that was always lit even on the warmest evenings and which pinked everyone's cheeks – as some of the happiest times of her life.

Roberto was away training with the Italian army, but Luca was often in the kitchen, leaving the room throughout the evening to check on the sheep or to do other chores. All her senses became more alert when he was around: she'd become attuned to the deep tones of his voice, acutely aware of the height and solidity of him, the planes of his cheekbones, the way his hair was short at the back and longer at the front, the way he smelled of earth and hay. It was most disconcerting, especially as she became annoyingly flustered when he was around. Sometimes she was certain she felt his eyes on her, but when she looked up he'd appear to be deeply engrossed in a book or whatever else he was doing.

She told herself her interest in him was because of what he'd said the previous year about Mussolini. She'd thought him ignorant and disloyal then but knew now there had been truth in what he'd said.

When Luca wasn't reading, he whittled away at pieces of wood, carving them into strange little figures just like those atop the columns in the church in Stia. The artist in her couldn't help admiring his skill as well as his intensity and focus as he worked. How could a man be so still one moment then filled with explosive energy the next? She'd seen him at work on the farm, accomplishing more in an hour than she imagined many did in a week.

When she asked him why he'd chosen the miniature gargoyles to carve he told her he'd been to look at them in the church after Margherita had shown him Flavia's sketch. To her secret delight, this time it was his turn to look abashed. Maybe he wasn't as immune to her as he liked her to think?

Too soon, the day of Margherita's wedding arrived. Flavia was due to return to Florence the following day and when she next came to Porciano, Margherita would be in her own home in Vallucciole, the cosy evenings in the farmhouse kitchen relegated to the past. Flavia wanted to slow time down. To stop it, even.

It was a perfectly still morning, the sky streaked with clouds like bowls of whipped cream into which raspberries had been stirred, as Flavia walked to the farmhouse to help Margherita get dressed. Despite the early hour, the Rossi home was a flurry of activity. Several women she didn't recognise filled the kitchen, speaking in excited voices and laughing. Pots of sauces bubbled over the flames from one side of the fireplace to the next. Haunches of cured ham, and bowls of cheese, fruit and tomatoes covered the entire kitchen table, ready to be taken to the village of Vallucciole where the wedding reception was to take place and where Margherita was to make her new home. Flavia hung back, inexplicably shy, for the first time feeling like an outsider.

It was Luca who noticed her. He caught her eye, grinned and strode towards her. 'I'm escaping. Too many women. Tell Margherita I've gone to tend to the farm. I'll be back in plenty of time to get ready. She needn't worry.'

When Flavia remained where she was, he tipped his head to the side. 'What's the matter? Why aren't you going in?' He placed his hand on her shoulder and looked down at her with his intense, almond-coloured eyes. At the pressure of his hand, her heart started its horrible racing and her mouth dried. If he noticed how flustered she was he didn't let on. 'You must know how much my sister depends on you,' he continued, 'how happy and honoured she is that you are here on her most important day.' When she still didn't move, he gave her a gentle shove. 'Go on. You know they all adore you.'

. . .

When it was time for Margherita to get ready, Flavia went with her. As her friend bathed, Flavia perched on the side of the bath, marvelling at how comfortable Margherita was in her own skin – utterly unembarrassed by her nakedness. Flavia washed her friend's back with soap she'd helped make from the previous year's leftover olive oil scented with lavender from the garden.

Once Margherita was out of the bath and dried, the other women piled into the bedroom to help her dress for her big day, clucking and pulling, adjusting, exclaiming, crying and laughing. When Margherita was dressed to everyone's satisfaction – no small feat – Flavia stood back to admire her. Behind her lids her eyes burnt, the way they always did when she wanted to cry but couldn't.

'You look so beautiful,' she told her friend.

Margherita turned away from the mirror, her normally confident expression doubtful. 'I hardly recognise myself,' she said softly, sounding awestruck.

More than ever, Margherita reminded Flavia of one of Botticelli's models. Her thick curls had been tamed by ironing tongs they had heated in the fire before Flavia had twisted Margherita's hair into a tight bun, which lay against the nape of her neck, some tendrils left loose to curl around her cheeks. The organza dress accentuated Margherita's curves in the most flattering way, the cream of the fabric contrasting with the light bronze of her skin. Flavia had lent her a set of pearls which matched the dress perfectly and almost seemed to glow as they lay against Margherita's throat. Although Flavia didn't think her friend needed make-up, Margherita's lips had been touched with red lipstick, making them seem even fuller than usual, and her eyebrows and lashes with dark liner. While her friend had been having her make-up done, Flavia had sketched her. She tore the page from the pad and handed it to Margherita. 'See how beautiful you are.'

Margherita's own eyes filled. 'You make me seem so.'

As the other women melted away to put the finishing touches to their own appearances, Margherita looked up at Flavia. 'You'll never stop being my friend, will you?'

Flavia took Margherita's small, strong hands in hers. 'Never. I will always do everything in my power to help you and those you love – as you would do for me. You can count on me. I promise, I will never let you down,' she whispered through the tightness in her throat. 'It is more likely you will forget about me, now you have Niccolo.' She tried to make her words light but failed. She couldn't pretend; she needed Margherita's love and friendship as much as her friend needed hers. Probably more.

'No, cara! I love Niccolo. More than anything. But a woman needs her friends too. And we are more than friends, are we not?' Margherita's eyes swam with tears, and she blinked them away. 'You are as dear to me as my sister.' She stood up and flung her arms round Flavia's neck, tucking her head under Flavia's chin. For a few moments they clung together. They might make promises to always love and help each other, but life was changing, people too, and Flavia had a terrible premonition even worse days were coming for them all. She shook the feeling away. She might not be able to control or predict the future, but she could help make this day one of the happiest of Margherita's life.

An hour later, Flavia sat alongside her godparents in the family pew in the church in Porciano, as her friend vowed to love, honour and obey her new husband. As they signed the register, Flavia's gaze drifted until it came to rest on Luca. The tallest man in the church, he was easy to spot. True to his promise, he'd changed out of his work clothes into a wool suit with a pressed white shirt buttoned up to the neck.

As if sensing her eyes on him he looked around, and she quickly averted her gaze to the church's most important painting. It was a triptych of the Annunciation by Bicci di Lorenzo, one of Italy's finest artists of the fifteenth century. Despite its undoubted value it was as safe in this little church as it would have been in the Uffizi, just as the paintings and Della Robbia terracottas in the church in Stia were.

By the time Flavia turned her attention back to the front of the church, Margherita and her new husband were making their way up the aisle, along which dozens of candles had been lit. There was no need for them; Margherita's radiance outshone that from the flickering flames.

The conte and contessa wished the couple happiness before slipping away. Their continued presence was neither expected nor wished for. However, they had offered their car to the newly wedded couple for the journey to Vallucciole, where Margherita was to make her new home and where the remainder of the celebrations would take place. Flavia, who had recently learnt to drive, would chauffeur them there, with Porciano's contribution to the wedding feast in the car boot. The rest of the guests would make their way to Vallucciole as best they could, but – given it was just over two miles through the forest – most would make the journey on foot. Travelling by car necessitated a much more circuitous route: the long winding road down to Stia, a right turn along the road past the flour mill for another couple of miles, and another right turn followed by three miles of lurching, bone-rattling unpaved road to the village.

Nonna, whose legs weren't strong enough for her to walk all the way to Vallucciole, and who had recoiled at the suggestion she might travel by donkey (apparently not appropriate for the grandmother of the bride – Flavia agreed entirely), took the front passenger seat. The newlyweds sat in the back. Throughout the journey Nonna held onto the dashboard with a vice-like grip, shrieking every time the car bounced over a bump, forcing Flavia to reduce her speed to not much faster than a snail's pace and making Niccolo and Margherita laugh. When they weren't kissing. Perhaps they didn't realise Flavia could see them in the rear-view mirror? More likely they didn't care!

When Flavia and her cargo eventually arrived at Vallucciole, she parked the car on the road above the village. Like Porciano, it was impossible to drive a car through the narrow streets, so the wedding party made their way down the cobbled path that led to the centre of the village where most of the guests were already waiting to greet the newly married couple. The villagers of Vallucciole – over a hundred of them in houses so closely squished together it was difficult to see where one home finished and another started – had come together to provide the wedding party with the best produce the area had to offer. In the small central area the village used as a piazza, white cloths covered tables groaning with food: *panzanella* made from stale bread soaked in water and dried before being mixed with cucumber, basil, tomato and onion; bowls of fresh pasta and *tortelli di patate*, the classic dish of the Casentino region; rounds of pecorino; mounds of sheep's cheese and ricotta mixed with honey and walnuts; platters of prosciutto; freshly baked bread; more bowls of lettuce; plump juicy tomatoes dressed with home-made olive oil; jugs of red wine from further down the valley; and on the centre table – the one nearest Niccolo's parents' home in which the newlyweds would have a room – an enormous wedding cake made by Margherita's mother-in-law, surrounded by fresh figs split open and stuffed full of more ricotta and walnuts. The women must have been cooking and preparing for days. Willing hands helped unload Flavia's car boot, and soon the tables threatened to collapse under the weight of food.

Lanterns containing tiny olive oil-fuelled lamps, to be lit once dusk fell, had been strung from every available branch from every available tree. Vallucciole had done Margherita proud. Here, even more so than Porciano, she was everyone's daughter, everyone's sister, as beloved as the dearest family member.

The afternoon passed in a blur of dancing, eating and laughing. Dusk was beginning to fall as Flavia flopped down on a doorstep to rub her aching feet.

There was a pause in the music and, leaning against the wall, she closed her eyes, letting the sound of the cicadas and the happy shrieks of excited children wash over her. Sensing someone standing near, she opened her eyes to find Luca grinning down at her. Fireflies sparked like a thousand lights in the semi-darkness. The village children, jam jars in hand, ran about trying to catch them.

'Hello,' Luca said, plonking down beside her. Flavia's heart tumbled inside her chest. Having removed his jacket, loosened the top two buttons of his shirt and rolled up his sleeves, he seemed more familiar to her than he had in the church. He smelled of soap.

'Margherita is so happy, it's as if the fireflies are celebrating with her,' Flavia mused. No champagne had been served tonight, but she had the same warm, fuzzy feeling as she'd had when she'd drank it at the party.

Luca grinned. 'It is why Vallucciole is called the Valley of Fireflies.' He looked over to where his sister was dancing with Niccolo. Margherita's arms were wound around her husband's neck, while his circled her waist. They beamed as they gazed into each other's eyes. 'Do you know fireflies only have a moment's brilliance before their light is extinguished forever?' Luca asked, his expression suddenly sombre. 'They use their light as a beacon to attract their mate. But once they have, they die.'

Flavia shivered. 'That's a horrible thought. Not one I'm going to dwell on. All that matters is that she's happy right now with her Niccolo, and there is no reason to believe she won't always be.'

'He'd better keep making her happy,' Luca said grimly.

Flavia turned to him in surprise. 'Why do you say that? Do you think he won't?'

'I wouldn't have let her marry him if I did.'

Flavia laughed. 'I didn't know she needed your permission.' She couldn't imagine anyone, not even Luca, denying her feisty friend anything.

'I am the head of the household. It is my responsibility to make sure she makes the right choices. If I hadn't been certain that

Niccolo will cherish her all the days of his life, I wouldn't have agreed to the marriage.' As if realising how puffed up he sounded, his face relaxed into a smile. 'Even if she'd shouted and stamped her feet and not spoken to me ever again.' She liked his smile, Flavia decided. Probably because he looked so much like his sister when he did.

'But I know they are meant to be together,' he conceded. 'Unlike some couples who get married because it's what Mussolini wants. Our esteemed leader thinks he can tax a man into marriage.' He was referring to the extra tax imposed on single men. 'What basis is that for something that should last a lifetime? Only love, great love, should tempt a man to join himself to a woman for the rest of his days.' He looked directly into her eyes. 'Don't you agree?'

Flavia's heart was pounding so hard she could barely breathe.

'Isn't that why we're here – to celebrate the wedding of two people who do love each other?' Her voice sounded strange even to her own ears.

He grinned and held out his hand for her to take. 'Then we should dance.'

He held her much closer than any other man she'd danced with. She rested one hand in his and the other on his shoulder, feeling his muscles bunch under her fingers. When he pulled her closer she didn't resist, letting her head rest against his chest. It felt solid, like a brick wall, and she had to fight the impulse to run her hands across it. Heat rose in her cheeks and travelled through the rest of her body. What would people think if they could read her mind? What would *he* think?

Thankfully, or disappointingly – she wasn't sure which she felt most – at that moment the pace of the music picked up and slowly, reluctantly, or so it seemed to her, he let her go. The wedding party started doing a country dance of the region. Flavia was whirled, laughing, from one partner to the next, as the villagers showed her where to put her feet, when to turn, when to spin. When the accordion players took a break she returned, out of breath, to the doorway where she'd rested before.

Moments later she was joined again by Luca. The only sign of his exertions was the damp lock of hair that flopped over an eye. She made room for him on their step – as she'd begun to think of it.

'You'll miss Margherita at the farm,' she said, hoping Luca would think her flushed cheeks were entirely down to the energetic dancing.

He shrugged. 'Nothing stays the same. Her place is with her husband and his family now. Isn't it what all women want? A home of their own – a family...'

'Not all women!' Flavia protested. 'The contessa's ancestor – the Abbess – led armies and ran her lands far better than her brother did. History has proved there is no reason a woman can't be as good as a man – better even. Look at Catherine de' Medici or Joan of Arc. There are hundreds of examples. Modern women too. Designers and artists, poets and writers...' She trailed off. Judging by his grin, she'd reacted exactly the way he'd expected her to. Why did she always have to be serious? Why couldn't she flirt a little – choose more lighthearted topics? Because, if she were honest with herself, with this man she could never pretend to be anything except herself. 'I would like to make a difference to the world before I leave it, be remembered for being more than just a wife and mother,' she finished.

He turned to face her, serious now. 'In what way?' It was as if he was seeing her – really seeing her – for the first time. His scrutiny made her feel even more hot and bothered. Yet she refused to look away.

'I've not the faintest idea,' she admitted. 'Perhaps I will know what it is when the time is right.'

Luca's eyes searched hers. 'I have a feeling you will. And that it will be something special.'

Flavia was aware that something had shifted between them. 'I always thought you disapproved of me.'

'Perhaps at first I did. I assumed any girl brought up alongside Italian nobles was bound to be spoiled. Have airs and graces at the very least. But you're not like that. You started changing my mind from the moment I found you in my mother's kitchen, looking perfectly content to be there.'

'I was happy to be there.' The air around them seemed to vibrate.

'You have stayed good friends with my sister. I never thought you would.'

She raised an eyebrow. 'And you were wrong about that too! I will always treasure my friendship with Margherita. We will still be friends when we are old and grey and walking with sticks.'

She took a nervous gulp of wine. It went down the wrong way, and she spluttered.

Brown eyes dancing, he reached across and wiped the corner of her mouth with the pad of his thumb. His touch gave her goose-bumps all over her body. She prayed he wouldn't notice.

To her relief, Luca leaned back on his elbows as he watched the wedding guests, and the moment passed. Children chased each other in circles as grandparents watched with indulgent smiles, women sat together talking animatedly and laughing, men stood in groups, drinking beer and occasionally picking up a child – not necessarily theirs – and tossing him or her into the air. These were the people Luca had known all his life, had grown up with, and no doubt he had kissed more than a few of the women. These were the people he felt at ease with. And so, she realised, did she.

'I too would like to leave my mark on the world,' he said, breaking into her thoughts.

'If there is a war will you join the army? Make your mark that way?' She wanted to know if he still felt the way he had the year before.

He shook his head. 'I will never fight for Mussolini and his Blackshirts.'

'Tell me why you don't support him.' She kept her voice low. Athleticism and prowess were at the heart of Fascism, and if anyone fitted that description it was Luca. 'He's given land back to the people and they have more to eat, are wealthier than ever before. He has built schools and hospitals, established camps for children who might not otherwise get a holiday.'

'I'm aware of that. I went to those summer camps. As did Roberto. I'd never seen my brother so happy as when he was there. All that dressing up in uniforms and marching with pretend guns. He was strong and fast even then. Everything Mussolini wanted in the youth.'

'And you?'

Luca took his time to answer. 'Even as a child I never saw the point in any of it. I didn't want to dress like everyone else. And as for it being a summer camp, to me the Tuscan countryside is a large holiday camp. But the kids from the cities loved it. Who could blame them?'

The narrowness of the step was such that they were close enough so that every cell in her body was excruciatingly aware of him, as if their bodies were magnets, straining towards each other.

'Admittedly Mussolini did some good, maybe a lot of good, to begin with,' Luca continued. 'At first he seemed determined to make a fairer society for everyone by making the majority wealthier and healthier. The landowners had had it all their own way for too long. But then he took everything too far. He began to behave as if he were a god and not a mortal man – insisting that Italy grows grain when we all know that crop does not do well in our soil. To farm it the farmers had to stop growing grapes and olives – crops that are part of their heritage and their souls, produce that did make money.'

The band struck up again, pulling her back to the moment. Engrossed in their conversation, Flavia had almost forgotten she was at her best friend's wedding. While they'd been talking the fireflies had disappeared, the moon now a golden jewel pinned to a cloak of a deep navy-blue sky.

'In the last years I don't like what I'm seeing – or hearing,' Luca continued. 'I don't like how Mussolini is Hitler's plaything. Those who still support him, like my brother, are deluded. Do people really think Franco is on the side of the ordinary man and woman?

Many believe Mussolini only sent troops to Spain because he wanted to get the army battle-ready. That's a terrible reason for young Italian men to die.' He looked off to the middle distance, then shook his head and turned back at her with a rueful smile. 'Enough about that. Margherita told me you've been working with refugees.' His obvious admiration sent a warm glow of pleasure through Flavia.

'But it is my work with the refugees, what they have to say, that scares me,' she said, before going on to repeat the stories of vast military parades the refugees had told her about. 'If even half the stories they tell are true then matters are very bad. They speak of camps, arrests, brutality, not just Jews disappearing but intellectuals, gypsies, people suspected of being homosexual too. Anyone the German government doesn't think fit to be German! And Mussolini sides with Hitler!'

She held his gaze, wanting him to know how strongly she felt, how frightened she was about what was happening in Europe. 'Jews are no longer citizens in their own countries. They must wear yellow stars on their arms to identify themselves as Jewish. They aren't allowed to own businesses, or sit on certain benches, or walk in the parks. They are without rights – like some sort of lesser people. For no other reason than that they were born into the Jewish faith. And now Mussolini is following suit. Italian Jews have been forbidden from attending university, made to add their names and addresses to registers, and we are not allowed to socialise with them as if they are not true Italians! Where will it end? Will Italian Jews be driven from Italy?' She shuddered. 'I believe Italy is sleepwalking towards a war alongside Germany.'

Given what Mussolini and his regime had done to her parents, he was capable of anything. She paused, tempted to tell him why she thought that. But she couldn't. She'd promised her godparents she wouldn't tell anyone.

'It is why I won't sign up if Italy joins Germany in a war,' Luca said. 'Italy does not need to gain territory in other countries at the cost of other people's lives. No, I won't fight unless it is for something I truly believe in.'

'And if people call you a coward for not fighting?'

He shrugged. 'It won't make any difference to me. A real coward is a man who does what he knows is wrong because he is too scared to do the right thing.'

Flavia wondered if he was always as open with his views. Not every Italian thought as he did. Many would think him a traitor to his country. However, she suspected it wouldn't matter to Luca what others thought. He was a man who would always say what he meant, without pretence or guile, without fear or care for the consequences, and she admired him for it.

'Aren't you worried someone reports you for saying these things?' If the Fascists could get rid of her mother and father without so much as a cry of protest, how much easier it would be for them to shut Luca up. However, her parents had been important people in their circles – when they spoke people listened, and that was what had made them dangerous, so perhaps nobody would take notice of what a young farmer had to say?

Luca looked incredulous 'Who? You? I doubt that.'

'Of course not me! I would never betray you – or any Rossi,' she added hastily.

'Then who? Not anyone in this village or in Porciano. I'd trust them all with my life.'

Flavia hoped for his sake that he was right. 'Be careful,' she said softly.

He leant into her, and her breath caught in her throat. She would never know what he might have said or done, as a girl with hair down to her waist came over and stood in front of Luca, placing her hands on her hips. 'Where have you been?' she pouted, ignoring Flavia. 'I've been looking for you. You promised me last night you wouldn't leave my side.'

'Don't go anywhere, I'll be back as soon as I can,' Luca whispered in Flavia's ear before allowing the girl to pull him to his feet.

Some of the magic went out of the evening. Flavia watched as they disappeared into the crowd and started to dance. It wasn't one of his talents. He danced like a skittish horse.

Happy her face was hidden by the shadows, she watched surreptitiously, her chin propped on her fist, trying to untangle her feelings. He was different: more complex, more thoughtful, more intriguing than she remembered – and she'd liked him even then. If she were honest with herself, she was drawn to him – as if being near him was where she needed to be. He seemed to like her back, but apparently he liked the woman he was dancing with better. That much was obvious. He'd gone off with her without as much as a backward glance. They'd moved closer, and the long-haired woman had her face lifted to his, his hands resting on her waist as he murmured something in her ear. Probably arrangements to spend the night together. Flavia sighed. Clearly she knew next to nothing about men.

What did it matter how he made her feel? She needed to remember what Margherita had told her about him. That he broke at least one heart a summer. She would not become one of his conquests. She stood and, spotting a laughing Margherita in the crowd, blew her a kiss and slipped away. Far better to keep away from Luca Rossi.

SEVENTEEN

As planned, the day after Margherita's wedding Flavia returned to Florence. Before she left she'd called at the Rossi farm to say her farewells. No matter what she'd told herself the previous evening, she was disappointed when there was no sign of Luca. No doubt he was asleep in the barn with his girlfriend!

One afternoon, shortly after their return from Porciano, Flavia's godparents asked to speak to her in the drawing room.

Her godfather was leaning against the fireplace with an arm resting on the mantelpiece, the other hand in his pocket, looking his typical urbane self. Her godmother was stiff-backed in her usual chair, beautifully dressed as always. Chaos might be swirling in the world around them, but one would never know.

'We have decided to go to Switzerland for an indefinite period,' her godfather said.

'Why?'

Her godmother ran a tongue over her lips. 'We are convinced Mussolini is determined to take us into another war alongside that abhorrent man, Hitler, and we don't wish to have any part in it. We have good friends in Switzerland who will be happy to have us to stay. You too, naturally.'

So they had the same fears she had. But if Italy was going to war alongside Hitler, she wasn't going to scuttle away at the first inkling of danger or discomfort. Not when people depended on her.

'I can't leave Florence. Not at the moment. I have my work. Is Sophia going?'

Her godparents exchanged a look.

'She has her training as a nurse to finish,' Lucrezia said. 'If there is a war she will be needed. So no, she will continue to stay here in Florence.'

'I am needed here too.'

'Please, Flavia. We very much want you to come with us. We fear for your safety. Remember what happened to your parents! We promised them we would take care of you. You can help refugees from Switzerland as much as from here.'

Flavia swallowed hard. She hated to deny her godparents anything, but she knew in her bones that right now Florence was where she needed to be. 'I am sorry. You have been very good to me. As good as any parents could be, but I can't go with you. I have my own life to live now.'

Her godfather straightened and sighed. 'We can't force you to come with us, and of course you will always have a home with us. But promise us, if – when – war does break out, that you will go and stay in Porciano. You will be much safer there. Even better, come to us in Switzerland.'

'I can't promise,' Flavia told her godparents, regretfully. 'But I will do my best to stay out of danger.' She would miss them. They had been part of her life for so long. Always there. She blinked away the tears that burnt behind her lids, and kissed them both. 'My mama and papa would be so very grateful for everything you have done for me. They made the right choice when they appointed you my guardians. Nobody could have taken better care of me.' Her voice cracked, and she took a deep breath, not wishing to cry and embarrass them all. 'I can't thank you enough, but it is time for me to follow my own path. Wherever that might lead.'

EIGHTEEN

May 1940

Flavia ran up the steps to the Villa Bencista, relishing the cooler air and the prospect of an evening with her friends. She found them on the wisteria-covered terrace, sipping tisanes.

'Flavia! You're here at last. We've been waiting for you,' Julia said, standing to kiss her. Natalia and Julia's new husband, Giuseppe, followed suit.

'What would you like to drink, Flavia?' Giuseppe asked, pulling out a chair for her.

'What you're having would be lovely.' As always when in the presence of her friends, Flavia felt herself relax.

As Giuseppe disappeared inside, Julia stared after him adoringly.

'Still enjoying married life then?' Flavia teased, pleased her friend had found the love of her life. She liked Giuseppe, found his solid presence reassuring. The last year had been strange and unsettling, her eighteenth birthday a subdued affair.

'I love everything about my life.' Julia smiled back. 'Giuseppe, this divine villa, living in Fiesole.'

Flavia could see why. Fiesole, a ten-minute walk from the villa, was only a short drive or bus journey from Florence, but so much cooler and quieter. And the villa *was* gorgeous. On a clear day like today, you could see all the way to the Duomo.

Julia and Giuseppe liked entertaining, so there were often other guests too. Some would only stay for lunch or dinner, others for the night or even the whole weekend, gathering around the piano after dinner to sing.

On this occasion, unusually, Flavia and Natalia were the only guests. It was how Flavia liked it best. That way they could talk without watching what they said. Although Mussolini hadn't imposed further restrictions on the Jews of Italy – certainly there had been no suggestion Italian Jews wear stars on their arms – not everyone approved of people breaking the law by socialising with Jews.

'I do worry, though,' Julia continued, frowning, 'now that Britain and France have declared war on Germany, Hitler will persuade Mussolini to join forces with him. I couldn't bear it if Giuseppe were called up.'

Natalia laid a soothing hand on top of Julia's. 'It's been months, and Il Duce has done nothing.'

'We will just have to hope Mussolini will continue to keep us out of it,' Giuseppe said, returning with a tray of drinks.

Flavia had her doubts. When war between Germany and France and Great Britain had been declared in September last year, despite all the hints of what was coming, Flavia had been outraged and shocked – her fellow Italians equally disapproving. It appeared most of her countrymen and women wanted war as little as Flavia did. Italy held its breath before carrying on as normal. As if what was happening in Europe had nothing to do with them, as if somehow war might pass them by.

Nevertheless, the government had taken measures to protect Florence and its treasures from bombs, and consequently the city, with its works of art covered and sandbagged, looked so different – like a bandaged and wounded warrior herself. Flavia had been in the Piazza della Signoria when they'd taken Cosimo de' Medici away on the back of a truck. It was all so unreal.

If Italy was in limbo, so was Flavia. It was no longer possible for people to leave Germany or its occupied territories, so the refugee centre had reluctantly closed its doors.

The dances, lunches and tennis that made up her days felt inconsequential and banal. She often thought of the long-gone Forestieri, the young men and women she'd met who were currently 'doing their bit' in defence of their countries. Her previous mockery of them made her feel small and ashamed. People were dying across the world, and she was twiddling her thumbs.

Flavia's godparents were settled in Switzerland, and Flavia and Sophia lived in harmony in the apartment in Borgo Santa Croce. Sophia, who was coming to the end of her nurse training, worked long hours at the hospital, and although their social lives were similar – dinner with friends, dances and lunches – they rarely intersected. With an increasing amount of time on her hands, Flavia had wondered whether she might train as a nurse too, but to her mortification the sight of blood made her nauseous. Instead, she'd put herself forward to work with the Red Cross. Should Italy join the war, it would be her job to roll bandages, count linen, dish out tea and sympathy. Not exactly the heroic role she'd envisaged for herself, but at least she'd be doing something.

In the meantime, Flavia had decided to drive on from Fiesole to the Casentino to visit Margherita. She'd only managed to visit twice in the last year, which wasn't as often as either of them would have liked. Although her godfather had left her his beloved car, she seldom used it as petrol was strictly rationed.

Since they'd last met, Margherita had given birth to a little boy she'd called Lazzero. Flavia hadn't been able to make the trip to Vallucciole for his baptism, so she'd been declared godmother in absentia – a responsibility she intended to honour.

She turned her attention back to her friends and joined in their lighthearted gossip, allowing herself the pleasure of the company of good friends and a cool mountain breeze.

Just before dinner was due to be served, the housekeeper brought a familiar figure to the veranda. Flavia's heart gave a leap of revolt. Captain Lambini! She knew he continued to invite himself to dinner at Julia's home in Florence, but to Flavia's knowledge he'd never been a guest at the Villa Bencista. Her hosts exchanged an uneasy glance, appearing equally surprised. The colour had drained from Natalia's face.

'Vincenzo! To what do we owe this pleasure?' Giuseppe asked, getting to his feet.

'Good evening, Julia, Giuseppe, Signorina Corsi.' He tipped his head in Natalia's direction. 'I'm afraid I don't know this other lady's name. I was passing and thought it would be pleasant to stop and pass part of the evening with you.'

'Then you must join us for dinner,' Giuseppe said.

Dear God, did Vincenzo remember Natalia from that day in Florence? Recall she was Jewish?

Natalia stood. 'If you don't mind, I think I'll skip dinner and go to my room. I have a headache coming on,' she said calmly. Only someone who knew her well would recognise the fear in her eyes. She slipped out before anyone could reply. Flavia wished she could say the same but knew, if she did, she'd only be antagonising Vincenzo and drawing attention to Natalia.

'Let's go in to dinner,' Julia said, plastering a smile on her face and taking Vincenzo by the arm. 'Tell me, how were my parents when you last saw them?'

Happily, Julia and Giuseppe kept the conversation going throughout the meal. Flavia could barely make herself swallow.

'You are very quiet, Signorina Corsi,' Vincenzo said when Giuseppe and Julia left the room – Giuseppe to go to the cellar for another bottle of wine, and Julia to check up on Natalia.

'I have nothing to say to you, Captain Lambini.'

'I see time has not changed your opinion of me. You still think yourself superior.' He looked at her if she were a naughty child. 'Perhaps if you took the time to get to know me, you would realise that I am a better man than you think.'

Flavia lifted an eyebrow.

'I am just a man who wants to improve the lives of his family and his countrymen and women.' He took a sip of wine. 'I wasn't brought up with privilege, you know. My mother was a simple woman who was married to a brutal man. I had to drag myself up, work two jobs while educating myself.'

Flavia felt a momentary flash of sympathy.

'Mussolini is the man who created the circumstances for me to do that. That is why he will always have my loyalty,' Vincenzo continued.

At the mention of Mussolini's name, Flavia's sympathy vanished. Anyone who supported a man who had innocent people murdered in his name didn't deserve a second thought. 'You don't have to explain yourself to me,' she said stiffly.

'But I will. I am now able to look after my mother, make life easier for her. Like any good son would wish to do. She can hold her head up in her village again.'

'Do you really think she is proud of you?' Flavia stood, pressing her palms against the table in a futile attempt to suppress her fury. 'You and your fellow Blackshirts are nothing but bullies. You beat and arrest anyone who speaks against you – or the regime. You have improved your lot on the back of other people's misery. As for your precious leader, Il Duce, you know what happened to my parents in his name. You—'

'Flavia,' Julia's voice came from the doorway, 'I think that's enough.' She turned towards Vincenzo. 'Do forgive my friend.'

'Please don't apologise on my behalf, Julia.' Flavia turned on her heel. 'I'll leave you to your guest. Goodnight.'

NINETEEN

The next morning Flavia apologised to Julia for arguing with Lambini. Julia brushed her apology aside. 'He left shortly after you went to bed. He was in a real funk. Look, cara, I understand how you feel. I would be happy to never set eyes on Captain Lambini again, but I agree with my father that it is better not to antagonise him. Especially when he could make life for Natalia and her mother difficult if he takes it upon himself to look into her.'

Flavia felt terrible. She'd never forgive herself if she brought trouble on Natalia. Hopefully Vincenzo wouldn't trouble himself looking into a woman he'd only met briefly.

When she reached Vallucciole, she left the car on the road at the top of the village and walked the rest of the short way down. She found Margherita on her veranda holding baby Lazzero on her lap. Despite the threat of war, her friend seemed more content than ever. Noticing Flavia, a beaming smile crossed her face.

'Flavia!' Margherita exclaimed, standing. 'I'm so happy to see you. It has been far too long.' She held out her son for Flavia to take. 'Meet your godson. My Lazzero.' She made no attempt to hide her pride.

Flavia held the baby gingerly in the crook of her arms. He was so small, his tiny features so perfect. The little boy gazed up at her with steady, large brown eyes. Judging by the way he gripped her finger, he was going to be strong. She was immediately smitten with him.

'We are going to have lots of babies,' Margherita said. 'If the next one's a girl I'm going to call her Flavia. After you. You will be her godmother too?'

'Of course.' Flavia was touched and honoured. It struck her how much she'd missed her friend. She would try to visit more often.

They were having drinks on the veranda when Luca appeared, carrying a large tub of pecorino. A slow smile spread across his face when he noticed Flavia, and – disconcertingly – a dizzy delight ricocheted through her body from the top of her head to the tips of her toes.

He still had the same air of confidence, but he seemed taller, better looking, more muscular than she remembered.

'It's been a long time,' he said. Had his voice always been that deep?

Only too aware that Margherita was watching them closely, Flavia couldn't prevent a blush from travelling up her neck and across her face.

Luca bent over Lazzero, pulling faces, making the baby coo with delight and giving Flavia time to collect herself. She didn't want him to see how he affected her.

Niccolo's nonna emerged from the house. From the way she greeted Luca, with gesticulating hands and shrieks of pleasure, anyone would have thought she hadn't seen him for months. Luca kissed the old lady soundly, complimenting her on how well she looked. She pretended to cuff his ear, and he backed away laughing. Flavia felt the familiar warm glow of being in the company of her country family, as she'd come to think of them.

Nonna swapped a basin of peas that needed shelling for a sleepy Lazzero. Margherita watched anxiously as the old lady tottered off with him but said nothing. It was beyond even Margherita to separate a nonna and her grandchild.

'Roberto's home for a few days,' Margherita said, as she ripped open a pod with the side of her nail.

Out of the corner of her eye, Flavia noticed that the village children had gathered around Luca. He tossed a little boy in the air, making him squeal with terror and delight. This was yet another side of Luca that Flavia was discovering. It was as if he were the sun and everyone else a planet revolving around him, as if being in his orbit was the most exciting place to be.

And she couldn't disagree. Just being around him made every cell in her body light up.

She forced her attention back to her friend. 'You don't sound too pleased.'

Margherita hesitated.

'Go on.' Flavia leaned forward. 'You know you can tell me anything.'

Margherita's expression was unusually solemn. 'He's changed – and not for the better. He was always, I don't know – different to the rest of us. But since he came back from Spain there's a coldness – worse, an anger – in him that wasn't there before. It's like he truly hates Luca now. He doesn't even try to hide it, not even for Mama's sake. And Luca has no time for Roberto either. They can barely manage to be in each other's company.'

'They're still brothers. Perhaps what he went through in Spain affected him more than was thought, and in time they will get along better.'

'I don't know. I don't think so.'

It wasn't like Margherita to be so worried, but there was little Flavia could say to reassure her friend. Flavia barely knew Roberto.

She popped a plump pea in her mouth.

Margherita took a deep breath. 'He says he intends to join the Blackshirts.'

Now that *was* shocking. No wonder her friend was upset!

Before Flavia could form a reply, Lazzero gave a hungry cry from inside, and Margherita went to feed him. Luca came to sit in her place. He looked at Flavia as if he were drinking her in. Was it possible she affected him, even a little bit?

She grew hot as it hit her – what she'd probably known for a long time but had not been able to admit even to herself. This man had her heart. He had stolen it piece by piece, without her being aware of it, but surely had it, and always would – whether he felt the same way or not. She wished she had a fan to cool her burning cheeks.

'I'm glad to see you,' he said. 'We've missed you.'

We? Not I? Flavia wasn't at all sure she could speak – she certainly couldn't think of a response to his comment.

Instead, she launched into her past work with the refugees – her frustration that not all of the people in danger had left when they still had a chance and her worries for those left behind.

Luca listened attentively while she rattled on – she just couldn't seem to stop talking. She went on to tell him how she'd thought of training as a nurse, but the sight of blood made her dizzy, so she was training as a volunteer with the Red Cross. She trailed off – mortified he'd think she was trying to impress him, which in a way she had been. While she'd been talking, she'd studied his expression surreptitiously, trying to read his thoughts, his body language for clues that he felt the same as she did.

In the meantime, Margherita had come back outside and was watching them both with a satisfied grin on her face. To Flavia's chagrin and disappointment, it appeared to be Luca's cue to leave her side.

For the rest of the visit Luca was occupied helping out in the fields, talking to the older men, assisting the women carrying water from the well. All the while Flavia was conscious of him in the periphery of her vision.

When it was time for Flavia to return to Florence, Luca walked her back up the path. He ran his hand reverently over the fender of her uncle's car. 'She's a beauty,' he said. 'I don't suppose I could drive it back?'

Finding his boyish excitement endearing, she couldn't bring herself to say no.

It was immediately obvious he'd never driven a car before. She showed him what to do, leaning across him to demonstrate how to let out the clutch while pressing down on the accelerator, blushing bright red as her leg became tangled in his. When he laughed, she scowled at him and pulled her leg away, keeping her body as far away from him as was possible in the confines of the front seat of the car. With Luca at the wheel, they jerked along the road. The look on his face, the concentration, the sheer determination! It was her turn to laugh at him. At first he pretended to glare at her, but he couldn't keep it up. They kept smiling at each other as they lurched all the way to Porciano. When they reached the end of the road to the farmhouse, he made no move to get out. Flavia felt short of breath, as if she'd been running up a hill.

'Will you come in and say hello to Mama and Rosina?' Luca asked.

Flavia was torn between never wanting to leave his side and putting as much space as possible between them. It was almost painful being with him, wanting to touch him but not daring to. Good sense won. She glanced at her wristwatch. 'I need to get back to Florence before night falls. Please pass on my love, and tell them I promise to visit the next time I am in Porciano.'

He leaned towards her and took her chin gently between his thumb and forefinger, and any thought of leaving disappeared. Was he going to kiss her? For months she'd imagined this moment; in her musings she always knew how she'd react, what she'd say, how she'd behave. Now she hadn't a clue. What was she supposed to do? Lean in? Purse her lips? She should have interrogated Margherita on the art of kissing when she had the chance. She swayed towards him, but at the last minute he looked over her shoulder, frowned, and with a regretful shake of his head pulled away. 'Stay safe, Bella,' he murmured, getting out of the car.

Burning with mortification, Flavia twisted in her seat to see what had caught his attention. It was Roberto. He was standing in the field, a bucket in his hands, looking as if he wanted to pour the contents over their heads.

TWENTY

AMELIA

Dusk wasn't far away when Amelia put Flavia's diary down.

Unlike Flavia, she'd known pretty much from the get-go that Cameron was the man for her. Her mind drifted to the day she'd met him.

She'd gone to the harbour for a swim that morning. He'd been painting his boat. Amelia had never encountered anyone down in the harbour before, although she had seen the boat moored there.

They'd given each other a polite wave, and – feeling slightly self-conscious – she'd stripped down to her bikini, left her clothes on a boulder and run into the sea.

When she emerged, practically blue with cold, Cameron strolled towards the rock where she'd left her towel and brought it to her. 'You don't think a wetsuit would help?' he'd said, grinning. 'The water's freezing.'

'I prefer swimming without.' She wrapped the towel around her shoulders. A sea breeze had sprung up, and she shivered.

'Look, you've turned blue. Why don't you come inside, dry off properly? I'll even make you a coffee.' He indicated the house behind him, located almost on the shore.

'I didn't know anyone lived there.'

'No one did. Until last week.' He gave another wide smile. 'I traded my London flat for it and the boat. Hope I don't live to regret it.'

Intrigued, Amelia accepted his invitation. She used his bathroom to change out of her wet clothes, pulling her jeans and long-sleeved T-shirt on over her naked body. They drank their coffee on a rock outside his cottage. He explained he'd worked in finance since leaving university but had had enough of the corporate world and wanted to try his hand at fishing. He'd been divorced for a couple of years – amicable, no children. He liked sailing, fishing and reading non-fiction. In turn Amelia told him she'd never been married, although she'd lived with someone in her twenties, had once worked in London but now worked mainly from home, loved swimming in the sea and spent most of her free time visiting galleries. It didn't take much to make her happy: sun, countryside, old books, friends, work. She'd never been a party animal.

He was easy to talk to, and she'd been drawn to him physically and mentally, but was frightened she'd make an idiot of herself by making it too obvious.

She'd been thrilled, although not really surprised, when he'd turned up at her door a week later, a wide grin on his face, a bottle of chilled white wine in one hand, a six-pack of beer in the other. Since she'd last seen him the weather had changed dramatically, and it was an untypical Scottish day – ferociously hot.

'I would have come sooner,' he said, 'but I've been in London all week, tying up loose ends.'

They took their drinks out to the deck looking out to the bay and the sea beyond. There had been no pretence from either of them – only a certain knowledge that they'd end up in bed together, and that all they were doing by delaying the inevitable was drawing out the pleasurable anticipation. Amelia knew – she didn't know how, or why – that she and Cameron were meant to be with each other, and that he felt the same. In a gap in the conversation, she'd wondered aloud about the women who, during a terrible storm in 1881, had waited anxiously on the cliff top, only a few metres from where they were sitting, for their fishermen to return –

only to watch helplessly as the returning boats were dashed on the rocks, their husbands, sons, fathers drowned in front of their eyes.

She'd been so smug that day, empathising with their grief, not for one moment ever believing that in six short years she'd be in the same position.

The crushing pain in her chest made her gasp, and she forced the memories of the past away.

She picked up the photograph of Flavia with the group, which she'd tucked back in the diary the day she'd first come across it, and studied it again. She was certain now the woman next to Flavia was Margherita, the little girl Rosina. Was that Luca standing behind her? If so, it was also him in the drawing she'd found in the trunk. In which case they did get together eventually. Did he break Flavia's heart? Or had something happened to him during the war, and Flavia couldn't bear the thought of a life without him? Was that why Amelia felt so connected to her? She stared out of the window, lost in thought. Making up her mind, she put the photo in her pocket. Perhaps she might find some answers at the farmhouse in the image.

She set off, locking the door of the castello behind her. She passed the village and turned right, confident from Flavia's many descriptions of the path that the track she was following would take her to the farmhouse. The sun was still hot, but the air was thick, and there were clouds in the sky, dark and swollen, hinting at rain to come – however probably not for another hour or two. At one time the valley must have been filled with farmers; now it had the air of a deserted Brigadoon, as if everyone had been plucked from their homes and deposited who knew where.

When she reached what she believed was the farmhouse, she pivoted on her heel to check she'd come to the right place. There was a low wall surrounding the house, and the view of the castello was exactly that in the photograph.

As Amelia made her way towards the door, a dog ran towards her, barking, the hairs on the back of its neck raised, stopping Amelia in her tracks.

'Toto! Don't be rude,' a voice called out, and a woman of around thirty, wearing a dress and Wellington boots, her hair covered by a scarf, emerged from the house and hurried towards her. The collie sat down, eyeing Amelia warily.

Amelia called out a greeting in Italian, and the woman greeted her back, her expression curious. Suddenly Amelia had no idea what to say, how to explain her uninvited appearance at the farmhouse.

'I am staying at the castello' – idiotically, she pointed to it as if the woman didn't see it every day – 'as a guest of the contessa.'

The woman broke into a wide smile. 'Yes, of course! We have seen you on the road. Welcome. Would you like to come in for a lemonade?'

'That would be great. As long as I'm not disturbing you?'

'No! Not at all. I was just thinking of having one myself. Please come in.'

Amelia followed her into a kitchen which was exactly as Flavia described in her diary. It was huge – almost the size of the flat she'd lived in before moving to Cove, with the same flagstones it must have had when Flavia visited, the same enormous wall-to-wall fireplace and, perhaps, judging by the pot marks and scars on the surface, even the same long, scrubbed wooden table. Amelia was ridiculously pleased it hadn't changed.

On the table there were several rounds of pasta ready to be rolled, and on the stove tomatoes were bubbling in an enormous pot. It wasn't just the bricks and mortar that hadn't changed.

'Sit down, Signora,' the woman said. 'I will fetch some lemonade.'

'Please, call me Amelia.'

The woman smiled back. 'I am Alessandra. This is my nonna.'

Sitting in a chair in the corner was an old lady, dressed all in black. She was so quiet that, until Alessandra pointed her out, Amelia hadn't noticed her. At first Amelia thought she was asleep, but then she peered up at her with bright brown eyes. There was something familiar about her, and Amelia's heart gave a lurch of excitement. Could this be Margherita? Was it possible she was still alive? Could the same family still be living here? That the farmhouse, the kitchen at least, hadn't changed would suggest that might be the case.

Alessandra set a glass down on the table in front of Amelia. She asked her grandmother whether she would like one too, but the old lady shook her head. 'Who is this?' she asked.

'A guest of the contessa,' Alessandra replied.

'Ah, the contessa.' The old lady slapped her hands together and gave Amelia a gleeful smile.

'How is she?' Alessandra asked Amelia, with a tender glance at her nonna.

'Good. Her daughter has just had a baby. She's gone to America to help with the other children.'

'She will be so happy to see them. We didn't think the baby was due so soon. '

'I think there were some difficulties. The baby had to be delivered early.'

'I'm sorry to hear that. The family has been good to us.' Alessandra wiped her hands on a towel. 'The contessa came to visit only a couple of weeks ago. She didn't mention there was anything wrong.'

'I understand everything is fine now,' Amelia reassured her. 'Beatrice emailed to let me know. The baby was born a little earlier than expected, that's all.'

Alessandra seemed genuinely relieved. 'That's good. When you see her, tell her that she and her family are in our prayers.'

'Of course.' Amelia took a sip of lemonade. It was delicious. Freshly squeezed, with perhaps a teaspoon or two of sugar added.

Nonna eased herself out of her chair and joined Alessandra at the table. 'Forgive us,' Alessandra said, 'but we must finish with the pasta before it dries out.'

As she thought about how to begin, Amelia watched in awe the rapid movements of Alessandra and her nonna's hands as they rolled, shaped and cut the pasta.

'Have you lived here long?' she asked Alessandra.

Alessandra laid the strips of pasta across the rim of a bowl. She smiled. 'Since my marriage. The farmhouse has been in my husband's family for generations. Going back to Nonna's grandparents' time at least. The farm was left empty for a while during the war, but Nonna and her mother came back a few years later.'

Amelia's heart gave a little kick. She took the photograph out of her pocket and showed it to Alessandra. 'I found this in the castello. I think it was taken here.'

Alessandra studied it before giving a small shake of her head. 'It's definitely this farm, but I don't recognise anyone. Perhaps Nonna will.'

She passed it to her grandmother who lifted it close to her eyes to study it. Suddenly, her face crumpled, and she started to cry.

'What is it, Nonna?' Alessandra cried.

But the old woman was sobbing too hard to reply, her fingertip touching each figure in the photograph in turn.

A perplexed Alessandra gave Amelia an apologetic look. 'I think you should go. Sorry if I appear rude but when Nonna gets like this...' She led her grandmother back to her chair, crouched by her side and took her brown-spotted hands in hers, murmuring soothingly. Alessandra turned back to Amelia. 'Nonna had a small stroke a year or so ago. She mustn't be distressed. It's not good for her.'

Appalled that she'd upset the old lady, Amelia stood. 'I'll see myself out.' She hesitated. 'Can I help? Do you need to get her to bed?'

Alessandra shook her head. 'My father-in-law will be in soon. He will help me.'

Amelia took a couple of steps towards the door, then turned around. She hadn't come only to leave without having any of her questions answered. 'Could I ask – what is your nonna's name?'

Alessandra frowned. 'Rosina.'

Amelia's heart skipped another beat. So at least one Rossi was still alive.

'Would you tell her I am truly sorry for upsetting her.'

But Alessandra had already turned back to her nonna.

Amelia let herself out of the farmhouse and tramped back to the castello. Rosina was bound to know more about Flavia. If only Amelia could think of a way of quizzing her that didn't upset the old lady.

TWENTY-ONE

The next morning Amelia decided it was time to visit the castello at Romena. As she drove through Stia she realised she still hadn't emailed Beatrice with an update on her progress. She'd do it later. Once she'd thought about what to tell her. She'd have to mention the letter. If she didn't and Kelly did, then Beatrice would be unimpressed. And what about the diaries and the box of personal treasures? There was no getting away from the breach of trust involved. Amelia wasn't looking forward to that conversation.

Although the Castello di Romena was a ruin, it was easy to see what it would have been like in its heyday – not dissimilar to Porciano's, but significantly larger and visibly more important. At the entrance, there was a sketch depicting how it would have looked in the mid-fifteenth century: the castle in the middle surrounded by walls, the small houses of the castle staff next, another wall and then the houses of the villagers. A board explaining the history of the castello and its link to the Guidi family – and how it was believed that Dante took his inspiration for his nine circles of hell from the Castello di Romena – standing alongside a replication of what the castello once looked like. Amelia scribbled some notes. She'd make sure the leaflet directed visitors here.

She spent some time on the ramparts, but Castello di Romena didn't call to her the way Porciano's did. Maybe because it was too much of a ruin, or perhaps because Flavia didn't live in it. Whatever the reason, she didn't sense the spirits of the past here the way she did in Porciano. She wasn't sure if that was a good or a bad thing. She left the castello and followed the track that pointed to the parish church of San Pietro.

As Beatrice had promised, it was a wonderful example of Romanesque architecture.

The interior was unlike any Amelia had seen before. Where normally there were pews there was only an empty space with a pretty rug and scattered cushions. Piped music and the smell of roses from scented candles filled the room. These weren't the only modern touches. The altar had been created out of the backs of old, possibly medieval, chairs. In the alcoves there were little offerings of fresh flowers and fruit. Although the church had a contemporary feel to it, this was the way it would have been in the twelfth century. Amelia couldn't help but contrast its openness and light to the church in Stia.

Hearing a step behind her, she spun around to find a man of roughly her age, dressed in faded jeans and a T-shirt.

'Hello,' he said in English. 'I see you're admiring our church.' He was very good-looking. He also had the kindest eyes Amelia had ever seen.

'It's very beautiful,' she replied in Italian. 'How did you know I was British?'

'You have that look. Despite your colouring. Your Italian is excellent, but would you mind if we speak English? I don't get as many opportunities as I would like to practise.' He held out his hand. 'I am Father Michael.'

Amelia couldn't hide her astonishment. She'd yet to see a man who looked less like a priest.

He appeared to realise what she was thinking and laughed, his eyes creasing at the corners. 'I know I don't look like one. That, I feel, is the problem with the Catholic Church. It's stuck in the past.

If we are going to get people to return to the Church, we have to make it more contemporary, more relevant to the needs of the current times.'

Which explained the cushions on the floor, the piped music and the alcoves. 'And is it working?'

He smiled. 'Come to a service and see for yourself. I'm warning you, there may well be standing room only.'

If all churches were like this, and all priests like him, she might well have done – even if she hadn't been to chapel since she'd left primary school and, more significantly, did not believe in God. She told him that. Even the bit about him not looking like a priest. To her mortification, a blush stole up her cheeks.

'I don't insist on either.' He smiled down at her. If he'd noticed that she'd turned beetroot, he didn't comment, but judging by the laughter in his eyes it hadn't escaped his attention. To Amelia's relief he had the grace not to say. 'The Church exists as much to bring people to God as to tend to those who already believe in Him.'

Amelia shook her head. 'I should warn you, nothing you can say will change my mind.'

Silence fell. She was the first to break it. She gestured to the bare walls. 'I couldn't help but notice there aren't any paintings or works of art here. There must have been at one time.'

'No doubt. At some point. However, this is how it would have looked when it was first built – minus the rugs and cushions, of course – to the original worshippers. Later I imagine there would have been paintings, but I suspect they were removed when the church fell into disrepair. They might hang in the Uffizi for all I know, or more likely just be stored there.' He shrugged in a typical Italian gesture. 'It would be impossible to get them back, even if I thought we should. To be honest, I like the simplicity of the bare walls.'

'Me too. Though I admit I'm astounded by all the amazing paintings and sculptures in these smaller churches. They must be worth a small fortune. Is no one worried they might be stolen? The church in Stia has wonderful terracottas by Della Robbia, for example.'

'What should we do? Remove them all? Our museums already have more than they could show in a lifetime. Besides, we would deprive the people who worship there of evidence of how God's beauty works through man. That would be worse than losing these pieces. The Catholic Church has always believed that works of art should stay in the places they were originally created for.'

'What happened during the war? Didn't the German army take them?'

'Now that's another story. Before the war started, the greatest artworks were removed and taken away. A great many were hidden in monasteries. Locals helped hide them. But you are correct. Many were stolen by the Germans.'

Once again Amelia was struck that a war that seemed so long ago to her had been a reality to Flavia.

They stood in comfortable silence for a while.

'Would you walk with me?' He smiled again. 'I promise not to try and convert you, at least not right now, but as I said, I welcome opportunities to practise my English.'

Amelia nodded. There was something about his presence that was a balm to her soul.

'Let me show you the grounds first, then perhaps we can have some tea?' His eyes twinkled again. 'I know how much you British like your cuppas.'

Amelia returned his smile. 'Where did you learn to speak English?' she asked, as they walked along the path and crossed over the road to the other side.

'In the UK. I did my theology degree at Durham University. I was very fortunate to get the chance to study there. It is a great city in a great country.'

'But you came back.'

'I couldn't survive without the Italian sun.' He waved his hand to encompass the valley. 'I have been blessed. I live in one of the most beautiful parts of the world. Every day I wake up to this and am reminded that each blade of grass, every tiny insect, every living thing is God's gift to the human race.'

Father Michael was right. It was beautiful. From where they were Amelia could see right across the valley to rolling hills, punctuated with the odd villa, farmhouse and copse of trees. The only sound was the rumble of a tractor in the distance. There was an undeniable sense of peace, a sense that whatever was going wrong with people's lives, here, at least for a while, they could find succour.

It would however take more for Amelia to find relief. She doubted that whatever had been broken inside her could ever be fixed.

'Is He not responsible for all its pain too?' she asked, unable to hide the bitterness in her voice.

He stopped and looked at her with his gentle brown eyes.

'You are suffering?'

'You could say that.'

'If you're waiting for me to say something like all will be revealed in due course – that God works in mysterious ways – you'll wait a long time. I don't know why some people suffer; I don't know what God's plan is. All I do know is that He has one, and I am just His means to bring people to Him so that somehow they will receive His comfort in this life.'

He didn't wait for Amelia to reply but carried on walking. 'Let me show you the rest. I think you'll get a better idea of what I mean then.'

Even more unusual than how he'd arranged the interior of the church was what he'd done in the remainder of the grounds. Apart from the main church, he had created numerous other sanctuaries: mini private chapels for one, bigger spaces with beanbags for small groups to meet and pray together. In all sorts of nooks and crannies he'd positioned benches, seats and tables, hewn from the natural rock or wood, each beside its own distinct sculpture ingeniously fashioned out of pieces of garden implements.

'I've never been to a church like yours. It's amazing.'

'I made as many different places as I could for people to sit and just let God into their heart.' He shrugged. 'Even if He doesn't come to them, I want them to feel a little of His peace.'

It *was* truly wonderful what this man had done. Amelia visualised him, bare chested, his muscles flexing as he lifted and dug, his brow furrowing as he created his unusual and astounding sculptures. Heat rushed to her cheeks again. It wasn't appropriate to think of a half-naked priest. She had to bite down on her tongue to stop herself giggling, but the bubble of laughter in her chest was like the sun coming out from behind the clouds. For the first time in months, she glimpsed the person she had been. Of course, there was no escaping the present. Her mood dimmed. Yet it was a suggestion that someday, a day so far in the future she could not imagine it, she might not feel the way she now did; that one day she would feel the sun's rays on her cheeks, hear the sound of children's laughter, and be glad.

'Are you here on holiday?' Father Michael asked.

She explained that she was staying at the Castello di Porciano, and what Beatrice – with Amelia's help – was hoping to achieve.

'I have met the contessa several times,' Father Michael said. 'Her ancestors used to own the land here, and she still takes an interest. At one time her parents and her grandparents worshipped here.'

It was like a light bulb going on in Amelia's head.

'If I were looking for records of the family – you know, birth, deaths, marriages – might I find them here?'

'You might. Why do you ask?'

'I'd like to know the date of death of Flavia Corsi. Apparently she died in the area.'

'Do you have her date of birth?'

She thought back to the diaries. Flavia was sixteen in 1938 and her birthday was inscribed in the dedication. 'The second of May, 1922. I believe she was born in Rome.'

'It's not very much information to go on.'

'I know, but could you try?'

'Of course.' He smiled. 'Shall we have that tea now?' he asked. 'You can tell me what's troubling you if you like?' He looked at Amelia as if he could see right into her soul and wasn't frightened by what he saw.

For an instant, she was tempted. Very tempted. However the moment passed, and she refused the offer of tea and bade him goodbye.

TWENTY-TWO

By the end of the second week Amelia had finished cataloguing the books. With Benedetto's words ringing in her ears, she'd checked each one thoroughly for documents potentially slipped between pages. She wasn't surprised when none of them coughed up an ancient manuscript. The brochure was taking shape too. She'd spent a couple of afternoons in the cafe in Pratovecchio, using its Wi-Fi to do research. She'd started with the Warrior Abbess, drafting a few paragraphs about the Castello di Romena and its beautiful church and grounds and explaining its connection with Dante and the Guidis. She'd emailed Beatrice, bringing her up to speed with her progress, mentioning Flavia's diaries but shamefully neglecting to say she'd been reading them. She'd also neglected to mention the letter, rationalising to herself that, if she did, she'd have to go on to tell her about the hidden key and that she'd opened the box of treasures, et cetera. All that was better left to a face-to-face conversation. So far Beatrice hadn't replied – no doubt preoccupied with her grandchildren.

It was time to visit the castello at Poppi. Amelia wanted to see it, check a few facts about the battle between the Guelphs and the Ghibellines and how it resulted in Dante's banishment from Florence. There was so much else she could include in the museum brochure – the monastery at La Verna, for example, where it was believed St Francis of Assisi got his stigmata; but that would be moving into travel-guide territory, when the contessa wanted the brochure to be centred on the more immediate vicinity and its history.

Amelia hadn't seen Kelly all week. The American had made no secret of the fact she'd like to be included in any trips. Amelia felt a twinge of guilt that she hadn't invited her to Romena, so she decided to ask Kelly if she fancied coming to Poppi. Amelia showered quickly and chose a cotton dress from the small selection of clothes she'd brought with her.

Kelly was delighted to be invited and eventually, after Amelia had had to cool her heels while Kelly fed the cats and changed into something 'more decent to be seen in', they set off.

When they reached the village of Poppi, Kelly told Amelia she had visited the castle several times already and would rather spend time looking at the shops, most of which appeared geared towards tourists. Very happy to explore the castello on her own, Amelia assured her she didn't mind at all, and they parted, agreeing to meet in the main piazza in a couple of hours.

The Castello di Poppi was much larger and far grander than the Castello di Porciano. It sat on top of the hill, towering over the village like a guardian dragon. Amelia paid the entrance fee and stepped into a large inner courtyard with a wide stone staircase and an internal balcony, still covered in part by its original decorated wooden ceiling. It was easy to imagine the ladies of the castle strolling along the balconies, arms linked as they chatted; or, in times of war, the men in their suits of armour clanging up the stairs, vital and full of themselves. Or, more likely, scared to death but unable to show it!

Next to the entrance, Amelia's attention was drawn to a statue of Guidi di Battifolle at the stairhead. Apparently he still haunted the castle. She thought of her knight back at Porciano and smiled. Maybe it was his ghostly presence she had felt.

Only a few miles from the Castello di Poppi, the first and last great battle of medieval times between the Guelphs and the Florentines had taken place. Had the women watched from the ramparts as the battle raged below, or did they cower in their rooms, terrified in case they witnessed their loved ones being hacked to pieces? Did they wonder at the pointlessness of it all? At some men's greed and insatiable thirst for blood? The waste of lives? No doubt the poor field soldiers were forced to fight for their dukes. Amelia imagined most of the men looked back up at the castle and wished themselves safe within its protective walls, anywhere but on that field.

There was nothing in the information displayed about the women. Not a single one was named. Yet these women were Guidis as much as the men, and were surely entitled to have their stories told too.

She strolled through the rest of the castle, taking in the ballroom and the upstairs apartments. In the chapel on the first floor there was a painting of St John the Baptist. It was more than a little gruesome: the body minus its head slumped in one corner, the decapitated head on a platter.

She climbed to the top of the bell tower, pleased that she could manage it without becoming short of breath – her morning runs were clearly paying off. The view from the top was astonishing. She could see across the whole of the Casentino valley all the way to her castello, as she'd come to think of it.

On her way out, Amelia took a quick look around the library. As Beatrice had said, it had to contain hundreds of priceless books and documents. Several were displayed in glass cabinets, the light subdued to protect them – making them difficult, if not impossible, to read.

Before leaving, she went into the little castle shop. Visitors, mainly Italian, were elbowing each other in their haste to buy the usual touristy stuff: guidebooks on the area, posters depicting Dante's image of the *Inferno*, plastic helmets and swords. She bought a postcard for Dad and a tea towel with a picture of the Castello di Poppi on it to post to her mother.

As she paid, she noticed, in an area of the shop that didn't appear to be used except for storage, half-a-dozen long shelves holding what had to be hundreds of dusty lever-arch files. On each spine a number was scribbled in pen.

'What are those?' Amelia asked, pointing.

The shop assistant flicked a glance behind her. 'Those what?'

'Those files.'

She shrugged. 'Papers. Documents. I don't know exactly. Every now and again someone comes and takes a file away. Not just anyone, of course. Someone with the right authority.'

Were those the unarchived documents Benedetto had told Amelia about? Languishing like old files in a council office. Surely not. Who knew what could be hidden in their depths? Perhaps the rumoured Dante papers? Amelia would give anything to get her hands on them. She reminded herself that looking for documents that may or may not exist wasn't why she was in Italy.

Outside, making her way down the narrow medieval streets towards the square where she and Kelly had arranged to meet, her attention was caught by a little girl, her blonde hair making her stand out from the crowds. Amelia's heart juddered. She was around four, the same age as Fiona. Amelia wanted to turn away, but she couldn't take her eyes off her. She was with a couple – her parents, Amelia assumed. The family were queuing in front of a gelati truck.

The father handed the little girl a towering ice cream and they started to walk away. Amelia couldn't stop herself from following. The parents were deep in conversation, and the child began to lag behind. She squatted to examine something of interest on the ground, probably nothing more exciting than an insect, but as she did her ice cream tipped and, almost in slow motion, fell to the ground.

It was as if someone had punched Amelia in the solar plexus. She wrapped her arms round her stomach. She hadn't always been as good a mother as she should have been.

One morning, after a busy week alternating between looking

after Fiona and working on a project that was way behind its deadline, she'd realised there was practically nothing in the fridge or pantry to eat. Cameron had been away the whole week fishing, and she'd planned to give the house a good tidy up, make something special for dinner and even light a few candles. Needless to say, she hadn't bought the ingredients for dinner, nor the candles, and the house looked like it had been caught up in a mini tornado.

Fiona had been in a fractious mood all morning, probably because she'd not had much attention over the last few days. It had been pouring with rain most of the week, so she couldn't go out to play. She was acting up, demanding cereal for breakfast then changing her mind and insisting on pancakes instead. Amelia was halfway through cooking the pancakes when Fiona appeared, wearing a dress over her shorts and with her shoes on the wrong feet. While she tried to persuade her that shorts *and* a dress weren't necessary, the pancakes had burnt and there had been no milk left to make more. A trip to the shops had become essential, but as Cameron had taken the car they'd have to walk.

Eventually Amelia managed to get Fiona's shoes on the correct feet, gave up on the shorts/dress combo, dumped the pancakes in the bin, and hauled a grumpy, tearful child out for the long walk to the local shops. Their progress was painfully slow. In the end Amelia picked Fiona up and carried her squirming child for the final half mile or so. On the way back, Fiona begged to be allowed to play in the park.

Amelia could remember feeling so frazzled; it was almost lunchtime, and the countless jobs she still had to do ran through her head. So she'd bribed Fiona. If Mummy bought ice creams (she ignored the guilty realisation that so far Fiona's entire consumption for the day had been a packet of crisps) they could eat them on the way home.

It was enough. Soon, ice creams in hand, they were heading back.

Then Fiona dropped hers. It landed with a splat, hitting the tarmac and immediately melting into a puddle. It crossed Amelia's mind to scoop it up and plonk it back into Fiona's cone, and she might have done had she not spotted a mother with two little boys, the kind of woman whose hair looked as if she'd just come out of the hairdresser's and whose children looked as if they'd been dressed for a photo shoot, walking towards them.

Fiona was beside herself at the loss of her ice cream and refused point-blank to take Amelia's. Amelia should have returned to the shop and bought a replacement, but that would have taken time she didn't think she had. Instead, she grabbed Fiona's hand and marched her heartbroken daughter home.

Why did she do that? It would only have taken a few minutes to return to the shop and buy a replacement. What would it have mattered if the house hadn't been tidy? Who cared about special dinners? It was those hours with her daughter which mattered, and she'd never have them over again.

The little Italian girl was still squatting over her dropped ice cream. Her parents hadn't noticed. They'd stopped to talk to a friend and were deep in conversation, smiling and gesticulating.

Amelia hurried over to the gelato stall and bought the largest ice cream available. Not knowing what flavour the girl had chosen, she asked for three different ones – vanilla, butterscotch and strawberry. She shoved a twenty euro note at the girl behind the counter, telling her to keep the change, and whirled round.

The child's crying had finally attracted the attention of her parents. The mother was squatting down next to her, saying something.

Amelia stopped in front of them and held out the cone, explaining that she'd seen what happened. Even while doing this, she could see how nuts her behaviour must look.

Then, unable to resist, she shoved the ice cream at the mother who, surprised, took it. Amelia reached across to the child and pulled her into her arms.

For a few wonderful seconds she rewound time and was

holding Fiona again. Her warm body tight against her, her beautiful face pressed into her shoulder, her small legs twined around Amelia's waist.

'I'm so sorry. I'm so sorry,' she whispered over and over. 'Mummy is sorry. Bad Mummy.'

At first the surprised child relaxed in her arms, then she wriggled and pushed Amelia away. Her mother, initially too stunned to move, was galvanised. She dropped the ice cream, scooped up her daughter and stared at Amelia with astonishment and fear.

Without the child in her arms, Amelia was bereft. She sank to her knees right there on the road, hunched over, and began to sob into her cupped hands.

She felt a touch on her shoulder. 'Are you all right?'

She looked up. The woman had passed her daughter to the father and was crouching next to Amelia. People had stopped to stare.

Amelia scrambled to her feet. 'I'm sorry,' she spluttered. 'I don't know what came over me.' She had just made the biggest idiot of herself.

'Hey, honey. What's going on?' Kelly's distinctive drawl broke through the babble of Italian.

The couple and their daughter moved away, and an old lady and a young man tried to explain. Amelia heard *crazy* (him) and *sad* (her) and *kidnapper* (him again). Kelly couldn't understand a word. She shook her head and taking Amelia by the elbow ushered her away.

'What in heaven's name happened there? Hang on – wait until we're in the car.'

Even if Amelia wanted to, she couldn't answer her. She was crying too hard.

Kelly opened the passenger-side door for Amelia. 'For once I think it's safer if I drive,' she said grimly, before settling herself in the driver's seat. She rummaged around in her supersized bag and brought out a wad of tissues which she handed to Amelia. 'Go on, get it all out, then have a good blow.'

She waited until Amelia's noisy, snot-filled sobs had subsided before she spoke again. 'You're not divorced, are you?'

Amelia shook her head. 'There was an accident...'

'When?'

'Almost eleven months ago.'

'You can talk to me,' Kelly said. 'I'm a listener.'

Amelia was quiet for a long time. Every moment of that day was carved into her soul. She closed her eyes, and she was back there. As if it had happened yesterday.

Cove, Scottish Borders

As the smell of coffee rose from the kitchen, Amelia stretched her hands above her head on the still-tangled sheets and smiled. Sunday. The best day of the week. She propped herself on her elbows and looked out of her bedroom window. For once the weather forecast hadn't been wrong. The sun was shining, the sea a calm deep blue. A perfect day for the picnic she'd planned for later.

Wrapping herself in her robe, she went downstairs. She found her husband in the kitchen pouring water from the kettle into mugs, humming under his breath. Amelia had never known a happier man. He turned to her and smiled, his nutmeg eyes crinkling at the corners.

'I was about to bring your coffee up. I thought I'd let you grab the chance of a long lie-in. God knows you get few enough opportunities.'

He was right. She didn't. Their daughter, Fiona, rarely slept beyond six and Amelia wasn't a morning person. Unlike Cameron, for whom it was the favourite part of the day – which, given he was a fisherman, was fortunate. Fiona was at the table, her little legs swinging in time to a song on the radio, the tip of her tongue just visible in the corner of her mouth. She was too engrossed in whatever she was drawing to acknowledge her mother. Amelia dropped a kiss on top of her head.

'Fi is going to be my helper today,' Cameron said, handing Amelia her coffee. 'We've got some chores to do in Leith, but after that we are going to the zoo.' He lowered his voice. 'Let you catch up on your work.'

Amelia had a project due in on Monday and wanted to go over it one last time. Make sure it was perfect.

Fiona lifted the page she had been drawing on and showed it to Amelia. Luckily, there were enough clues to what the blob was supposed to be for her to hazard a guess.

'A panda!'

'A panda mummy!' Fiona acknowledged. 'Daddy said we can go and see her once we have finished our chores. She is going to have a baby soon.'

Amelia raised an eyebrow at Cameron and smirked, wondering how he would address the inevitable question when it came up.

When Fiona ran upstairs to get dressed, Cameron took Amelia's coffee mug from her, placed it on the kitchen table and circled his hands round her waist, pulling her against him. Dark haired like a pirate, solid and reassuring, Amelia loved him as much as she did the day they married six years ago. More, if that were possible.

He pushed the edges of her dressing gown apart with palms roughened by the pulling of sea rope, landing kisses on her throat, her collar bone, between her breasts and inching down towards her navel. As always when he touched her, her body thrummed with desire.

She placed her palms on his chest and stepped back. 'Fiona,' she whispered. 'She could come back downstairs any minute.'

Cameron gave her a final kiss and closed her robe with a smile of regret.

'Later,' Amelia promised.

After they'd left, Amelia tidied away their breakfast things then settled down at the kitchen table to work. When they'd decided to live together, they'd moved into her home and rented out his. She loved this house, with its outlook directly onto the sea and its secret path to Cove harbour.

For the rest of the morning and most of the afternoon, Amelia worked steadily, only stopping briefly for a sandwich. The sun had been blazing all day, and she knew Fiona would be looking forward to spending an hour or two playing on the sands down at the harbour. Satisfied the book was in good shape, Amelia emailed it to the publisher, packed a cool bag with small cartons of orange juice, some fairy cakes she'd bought the day before and ham-and-cheese sandwiches. In another bag she slung a couple of old towels, a bucket and spade, and plastic armbands.

Five o'clock came and went, but there was still no sign of Cameron and Fiona. Amelia reminded herself that the roads into Cove were narrow and windy and used by farm vehicles. Getting stuck behind one could double the travelling time. Nevertheless, she felt a prickle of unease.

She called Cameron's mobile. It immediately went to voicemail. That wasn't unusual either. Reception in this part of Scotland was notoriously unreliable. Amelia visualised them stuck behind a tractor, Cameron's long fingers tapping impatiently on the steering wheel, Fiona chatting away from her car seat in the rear.

She kept trying to get hold of Cameron on his mobile. As before, it went to voicemail asking her to leave a message.

She switched on the radio and tuned it to the local station. If there were roadworks causing delays, it would be mentioned on one of the traffic bulletins. Taylor Swift and Ed Sheeran were singing 'Everything Has Changed'. When the song finished, the radio presenter came back on. There was some sort of quiz. A man on the other end of the phone had to answer questions based on music of the sixties. If he got six or more right, then he might be in with a chance to win a DAB radio. Then Amelia remembered it was Sunday. Did they even have traffic updates at the weekend? She didn't think so. But if there had been an accident – please God no – surely that would be reported?

As time crawled on and Cameron didn't return her call, the sick sensation in Amelia's stomach grew, and her messages became increasingly angry and frantic. It took all her self-control not to fling the phone at the wall. Why wasn't he answering?

It was almost eight when the doorbell rang. Amelia's heart stopped. Through the frosted glass she could see two people. She couldn't be sure whether they were male or female, but deep in her gut she knew they were bringing news she didn't want to hear.

She wouldn't answer the door. If she didn't they'd go away.

She thought of the day the planes flew into the twin towers. She'd been a child when it happened but had watched a documentary about it a few years ago. Although she knew what was going to happen, she kept hoping that this time it would be different, that somehow at the last minute the planes would swoop away and miss altogether.

Did the people inside know they had only a few seconds left to live? Or did they keep hoping right up until the last minute that it was a bad dream, or that something would happen and the plane wouldn't crash after all? That somehow everything would still be all right. That's how she felt now. She wanted to press the pause button, freeze her life; even better, rewind it.

The doorbell rang again, followed by loud knocks. Her heart lodged in her throat as she opened the door to two police officers with sombre faces: a woman in pale-blue shirt and black tailored trousers, and a man in uniform. Still Amelia clung to a gossamer thread of hope. They were here about a car break-in or had come to the wrong door; they were looking for Mr and Mrs McInnes or, more likely, the Williamses, whose teenage son was always getting in trouble. Amelia would smile and point them in the opposite direction. Or perhaps they'd come to tell Amelia her father was dying, and she needed to hurry to the hospital. She was ashamed of how much she preferred this to be true. She held onto the doorframe, knowing that without its support her legs would give way.

'Mrs Simpson?' the woman in plainclothes asked.

Although Amelia wanted to slam the door in her face, she nodded.

'I'm Sergeant Halliday, and this is my colleague, Constable Bain.' She held out a card, and Amelia took it from her. The photograph blurred. It could belong to anyone. But she had no doubt the woman officer was who she said she was.

'May we come in?' Sergeant Halliday asked so very gently. A seagull squalled.

She didn't need to say any more. Amelia knew her plane was going to crash.

Amelia faltered to a halt. Reliving that day had brought back every excruciating detail. She became aware Kelly's arm was around her shoulders. She swallowed. 'My gut was right. There had been an accident. My daughter died at the scene.'

'You poor, poor honey,' Kelly said.

The sympathy in her voice made Amelia bawl all over again.

'Look, don't take this the wrong way but perhaps you should see a doctor?'

'No!' Amelia practically shouted. 'There is nothing anyone can do to stop the pain!' She drew a shuddering breath and softened her voice. 'I'm sorry. I'll be okay. I'm just overtired. I haven't been sleeping well.'

Kelly looked doubtful. 'If you won't see a doctor, maybe you should speak to someone. These things are better out than in, as they say.' She paused. 'I'm going to Elba for a few days. Why don't you come with me? Get a break.'

Amelia blew her nose and managed a weak smile. 'Really. I'll be fine. I can't. Anyway, a good night's sleep is all I need.'

Kelly touched Amelia's face with the palm of her hand. 'If you're sure. But I still don't like you being on your own in that big empty castle. Isn't there anyone who could come and stay with you? I don't think Beatrice would mind.'

'You won't tell her, will you?' Amelia twisted in her seat and held Kelly's gaze. 'It was a blip. That's all. It was seeing that little girl... I'll be okay, I promise.' When Kelly continued to look unconvinced, she blurted, 'Remember that letter we found in Flavia's coat?'

Kelly stopped in the act of turning the ignition and turned to face Amelia.

'Sure.'

'I haven't found a document or anything – so don't get your hopes up – but I have found some diaries that belonged to Flavia.' She didn't mention that it was the day she arrived.

'Flavia left diaries?' Kelly's gaze sharpened. 'Awesome. What do they say?'

'I haven't finished reading them. They're mostly about her life in Florence and in the Casentino. They're fascinating. There are doodles in the margins too – she was an excellent artist.'

'Hey, back up a little. When did you find them?'

'I stumbled across them when I was looking through her clothes. They were in a false compartment at the bottom of one of her trunks.' Amelia ran her tongue over dry lips.

'What does Bee have to say? Is she excited?'

Amelia was acutely aware of the heat stealing up her neck. She was beginning to regret saying anything. 'She knows I found them but not that I've been reading them.'

'Shit, girl.'

'Please don't say anything to anyone about them until I've spoken to her.'

Kelly drew the tip of her finger across her mouth, indicating her lips were sealed. It was clear she was almost as excited as Amelia had been to know what was in the diaries.

'Do you think they're the journals Flavia's aunt referred to in that letter? Does she say anywhere what it was she discovered?'

'Not in what I've read so far. But I think there must have been other entries at one time.' Amelia explained about the ripped-out pages. 'I'm guessing she destroyed those as her aunt asked.'

'Oh well.' Kelly's face fell. She started the car. 'Perhaps something will turn up yet.'

'There's something else.' As the car moved off Amelia explained about the box, the key in the collar of Flavia's coat, finding the ring and the sketch and the christening gown. 'I wonder why she locked those away?' she murmured almost to herself.

Kelly flashed Amelia another of her penetrating looks. 'Makes *me* wonder what else she might have hidden – and where.'

TWENTY-THREE

That night Amelia dreamt she was standing in a field filled with poppies. She didn't know why she was there or how she got there. Suddenly a mist came down, so thick she couldn't see her hand when she raised it to her face.

Then, through the mist, Fiona appeared. She was holding her hands out to Amelia and smiling. Joy flared. Her daughter wasn't dead after all. As suddenly as the mist had fallen, it cleared, revealing a deep gash in the earth. Her daughter didn't see it. Fiona, her face lit up with love and relief, cried *Mummy!* and started to run towards Amelia. A few more steps and she'd fall into the chasm.

Amelia tried to shout for her to stop. To stay where she was. But it was as if her lips had been stitched closed. She needed to move, to intercept her child before she fell; but although she mustered every ounce of strength, it was as if her feet were encased in cement.

The drumming of horse's hooves came from the left, and a woman wearing body armour, her cloak flying behind her, thundered towards them. In the second before Fiona reached the hole the woman grabbed her and lifted her onto the horse, holding her in front of her. The horsewoman – the Abbess – stared at Amelia for a long moment, before shaking her head despairingly and galloping away.

Appearing before them was the castle of Porciano with its walls still intact. The Abbess's horse gathered itself and with one almighty effort leapt over the castle walls.

Amelia screamed her daughter's name, wrenching herself from sleep. She lay, her heart hammering in her throat, awash with loss and regret.

Eventually her pulse slowed. She tried the light switch, but nothing happened. Had there been another storm? She fumbled for her phone before remembering she'd left it on the dining room table. Instead, she reached for the box of matches next to her bed. It took several attempts before her shaking fingers could successfully strike a match. She lit the candle. Its weak flame sent shadows scuttling across her room.

She sank back on her pillow, and gave in to tears, her face turned towards the candle. A breeze flowed over her, making the candle gutter. It took a while to realise that the breeze wasn't coming through the window – it was closed – but from beneath the doorframe. The night was perfectly still without a breath of wind. So what had caused the power to fail? Floorboards creaked somewhere in the castello.

Her heart started its painful beating again. Somebody or something was inside the building. She tossed the covers aside and pulled the sweatshirt she'd left on the chair over her head, her fingertips brushing against her pendant as she did. She wasn't about to hide in her room and wait for whoever it was to leave. She flipped the light switch again, but the electricity remained stubbornly off. It appeared the supply was more fickle than Beatrice had let on.

Where to start looking for an intruder? Up or down? She'd left her phone on the dining room table, so that's where she'd start.

Holding the candle in front of her, its flickering flame doing little to illuminate the depths of the castello's corners, Amelia made her tentative way downstairs. She tried each light switch she passed, leaving them in the on position in case the electricity came back on. She found her phone, switched on its torch, and blew out the candle.

Just then she heard a woman's voice say *Take care* in Italian, as clearly as if the person were standing right beside her. She strained to see beyond the pool of light from her torch, but a quick search of the room confirmed there was no one there. If she'd thought she couldn't be more frightened, she was mistaken – she was terrified. She took deep, calming breaths, muttering to herself that only people in the throes of psychosis thought ghosts went around giving advice. The words were her own – from inside her head. Nonetheless, she remained rooted to the spot for what felt like hours but could only have been minutes. The voice didn't come again.

Gathering her courage and forcing herself on, she took the stairs down to Dante's Hall and crossed the room, using the torch on her phone to inspect the darkest corners. There was nowhere to hide here. She inspected the high gallery. As far as she could see it was empty.

She was being ridiculous. No one could get up there, and if they did there was nowhere to hide. She made her way slowly down the next flights of stairs until she reached the lowest floor, all the while fighting the childish impulse to run back upstairs and leap into bed, pulling the covers over her head.

She peered into the thick darkness beyond the circle of light from her phone. The beam didn't reach far enough to illuminate the door on the far side, but it was enough for her to make out a shape in the shadows. Her heart stopped – then started its painful beating again. It was only Piero the Gouty! All the same she shot across the room and lifted his visor to check there was no one hiding inside. Thank goodness there was no one to see her. They'd think she'd lost it.

'Hello?' she said out loud, her voice pathetically feeble. She sucked in a gulp of air. 'Is anyone there?' she said, more firmly. There was no reply. The boxes and trunks were where she'd left them. She threaded her way through them and towards the door. It was closed, the key still on the hook beside it. She reached out to the heavy handle and turned. Nothing happened. She tugged the door, but it didn't budge. It was still locked. Of course it was. Since Benedetto had let himself in the other day she'd made sure it was. Her legs felt as if they were about to give way, and she leaned against the door, a leaden sick feeling in her stomach.

At that moment the lights blazed on, and she blinked, momentarily blinded. As her eyes adjusted, she scanned the room. Everything was as she'd left it. Except... Her heart gave a sickening kick. The trunk containing Flavia's clothes was slightly ajar, a piece of cloth trapped by the lid. She knew she hadn't left it like that.

But there was no other possible explanation. She must have left it open. She hadn't been thinking straight when she arrived home yesterday after her shameful display in Poppi. Unless – an electric chill ran across her skin – someone besides herself and Beatrice had a key. Beatrice had said not. Didn't mean it wasn't possible. But who would let themselves in in the middle of the night only to creep away again? Who would be looking in Flavia's trunk, and what were they looking for? It came to her in a flash.

Kelly. It had to be. Searching for the diaries, so she could find clues about the document she seemed certain was hidden here. In which case, she must have a key.

No. That was just paranoid. Kelly was lovely. Someone Beatrice trusted.

All the same, Amelia dragged the heavy wooden chair she used when working down here across to the door and wedged under it the door handle.

She hadn't checked the rooms above her bedroom. Oh God, what if the intruder was still on the floors above her or on the ramparts, waiting for her to go back to bed? Spotting the rusty spade still propped against the wall, she carried it up the interminable flights of stairs making sure every light was on, shining her pathetic excuse for a torch into the shadows of the mezzanine, and the corridor running along from her bedroom, before taking the final flights of steps to the roof. She paused at the door and checked it was locked. Perhaps she should wait for the morning to discover if anyone was lurking there. But some of the bedrooms in her corridor allowed access to the lower ramparts. He – or she – could easily slip back in that way. There were so many places to hide in the tower.

She needed to look. Summoning her courage, she eased the door open and stepped onto the ramparts and into falling rain. A quick search persuaded her there was no one there either. Taking advantage of her bird-like view, she scanned the grounds. She couldn't see anyone hiding in the shadows, no figure looking up, no car lights, no suggestion of anyone making a speedy exit from the grounds. There was, however, a light in Kelly's cottage. She was awake too. If she had been in the castello, she was back in her own house now. Amelia's head pounded. She wanted nothing more than to lie down and go back to sleep.

Having convinced herself she had simply allowed her nightmare to frighten her, she returned to her room.

The moment she stepped inside, a chill swept across her skin. There, spread out on her pillow, was the christening gown belonging to Flavia.

For a long time Amelia sat on the bed shivering, her knees pulled up to her chin. How did the gown come to be in her room? Who put it there? It had to have been Kelly. She was the only one who knew about Amelia finding the christening gown, the only one who knew about Fiona, the only one who might guess how finding the gown on her pillow would affect Amelia. But why would she want to upset her? It was one thing suspecting Kelly of trying to find a document, quite another to think she wanted to torment Amelia. And how could she have done it? She would have had to have gotten in somehow, started her hunt and stayed hidden in the rooms or any of the nooks and crannies on the floors above Amelia's or on the ramparts, creeping into Amelia's room while she was searching the lower floors. And how did she get out again? She didn't pass Amelia on the stairs and couldn't have used the lift, as it made too much of a racket and Amelia would have heard it. She must have left the same way – hiding in the shadows as Amelia went up and down – playing a game of cat and mouse with her.

One thing was certain; someone had waited until she was asleep before letting themselves into the castello, hiding from Amelia with ease until they'd done whatever they needed to do. Amelia inhaled sharply, remembering the figure she'd seen looking up at her the night of the storm. She hadn't actually recognised the figure as Kelly, but it had to have been her.

She yanked on a pair of jeans and a T-shirt and ran downstairs and let herself out of the castello. At some point it had started to rain heavily, and within seconds she was drenched.

She banged on Kelly's door.

Almost immediately, as if she'd been expecting Amelia, Kelly opened it. She was wearing a dressing gown, her hair hidden under a turban fashioned from a towel. Either she'd just had a shower – or just changed out of soaking wet clothes. Her eyes widened when she saw Amelia.

'Amelia! What is it? What's wrong?'

Amelia hesitated. Kelly's surprise appeared genuine.

'For God's sake. Come in out of the rain.' She took Amelia's arm and tugged her inside, closing the door behind her. 'Sit down. I'll get you a towel.'

Amelia was shaking, adrenaline still coursing through her body. Her eyes started itching, and she sneezed.

Kelly disappeared, returning a few moments later with a towel and a glass of brandy which she thrust into Amelia's hands. Her hands were trembling so badly the brandy splashed on her jeans.

'Now. Take your time. Tell me what's happened.'

Amelia saw nothing but concern in her eyes. However, somebody had been in the castello.

'Were you in the castello tonight?' she demanded.

Kelly frowned. 'Tonight? Why on earth...?'

'Someone was inside.'

'Are you sure?'

'It was you, wasn't it?'

'Me?' Kelly seemed genuinely bewildered.

'Yes. You.' Amelia's teeth were chattering so hard she was barely coherent.

Kelly shook her head. 'Amelia,' she said softly, 'take a breath. Go back to the beginning. What makes you think I've been in the castello?'

'You're wet.'

Kelly gave a bark of laughter. 'I've just come out of the shower. Don't you remember I told you I was going to Elba for a few days?'

So she had. Amelia had forgotten.

'And as usual I've left everything to the last minute.' Kelly pointed behind her. 'I haven't even finished packing yet.' Her suitcase was open on the floor, half empty. 'Lucky for me I've never been an early-to-bed sort of gal.'

That all might be true. Didn't mean she wasn't in the castello, however.

'I saw you. Outside. The other night. The one of the storm. You looked right at me.'

'Amelia, whoever, *whatever* you saw, it wasn't me.'

'But someone *was* in my room,' Amelia insisted doggedly, only too conscious of how she looked, how crazy she sounded.

'Why on earth would I break into the castello?'

'To look for Flavia's diaries, and whatever you think she hid.'

'Did you see me?'

'Well, no,' Amelia admitted, wiping her running nose. 'But you could have slipped by me without my noticing.' There were several places she could have hidden as Amelia hurried past.

'And how would I have got in?' Kelly sighed. 'It wasn't me – I promise.'

Kelly must have seen Amelia bury the key in the plant pot when she went for her runs. It was the obvious answer. How stupid of her to leave it behind.

'You could have taken the key and made a copy.'

Kelly laughed again. 'I'm not a spy in a Cold War drama. I

don't go around with putty in the palm of my hand just in case I get the opportunity to take an imprint of a key, so I can let myself in in the middle of the night to look for mysterious documents that probably don't even exist. Come on, Amelia. You know that's just crazy.'

The word *crazy* hung in the air. One of Kelly's cats stretched lazily and jumped to the floor.

'You've not been yourself, sweetie,' Kelly continued. 'You admitted that. It's understandable. The castello can't be good for someone who feels as low as you do. Perhaps you should reconsider whether Porciano is the right place for you at this time? Maybe you should go home to the UK?'

'I know what I saw,' Amelia mumbled like a sullen teenager. But she was beginning to have doubts. Why would Kelly want to torment her? She decided not to mention the christening gown left on her pillow. She'd made a big enough idiot of herself.

'You can't have seen me because I wasn't there.' Unable to keep the exasperation from her voice, Kelly opened the door. 'Seriously, Amelia, I think you should go home. Back to Scotland. You're not well. Not well at all.'

Amelia trudged back to the castello. Kelly sounded so adamant it hadn't been her in the castello. But if not her, who?

Was it *Flavia* who left the christening gown? Flavia who'd whispered a warning to her?

Thinking that truly was nuts. An overactive imagination was one thing – believing in ghosts that could physically move things around was quite another. The only possible explanation, which didn't exactly reassure her, was that she'd sleepwalked. That, during the night, possibly while she was dreaming of Fiona, she got up, went downstairs and took the christening robe to bed in a subconscious longing to hold her own child again.

There was one other explanation. One she was even more terrified to consider. What if she was beginning to lose touch with reality? What if she ended up back in the psych ward? She must not, under any circumstances, let herself sink back into depression. Her obsession with Flavia had to stop. She must get out more, exercise harder, leave Flavia's diaries alone. She had to stay well.

Her resolve lasted less than twenty-four hours.

The next afternoon, after she'd finished working for the day, she returned to Flavia's diaries. In the cold light of day, with the sun streaming through the windows, she'd convinced herself that last night's fears were childish and ridiculous. She couldn't have closed the lid of the trunk properly. The creaks and groans she'd heard weren't made by an intruder – or ghostly spirits. They were the natural settling of a very old building. And if she *had* sleepwalked, it didn't mean she was losing it. Lots of people sleepwalk without being mad.

Neither was she being haunted by Flavia's ghost. Her fascination with her was perfectly understandable. Like Amelia, something had driven Flavia to the point of despair. It was only human to want to know what that had been.

Amelia settled herself on the pile of cushions in the window seat with the diary she was currently reading.

Perhaps when she found out what had happened to Flavia she'd stop obsessing about her.

TWENTY-FOUR

FLAVIA

Florence, Autumn 1940

Flavia sat on a *panco* in the Piazza della Repubblica, watching little boys in Fascist uniform collect scraps of metal for the war. Italy was at war. While she knew it had been coming, it still felt impossible.

To most Italians' embarrassment, Il Duce waited until the British had been chased back across the Channel, and Germany was at France's door, before declaring war on Britain and France.

Everything changed then.

Just over twenty-four hours after Italy declared war, Turin was bombed, followed by Genoa, Milan, Naples and Taranto, with hundreds of civilians killed. Shelters had been built across the cities, and air-raid sirens went off frequently day and night. At first every time one had sounded Flavia had joined her fellow Florentines taking shelter, but there weren't enough shelters for everyone and, as it became clear that the British weren't particularly interested in bombing Florence, she stopped going, relying on her boarded-up windows and the night-time blackout to keep her safe.

Within days, Italy's ill-equipped and underprepared army was fighting in North Africa and suffering terrible casualties.

Although she was horrified by what was happening, Flavia wanted to do her bit. So, the day after Italy entered the war, Flavia started working full time as a Red Cross volunteer at the hospital. Soon injured Italian soldiers were pouring into hospitals across Italy. Her job was to make the wounded soldiers as comfortable as possible and write letters to their families to let them know they were recovering or had died. Regardless of the way the soldier had met his end, Flavia always wrote that they hadn't suffered.

Sophia, her nurse training completed, was working on a hospital ship. Following Italy's declaration of war, Jews had been moved to camps across Italy, and – although it was a disgrace that Italian Jews had to leave their homes at all – apparently conditions in these camps were comfortable. Nevertheless, Natalia had refused to leave Florence, choosing to move instead to an apartment that belonged to a sympathetic friend.

Flavia had only exchanged a couple of letters with Margherita since she visited her in the spring – mail was sporadic and heavily censored. Niccolo had been called up and was fighting somewhere – nobody could say where. Her friend rarely mentioned Luca, only saying that he continued to work the farm. Thank God he hadn't joined up. In her bleakest moments Flavia thought back to the summer of Margherita's wedding, reliving the happy evenings in the kitchen, the time in the car they'd almost ended up in each other's arms, every conversation they'd had.

Flavia sighed and returned her attention to the little boys collecting metal and drawing amused looks from passers-by. One stalwart was blowing a trumpet, as if calling his regiment to arms. Flavia stood and tucked her drawing pad under her arm, but before she could take a step, a military vehicle drew to a halt right in front of her. Lambini! She hadn't encountered him since the dinner at Villa Bencista before the war, but she'd seen him a few times still wearing the uniform of the Blackshirts, sitting in the back of his chauffeur-driven vehicle as if he were Mussolini himself. He'd grown a moustache very similar to Hitler's and twirled a baton between his fingers.

He jumped out of the car and, stopping in front of her, clicked his heels together – who even did that? – and sketched a bow. He looked ridiculous. As ridiculous as the goose-stepping the Italian army had adopted in a thinly veiled tribute to Hitler. She noticed he'd been promoted to major. If it were possible, he was even more pleased with himself.

'How are you, Flavia?' he asked, infuriating her by his use of her first name.

'I am as well as can be expected in these difficult times.' She tried to make it clear by her tone that she had no wish to talk to him. She'd heard reports of him over the months, and none of what she'd heard had made him any more appealing – his strong arm and thuggish behaviour had only increased after Italy had entered the war.

'I believe you are caring for our brave soldiers.'

How did he know how she spent her time? She knew he still visited the Villa Bencista occasionally, but Julia never mentioned he'd asked about Flavia.

'How are the conte and contessa?' he continued when she didn't reply. 'I understand they ran away to Switzerland as soon as it looked as if war was imminent.'

Odious, odious man. 'They are visiting friends there.'

'True Italians would stay in their country when she is suffering.'

'And you,' she queried, looking him directly in the eye. 'Not fighting, like the rest of our poor young men?'

He flushed with anger. 'There is more than enough to do here. Upholding the rule of law becomes even more important when there is a war on.' He had the temerity to stroke his moustache as he spoke. Was his behaviour copied straight from an American movie? Flavia smothered a giggle. If he only knew how silly he looked.

He cleared his throat. 'Let's not argue. I think we got off on the wrong foot before. Let me take you to dinner. There is a place not too far from here that saves the best Italian steak for me and my guests.' It was the first time he'd appeared uncertain.

Food was rationed, especially meat, butter, flour and cereal, although a black market flourished in the cities for those who could afford it; therefore it had been a long time since she'd had a decent meal out, let alone a *bistecca alla fiorentina*. However, she'd rather starve than eat a single morsel in his presence.

'No, thank you. I prefer to dine with friends.' She made no effort to keep the contempt from her voice. The idiot seemed completely taken aback by her refusal. When was he going to accept she wanted nothing to do with him?

'I suggest you may wish to reconsider. You may still think yourself above me, but war makes equals of us all. This war may go on for some time, and I have the contacts and the wherewithal to make life a great deal easier for you and those you care about. Especially your little Jewish friend.'

So he did know who Natalia was. Dear God.

'I have Il Duce's ear, you know,' he continued, having regained his equilibrium. 'I can even make sure the hospital where you work gets more than its allocated share of supplies.'

He was selling food and other scarce commodities on the black market! She might have known! She was so disgusted she could hardly speak.

'I wouldn't have dinner with you if you were the last man on earth. You are despicable. No gentleman would behave as you do. Do you think, for one moment, that people will forget what you've done when the war is over? Everyone will have to account for their actions then.'

His expression darkened. He grabbed her upper arm and yanked her towards him, close enough for her to smell his stale breath.

'We are talking about here and now,' he hissed. 'Who knows if any of us will survive the next few months, let alone the war?'

She tried to break away, but he was too strong.

The children had stopped what they were doing and were

looking their way with frank curiosity, as were several other pedestrians.

Lambini released her so suddenly she stumbled, only just managing to keep on her feet. 'I know where you live,' he said. 'And your Jewish friend. Don't forget that.'

TWENTY-FIVE

Spring 1943

The months and years that followed were the darkest of times. War was twice as bloody as Flavia could ever have imagined. As Italy suffered defeat after defeat, more wounded flooded into hospitals across Italy. What she came face to face with every day filled her with anger and despair. Young men, who should still be working in fields, factories and offices, were brought in with the most terrible injuries. Nearly all of them cried for their mamas. The nurses did their best to ease their pain with morphia, while Flavia and the other volunteers tried to comfort their minds with a soft word and a gentle touch. It was never enough. No sooner did one leave, or die, than another was admitted. Not all were strangers. Flavia had met many of the officers socially in the past; one or two had even taken her to dinner. She did what she could to get through the long hours, often going straight to bed after another heartbreaking shift. She'd let her twenty-first birthday pass without notice. What was there to celebrate anyway?

Whenever she had a break in her day, she went to the church to pray. She was never alone; there were many, many women praying there too. They knelt, rosaries in hands, eyes lifted to the

Madonna – begging her to make the war stop. They hated what it was doing to Italy and their fathers, sons, husbands and brothers. She continued to sketch, but her recent drawings were dark and gave her little pleasure. Aunt Lucrezia wrote when she could – as did Sophia.

Flavia was given one day off every fortnight, and, although she was often so exhausted she could barely stand, she tried to make the most of it, attending dances and dinner parties whenever she was coaxed by friends. The British and American men had returned to their own countries, but many Italian men she knew came when they could, dressed in their officer uniforms. However, her heart wasn't in it. Julia teased her, telling her she would die an old maid if she didn't fall in love soon with one of the men who asked her out. Sometimes she was lonely and wished she had someone to share her life with; but no one made her skin tingle and her heart beat faster the way Luca had.

She'd thought a great deal about him in the intervening years since that near-kiss, wondering if he'd fallen in love, if he was happy, if he ever thought of her. She knew it was pointless letting her mind go in that direction. If he'd felt the slightest smidgen of affection for her, he would have found a way to see her. All the same, her heart paid no attention to her head, and far too often he found his way into her dreams.

Whenever she had a night and day off together, Flavia visited Julia in Fiesole. Julia had a new project. Across Italy, mothers terrified of their homes being bombed sent their children to anywhere they thought they might be safer, and Julia was happy to take them in. Some poor mites were orphans, their whole families having died in a raid.

Julia had a separate outbuilding which she used to house the children, who ranged in ages from two to fifteen, and had employed a nurse and teacher to look after them. According to her, some arrived at the villa without clothes or the most basic necessities, and many hadn't eaten for days.

It broke Flavia's heart to see them – especially the orphaned children who did not have families they could return to when the war was over. It brought back the horrible days after her own parents had been killed, the sense of dislocation and bewilderment she'd felt. Despite the care of her godparents, it had taken years for her world to feel safe and secure again.

She spent as much time with the children as she could, unable to resist picking up the toddlers who lifted their arms for attention, cuddling them in turns in her lap, helping to put them to bed, reading to the older children as they sat in a semicircle at her feet.

She wondered again whether she would one day have children of her own.

TWENTY-SIX

The war against Britain and France had been going on for more than three years when, astonishingly, that summer Il Duce was arrested, and a new government established. Over the course of the war people had become increasingly disillusioned with Mussolini and the war he'd dragged them into. The Italian army had suffered defeat after defeat – often against far inferior numbers – and Italian soldiers had been killed in their thousands. Most Italians believed the war was lost anyway given that the Allies had taken Sicily.

A few weeks after Mussolini's arrest, the new government surrendered to the Allied forces, and the following month Italy declared war on Germany. Confused Italian soldiers tore off their uniforms and fled back to their farms and villages. Then, in another head-spinning turn of events, the Germans took Rome, liberated Mussolini from prison and established him as governor of the Italian Social Republic – a Nazi puppet state – in the north, while they took control of central Italy, including Florence. As the German occupiers started hunting down the Jews, aided by the Italian SS, Jews who had remained in Italy went into hiding or scrambled to escape. Some managed to cross the border into

Switzerland, but many were arrested and deported to labour camps. The camps had been fairly benign under Mussolini, but that changed with the occupation. To everyone's horror the Nazis had built a crematorium at San Sabba and were sending Jews there in their thousands.

The German troops were a menacing and unpredictable presence in the city. When horrifying rumours of the cold-blooded murders of dozens of Italian Jews near Lake Maggiore reached Florence, Flavia begged Natalia to go into hiding. But her friend refused point-blank to be evicted from her home city – especially when she had a frail mother to care for. She did however agree to move to an address where her name hadn't been registered.

Following the occupation, Flavia's services were no longer required at the hospital, which would now only admit German soldiers and was now largely staffed by German nurses. Florence no longer felt like her city, no longer felt like home. As so often they did these days, her thoughts turned to the Casentino valley and her friend there.

Flavia hadn't seen Margherita since Italy had changed sides, and longed to see the friend from whom she hadn't heard since the birth of her second child, a daughter.

However, there was nothing stopping her from going to see her now. There was still a half tank of petrol in her godfather's car. And who knew when the German army might confiscate it for their own use? All of a sudden, she was seized with an urgent need to be with her friend.

She packed an overnight bag, chucked it in the car and drove towards the mountains. The road into Florence was choked with convoys of German vehicles, and she was stopped three times and asked for her identity papers. She had to hide her impatience to be on her way, forcing herself to be charming to men who would shoot her or her fellow countrymen and women without compunction. But finally she reached Vallucciole. She parked her car on the road and hurried down the path winding its way through the village.

The open area that served the village as a piazza seemed much as it had the last time Flavia was here, apart from the conspicuous absence of young men. Women peeled vegetables, or prepared fruits to jar. Children played tag, the older villagers watching them with benevolent amusement. Something inside Flavia stilled. She hadn't known how anxious she'd been until she found herself among the people she considered friends, almost family.

She craned her neck, eager to catch sight of her friend. A group of women gathered in front of Margherita's house chose that moment to disperse in different directions, and it was then Flavia saw her.

She was shocked to her core. The once-vital Margherita looked like a wraith.

Not just because her clothes, like those of most Italians, had been mended over and over until they were barely more than rags, or that she'd lost a great deal of weight – everyone had – but because her once-sparkling eyes were dull and lifeless; her radiant smile was absent as she caught sight of Flavia. She moved like an old woman as she rose from her chair and came towards Flavia.

Flavia opened her arms, and Margherita stepped into them. They held each other close.

'Tell me what's wrong,' Flavia murmured into her friend's ear. 'What's happened?'

Her friend pulled away and gave Flavia a tremulous smile. 'You know me so well.'

A person didn't have to know Margherita to realise that she was a woman whose world had fallen apart.

'It's Niccolo,' Margherita whispered. 'He's been killed.' Her voice cracked and tears streamed down her face.

'Oh, no! When?' Flavia thought of the last time she'd seen Niccolo, his face shining with happiness and love. She ached for her friend. Only a few years ago she'd been so happy, the sun seemed to shine out of her.

'In one of the last battles against the British' – her mouth twisted – 'when we were on the side of the Germans – now our occupiers. Nothing makes sense anymore!'

But that had been months ago. Flavia wished she'd known. Nothing would have stopped her coming to comfort her friend then.

'Why couldn't he have deserted? Come back to me and his family?' Margherita continued bitterly.

'I am so very sorry,' Flavia said, enveloping her friend in her arms again, hugging her now-slight frame close and wishing she could take some of the pain from her.

A small body inserted himself between them. 'Mama!' complained a little dark-haired boy. 'Who is this lady?'

The two friends broke apart. 'This is your godmother, cara,' Margherita said, brushing her tears away with the hem of her apron. 'Your and Flavia's godmother. Mama's good friend. Like your sister, she is also called Flavia. She has promised to always look out for you and your sister.'

Shame burned Flavia's cheeks. She hadn't done too good a job of that so far. What kind of godmother saw her godchildren so rarely they had no idea who she was?

Margherita's daughter hung back, regarding Flavia shyly through dark lashes.

'I'm very pleased to see you again, Lazzero, and very happy to meet you, Flavia.'

Margherita gestured for little Flavia to come to her. She tucked her children into her side and gave Flavia a tremulous smile.

'I can't be too sad when I have Lazzero and little Flavia to care for. I only wish that they had a chance to get to know their father properly.' She gave a shaky smile. 'Of course, I am not alone. Many here have lost someone – a brother, a father, a husband. We are rapidly becoming a village of women, children and old men.'

'Luca?' Flavia asked, her heart in her throat. There was no sign of him in the village.

'Helping Paolo bring in the chestnuts from the huts,' Margherita said with a vague wave in the direction of the forest.

Relief flooded through Flavia. 'He's all right then? He didn't join up?'

'He's fine,' she looked away, 'and he didn't join the army. He's needed at the farm, particularly when Roberto isn't around to help.'

Despite her best efforts, she'd never been able to stop thinking about Luca. Over the years she'd been out to dinner with a couple of men, met more at friends' homes, but none of them matched up to Luca. She wanted to like them – they were decent, straightforward, charming men who were keen to be seen as more than friends. To her shame she found herself constantly contrasting them with Luca, finding them boring and insipid in comparison. When she'd been volunteering with the Red Cross and was faced with death and dying on a daily basis, she'd thought of going to him, presenting herself to him like a cake on a platter, like some of the women she knew did. Why not, when neither party knew if they would live to see another day? What if she died never knowing what it was like to be loved?

Of course, she hadn't gone. She could never humiliate herself like that. Over time her regret turned to relief, and she gave up her fantasies. She might still have her virginity, but she also had her pride.

She turned her attention to little Flavia, who was delightful; she had her mother's (previously) sunny disposition and mischievous eyes. So too was Lazzero. Even at three and a half, Flavia's godson looked a lot like Luca. They had the same deep brown eyes.

'You must be relieved Luca didn't join up.' Flavia couldn't resist asking after they'd shared all their news and were in the kitchen. Flavia was holding little Flavia on her lap while Margherita made pasta from ground chestnuts – the substitute for real flour, which had become impossible to find outside the black market.

Margherita's gaze dropped as she became absorbed in rolling out the dough. That was strange: her friend could make pasta with her eyes closed. Every time she asked about Luca over the last few years her friend had been evasive, rarely giving her a straight answer. Flavia couldn't shake the feeling Margherita was withholding something from her. Perhaps Luca had fallen in love, and Margherita suspected hearing that would break Flavia's heart.

'Of course I'm glad he's not in the army,' Margherita replied after a long pause. She sighed. 'He's worried about us. He wants me to take the children and go back to the farm and live there.'

'Why don't you?'

At last, Margherita met Flavia's eyes. 'Because my home is here. With Niccolo's family. With his nonna. I can't leave her to manage on her own. And his brother, Paolo, needs me too.' Niccolo's mother had died unexpectedly near the beginning of the war. 'We look out for each other, help one another. Nonna is getting frailer every day and quite forgetful too.'

'And Luca? Is he married?' This time it was Flavia who wouldn't meet Margherita's eyes. She bounced little Flavia on her lap and the girl squealed with delight.

When Flavia glanced up, Margherita gave her the mischievous smile she hadn't seen for so long and had so badly missed. It was only fleeting, but for that moment Flavia allowed herself to believe that one day, when this was over, everything would get back to normal and they'd be able to live the lives they were meant to live.

'Why are you always so interested in Luca?' Margherita asked. She narrowed her eyes. 'Have you fallen for him?'

When Flavia blushed, Margherita clapped her hands together and laughed. 'You have, haven't you? No, he isn't married, doesn't even have a serious girlfriend. Maybe he's been waiting for you? I would be so pleased if he loved you back. That way we could be real sisters!' Her expression grew serious. 'What would your godparents say though? I don't imagine they would be happy.'

Flavia's gave her friend a wry smile. 'It's not something either you or I have to worry about. Luca and I have barely spoken, nor seen each other in almost three years, and who knows when I will see him again.'

Perhaps when she saw Luca again, she'd realise she'd built an image of him in her head that bore no resemblance to the actual man.

Little Flavia grabbed a lock of her godmother's hair and yanked, making Flavia wince. 'Luca will likely be married and have a brood of children by the time we next see each other,' she said, untangling her hair from the little girl's fist.

Or, Flavia thought, suppressing a shiver, *they could all be dead*. She shook her head to dispel the thought. She mustn't think like that.

'How is your mama?' Flavia asked. 'And Rosina? She must be a help to you with the children?'

Margherita's sigh seemed to come from the bottom of her boots. 'Mama and Rosina have gone to stay with Mama's sister in Poppi.'

Flavia frowned. 'Why?' Why would Signora Rossi take her youngest child and leave their farm to move to a village further away from her daughter and grandchildren? Even if it was still in the valley.

Margherita's eyes filled. A tear trembled on her lash before sliding down her cheek. 'I am ashamed to tell you. We are all so ashamed. Not only did Roberto become a Blackshirt, but he has turned against his own people and stayed on the side of the Germans. Mama can't bear to look at him, but now he's based in Florence she can't stop him visiting the farm whenever he chooses. That's why she and Rosina have gone to stay with Mama's sister. They will come back when the war is over.'

Flavia's heart ached for her friend. Not every Italian had discarded their uniforms and headed for the hills when Germany occupied Italy. Some, despicably, like Lambini – and clearly Roberto too – stayed on the side of the Nazis, proud to stand with them instead of against them.

She stood and hugged her friend again, little Flavia squished between them. 'Oh, Margherita, I am so sorry. What does Luca say about this?'

'What can he say? He is disgusted of course, wants nothing to do with Roberto, would kill him, I suspect, if he got the chance.' She pulled away from Flavia's embrace and clamped a hand over her mouth. 'Please forget I said all of that. Let us speak of happier matters.'

Suddenly Flavia knew what she needed to do. Her friend was grieving, struggling to look after her children as well as Niccolo's nonna. Without the help and support of her mother or sister, it had to be hard. War had stopped renovations on the castello, but enough had been completed to make it possible for Flavia to live there. After all, there was little reason to stay in Florence, and in Porciano she'd be able to help Margherita with the children – children she'd made a sacred promise to look out for.

When she told Margherita what she planned and her friend's face lit up, she knew she'd made the right decision. But first Flavia had to return to Florence to pack what she needed.

The next afternoon, Flavia was walking beside the Duomo, having shopped for some thread and buttons to take with her to Porciano, when she saw a large army truck surrounded by soldiers. She recognised Maggiore Lambini straight away. He was standing next to a German officer, and the pair of them were studying a clipboard. She stepped into a doorway so she could watch unobserved.

Every so often, Lambini would shout out a name and address, and a soldier would charge off. At the same time other soldiers would return, marching Florentines at gunpoint and directing them into the truck. Recognising a particular family, Flavia's blood froze as she realised what was happening. The Germans were rounding up Jews to deport to their dreaded camps. It was said some Jews didn't even make it to there but were executed for 'trying to escape' or 'not obeying orders'. Italians suspected of helping them suffered the same fate. There were posters everywhere warning people what would happen to anyone aiding Jews.

A thought struck her. Natalia and her mother! What if their names were on the list? What if the Germans had discovered where they were hiding? Lambini had said he knew. Her friend was in terrible danger.

It was too late to do anything about the people who had already been arrested and were even now being herded into the back of the truck at the point of a bayonet, but hopefully not too late to save Natalia and her mother, Martina. Careful to ensure Vincenzo didn't see her, Flavia hurried off towards the Via del Moro where Natalia and Martina currently lived, walking as fast as she could without attracting attention.

She was breathing deeply by the time she arrived. To her relief, Natalia answered the door almost immediately.

'Thank God,' Flavia said as Natalia glanced up the street before ushering her into their apartment. 'Is your mother here?'

'She is. She's not been feeling well so hasn't been going out and about much.' Noticing Flavia's agitation, she gave Flavia a startled look. 'Why? What is it?'

'The Germans are rounding up Jews living in the area. Pack a bag. Your mother too. You both need to leave.'

'Leave Florence? To go where?'

Where indeed? Not to Flavia's apartment. Vincenzo knew that she was friends with Natalia and knew where Flavia lived. She wouldn't put it past him to look for Natalia there.

There was only one place. Porciano. Not the castello – the women would stick out there like sore thumbs. But they could live in one of the houses in the village. There, the women would blend in, and no one would give them away. Flavia would bet her life on it.

'To the Casentino. You'll be safe there. Safer there than here anyway.'

Natalia quickly grasped the urgency of the situation. 'I'll pack a couple of suitcases.'

'Just essentials for now. I'll fetch my car. Meet me outside the Palace Medici Riccardi in twenty minutes.'

Flavia sped back to her apartment. Luckily she'd packed the night before, so it was only a matter of throwing her bags into the boot of her car. However, by the time she picked up Natalia and Martina from the agreed meeting place, it was getting late. They'd never be able to make it all the way to Porciano before curfew. They were horribly conspicuous as it was.

There was only one thing for it. Stay the night at Julia's villa in Fiesole and make plans from there.

TWENTY-SEVEN

AMELIA

Amelia closed the diary. The October 1943 entry was the last one. The last few pages had been torn out, most likely destroyed as Flavia's aunt had asked. What secrets had they contained? Had the women made it to Porciano? One way or another, Amelia's journey with Flavia had come to an end. Maybe just as well. She wasn't sure she could bear to know what had happened to them.

Over the next few days, between working, she went for long walks and continued to go for runs. The brochure was taking shape, all of the books were catalogued, and the mock-ups of the display boards were pretty much drafted. During the day, when not working, she drifted around the castello, sitting in different window seats to alternate the view – or climbed up to the ramparts to sit in the sun.

Which was not to say that she didn't think of Fiona and Cameron. She did. Memories punched through in unexpected moments, making her gasp with pain. Yet, recently, there had been the odd occasion when remembering made her smile rather than double up in agony.

But any progress she thought she might have made with her mental health was blown out of the water when one night she woke to find herself at the desk in the sitting room. She had no idea how she'd got there. She had a pen in her hand, which was resting on a piece of paper scrawled with ink. Blood thumped in her temples. She couldn't quite make out what she'd been writing. One scrawl looked like it could be *Flavia*, another *Keep looking*, but she could be completely wrong. They could just as easily be doodles. She told herself that's what they were. But there was one thing she couldn't explain away, and it frightened her to death. She was wearing Flavia's deep-blue evening dress.

It was happening again.

They found her in the lay-by where the accident happened, curled up among the bunches of decaying flowers still wrapped in their cellophane. She'd no recollection of getting into her car, or of the drive, all she remembered was a desperate need to find Fiona. Although her father had been watching her like a hawk since she'd moved back in with him after he'd intercepted her at the cliff, he couldn't watch her twenty-four seven. Apparently, she'd waited until he went to the pharmacy to pick up her prescription, before leaving the house.

She'd vague memories of flashlights and urgent voices. Of muffled static on walkie-talkies. Of being lifted and placed somewhere – a car? An ambulance? Of blue lights casting an eerie glow over the face of the girl who was fussing over her. She remembered a sense of outrage that she wasn't being left alone, a prick in her arm, then nothing – until she came to in the acute psychiatric ward.

She forced her attention back to the present. She was becoming unwell again, losing the ability to distinguish between what was real and what wasn't. Her obsession with Flavia had to stop.

Yet she knew it wouldn't. Her need to find out what had happened to her was too overwhelming. It was as if something was driving her on. Or *someone*. Flavia's spirit? Perhaps people didn't totally disappear when they died. Amelia had read somewhere that there was only a finite number of atoms in the world, and that they were constantly forming and re-forming and that, when someone died, all the atoms that made up their body got released into the universe and eventually joined up with other atoms to form something else. Before the accident she would have dismissed such a notion out of hand, but now it was a comforting thought. Fiona could still be part of the world.

As for Flavia, maybe her atoms were part of the castello. Perhaps when Amelia found out what really happened to her, her spirit would leave Amelia alone.

She sucked in a deep, shuddering breath. Fuck it. What did she have to lose? If it was all in her imagination, then she was okay living in a fantasy world. The real one wasn't too brilliant.

'Okay, Flavia – you're on,' she murmured into the half-light. 'If I find whatever you want me to find – discover whatever it is you want me to discover – will you leave me in peace then?' Amelia had definitely crossed a line – speaking to a dead woman as if she were in the room with her and could reply. But here was the thing: she no longer cared if she was crazy. It no longer mattered if she wasn't sure what was real and what wasn't.

But what did Flavia want Amelia to look for? And where to look? The possibilities were endless. Flavia had lived in many places: her aunt and uncle's home in Florence, the castello of course, and possibly other places Amelia didn't even know about. There were the cottages belonging to the castello, including the one Flavia and her godparents had stayed at in '38, not to mention the many churches and buildings nearby. She might even have given whatever it was to someone for safe keeping. *If it even existed.* She shook the thought away. For the time being she was going to assume it did.

Having changed out of the dress and armed with a pot of coffee, she started her search in the basement and worked her way up. Although she'd looked through all the boxes and trunks, she checked them again. Next, she searched Piero the Gouty, including his armoured feet and metal gloves. Nada. She scanned the walls, top to bottom, looking for a loose piece of stone or a fissure. She didn't see any. Furthermore, the walls were so high she couldn't imagine Flavia scaling the rough stonework to prise a stone loose. A skilled rock climber would find it difficult even with ropes.

The next floor up – the one that was to house the museum – had the only wooden floors in the castello. The thick planks, scuffed and darkened with age, and more than a foot wide, would have been laid, or more accurately re-laid, at the time of the renovations. Which suggested a space between them and the supporting trusses.

Getting down on her hands and knees, Amelia began her search nearest the door, running her fingers over each and every plank, probing for a loose board or a cut in the wood. It took her a good hour to check the whole floor. Another dead end.

The clock was creeping towards midday, and she dimly registered that she was getting hungry, but she didn't want to stop. She climbed to the next floor and emerged into Dante's Hall. This floor had edge-to-edge flagstones and therefore no way to hide anything under them. She looked up at the wooden balcony at least three metres off the floor. It was a simple structure of wood with cross planks underneath for strength. If she couldn't get up there, neither could Flavia.

There was only one more place to search in this room: the enormous inglenook fireplace. However, would Flavia have risked hiding anything where a fire might have been lit? Unlikely. All the same, she ran her hands across all the bricks in the front and sides of the fireplace before stepping into it and doing the same on the inside. She could only reach so far. Even on her tiptoes Amelia was a good bit shorter than Flavia. How high could she have reached? Supposing she hid whatever it was herself and didn't ask someone to do it for her? It was dawning on Amelia how hopeless the task she'd set herself was.

Grabbing a hard-backed chair, she put it in the fireplace and stood on it. Stretching as far as she could, she still couldn't feel any loose stones or gaps. Another blank. She wanted to scream with frustration. She should be working instead of spending all this time looking for something she might never find; that might even have been removed some time ago and hidden somewhere else.

She also knew she wouldn't – couldn't – stop until she'd searched the castello from top to bottom.

By late afternoon Amelia had searched everywhere she could think of – even, shamefully, Beatrice's bedroom. She was acutely aware this was exactly how people who had lost touch with reality behaved, but she no longer cared. The need to search for the thing Flavia wanted her to find was too strong.

But she'd failed. She'd let Flavia down. Then, suddenly, the thought came into her head as if placed there. *Go back to the diaries. The clue is there.*

She took them over to the window seat in the sitting room and read them all over again – up until the last entry and the ripped-out pages. *What bloody clue?* She resisted the impulse to hurl the note-books across the room. She needed more information if she had a chance of succeeding. And the only person she could think who might be able to help her was Rosina. She had to know something that would help.

Although Alessandra had made it clear she didn't want her to talk to Nonna about the past, she hadn't said Amelia wasn't welcome to come again.

Ten minutes later, Amelia was at the farmhouse. She knocked on the door, gently at first, and then – when there was no reply – more firmly.

A few moments later the door was opened by Rosina. Her face was crumpled, her eyes bleary as if she'd just woken from a long nap. 'I wondered when you'd be back,' she said, to Amelia's surprise. 'Come on in.'

Amelia followed her into the kitchen. Happily, it appeared she'd caught Rosina on her own.

Rosina lifted a glass from a shelf above the sink and poured Amelia a tumbler of lemonade. All this took several agonising minutes. Amelia would much rather not be there when Alessandra returned.

The old lady placed the glass on the kitchen table on top of a knitted coaster and nodded at Amelia to sit. Amelia looked around. This was where Luca had lived – where Flavia spent many happy hours. The room really hadn't changed. It was easy to visualise Margherita and her mother at the table making pasta, the women gathered to sew Margherita's trousseau; to see Luca in his chair as he whittled at wood.

A photograph on a shelf caught her attention. It was almost hidden by the usual gallery of family photographs – probably why she hadn't noticed it the last time she'd been here.

Wearing the simple cambric shirt of the time, and breeches, he was leaning against a car, smiling directly at the camera, looking at the person who was taking the photograph as if he or she filled his universe – as if just looking at whoever it was made him happier than he had ever been before. Suddenly it was her taking the photograph. The sun was shining, and Luca and Amelia were clinging together in some kind of embrace – one that stretched across the distance that separated them. She could smell his body scent, a blend of fresh sweat and hay, and it wasn't unpleasant. Desire pooled in her belly. She knew that not long ago she'd been lying naked with this man and wanted to do so again. Which was weird, more than weird. The only man she'd slept with, let alone desired, had been Cameron. Her chest tightened. Could it really be possible she would never hold him again?

'Are you all right?' Rosina's soft voice came from behind her.

'Yes. Thank you,' Amelia said quickly, aware she was trembling. She gave herself a mental shake as she searched for a way to ask her what she wanted to know. She needed to tread carefully so as not to upset the elderly lady. She pointed to the photograph on the bureau. 'Is that Luca – your brother?'

'Yes, my beautiful brother.' Rosina shuffled over to the shelf, lifted the photo and studied it with a sad smile.

'He was very handsome,' Amelia said.

'The girls all thought so.' The old lady's mouth curved in a smile. 'But in the end he only had eyes for Flavia.'

An electric shock ran along Amelia's skin. She held her breath, waiting for Rosina to continue.

The old woman placed the photo back on the shelf and sat back down. Behind the wrinkled face, Amelia saw the determined young girl she once was.

'Why are you here?' Rosina asked. Her eyes weren't unkind, only curious.

There was little point in beating around the bush. 'I've been reading about Flavia and have become very interested in her. I know she was very friendly with your family, particularly Margherita. Is Margherita still alive? Or Luca? Is there anything you can tell me about them? Did they ever get together? I mean...' *Oh God, that wasn't the most tactful way to phrase it.*

Rosina's eyes blazed. 'Young people! You think other people's memories – the past – is yours to look into, to rifle around in like a bag of pegs? A source of entertainment? Sometimes it is better to leave the past behind. Not think of it. I wish I could choose what to remember, what to forget. I wish I could forget what my brother did.' Tears poured down her cheeks, and she rocked silently back and forth in her chair. Aghast at being the cause of this reaction, but unable to stop now, Amelia patted her hand, murmuring meaningless, soothing words, until her sobs subsided.

'What did Luca do, Rosina?'

'Not Luca! He was a hero. Roberto!' Rosina cried.

At that moment Amelia heard the crunch of gravel outside.

'What did Roberto do?' she asked Rosina urgently. 'I know he was a Blackshirt. Is that what you mean?'

'My fault. My fault.'

'What's your fault?'

Before she could reply, Alessandra and an older man, Toto at their heels, entered the room. Taking in the scene and Rosina's distress, the man's face darkened with anger.

'Nonna!' Alessandra cried, hurrying over to her grandmother.

The man Amelia assumed to be Alessandra's father-in-law and Rosina's son glared at Amelia and placed a hand under her elbow, forcing her to her feet. 'Forgive me, Signora, but you must go. Alessandra explained to you that my mother is not to be worried and harassed.' As he talked, he propelled Amelia to the door. He might be in his sixties, but he had the strength and speed of a man half his years. Probably from working the land since he was a child.

'I must insist that you do not come here again,' he said, only loosening his grip when they were outside and well away from the house.

'I'm so sorry. I didn't mean to upset your mother.'

He released her arm with a grunt and flushed, as if regretting his reaction. 'I don't mean to be rude. It is not the Italian way not to make visitors welcome, but my mother is elderly and hasn't been well. She must be kept peaceful at all times.'

'I do understand. And I apologise again. Would you say goodbye to her and Alessandra for me?'

He nodded brusquely and went back inside. Amelia was mortified and ashamed she'd upset the old lady – particularly when she hadn't even got the suggestion of a hiding place from her. But it hadn't been an entirely wasted trip. Now she knew it wasn't Luca's name or even Flavia's that had upset her. It was Roberto's. He must have done something unforgivable. But what? And why did Rosina think it was her fault?

TWENTY-EIGHT

Amelia let herself into the castello and headed upstairs, still musing over Rosina's words.

Rosina must have known her brother was a Blackshirt, but she couldn't possibly think his decision to become one had anything to do with her. What then? Every family had their secrets, things they regretted. Amelia knew *that* only too well. So what was Rosina's?

Deep in thought, it was some time before Amelia became aware that she could hear a cat crying. It was coming from inside the castello. From one of the lower floors.

So that's why her eyes had started itching. How the hell had it got in?

Mystified, she went downstairs to Dante's Hall, but there was nothing to be seen. Yet she could definitely hear a cat in distress. This time the sound appeared to be coming from somewhere above her head. The penny dropped, and she looked up at the suspended balcony. Sure enough, one of Kelly's cats had managed to find its way up there and was stuck. He must have slipped through the door when she'd left for the farm.

She did everything she could to coax him down, making encouraging cat noises and holding out a chunk of tuna from her previous night's supper. To no avail. The cat was not coming down on its own. It wasn't as if she could ask Kelly to help, she was still in Elba. Neither could she leave the terrified creature up there until Kelly returned.

How did he get there in the first place? She'd never seen a cat climb a vertical wall; they could go straight up trees, but that was only because they could cling to the bark with their claws. There was no such purchase obvious on the smooth stone. She peered closer at the wall. Jutting out, by only an inch or two, were a series of small rectangular stones that most likely supported the long-gone steps at one time. They were narrow, too narrow for a human foot, but just about the perfect size for a cat.

She knew now how the cat got there, but not how she was supposed to get him back down again.

The cat mewed plaintively. Perhaps if she left him he'd find his own way down? However, she couldn't bring herself to do that.

She recalled seeing a ladder in the basement, so she used the lift to carry it up. She placed it against the balcony, making sure it was steady before clambering up.

The cat padded towards her, purring, its tail straight up, and she stroked it for a while before sneezing explosively.

'Sorry, Puss,' she said. 'You can't stay here. And neither can I. We both need to get down.'

At that moment the cat jumped out of her arms and leapt down the projections on the wall, landing at the bottom and looking up at Amelia as if expecting to be applauded.

If she'd waited, he would have found his own way down eventually.

She knelt on the stone bench and looked out of the window and towards the village, thinking how odd it was to have a window seat no one could use. As she turned away from the window, a thought struck her. When Flavia lived here, renovations were still under way. In which case there must have been scaffolding on the inside of the building. Or, at the very least, ladders. If she could use one to get up here, so could Flavia. Where better to hide something than somewhere it was difficult to reach?

Amelia scanned the walls in front of her but saw nowhere obvious to hide anything. She knelt and peered underneath the stone seat. It was too dark to see anything under there. She took her phone from her pocket and used its torch to illuminate the space. With a surge of excitement, she noticed a place where the mortar was slightly different to that used elsewhere. It was carelessly done, amateurish, as if done in haste. No one would ever have noticed unless they were looking for it.

She scrabbled at the mortar with her fingers, clawing and scratching until her fingertips were bleeding, yet she'd made not the slightest bit of progress. She needed a tool of some description.

After fetching the sturdiest knife she could find, Amelia used it to chip away at the mortar.

It took forever, but eventually she'd loosened the piece of stone sufficiently to remove it. She edged it out and behind it, just as she'd hoped, was a space, inside which were papers rolled into a cylinder. Carefully, she lifted them out.

Needing both hands for the return journey, Amelia tucked the cylinder down the back of her jeans. At the bottom, she retrieved it from her waistband and pulled on her cotton gloves. Very carefully, she smoothed out the sheets of paper. Her hands were shaking so much she was terrified she'd tear the fragile sheets. Her breath caught. She was looking at the ripped-out pages of Flavia's diary, the first page starting mid-sentence – exactly where it left off with Flavia at Fiesole with Natalia and her mother.

Upstairs, she sank into an armchair and began to read.

TWENTY-NINE

FLAVIA

Fiesole, October 1943

'Flavia! Natalia! Signora Esposito!' Julia exclaimed. 'What are you doing here?' They'd made it with only moments to spare before curfew.

As she took in the sight of the three women on her doorstep, small suitcases in hand, Julia grasped the situation at once. Darting fearful glances over their shoulders, she ushered them in.

She wouldn't allow them to speak until she'd shown Martina where she could rest and served her friends tea and wine. She listened attentively as Flavia described what had happened and why it was imperative Natalia and her mother get out of Florence.

'I know it's dangerous for you for us to be here,' Flavia said, 'but it's too late to continue to Porciano.' She'd made sure Julia wasn't entertaining before approaching the house.

Julia shuddered. 'We should have known it would come to this – we've had enough warning. The Nazis are capable of anything. But to think Italians are helping them kill fellow countrymen. I could put a bullet in Vincenzo's head myself.' The remaining colour left her face. 'I wish I could offer you and your mother the use of Villa Bencista, Natalia, but Vincenzo could appear anytime. Happily, the bastard is being posted north – no doubt a reward for his loathsome collaboration with the Germans. He leaves any day now – and I expect he'll come to pay his respects. He likes to drop in unannounced.' Her mouth curled in distaste. 'You know, I think he actually believes Giuseppe and I are his friends.'

'We only stopped here because of the curfew. We need to get Natalia and Martina to Porciano as soon as possible,' Flavia said. 'They'll be safe there.'

'Of course you had to come, but you're right, you can't stay long. You should leave before light.'

But how to get Natalia and Martina from Fiesole to Porciano? The short drive from Florence was one thing; they weren't overly conspicuous among the other travellers. But given the constant stream of German soldiers heading south, the road from Fiesole to Porciano would be much more dangerous. Far more likely they'd be stopped and asked to produce the appropriate papers. Then the two women would be arrested and almost certainly Flavia with them.

'How can you be certain the people of Porciano won't betray us?' Natalia asked.

'Because I know them and trust them,' Flavia reassured her. 'I could take your mother first and if I see a roadblock hide her in the boot of the car. I could return later for you, Natalia?'

Giuseppe, Julia's husband, was away from home and therefore couldn't help.

'It's too risky,' Julia objected. 'What if you were stopped and they searched the car? They might well shoot you both there and then.'

Julia had a point.

'Then there is only one other option. We'll have to walk.'

'But it's miles on foot!' Natalia protested. 'Mama isn't strong enough for such a journey.'

'The refugees we helped at the centre managed longer routes,'

Flavia reminded her. 'We could take Julia's mule and travel through the night. I can lead Diablo with Martina on his back,' she added, the plan coming together in her head.

Natalia chewed on her lip. Flavia could only imagine how difficult this was for her. 'It's hard to keep a mule quiet,' she replied after a moment. 'But I agree, I don't know what else we can do.'

'It's decided then,' Flavia said. 'It's a chance we will have to take. Neither option is without risk.'

Natalia went to let her mother know the plan while Flavia and Julia pored over the map, identifying the best route for Flavia and her charges to take. Most of it would be through the forests and away from the road. There were a couple of bits where they would have to cross open country, but as long as they waited for cloud cover they might manage it. The route, as long as they made good progress, could be covered in one night, and if they were delayed along the way for whatever reason then they'd just have to find somewhere to sleep and hide out until it was safe to continue their journey.

'And if you are caught? What will you say?' Julia asked, her dark eyes anxious. 'Natalia and her mother don't have the correct papers. I don't know, Flavia. It seems too risky. You know what the Germans do to those who help Jews.'

'I don't have a choice. I have to do this,' she said and folded the map, having memorised the route. 'Look at it this way. If we were in the south, we'd be in danger of being bombed. War carries risk for us all. Why should I take less than my share?' Flavia took her friend's hand. 'You are doing your bit to help. How can I do less?'

And so, it was decided. They would go that night. They probably wouldn't get better conditions even if they could afford to wait.

Flavia tried not to think about the danger as they prepared for the journey. It was no use trying to pretend, even to herself, that she wasn't scared. She was terrified. But she didn't want the others to see. She placed her hands on the table and pressed down to try and stop them shaking.

The three of them were in Julia's dimly lit kitchen, each preoccupied with her own thoughts. They'd plotted the route in minute detail and talked everything through several times. Now there was nothing left to say.

Julia's lower lip was caught between her teeth. Natalia whistled softly and tunelessly, as she did whenever she was concentrating. When they did speak it was in whispers, although there was no one to overhear them. None of them were under any illusion what would happen if they were caught. Being out after curfew carried stiff enough penalties, but to be discovered aiding Jews... Flavia suppressed a spike of terror. The important thing was not to let the fear prevent her from seeing this thing through. She could choose; Natalia and her mother could not.

She wrapped a chunk of pecorino and a small loaf in brown paper and placed it in a canvas satchel, along with a sharp kitchen knife to slice the cheese.

Silently, Julia passed Flavia flasks of water and coffee to add to her bag and started to tidy the kitchen, returning the cheese to the larder and wiping down surfaces.

Julia added a torch – only to be used in emergencies – to the satchel. Earlier they'd discussed when to set off and had agreed on ten o'clock. Hopefully the German soldiers would be relaxing in their barracks.

Just before ten, satisfied they had prepared as best they could, the three women gathered in the front hall, shrugged into dark coats and pulled on woollen hats. They had dressed earlier in dark trousers, thick socks and layers of jumpers. If they had to sleep outside overnight they wouldn't freeze. Natalia was to leave the rest of her and Martina's belongings at the villa. Flavia would collect their suitcases when she returned for her car.

Flavia's stomach was in knots, her pulse drumming in her

throat. Her friends' eyes were wide, their faces pale in the light of the flickering oil lamps.

As she waited, Natalia's mother muttered prayers under her breath in a constant flow. Natalia crouched by her side and spoke to her in a low, reassuring voice. The older woman grabbed Flavia's hand and held it in both of hers, speaking rapidly in her own dialect. She had been born in the south, travelling to Florence to come and live with her daughter after Naples had been badly bombed by the Allies at the beginning of the war.

'Mama thanks and blesses you for what you are doing for us,' Natalia translated. 'She knows you are putting your own life in danger. She has prayed for us all.'

'Italians are risking their lives all the time,' Flavia said. She breathed deeply, lest her trembling voice betray her. 'We will be fine as long as we move as quickly and as quietly as we can.'

In the yard, they saddled Diablo the mule, tying the bag of provisions to his saddle.

This was it, Flavia thought as she pulled the knot tight, and Natalia helped Martina onto the beast's back. There was no going back now. She wouldn't dwell on being caught, or what the Germans might do to her or the other women. If she did, her courage might fail her.

Following a quick hug and a whispered *good luck* from Julia, they set off, eschewing the road for the woods. The moon was bright enough for them to make out the silhouettes of the trees, but there was enough cloud skating across it to offer them the protection of darkness when required. The path began in the forest, and at first their steps were tentative; they stopped and held their breath at the slightest sound. Once more Flavia had cause to thank Margherita. On their walks in the woods, Flavia had learned to distinguish the different sounds of the forest: the crunch of dry twigs underfoot, the rustle of brittle leaves through the trees, the varying calls of bullfrogs and toads, the haunting screech of an owl in flight, the grunt and crash of a wild boar snuffling for food. If Flavia hadn't been able to differentiate between the natural sounds of the forest and the noises humans made, she suspected they would have halted every few inches, petrified that a German unit was close by, and therefore made no headway. As they relaxed, they made better progress. The most dangerous time was when they had to cross an open field. They waited in the woods until the clouds covered the moon before, hearts in throats, hurrying across the field as quickly as possible.

They were halfway to Porciano when Flavia froze, her senses on high alert. Something was different. There it was again – a subtle shift in the air that she was certain hadn't been caused by the wind. She signalled Natalia to stop and held her breath as she listened for the sound to come again.

Suddenly a hand covered her mouth, and she was pulled against a hard body. She could see other shapes moving as Natalia and her mother were captured too. Flavia could make out enough of the shadowy figures to see they were holding rifles. She tried to scream, but the hand over her mouth prevented any sound escaping. She kicked her legs, but the man holding her was tall enough to lift her feet off the ground, and she realised she was flailing at air. She wished she'd thought to keep the kitchen knife in her pocket. What use was it tucked away in her bag?

She found a fleshy bit of palm and bit down hard. Her assailant cursed under his breath.

'Stop it,' he growled in her ear. 'Quiet, or you'll get us all killed.'

She recognised the voice immediately. Luca? What was he doing out here?

'If you promise not to scream, I'll let you go,' Luca continued.

When she nodded, he removed his hand. Before she could as much as gasp, he spun her round to face him.

'Flavia! What the hell are you doing out here?' he hissed.

'I could ask the same of you!' Flavia hissed back. Yet there was a sense of inevitability to the pair of them meeting here in the middle of the night in the depths of a forest.

'You and your friends have been making so much noise I'm

surprised there isn't a platoon of Germans surrounding you,' Luca continued, as if she hadn't spoken. 'As it is, they're only just up the road. Christ, you could easily have stumbled right into them. We were tracking them when we heard you.'

'We've been careful,' Flavia protested weakly. Learning they'd almost walked into the arms of a German unit made her already-shaky legs feel as if they were going to give way underneath her.

'We've been on your trail for the last half an hour.' Luca continued to glower at her. 'You've been stumbling through the woods as if you're on some bloody picnic.'

The moon slid from behind the clouds, and the figures took on shapes. There were at least ten of them, men and women, and yet Flavia hadn't heard a thing. They were dressed in dark shirts tucked into trousers, the men with caps, the women – some surely still in their teens – with their hair hidden under dark scarves.

'You're with the partisans!' It all fell into place. The shifty, evasive expression on Margherita's face when Flavia had asked about Luca, and her reticence to talk about him or mention him in her letters all made sense now.

'Not now, Flavia. We need to get away from here.' Luca kept his voice to just above a whisper. 'We can talk properly when I'm sure we've put enough distance between us and those German bastards. I'm going to let the mule loose. If they hear anything they'll assume the animal was to blame.'

He whistled quietly and his fellow brigands, taking Natalia and Martina with them, slipped into the darkness.

'Where are they taking my friends?' Flavia demanded.

'Don't worry, they'll be looked after.'

Flavia's head was still whirling. It appeared Luca was the leader of the group. He'd been so adamant he wouldn't fight it hadn't crossed her mind that he would join the partisans. But of course, it was exactly the thing he would do.

She had so many questions, but – as Luca had said – now was not the time for them.

He held her hand in a firm grip. 'Stay right behind me,' he ordered. 'Step where I step.'

Once they had crossed the fields and re-entered the woods, and were as far away from the roads as it was possible to be, he called for a rest. It was obviously for their benefit, as Luca and his fellow partisans showed no signs of fatigue.

'Tell me what you're doing out here,' he asked, pulling her down onto the roots of an ancient fig tree. 'Who are those women? Christ, Flavia, do you have any idea of the risk you're taking?' His expression was grim, his full lips pressed together in a flat line.

'They're friends – Jews. They had to get out of Florence. I'm taking them to Porciano. They'll be safe there.'

He stared at her in astonishment before his mouth curved in a smile. She was almost certain she saw approval in his eyes before his expression grew grim again. 'That's a job better left for people who know what they are doing. You could be shot if the German bastards found you.'

She shrugged. She knew it, had accepted it, and didn't need to be reminded of it. 'What about you? If you're with the partisans, you risk your life every day,' she parried.

'But I know what I'm doing. I don't take unnecessary risks.'

She didn't believe him. She'd always sensed Luca was a man who liked nothing better than to flirt with danger.

'How long have you been doing this?' she asked now.

His eyes creased at the corners, and he gave a rueful shake of his head. 'That's the first thing you want to know?' His expression turned serious again. 'From the beginning. As soon as Mussolini sided with the Germans.'

'Margherita knows, doesn't she?'

Luca nodded. 'I wish she didn't. We were careless when we started, stored our weapons in the village. It was reckless. We placed the whole village in danger.'

'Why didn't Margherita tell me? Did she think I'd betray you? Her brother!'

'Of course not. But she does know when to keep her mouth

shut. It's dangerous for anyone – any villager – to acknowledge they know one of us, let alone help us.'

'Hey, Liberte – is that your girl?' one asked. Flavia looked across at them. Natalia and her mother were drinking from the flasks of coffee, apparently unperturbed at being surrounded by the men and women who had accosted them.

Luca grabbed her hand. 'Come with me. Somewhere we can't be overheard by this lot.'

He led her deep into the forest and pulled her behind the trunk of a chestnut tree. Her pulse was still racing, but it was no longer from fear.

He brushed her hair from her eyes and placed his palms on either side of her face. He looked at her long and hard. She held his gaze. She couldn't breathe. He traced her lower lip with the pad of his thumb, making her body thrum. 'My brave, reckless love. You have no idea how often I have thought of you, watched you when you came to visit Margherita. It took all my willpower not to come to you.'

Her back was against the tree, Luca so close she could feel his breath on her skin.

Was he playing with her? In the middle of a forest with the enemy not too far away. The sheer craziness of the moment didn't escape her.

'Then why didn't you?' she challenged.

'I didn't want to put anyone in danger. The Nazis mustn't think the villagers of Vallucciole are helping us.'

He cupped her chin with his hands and tipped her face towards him. He smiled down at her. 'Did you miss me?'

Miss him? The nerve of him! If he'd wanted to see her that badly he would have found a way. He could have written, even come to Florence, but he hadn't, not once!

'Like a wild boar misses a boil on its backside!'

He laughed again. 'Still got an answer for everything.'

Bending his head, he pressed his lips on hers. Their first kiss was everything she'd ever dreamt it would be. Gentle at first, then deeper, as if he'd been waiting to kiss her forever. She wound her arms round his neck and pressed her body against the solid, muscled length of him. Certain she could feel his heart beating against hers, she could think of nothing except for the sensations shooting through her. When they eventually drew apart, she struggled to catch her breath. He gave her a regretful smile. 'Don't keep looking at me like that...' He kissed the tip of her nose. 'Otherwise, I'll never get you to safety before the sun rises.'

Dawn was still a couple of hours away when they reached Porciano. Luca and his brigade melted into the shadows. As Natalia and her exhausted mother stayed out of sight, Flavia tapped gently on the door of Signora Cecchini. Her eldest son had been killed early on in the war, her other son days before Italy surrendered, and she blamed Mussolini. Flavia was certain she would help without hesitation.

'Signorina Corsi!' The older woman glanced over Flavia's shoulder. 'What's wrong?'

'I am sorry to disturb you, Signora. My friend and her mother need somewhere safe to stay where the Nazis won't find them. Can you help?'

'Of course, of course. I have more than enough space.' Her two daughters had married and were living elsewhere; Martina and Natalia would be company for the still-mourning mother. Flavia gestured for the two women to come forward.

Signora Cecchini hustled them inside, insisting Martina – younger, but frailer – take the best chair.

'You will be hungry. I will make breakfast. While you are eating, I will organise clean linen on your beds.' Clicking her tongue, she bustled into her kitchen. The clashing of pots and plates suggested she was wasting no time.

As Flavia prepared to leave, Natalia grasped her hands. 'I'll never forget what you did for us.' Her voice was raw. 'Risking your life...'

Flavia hated that Natalia felt she should be grateful. 'The boot could have so easily been on the other foot,' she told her friend. 'In which case you would have done the same for me.'

Natalia gave her the ghost of a smile. 'I hope so. None of us can be sure what we'd do when faced with difficult choices.'

Flavia kissed her friend on the cheek. 'Get some sleep. I'll see you soon.'

THIRTY

The sky was tinged with rose when he landed soft as a cat on the Juliet balcony leading off the kitchen. Flavia had only just got back to the castello and was brewing coffee – otherwise she might not have heard him until he was actually inside. As it was, her heart had leapt to her throat. At first she was baffled as to how he'd got there, but then she remembered the scaffolding that remained on the north side of the castello.

'You climbed all the way up here?' she asked, opening the door for him, her heart racing – and not just because of the fright he'd given her.

He grinned. 'The wooden beams make a handy ladder. You should be on your guard in case anyone else attempts to get to the princess in her tower.'

Flavia turned off the gas under the coffee pot and smiled at him. 'I was furious when Margherita told me you called me that.'

'It was only because I was in awe of you.' He gave a bemused shake of his head. 'I thought you were the most beautiful woman I'd ever seen.'

He kissed her again, this time more urgently, running his hands through her hair and down her back. She responded, winding her arms around his neck, wanting to press every inch of her body against every inch of his.

He groaned and pulled away, holding her at arm's length. 'Perhaps I should go.'

'You're not going anywhere,' she murmured, bunching his jumper in her fist and tugging him towards her.

He lifted her and sank down on the sofa, still holding her in his arms. She snuggled into him, resting her head against his chest. She realised she'd been waiting for this moment all her life. But first, there was something she needed to know.

'Am I just another conquest to you?' she asked. 'It won't change what is about to happen, but I need to know.'

'I will never want another woman as long as I live. It's been you for years. I think it's always been you.' She knew from the way he held her gaze he was telling the truth – that, to him, she was different to all the women who had come before, and that he would never deliberately hurt her.

'If you had feelings for me for years, why didn't you kiss me that day when you drove my uncle's car?' Although she said it lightly, she truly wanted to know.

'Because I didn't want Roberto to know how I felt about you. He might be my brother, but he'd gladly destroy anything I cared about. It is even more important now that he doesn't discover how I feel about you.' He tilted her chin. 'But how do *you* feel? You could have anyone.'

He was everything she wanted. All she needed was contained within him. Him, her, together, it was inevitable. A life with him was the life she was meant to have.

She touched his face, his unshaved skin raspy under her fingertips. 'It's always been you for me too, although I didn't always know it.' She sat up and, looking him directly in the eyes, tugged his jumper over his head. It wasn't long before they were both naked on the floor. She wasn't quite sure how they'd got there.

They moved together, her body instinctively following his lead. He was gentle to begin with, but she whispered words in his ear, gripped his shoulders with her hands, his hips with her knees, wanting to absorb him into her, wanting him to lose himself in her. He responded with another groan, his need mirroring hers, their mouths and hands all over each other's bodies, until at last she let go, giving in to sensations that rocked her to her core.

Later they lay entwined, covered in sweat, their ragged breathing audible above the sound of the wind. Flavia had never been happier. He was the missing part of her life. If she only had a few hours left to live she would choose to spend them with him.

They talked then, the way she imagined that lovers had throughout the ages. She told him things she hadn't even shared with Margherita. About her parents, how she hadn't known that they'd been murdered until she was seventeen, how despite the affection of the Corsi family she'd felt lonely until she'd met Margherita, how much she longed to be part of a family again.

In turn he told her that he too had known they were meant to be together from the day he'd driven her home. He spoke of his dreams, his wish to develop the farm, so that his family's cheese would be sold all over Italy, perhaps all over the world. His belief that, with her by his side, he could accomplish anything.

After they'd made love again, he told her about forming his group of partisans. How he knew who would be keen to help and who could be trusted. How they'd become experts in moving silently through the forests and mountains, trained themselves to creep up on Germans and kill them before they even realised they were there.

Flavia shivered. She'd always sensed he could be ruthless if he had to be. If she were honest, perhaps this dangerous side to him was part of his attraction. Life with Luca would never be boring. 'And the women in your group? Do they kill too?'

'We are all the same. The women don't ask for, or get, special treatment. Mainly they take fugitives across the borders, but if they walk into a trap they need to know how to get out of it.'

Flavia felt a pang of envy for these women she'd met so briefly. They'd spent months with Luca. 'Have any been your lover?'

Luca grinned down at her. 'If I said yes, would you be jealous?' She refused to answer that.

'No,' Luca continued. 'I would never take a lover from my band. As their leader it wouldn't be right. Anyway, most of the time it is too cold and uncomfortable to even think of those things. But danger brings people close, so I have no doubt there are lovers among them. I'd prefer it if there weren't. Love makes a man and a woman take more risks than they normally would.' He fixed his dark eyes on her. 'They are the best men and women I have ever met. They would die for me, and I for them. It is my responsibility to keep everyone alive.' She knew this was no casual boast. Luca could only ever say what he meant.

'Who knows you're with the partisans?' she asked.

'All of Vallucciole – unfortunately. It would be safer for them if they didn't. If the Germans discover the villagers know who some of us are, God knows what they would do to them. We stay away from Vallucciole now. Margherita and the other women bring food to us though, so we eat well enough.'

'Where do you live? At the farm?'

'Yes. Whenever there is a chance Roberto might come home on leave. When we're on a mission we live in the mountains. When it's colder we use the chestnut huts.'

Almost every farm had a hut where in winter they roasted chestnuts. Some were right next to the home, others in the fields and forests.

'Do I know any of your partisans?' she asked.

Luca shook his head. 'We all have special names for each other. I can't tell you their real names. It is too dangerous. For them. And for you.' He kissed her again. 'Enough talking for now.'

She took him to her room where they made love again. Now they had found each other, it was as if they couldn't get enough of one another. He stayed all that day and through the early part of the night. They sat on her bed and ate bread and cheese and drank red wine. They laughed and explored each other's bodies with joy and pleasure. When Luca rose from her bed and started to dress, she knew he was going to meet his band of partisans. She tried not to show how terrified she was for him.

'I want to come with you,' she said, getting out of bed to stand behind him, unashamedly naked, winding her arms around his waist and placing her cheek against his back. 'I can help.'

He turned and held her away from him. 'No. I don't want you in danger. Ever again. In future if anyone needs help, find a way to let me know. Leave a tea towel on the kitchen balcony during the day or a small light at night, and I'll come as soon as I can.'

'And wait for you to come to the rescue?' Flavia retorted. 'If the women of the Casentino can risk their lives so can I.'

'I forbid it.'

She laughed. 'Forbid it! My darling Luca Rossi, surely you know me well enough by now to know you can't forbid me anything. If you don't let me help you, I will find another way to be of use. You can have your war, but I shall have mine.'

THIRTY-ONE

November 1943

It was three nights before Luca came again. Flavia had worried about him and his group of partisans constantly. She let him in and hugged him fiercely. He smelled of the forest and wood smoke. He held her as if she were the most precious thing in the world and he couldn't bear to let her go.

When he finally released her, she led him upstairs by the hand.

'I can't stay long,' he said, as she guided him towards her bedroom. He kissed her between each word.

When they were finished making love, they took some blankets up to the ramparts and used them to make a bed. He propped himself against a wall and held her in his arms. They were quiet, looking at the moon and the thousand stars in the black sky, listening to the calls of wild boar and wolves.

'I've been thinking of what I can do to help,' Flavia said after a while. Neither of them had spoken of the rumour hundreds of resistance fighters had been captured and taken to San Sabba, where they'd been tortured to death.

'No.'

'No?' She turned to face him. 'I'm no longer the innocent girl you once knew. If you need someone to take soldiers, fugitives, anyone who needs help, I will. If you don't let me help you, I will find another group. There must be others.'

'There are. Not all of them do it for the right reasons.' He was quiet for a long while. 'It will be dangerous. At least if you are with my band I can watch over you.'

'I don't want you to worry about protecting me. If I can do something, just tell me what it is.'

He sighed. 'I see it's pointless to try and stop you.' He kissed the top of her head. 'We often hide Allied soldiers in the forest. Some have escaped from prison camps, others are airmen whose planes have come down, or soldiers who have become separated from their regiments. They all want to get back to their country so they can continue to fight. It's not safe for them to keep them in the forest too long, especially now it's winter. We need people to check which routes are free, and sometimes we need help to guide the Allied soldiers. Many of them have been hurt or are ill.'

'I could hide them here in the castello until it's time to move them on.'

He stroked her hair. 'I thought about using the castello as a hiding place for the men before you came back to Porciano but decided it has too many disadvantages. If we post a watch on the ramparts we can see the Germans coming for miles. And there is the scaffolding as a way out. But if the Germans did manage to creep up on us we would be trapped and easy prey. I decided sticking with the safe houses was better. Mostly barns or chestnut huts. We only ever need them for a night or two. Long enough to let our charges rest and recover before we pass them down the line. Although the more we have, the better – using the same one too often carries risks.'

Instantly Julia came to mind. Her villa was well placed; far enough from Florence to be out of the Germans' immediate vicinity, yet close enough to get the men – or women – onto trains or boats and away. Surrounded by forest, it also had a number of outbuildings with views of the road in and out of the villa. She didn't see how the Germans could approach it without being seen even if they travelled on foot, so there would be time to warn everyone to hide. The children might be a problem, but if the partisans and their charges kept out of their sight they'd be safe enough. As long as Vincenzo remained in Italy's puppet state in the north, he wouldn't be a problem.

'I might have an idea.' She turned to face Luca. 'But I need to speak to the person first and see if they agree. I'll do it tomorrow. How do I get word to you?'

'I will come back as soon as I can.' He looked deep into her eyes. 'I don't want you to take unnecessary risks. Knowing you are safe keeps me alive.'

With her car still parked at Julia's, Flavia took the bus to Fiesole the next day. For the first time, passing the convoys of German trucks made her nervous, as if the Germans could tell she had tricked them once and was determined to do so again.

She heard the sound of childish laughter before she'd crossed the garden and reached the front door. It seemed that, no matter what children had to bear, their natural high spirits couldn't be kept down for too long. Although some of them might have more food and freedom to play than they'd had at home, of course they would far rather be in their own homes with their mamas and papas and the rest of their families. She knew that only too well.

Julia was delighted – and relieved – to see her.

'Thank God,' she said, taking Flavia by the arm and leading her into the library. 'I was terrified they might have caught you.' She kept her voice low. 'Vincenzo came that afternoon to say goodbye. My God – if Martina and Natalia had still been here! I'm thrilled the bastard has gone north. I'd be delighted if I never laid eyes on him again.'

Flavia felt exactly the same. More importantly, Vincenzo's absence meant she was free to put her idea to Julia. 'Natalia and her mother are both safe, but I need to talk to you. In private.'

Julia looked intrigued, but before she could question Flavia, a little boy came running over, throwing his arms round Flavia's legs. He clambered into her lap, as a sad-looking youth called Bruno brought them tea.

'He's from Milan,' Julia told Flavia when Bruno retreated. 'His whole family was killed in a bombing raid there last year. He barely says a word, but he likes to help in the house.' She grimaced. 'I think he believes that we will send him away if he doesn't try to earn his keep. I've tried and tried to tell him that he can stay here as long as he likes, but I can't convince him.'

So many lives destroyed because of the egos of two men. 'What will happen to the children when it's all over?' Flavia looked down at the child in her lap. He'd fallen asleep, thumb in his mouth.

'The lucky ones will return to their families or extended families. I hope that is what will happen to Angelo.' She nodded towards the boy on Flavia's lap. 'Others will be adopted. As for Bruno' – Julia shrugged – 'I think he's too old to be adopted, and as far as I'm aware he doesn't have any family still alive. We shall see. If all else fails, he can have a home here.'

Flavia lifted the sleeping Angelo from her lap, laid him down on one of the sofas and closed the doors and windows leading to the hall. Satisfied they couldn't be overheard, Flavia told Julia about Luca and his partisans finding them in the forest. She didn't mention they'd become lovers. She wanted to hug that particular secret to herself for the time being.

'I want to help them get fugitives to safety,' she told Julia. 'The journey can't always be made in a single night. And with winter on the way, the forest won't always offer adequate shelter – particularly not for men or women who have been injured or who are sick. Could Villa Bencista's outbuildings be used to hide them for a night or two?'

Julia chewed on her lower lip. 'What about the children?'

'We will have to make sure they're never made aware of what we're doing. If you think there is any danger to them, then of course we should abandon the idea.'

Julia was quiet for a while. 'We could use the outbuildings furthest out, the ones on the edge of the forest. They're on the opposite side of the children's house. The road to Florence can be seen from them. And if we posted someone to the rear of the house we'd get advance warning of any vehicles coming from the other direction. It could be done. I'd have to check with Giuseppe, but I am sure he'll agree. We both want to do anything we can to bring this war to an end, and if getting fugitives safely out of the country and soldiers back to the fight is what it takes – then we will do whatever we can.'

Flavia hugged her. 'I knew you would help.'

Julia stood and started to pace. 'We will have to keep them well away from the children. They will have to come in the night and stay hidden from everyone apart from myself and Giuseppe. When it is time for them to go, they must leave in the night too.' The animation left her face and she spread her hands wide. 'But where am I to get food for them? It's a struggle to feed ourselves and the children as it is.'

'We will find a way to feed them, Julia. Many of the farmers in the Casentino have hidden food from the Germans and will, I'm sure, be happy to share.'

She was excited, and she could tell Julia was too. It felt good to be doing something important against the German occupiers.

THIRTY-TWO

Flavia shivered, and not just with cold. Tonight she'd be helping to guide a British pilot and his navigator whose plane had come down on the other side of the mountain.

Over the last few days Luca had taken Flavia into the forest above Porciano. He taught her how to move through the woods without making a sound. She learned how to tread carefully, alert for twigs that might snap underfoot; how to cover her tracks by brushing over where she'd trod or by wading through the river. He taught her how to use the stars and moon to navigate by, making her go over everything repeatedly until he was certain she was as well trained as the rest of his brigade. When it rained or was windy, and there was little chance sound would carry, he also taught her how to shoot. Despite the fear, the sheer craziness of that time, she cherished every moment.

Finally, Luca had reluctantly agreed she was ready.

Since this was Flavia's first mission, Luca insisted on coming too. As he'd predicted, the moon was full enough for them to see their way, with enough cloud to hide should they need to. She should have gone to bed for a few hours – God knew when next she'd get some sleep – but she'd known it would have been a waste of time. She was too anxious. Recently there had been reports of executions for far less serious offences than the one they were about to commit. She hoped if she were ever captured she'd be shot on the spot. Better a quick death than one by torture. She had no real way of knowing for sure if she might be the one to break, the one to give up names and secrets that put other lives in danger. She'd rather die a thousand deaths than do that. She pushed the thoughts away. There was no point dwelling on something that might not happen, no turning back from her mission now. A thrill of excitement ran up her spine, overriding her fear. If she could save even one life, help a single pilot or soldier to return to battle, then it would all be worthwhile.

She set the coffee pot on the stove and, while she waited for it to boil, she wrapped some prosciutto and bread in a linen cloth before placing it in the backpack she would carry. She was already dressed in dark trousers and sweater and had wrapped her hair in a scarf. She'd borrowed one of the padded jackets Lucrezia had left behind, along with wool-lined gloves. There was always a chance they would be sleeping out that night.

When it was time, she pulled on her stout walking boots and, ignoring the road, made her way to the woods above the castello where she was to meet Luca and his partisans. They were there already, the two airmen with them. Hunched in their overcoats, the airmen looked pale and gaunt. They grinned and gave her the thumbs up, and she thought back to her contempt for the Anglo-Fiorentini – could it really be only a few years ago? – and felt ashamed. She'd looked down upon the young British men, thinking them superficial and self-obsessed. How wrong she'd been. These same men were doing whatever it took to get back to Britain so they could risk their lives all over again. To help Italy! A country that had taken up arms against them.

Luca gave her a quick smile. 'Follow close behind me,' he whispered.

As their little group made their way, Flavia concentrated on memorising the route – the steep bits, the places where there was a river or stream to cross, the safest places to rest. Most of the time they were away from the road, sheltered by chestnut trees, the sounds of their movement dampened by the forest. The only real potential source of danger was when they had to cross open fields. Depending on their route there were safe houses which Luca had made her learn by heart. It would be safer to sleep in the forest, but if the weather worsened they were more likely to freeze to death than be discovered by German soldiers.

At one point the sound of rustling stopped them in their tracks. When a wild boar plunged out from the trees, they laughed off their unease.

Flavia thought back to her earlier hope that she wouldn't be scared; she'd done it once, so she could do it again. But all the fears of her first trip with Natalia and her mother were still there. Even with the comforting presence of Luca and his partisans, she still had to fight the fear that somehow she wouldn't be able to go on, that she'd freeze, give in to panic – become the burden rather than the helper. As if sensing her anxiety, Luca would reach out to grasp her hand, reassuring her with his touch.

Flavia's anxiety was unwarranted. This first trip went off without a hitch, ending at a farmhouse where they passed the airmen on to another group of partisans who would take them the remainder of the way.

The following journeys were less frightening. Perhaps because she either had Luca or one of the other partisans with her. After months, if not years, of living in the mountains, they knew every inch of the terrain. They knew the places to avoid as well as the houses they could rely on for shelter if needed. Furthermore, many of the men they were helping to safety had already spent several nights either in POW camps or in the open. They were battle-hardened and fearless.

The trick, Flavia had discovered, was to ignore the voice in her head that told her to run, or hide and stay hidden, to let others take the risk. Instead, she focussed only on getting where they needed to as quickly as possible.

Often, progress along the route was dangerously slow. Not all of the men were as fit as they once had been. Some had endured weeks, even months, in camps with little to eat. Others had been injured as they bailed from their plane, or been shot and tortured in previous escapes.

More than once they were forced to make use of a barn when dawn came too soon. Spending the day hiding, listening for the sound of German trucks, was horrible. Nothing Flavia learned about the Germans lessened her hatred for them. On the other hand, her admiration for the Allies continued to grow. Many of the men she helped were barely out of their teens, yet they showed nothing but courage, consideration, and – in whatever way they could communicate it – humour. Despite the sporadic episodes of paralysing fear, she felt truly alive during these expeditions, and she knew this was what she was meant to do.

Luca wasn't always with them. His role with the partisans was to strike at the Germans whenever they could. She knew he was involved in ambushes and sabotage, and that each time he participated in a raid he risked his life. That terrified her more than anything.

Whenever they had a chance to spend time alone together, he left her in no doubt that she was his world, his love, his everything. But she couldn't shake the sense of their future being fragile. She tried to imagine them old and grey, surrounded by their children and grandchildren, but she couldn't see beyond the immediate moment. Even though she wanted the war to be over, she felt an equally strong desire to freeze time.

One night, after they'd made love, she crept from their tangled sheets and taking her sketch pad from her dressing table she curled up in the chair facing the bed. Tucking her feet under her, she lifted her charcoal pencil and began to draw. Her pencil flew over the page, trying to capture his extraordinary beauty, his extraordinary courage. His eyes opened. He hooked his hands behind his head and studied her through half-closed lids. She finished her sketch, wanting to record the moment on paper the way it was imprinted on her mind. As if by doing so, she could make him immortal.

When he smiled and reached out for her, she put her pad away and went to him.

One morning in February, they were in Margherita's kitchen making pasta from chestnut flour when Margherita stood back and scrutinised Flavia from top to bottom. She frowned.

'Are you going to have a baby?' she asked, and immediately answered her own question. 'You are, aren't you?'

'Why do you say that?' Flavia replied, taken aback.

'Because I can tell. Look at your breasts. They are much larger than usual. Have you been feeling queasy?'

At that moment Flavia knew. She had put the fact she hadn't had a period for the last couple of months down to the stress of helping the partisans and that there was less to eat, even in the countryside where they managed to conceal some of their produce from the Germans.

Joy spread through her like the warmth of the rising sun. She was going to have a baby. Luca's baby. Their child. She hadn't planned to get pregnant, but now that she was...!

She gave a shriek of delight, and she and Margherita fell into each other's arms. They hugged and laughed and cried.

Eventually Margherita held her at arm's length. 'You must start taking care of yourself. No more night-time trips,' she said sternly.

Of course, Margherita knew Flavia was working with the partisans. Her friend missed very little. Hadn't she just proved that?

'What do you think Luca will say?' Margherita continued, smiling again.

Flavia wasn't sure. She *hoped* he'd be pleased. She had no doubt he loved her, but marriage and children had never been discussed. They'd been too intent on the immediate future, on each day as it happened. Perhaps they'd been frightened to jinx what they had by thinking too far ahead?

Flavia smiled back. 'There is only one way to find out.'

Before Flavia left, Margherita went into her bedroom, returning with a tiny white embroidered gown. 'Take this.' She held it out to Flavia.

Flavia recognised it immediately. It was the christening gown she'd helped sew in the farmhouse kitchen; each stitch sewn with love. She'd thought about those warm summer evenings often; it had been such a happy time. It was perfect that her baby would wear it too.

Margherita hugged Flavia fiercely. 'Promise me you'll be careful.'

It was the middle of the night when Luca next came. Seeing him always took her breath away. He was just so sexy – with his woollen hat pulled low over his thick hair, framing his beautiful face, a beard that tickled, his gun stuffed down the back of his trousers. She could imagine him dressed like Cosimo de' Medici, his cloak streaming behind him as he strode through the streets of Florence. Or even as a Roman gladiator. Maybe he'd been born into the wrong time and wrong place. Or exactly the right time and the right place. He wouldn't be the man she loved if even one facet of him was different. And she did love him. In her wildest dreams she could never have imagined how much. He loved her too. He didn't have to say the words for her to know it.

After he kissed her, she made him coffee and brought it to him. He was sprawled in an armchair grinning up at her, his whole being focussed on her as if nothing and no one else mattered.

All the same she was nervous.

He reached out to pull her to him, but she whirled out of his reach. He gave her a puzzled look.

'I have something to tell you,' she began.

He cocked his head to the side. 'I'm listening.'

Her mouth was suddenly dry. 'I hope you'll think it's good news.'

'Are you going to tell me, or do I have to guess?' he said, laughing.

She ran her tongue across her lips. 'I am going to have our baby.'

Her words took a moment to register. When they did, he jumped to his feet, grasped her by the elbows and looked at her in wonder. 'Are you sure?' he asked huskily.

'Yes.'

'How long have you known?'

'A few days.'

'We must marry – immediately.'

'*Must* marry...?' She stepped out of his arms. Not exactly the romantic proposal she had been hoping for.

His eyes widened in surprise then he grinned, lifted her off her feet and swung her around. 'I love you, I love you, I love you. I will never, ever stop loving you. You would make me the happiest and proudest man in the world if you would agree to become my wife.'

Why had she ever doubted him?

He set her back on her feet, kissed the dip of her neck, and looked at her. His expression clouded over. 'No, we can't. It isn't safe for you to marry me. If the Germans find out, you could be in danger. They are searching for Liberte and his band and will do anything to get us. If they discover we are married, they might arrest you and interrogate you. I can't take that chance.'

'I would never betray you. Any of you.' If it came to that she would find the strength from somewhere. *Even if your baby died with you?* a voice crept into her head. She pushed it away.

Luca placed the tip of his finger under her chin and tilted her face so she was looking directly into his eyes. 'Which is why I can't put you in danger. I know you'd rather die before you'd give any of us up. And now there is a greater reason for you to stay safe.' He placed his hand on her stomach. 'We have our child to think of.'

'This war can't continue much longer now the Allies are

advancing through Italy,' she said. A month earlier British and American forces had landed in their tens of thousands at Anzio, only thirty miles from Rome.

'It will take time for our country to be fully liberated,' he continued, starting to pace. 'And if something happens to me I don't want my child to be born out of wedlock.'

She'd never seen him so conflicted.

'We will marry in secret,' Flavia said firmly, making the decision for him. 'At the church in Romena. My family knows the priest there well. I will go and see him. The priest in Porciano would never betray us, but it would be impossible to keep our marriage a secret from the villagers, not when the church is in view of practically every house.'

Luca's frown deepened. 'No one, not even my mother, must know we are married until this war is over. It could get back to Roberto. He might be my brother but I don't trust him. Even if he didn't tell his Blackshirt friends there are others who want to keep on the side of the German occupiers – traitors who will be dealt with when this is all over.'

This ruthlessness was a side of Luca that still shocked her. But he'd been changed by the men he'd known who'd been tortured and executed.

He sat on the sofa and pulled her down beside him. 'I wish we didn't have to marry in secret. I don't want people believing you are having a child by someone who didn't care enough to marry you.'

She smiled up at him. He was more of a prig than she realised. She loved that she was still learning about him. 'Let them think what they like. We won't be able to hide it forever – people will notice when I begin to show. Now what about Margherita? Will she be our witness?'

Luca shook his head. 'We can tell her we are to marry, but I don't think she should come to the marriage ceremony. It will have to take place at night if we are certain not to be seen, and she might be arrested for being out after curfew.'

Although disappointed, Flavia knew he was right. She brushed his hair from his forehead. 'One day, we will have the most enormous wedding for all our friends and family.'

Luca grinned. 'People will talk about it for years.' He turned serious again. 'After we marry you should go to your family in Switzerland. You'd be safe there.'

'I won't leave here. I won't leave you.' She gripped his hands and held his gaze. 'Don't ask me again.'

'Will you tell the conte and contessa?' he asked.

'No. There will be time enough to let them know when all of this is over. After everything returns to normal.'

'They won't be happy when they hear we are husband and wife.'

'Perhaps not,' Flavia answered honestly. 'But they'll get used to the idea.' She laid her hand on his thigh. 'It's not something to worry about now. We are in the midst of hell, millions of innocent people have been killed.' She suppressed a shiver. How many more would die before it was over? 'I am certain they'll be content I'm safe and happy.'

'And you? How do you feel about being a farmer's wife? It is not a life you are used to.'

'You know it won't bother me. I've slept rough, gone without food or water...' She smiled up at him. 'Most importantly, I'll be with you. That's all that matters. I'd live in a chestnut hut if it were the only way for us to be together.'

He grinned again. 'My love, you could never live in a hut and I'll make damned sure you'll never have to.' His mood changed once more, and he started pacing again. 'You have to stop your work with us. It's too dangerous.'

'I will. After the next trip. There's no one who can take my place until after that. I'll go and see the priest in Romena tomorrow. I'll arrange everything. All you'll have to do is be there.' She stood and tugged at his hand, pulling him to the floor. And there on the rug, in front of the fire, she started to remove his clothes, interspersing every undone button with a kiss on his exposed skin.

Sex had always been passionate, fierce, as if both were trying to impress the other upon their skin, as if every time might be their last. This time it was slower, gentler, as if he was scared he'd break her. As they lay together, an owl hooted. A chill swept across Flavia's skin. She should be feeling blissfully happy. Instead, she had the terrible sense there would be no *happy ever after* for them.

THIRTY-THREE

They married a few nights later. The Pieve di Romena was lit by only by a few candles which had been placed on the floor so that the light couldn't be seen from outside. Flavia was wearing her best day-frock, Luca was in a suit. It was old and worn, but she'd never thought him more handsome, never loved him more. The priest didn't waste much time; they were breaking curfew and, even if they weren't, the Germans could patrol at any minute. It was why Luca's band of partisans kept watch outside, as silent and still as the shadows. Soon Luca was placing the gold ring that had belonged to his grandmother, and her mother before that, on her finger, and they were man and wife, promising to care for each other in sickness and in health for the rest of their lives.

They rode back to the castello – where else could they spend their wedding night but in the tower? – on the only remaining farm horse. Flavia perched in front of Luca, her head resting against his chest. So, after everything she'd told herself, she too was a married woman. It no longer felt like second best to her. She was meant to be with him. Whatever the future held, it was fitting and right that they faced it together.

'Happy?' she asked, swivelling so she could see his face.

'Happier than I thought possible. Everything I could ever need or want is right here in my arms.'

They reached the castello without encountering trouble. Luca's brigade, after a number of innuendos and cheeky grins, melted back into the forest.

Before Flavia had left the castello for her wedding, she'd set a fire in the grate. While Luca got it going, she laid the cheese, ham and bread Margherita had given her earlier that day on a small table in front of the sofa – along with a flagon of red wine. After she'd done that, she lit some candles and placed them on the table too so that their light wouldn't be seen in the windows.

She kissed Luca. 'Wait here for me. I'll be back down in a few minutes.'

He circled her waist, and together they fell back on the sofa, Luca raining kisses on her until she could barely breathe. Reluctantly she pushed him away. She wanted this day, this evening, this night, to be perfect. She'd planned every moment in her head.

'I won't be long,' she promised.

She ran up to her room and slipped on a favourite gown she'd brought to the castello. It was the full-length blue silk, cinched at the waist with a matching sash. It was tighter round her breasts and stomach than the last time she'd worn it, but otherwise still fitted perfectly. She studied her reflection in the mirror. Her cheeks were flushed, her eyes bright. She knew she'd never looked more beautiful, and she was glad.

The fire was blazing by the time she returned downstairs. Luca had poured two glasses of wine. He handed one to her, his eyes filled with awe.

'I can't believe how lucky I am. I can't believe you are my wife.'

'The princess came down from her tower after all?' she teased, clinking her wine glass to his.

Placing her glass on the table she wound up the gramophone and put a record on.

'Dance with me,' she said, holding out her hands to him.

They moved together, her fingers flat against his chest, his lips on her hair, their hearts beating in time. They fitted together. It would, she knew, be a fiery relationship. They were Italian after all. There would be times when he would try to bend her to his will, as she would try to bend him to hers. They would both have to learn to compromise.

Afterwards, they took the half-drunk flagon of wine and the remains of their meal up to the top of the turret. It was their favourite place. The moon was a white orb in a dense black sky. They sat on cushions, she between his legs, her back to his chest. He wrapped a blanket around his shoulders so that they were cocooned together, protected from the frosty night.

For the first time they spoke of the future. They wondered out loud what their child, boy or girl, would look like. She, or he, would have their courage, her looks and brains, everything else could be his, she laughed. Their child would be brought up in a fairer world, have the formal education neither of them really had. Flavia would teach her about art, Luca would take him shooting wild boar. They talked until Flavia grew sleepy.

'Perhaps you should stay with Margherita in Vallucciole,' he murmured as her eyes were closing. 'She can keep an eye on you for me.'

'Perhaps. Later. When I am closer to giving birth.' The castello was their fortress against the world, and she intended to keep it that way for as long as she could.

THIRTY-FOUR

March 1944

When Flavia heard the banging on the door she'd thought it was Luca. All day the wind had howled around the castle, whining and whistling through doors and windows, hurling clumps of snow against the glass. As night fell she'd fretted about Luca and his fellow fighters out in the freezing cold. Almost immediately she knew it couldn't be her husband. He would never draw attention to his visits like that.

She wondered who it could be. Someone in trouble perhaps? Or – anxiety clawed her chest – someone coming to tell her Luca and his fellow partisans had been captured?

Her heart was in her throat as she ran down the stairs, the light from her oil lamp casting eerie shadows on the wall.

To her horror she found Vincenzo on the doorstep, Roberto at the wheel of an army vehicle. One of them here in Porciano was alarming enough, but both! And together. She hadn't heard the vehicle approaching. The wind must have drowned out the sound of its engine.

She made herself as tall as she could and stared at Vincenzo, trying not to let him see how terrified she was. Dear God, had he come to tell her that Luca had been arrested, executed even? Had Roberto found out about her and Luca and told him? Surely, whatever bad feeling there was between the brothers, Roberto would never betray Luca. Even so it was dangerous that Roberto was back in the valley. Who knew what secrets he would ferret out from people in an area he knew like the back of his hand.

'Why are you here?' she asked Vincenzo, relieved to hear her voice sounded disdainful rather than frightened. She made no attempt to stand aside so he could enter.

'Can a man not visit an old friend?'

They weren't friends. They both knew that.

'It's late. I was in bed.' She pulled her robe tighter, conscious of his hot, greedy eyes on her.

'May I come in?'

'As I said. It's late,' she repeated. She had a very bad feeling about him being there. What if Luca had chosen this time to come? What if he still came? She took a deep breath to calm herself. Luca would see the vehicle and instantly know it wasn't safe. Thank goodness she had taken her wedding ring off and was wearing it around her neck on a chain.

'I don't plan on staying long,' Vincenzo persisted, moving closer to her. She had no choice but to step back and let him enter. Thankfully Roberto remained in the car. She didn't think she could manage to hide her dislike of him too.

Vincenzo followed her up the stairs, so close she could feel his breath on the back of her neck. When they reached the sitting room, he sat down without her asking him to.

'I don't suppose you have any coffee?' he asked. The innocuous request should have made her feel relieved, but it didn't. He was making it clear he wouldn't be leaving until he was ready. Although she desperately wanted this man out of her home, she mustn't show him how she felt. It could be dangerous.

'I'll put coffee on, but before I do, if you'll excuse me, I'll go and dress.'

He smirked at her. 'Really, Flavia, there is no need. This war –

well, it has changed a great deal, don't you agree? Nothing is the same. People are not as formal, are more inclined to be friendly with those that once they could never imagine being friends with. People even take lovers where they would never have dreamt before.'

He leered at her, running the tip of his tongue along his lips. Was he insinuating she might take him as a lover? What made him think she would consider him now when she wouldn't consider him before? Or, dread made her stomach churn, was he referring to her relationship with Luca? Dear God. Did Vincenzo know about them? They'd been careful, but in a valley this size it was difficult to keep secrets. Or had someone let something slip to Roberto?

She mustn't panic; it would surely show in her face if she did. At that moment she caught sight of her diary, left where she'd been writing it, on the dining room table. She didn't think it was possible for her heart to beat faster. What if Vincenzo saw it and insisted on reading it? He would know everything then. Dear God, how could she have been so stupid to have left it lying about? As soon as she could, she had to get it out of view. In the meantime, she mustn't so much as glance at it again – or draw his attention to it in any way.

She raised an eyebrow. 'Things haven't changed so much that I am comfortable entertaining in my nightclothes,' she replied. 'Now if you'll excuse me.' She could scoop up the diary, hide it in the folds of her dressing gown, hide it in her room.

But as she moved past him he grabbed her wrist. He held it so tightly she suspected there would be bruises there tomorrow.

'Why so frightened, Flavia? I am here only to help you. To make sure you stay safe. Make sure you do the right thing.'

'What on earth do you mean by that?' Her mind was skittering all over the place. She looked pointedly at her wrist.

His lips curled in a sneer. 'You know as well as I do that your family is not on the right side. Your mother and father were traitors who thought they could mock Il Duce and his vision for Italy. As for the conte and contessa, they would have been better remaining here and making friends with the Germans. Germany is going to win this war. Anyone who doesn't know that is making a mistake.'

White-hot fury surged through her. He wasn't fit to lick her godparents' boots, let alone those of her parents.

'Is that why you stayed with the Germans?' she spat. 'To be on the winning side?' She drew in a breath, forced her fists to uncurl. She mustn't antagonise him.

'Of course. What other reason could there be? When this war is over, people will be needed to govern Italy. People like me, with the skills and the contacts I have.' His eyes raked over her as if she were little more than a mannequin. 'And it would be better – easier – for you and yours if you kept on my side.'

Her stomach turned over. 'I am perfectly happy with the way things are.'

'You wouldn't want me to tell my German friends about your lover,' he continued, as if she hadn't spoken.

She only stopped her legs from giving way by gripping on tightly to the sides of the chair. *Dear God, he did know!* It took all she had not to look at her diary again. Within its pages was all the evidence he would need – if he needed any more proof.

'I can't imagine what you mean,' she said, trying to keep her voice from shaking.

'Roberto tells me his brother has more than a passing interest in you. You should know that the Gestapo are very interested in talking to Luca Rossi and his band of thieves. Where is the elder Rossi anyway? Roberto says he hasn't seen him since he returned to the farm.'

She thought quickly, keeping her expression as bland as possible.

'Roberto is lying. He is jealous. I know Luca only because I am friendly with his sister.' Even as she said the words, she realised she might have made a mistake. The last thing she wanted was to draw attention to Margherita. She'd heard terrible stories about what the Gestapo did to those who they only *suspected* of having information relating to the partisans. Proof of guilt wasn't necessary for someone to get a bullet in the head or to be taken to a German prison, never to be seen again.

'Not everyone agrees with what the partisans are doing, you know,' she continued, forcing a smile. 'Many of us, particularly landholding families, believe they are little more than thieves and cowards. As for Luca – he is a peasant, and I have been raised alongside aristocracy. I would hardly take him as a lover.' She put as much contempt into her voice as she could muster. Some of what she said was true. There were many Italians who had no time for the partisans, believing they only brought trouble.

'His sister is a peasant too, yet you are friendly with her.'

'We were friendly when we were children – when the differences between us didn't matter. She asked me to be godmother to her children when I was still very young. I carry out the duties, little more...'

Such a wicked betrayal of a friendship that meant more to her than almost anything! But she would say – would *do* – anything to keep Luca and his family safe.

Flavia moved closer to the dining room table. 'Look, Vincenzo, I think we got off on the wrong foot. You have a job to do, and I'm but a woman who doesn't really understand politics. Why don't you feed the fire while I dress?' She forced a smile. 'There is some French cognac over there on the shelf. Help yourself to a drink while you are waiting.'

He gave a self-satisfied smirk, crossed over to the shelf and lifted the bottle. As soon as his back was turned, Flavia slipped her diary between the silk of her dressing gown and her skin.

She ran upstairs, removed her other diaries from her dressing table and shoved them under her mattress. Once that was done, she dressed quickly in a skirt that came to well below her knee and a blouse that buttoned up to the neck. She finished off her outfit with one of her godfather's cardigans she sometimes used as a bed jacket. She surveyed her image in the mirror with grim satisfaction. She looked almost twice her age.

By the time she returned to the sitting room, Vincenzo had

stoked up the fire and helped himself to a good third of the decanter of cognac. He appeared thoroughly pleased with himself. Flavia made coffee and brought it through.

'I thought you'd be interested to hear that the Germans are to take up residence in Porciano. I stopped them from requisitioning the castello. I told the commander of the German regiment that the tower would not be a suitable place for them, unfinished as it is. They have agreed to occupy the houses instead. They will use the church as a mess for the troops.'

If he wanted her thanks for dissuading the commander from occupying the castello, he wasn't going to get it. Her mind raced as she processed the implications of having the German army stationed so close. It was terrible news that they were coming to Porciano. Natalia and her mother would no longer be safe, and it would be even more dangerous for her and Luca to be together. While Vincenzo was talking, she thought of other places she and Luca could meet. She would have to find a way to go to him, otherwise nothing would stop him coming to her.

She refilled Vincenzo's glass. 'I'm sure the villagers will do their best to make the soldiers comfortable.' What else could they do?

Vincenzo left at last, promising to return when his duties permitted. When she was sure he had gone, Flavia collapsed into a chair, her heart beating painfully. If Vincenzo didn't know for certain about her and Luca, he clearly had his suspicions.

If Vincenzo *had* spotted her diaries and read them, or noticed the wedding ring she wore around her neck, or even found her sketch of Luca, he would have known the truth immediately: that she and Luca were together, and that he and his group of partisans were operating out of the valley. How could she have been so careless? Who knew what destruction she might have brought to all her friends – not just Luca? As for the document she'd found...

On one of the long nights when she was waiting for Luca but he didn't come, she'd been looking through an old, battered suitcase filled with papers belonging to her godmother when she'd come across a yellowed, brittle manuscript. She couldn't be sure, but she thought – judging by the style of writing and the style of Italian, as well as the age of the paper – there was a chance it may have been written by Dante. She knew he'd stayed here when he'd been exiled from Florence. If the papers were part of a missing body of his work, they would be extremely valuable. She'd written to her godmother explaining she believed she'd found something of significance. Aunt Lucrezia had replied, warning her to be careful and to hide what she'd found and to destroy any evidence of her find.

Preoccupied with other matters, she'd ignored her godmother's advice in every regard. She couldn't bring herself to destroy her diaries, but she did need to hide them and the documents somewhere they would never be found by the Blackshirts or the Germans. However, someone had to find the documents, sometime in the future, if ever she was unable to retrieve them herself.

There were so many things to think about, so much to do. She took a deep breath. Time was critical. Every wasted moment might bring destruction down on them all. The Germans were coming to Porciano, so her immediate priority had to be Natalia and her mother. They were no longer safe; Vincenzo might recognise Natalia, and Roberto would certainly know they didn't belong to the village. They had to be moved – sooner rather than later.

She thought for a moment, coming up with a plan. First things first. Making sure the coast was clear, she hurried across to the priest's house. As quickly as she could, she explained about Vincenzo and Roberto's visit. Father Sebastian grasped the situation right away. He sent someone to call the heads of the households to a meeting.

'We can hide the women with the nuns in the monastery in Stia,' Father Sebastian suggested, while they were waiting. 'They will be safe there.'

It was the perfect solution. Trusted priests and nuns had a network of safe places all across Tuscany, and most likely the rest of Italy too. Who would notice two more among their number?

The villagers assembled quickly. Naturally they weren't at all pleased the Germans were coming to Porciano. It was bad enough having troops in nearby Stia.

'They will rip everything out of our church,' Pietro, one of the older villagers, muttered. 'Or destroy it.'

He was right to worry. It was well known that the Germans pillaged Italian treasures wherever they went. They had no respect for the churches and chapels of Italy.

'We can't let them take our triptych of the Annunciation,' Father Sebastian said. 'It is the only thing of real value in the church.'

As the talk went on around her, Flavia thought about the papers she'd found and where she could hide them, assessing and discarding one place after another. The men eventually decided that the painting should be taken to the church in Stia, which was right next door to where the priest lived. They hoped it would be safer there. They couldn't be certain, but they all agreed it was worth taking a chance. Perhaps, hanging in plain sight, the Germans would not realise that it was painted by Lorenzo di Bicci.

At that moment Flavia knew where she could hide the documents she found. In the meantime, she had to warn Natalia and Martina, and persuade them to stay with the nuns. As soon as she'd done that, she'd return to the castello and hide the evidence of her marriage too.

THIRTY-FIVE

A week after Vincenzo's visit, German troops moved into Porciano, occupying the three largest homes in the village. Surprisingly the soldiers weren't too bad. As long as the villagers kept to the curfew, they largely left them alone. It did however make it more difficult for Flavia to leave the castello without being seen. Although its front door faced away from the houses the German soldiers lived in, and wasn't visible from the priest's house, it was nevertheless high and exposed. To make matters worse the Germans had requisitioned the home of Signora Lisio, who occupied one of the larger houses, and forced her to operate it as a trattoria to serve his men. The troops often stayed up late eating and drinking, coming outside to relieve themselves. Consequently, Flavia had to be very careful whenever she left Porciano to meet up with Luca. Fortunately her friendship with Margherita and her visits to Vallucciole provided the perfect cover.

The German troops had been in Porciano for several weeks, and spring was well on its way, primroses and violets giving splashes of optimistic colour in an otherwise dark world, when Flavia heard about the brave, but ultimately doomed, attempt at resistance against the German occupiers by a small group of poorly armed rebels.

A handful of partisans had joined Italian soldiers and army officers, along with twenty-nine escaped POW Allied soldiers, and taken on over two thousand Nazi and Fascist troops in San Martino near Rome. They'd managed to shoot down two German planes before being forced to disperse. In retaliation the Germans had burnt the church from which they launched their offensive to the ground, as well as a nearby village. But what chilled Flavia to the soul was that six partisans had been captured, tortured and executed.

Although she knew it was unlikely Luca had been involved, at the first opportunity Flavia risked going to his farm to look for him. When she didn't find him there, she searched for him in the forest – but without success. Increasingly fearful, she'd continued on to Vallucciole, and to her relief her friend had promised that Luca was safe – she'd seen him the evening before, when he'd slipped down to see her. Signora Rossi and Rosina had been there too, although they'd since returned to Signora Rossi's sister in Poppi. With Roberto back home they wouldn't be returning permanently anytime soon.

It was almost curfew by the time Flavia got back to Porciano. She had just turned the corner and was crossing the lawn in front of the castello when a figure stepped out from behind a tree.

'Roberto!' It was as if thinking of him had made him appear. 'What...' Before she could finish, he grabbed her arm and hustled her behind part of the wall and into the shadows. 'Where the fuck have you been? I've been waiting for you.'

The expression on his face brought her out in a cold sweat. 'What is it?'

He put his fingers to his lips and darted a quick look over his shoulder. 'Please. You must listen very carefully to what I have to say. Two German soldiers have been murdered by partisans, and the Germans have decided to rid the valley of the partisans once and for all. They intend to raid Vallucciole at dawn tomorrow to search for them. You must go there and tell Margherita and her children to stay indoors – or preferably hide in the forests. If they do, they will be safe.'

Nausea rose in Flavia's throat. 'And the men?'

'They must take their chances.'

'We must both go and warn them. Right away.'

Roberto's eyes stretched in disbelief. He was like a little boy caught up in a game he was only just realising he didn't want to be part of. He collected himself quickly, sneering at her. 'Don't be stupid. If Major Lambini were to learn I'd passed on this information he'd have me shot on the spot. You must hurry – get there before they do.'

Before she could ask him more, he slipped away.

Flavia remained in the shadows, taking deep breaths to control her panic. She had to warn Margherita and the rest of Vallucciole. There was no time to waste.

Pivoting on her foot, she was about to turn back towards the forest when one of the German soldiers emerged from behind a chestnut tree, doing up his trousers. She froze. Had he overheard Roberto warning her?

'You need to go inside, Signorina,' he said, politely but firmly. 'You must be aware it is almost eight. The curfew?'

She racked her brain for an excuse to be out but knew nothing she could say would persuade the soldier to let her go. He kept his eyes on her until the door closed behind her. She'd no choice but to wait until everyone was asleep and sneak out then. There would be soldiers on patrol throughout the night, so she'd have to choose her moment. Whatever it took, she would find a way to warn them. She had to.

THIRTY-SIX

AMELIA

Frustratingly, the remainder of the pages in Flavia's diaries were blank. Amelia stared out of the window, her mind whirling. Flavia must have been so panicked, desperate to get to Vallucciole in time to warn the villagers. Amelia wanted to believe she had. After all, she'd been brave, resourceful and in love.

She'd also been pregnant. The christening gown wasn't a family heirloom but intended for *her* baby. Amelia knew without a shadow of doubt that there was no way Flavia would have killed herself if she were expecting a child.

She should go to Vallucciole. Someone there might be able to tell Amelia what happened to them all, maybe even where she might find Luca and Flavia's child. Margherita or Luca might even still be alive. Why hadn't she thought of going there before now?

Excited by what she might learn, she changed out of her grubby clothes into clean jeans and a long-sleeved T-shirt, applied some lipstick and brushed her hair. It was important she looked normal to whoever she might find there.

She wasn't going to attempt to walk through the forest – even if there was still a path. She couldn't trust herself not to get lost. Consulting the map of Tuscany she'd found in the castello, she realised the route by road would be the same as the one Flavia drove the day of Margherita's wedding.

On her way to the car, she glanced over at Kelly's door. It was open. She must be back from Elba. She should apologise for the way she'd behaved the other night.

Taking a deep breath, she tapped on the door and, hearing an 'enter', walked in. Kelly was in the kitchen opening tins of cat food.

'Oh, hi.' Unsurprisingly, her expression was wary as if she expected Amelia to launch into more accusations. Using a fork, she scraped the contents of one of the tins into a metal bowl.

'I'm sorry about the other night,' Amelia said. Kelly placed the tin opener on the counter and turned to face Amelia. 'I don't know what I was thinking, accusing you like that,' Amelia hurried on.

A smile touched the corners of Kelly's mouth. 'I *was* a little taken aback.'

Amelia struggled to find an explanation for her behaviour that didn't place her in an even worse light. 'I'm okay now. You were right. I let the atmosphere of the castello get to me.'

Kelly's expression softened. 'You've had it tough recently. What you've been through would be enough to drive most people crazy.' She didn't seem to appreciate that her choice of words didn't comfort Amelia. 'Rattling around that enormous place all by yourself, who wouldn't start imagining a whole bunch of stuff?'

I didn't imagine the christening gown on my pillow, Amelia was about to protest, just stopping herself in time. It *was* still possible she'd put it there herself.

'Are you sure you wouldn't prefer to stay here with me? I'd be very happy to have you,' Kelly continued.

'Oh, no. Really. Thank you for the offer but I like living in the castello. Everything's been fine since you left.'

She raised an eyebrow. 'You're not implying—'

'No, no. Of course not.' Amelia had to stop digging holes for herself. 'What I meant was – I've been all right. Much better.'

'Awesome. I was worried about you all the time I was away. I kept wondering whether I should ring Beatrice.'

Amelia's breath caught in her throat. 'Did you?'

'Nah. I decided it was none of my business.'

Thank God. Amelia would hate for Beatrice to feel alarmed about the unhinged woman living in her castle when she was thousands of miles away.

Kelly held up the coffee pot. 'Stay?' Thankfully she didn't seem to bear a grudge.

'Could we make it another time? I'm on my way to Vallucciole.'

Kelly's eyes widened. 'Why the heck would you want to go there?'

A creeping sense of dread crawled up Amelia's spine. 'What do you mean? Why shouldn't I?'

'There's nothing there apart from a few ruins. The whole village was wiped out during the war.'

The breath left Amelia's body. She clutched the back of one of her chairs for support. 'Are you sure?'

Kelly nodded. 'Worst German atrocity in the Casentino in World War Two.'

No longer excited, but filled with trepidation and fear, Amelia set off down the road to Stia, her hands trembling on the steering wheel. Instead of turning left, which would take her into the town, she turned right, and a few miles further on took another right.

The road became rougher and narrower, and she was forced to slow down to a snail's pace. The car hit a pothole and juddered, and Amelia prayed she hadn't damaged it. If she broke an axle, she would have to walk back to Porciano. It was unlikely she'd get a lift. Since turning onto the road, she hadn't passed a single vehicle. It was as if no one ever came this way.

It was heavily wooded on both sides of the road, but every now and again there was a gap in the trees, allowing glimpses to the valley below. She visualised Luca and the partisans bending low, weapons in their hands, moving unseen over terrain they knew like the backs of their hands.

As she crawled past a small, simple church on her left, she noticed a plaque outside, of the type often seen next to a place of interest. She pulled over and got out.

The air was still, the road shaded by large chestnut trees, the sunlight barely filtering through them. Up here, with the forest closing in on her, it felt as if she were the only person alive in the world. All of a sudden, Amelia was suffused with a stomach-churning mix of dread, sadness and terror.

The plastic cover of the plaque was covered in dew. She used the sleeve of her blouse to wipe away the moisture. Her breath came in short, painful gasps as she read.

The words were simple and to the point. This was where one of the worst atrocities happened in 1944. The German army, in retaliation for the killing of two of their soldiers, and suspecting the village of harbouring partisans, burnt it to the ground. Before they did, they gathered the men and took them into the hills, where they were all executed. The women and children were not spared either. In total a hundred and eight villagers were slaughtered.

A hundred and eight men, women and children. Murdered. So Flavia hadn't made it in time! Amelia fell to her knees in front of the plaque and covered her face with her hands as an image filled her head, so powerful it made her cry out. She saw Margherita on her knees, hanging onto the coat of a German soldier, screaming and begging for her children's lives. Behind her an old lady, her face white with terror, had a little girl by the hand.

She tried to push the unbearable images out of her head, knowing she really would go mad if she let them stay there. Almost immediately the images of the past were replaced by the memory of the day after she lost her child.

The sergeant and the constable were waiting for Amelia and her father at the entrance to the mortuary, their faces appropriately sombre. But Amelia could tell that only moments before they'd been sharing a joke. There was still a trace of laughter in the sergeant's eyes, and the constable wasn't quite quick enough to settle his face into the appropriate mask of compassion. Fury washed over Amelia. How could their lives be going on as normal? No doubt Sergeant Halliday got up that morning, rising from the arms of a husband or lover, showered, perhaps had tea brought to her while she was doing so, breakfasted together with him – or perhaps he cooked while she got the children ready. Amelia didn't know. At any rate she would have woken to a world little different to the one she lived in yesterday. As for Constable Bain, he too would have shaved and showered, perhaps humming to himself, stopping off for the takeaway coffee he was holding in his hand. He placed it behind a bin as if Amelia had caught him smoking a spliff.

Amelia wanted to launch herself at them, pummel them with her fists. She had to dig her nails into the palms of her hands to stop herself.

'We'll go through in a moment,' Sergeant Halliday said, and took a breath. 'You do know your daughter has had a post-mortem?'

Someone in a white coat got up this morning, his life unchanged, took a knife to her child's scalp, peeled down her face, opened her skull, removed her brain and other organs, and took samples before squashing them back in and sewing them up.

She should have been there for Fiona, holding her hand, murmuring to her. She should have been there.

Her heart felt as if someone had reached in through her chest wall, pulled it out and taken a cheese grater to it. It took everything she had left to stop the silent scream that was reverberating around her head from escaping and ringing through the room.

The door opened and the pathologist stepped out. To Amelia's surprise she was young, not much older than her. She took Amelia's hands in hers. 'I am so very sorry, Mrs Simpson.' There was no mistaking the pity in her voice.

'I'm Dr Katherine MacDonald.' She gave Amelia's hands a

gentle squeeze. 'I don't have children,' she said softly, 'but I have looked after your daughter as if she were mine.'

Looked after? For a second, a blissful, giddy second, Amelia thought she meant that Fiona was still alive – that it wasn't a mortuary they were about to enter, but a small ward, where she had been caring for her child until such time Amelia could come and take her home.

'She has a bandage on her head,' the doctor continued. 'I'm sorry about that – but otherwise she looks as if she's asleep.'

'Ready?' Sergeant Halliday asked. Amelia's feet felt as if they were stuck to the floor.

Amelia's father rested his hand on her shoulder. 'You don't have to do this. I can do it for you.' He looked at Sergeant Halliday, who nodded.

Filled with a momentous fury, Amelia rounded on her father. 'It is my job,' she ground out. 'I am her mother.' Until she saw Fiona for herself, she would not accept she was dead.

Dr MacDonald opened the door and stood aside. Beyond her Amelia saw a trolley, with a small, sheeted body. She stepped forward, and the others followed behind her.

The pathologist stood at the head of the trolley. Her hand hovered over it, and she looked at Amelia. 'Ready?' she asked.

She would never, ever be ready. But once again she nodded. Her head felt too heavy for her neck, she was gripping her hands together so tightly she'd drawn blood. Dr MacDonald lifted the sheet, exposing the head of the body underneath. Amelia felt another flare of hope. It didn't look like Fiona – always-in-motion Fiona – her face usually split in a wide grin. This face was pale as marble except for the blue-tinged lips. Her eyes were closed, her fair hair covered by the bandage Amelia was warned about. Her heart might have splintered before, but now it was as if someone had taken a knife, plunged it into her guts and was twisting it around and around.

She clamped both hands over her mouth to trap her screams inside.

They waited silently. Amelia gathered herself and reached out to touch her daughter's cheek. It was cold, waxy underneath her fingertips.

'Is this your daughter, Mrs Simpson?' Sergeant Halliday asked.

Her face was moving in and out of focus.

'Yes,' Dad answered for her. 'It's Fiona.'

The doctor made to cover her little girl's face with the sheet again, and when a whimper escaped Amelia, the doctor stopped. Amelia reached under the sheet until she found Fiona's cold, white hand. If she could, she'd let the breath and blood flow from her body into her child's. She closed her eyes and let herself believe that, as long as she clung to her daughter's hand, she would never have to say goodbye.

Amelia had no idea how long she stayed on her knees– it could have been minutes or hours. Eventually she got up, using the plaque for support as if she were an old woman. Part of her wanted to get into the car and turn it round, never ever to come back, but another, stronger part needed to see where the murders took place.

Leaving the car where it was, she followed the road, searching for evidence of the ruins. A couple of hundred yards up the road, almost hidden by bushes and vegetation, she found an overgrown path. If she hadn't been looking for it, she'd never have known it was there. She picked her way down. The walls of the destroyed homes were pockmarked with bullet holes. She ran her fingers along the stone, wondering which one had been Margherita's home.

Vallucciole hadn't been forgotten. Among the ruins and rubble someone had made a garden in an empty plot, and nestled in crannies in each of the ruined houses were flickering candles – lights for the dead. Amelia's heart felt as if was about to explode. People still came here to remember their loved ones.

Amazingly a house still stood amid the ruins, and it looked as if it was occupied. Washing hung in the back yard and the windows were curtained. Perhaps one of the villagers had survived? A son who was away fighting? A woman gone to the well to fetch water? But who would continue to live in a place filled with so much pain and horror? Perhaps someone had bought the house to use as a second home, not knowing what they were purchasing?

Amelia knocked on the door but got no reply. She circled the house, peering in the windows. If anyone did live here, they weren't at home.

THIRTY-SEVEN

Over the next few days Amelia could barely function. She told herself repeatedly not to think of Fiona or the murdered children of Vallucciole. But she couldn't stop. Like the days, weeks and months following the accident, she couldn't find the will or energy to shower or dress. Instead, she wandered the castello like one of its ghosts.

They were all around her. Dante in his signature red cap stood by the window looking towards Florence, dreaming of his Beatrice; the Warrior Abbess, her dark cloak gathered around her, haunted Amelia's bedroom, once her own. There were others she couldn't name: women in red and purple velvet, hair gathered up in gold-braided net. There were children too, playing in the castle grounds or running up and down the stairs, brandishing wooden swords. The castle walls rang with the sounds of their laughter.

Most of all it was Flavia she saw. She was everywhere, always by Amelia's side.

Not all of these ghostly presences were benign. Vincenzo in his black shirt was there too, leaving a trail of evil in his wake.

At first Amelia thought them creations of her over-imaginative brain, but they'd become more real to her than she was to herself, and she'd begun to believe that if she let them live with her, soon they'd be joined by the one she longed for most.

She lay in bed clutching her daughter's photograph, her thoughts spinning from Fiona to Margherita and her children and back to Flavia. She knew she was sinking back into that deep, dark hole she'd only so recently pulled herself out from. She also knew if she went under this time she might never find the will to climb out.

She kept hearing Flavia's voice in her head – the woman would *not* leave her alone. *Don't let me down, don't let everyone down. You can get through this. You must. Be brave.*

If only she could.

Her fingers found her father's pendant, and it was as if some of Flavia's courage flooded into her. Flavia was right. She couldn't hide from life forever.

Amelia pushed the bedcovers aside. She owed it to her daughter not to give up, however much she wanted to.

She hauled herself into the shower and stayed there long after it had run cold. She dressed and forced down some bread and coffee, thinking hard. What did Flavia want her to do?

Mug in hand, she picked up the pages that had been ripped out of Flavia's diary and took one over to the window seat. Something had jarred when she'd read one of the entries. What had it been? She read through them again. She was almost at the end when... Bingo!

Flavia had named the wrong artist when she'd talked about hiding the triptych – the same one that still hung in the church in Stia. The first time she'd mentioned the painting she'd attributed it to Bicci di Lorenzo, which was correct. The second time, when she'd been talking about moving the painting to Stia, she'd attributed it to Lorenzo di Bicci, who was also an artist – the father of Bicci di Lorenzo, as it happened. It was an easy mistake for some, but not for Flavia, who not only knew her artists but this particular painting well.

Amelia's mind raced. Flavia had written about hiding something in plain sight. Could the painting hold the clue?

Too filled with restless energy to drive, she jogged down to Stia and came to a panting halt in front of the church. It was lunchtime so the streets were almost deserted. Hopefully the church would be empty too.

The heavy doors opened with a groan, and Amelia plunged into the cool, incense- scented gloom of the church and fumbled for the light.

Sucking in a breath, she stood in front of the painting. If she was wrong, if it was alarmed, she was about to get herself into a whole world of trouble.

She inched closer, hardly daring to breathe, ready to bolt if the alarm went off.

She was right in front of it, and the alarm still hadn't sounded. Unless it was silent, wired directly to the police? Even if it was, it would take time for them to get here.

Amelia took a steadying breath. If there was a clue in the actual painting, she couldn't work out what it was. She ran her fingers along the sides of the frame. The triptych stood ever-so-slightly clear of the wall, and she tucked her fingertips behind it, feeling along the backing paper until, along one edge, she felt a piece that had come away. She checked behind her, but she was still completely alone. Using her fingers as pincers, she inserted them into the space. When they connected with a sharp edge, she eased her hand out. It was a folded manila envelope. She took the package over to a pew and opened it to find a sheaf of yellowed parchment filled with barely discernible writing in faded ink. But it was the sight of Flavia's handwriting, cramped and blotched in places as if by tears, on the back of the envelope that made her pulse leap. Heart in mouth, she started to read.

THIRTY-EIGHT

FLAVIA

13 April 1944

Dressed head to toe in black, her hair hidden by a woollen hat, Flavia reached under her jacket to tuck her pistol into the waistband of her trousers. The German soldiers, as was their habit, had stayed up late drinking and so she had been forced to wait, anxiously pacing the ramparts until she was sure they were, apart from the single guard, asleep.

It had been three in the morning before she was able to set off towards Vallucciole. The journey took forever. The moonless night was pitch black, but she was reluctant to use a torch in case anyone saw the light. But without the familiar landmarks to guide her, she became disoriented, discovering once to her frustration and panic that she'd walked in a circle, wasting time she didn't have. She had to get to the village before the Germans. Throwing caution to the wind she started to run, tripped, and crashed to the ground. Tears stung her eyes. She wanted to howl with frustration.

She stayed there, wasting more precious minutes, gulping for air. Terrified the sound of her fall might have attracted the attention of a German soldier, she staggered to her feet, biting down on her lip to stop herself crying out when she put her weight on her ankle. She had to keep going. She couldn't risk not getting there in time. She hobbled on, focussing on putting one foot in front of the other, telling herself that if only she could make this step, then the next, she could make it all the way.

She kept praying to God to keep everyone safe.

She knew she was near the village when its small church emerged from the darkness. Almost immediately her relief turned to despair when she heard something that turned her blood to ice: the rumble of German engines coming up the valley. They weren't due until dawn! Had Roberto deliberately misled her? She had to go faster. Had to get to the village before them.

Suddenly someone stepped out of the dark and clamped a hand over her mouth, pulling her against him. She struggled, but his grip was too strong.

'It's me, Flavia. For God's sake, keep still,' Luca said in her ear. Only then did she recognise his unique smell of woodsmoke and hay.

Dizzy with relief, she sank against him; she probably would have fallen to her knees if he hadn't held her. She let herself relax for a moment in the safety of his arms.

'How did you know it was me?' she whispered, turning to face him.

Even in the dark she could see his smile. 'I would know you anywhere.' Then he grew serious. 'What the hell are you doing out here on your own? In the middle of the night!'

She grabbed him by the arms. 'Where have you been? I've been trying to find you.'

'I've just come back from taking some men over the mountains. Why? What's the matter? Are you all right? Is the baby...?'

'No, no. I'm fine. So is the baby.' She quickly filled him in on Roberto's visit to the castello, about the killing of the German soldiers and the plan to seek retribution on the villagers.

'It will be light soon,' she hurried on. 'The Germans are on their way. We don't have long. We have to tell everyone to hide.'

To her relief, he grasped the urgency of the situation immediately. 'Fuck. I hadn't heard about the German soldiers. That's not good. Some of the other partisan groups don't always think before they act. Come on, we need to get moving.' He grabbed her hand and tugged her along.

With Luca leading the way they made much better progress, but the sky began to inexorably lighten. They were almost at Vallucciole when Luca yanked her down behind a tree. To Flavia's horror she saw army trucks parked by the side of the road. The Germans were already there and must have been for some time. The sound of voices carried up to them, the actual words indistinguishable to Flavia.

They crept closer until they were able to see what was happening. The villagers had been dragged from their beds and herded outside, the men with shirts half tucked in, braces hanging loose, the women in nightgowns, feet thrust hastily into slippers, holding babies in their arms and older children by the hand. The rising sun was turning the pigeon-grey sky blue. Margherita was there too with little Flavia and Niccolo's nonna, who had to be supported by Margherita. The men were made to stand with their hands laced behind their necks. Flavia saw Paolo, Niccolo's younger brother, among them. The soldiers prodded them with their rifle butts, shouting questions at them. Flavia clearly heard the word *partisan* above the crying of the women and children. The village men stared back in stubborn silence.

The German soldiers yelled at the men to form a line and, using their bayonets, directed them up the hill. An old man fell down. Paolo helped him back to his feet.

The line started off, some of the soldiers going with them, the remainder staying behind.

'Wait here,' Luca said, unhooking his rifle from his shoulder. He looked at her for a long moment. 'Go back to the castello – as quickly and as quietly as you can.'

Realising what he intended, she was gripped by terror. She clutched his arm, certain if he went she would never see him again.

'What can you do?' she pleaded. 'There are too many of them.'

He looked across to the village and was quiet for a while. Pain blossomed in her chest as she realised he was focussing on what he needed to do. He turned back to her, and as he looked deep into her eyes regret darkened his. He held her face between his hands. 'I love you. I will always love you. These last months have been the happiest of my life...'

'No, please, don't ...' She shook her head from side to side – she wasn't ready for this, she wasn't ready to lose him, would never be ready. But deep inside she knew begging him was hopeless.

'Promise me you will go home.'

She sniffed the tears away and lifted her chin. 'I'm coming with you.' She managed a twisted smile. 'Whither thou goest...'

'You can't,' he said urgently. 'Cara, you mustn't! Whatever happens you have to stay alive. Not just for my sake but for our child's. You have to promise me.'

Torn, she looked up at him in anguish.

'I can face anything,' he continued, 'as long as I know that you and our child live.' Dropping his hands to her hips, he bent, pressing his lips first to her stomach and then to her mouth. He gave her one last long look, brushing her tears away with the pad of his thumb. Before she could stop him, he turned away and crouching low, his rifle by his side, ran along the road.

Flavia stayed where she was. Despite her promise to Luca, she couldn't go back to the castello until she knew everyone was safe. She dragged her gaze back to the village. It was then that she saw them. Roberto and Vincenzo. They were standing by the German officer, both clearly party to what was going on. Anger and disbelief coiled inside her chest. How could they? These villagers were their people. Fellow Italians.

The next bit happened quickly. Two soldiers grabbed one of the younger women – Flavia recognised her as Victoria, a feisty brunette – and dragged her away. Another soldier took hold of a pleading woman – Maria, a mother of three – threw her to the ground, pulled her nightgown above her head and dropped on top of her. It was as if that was the signal. More and more soldiers grabbed women and, as they screamed and clawed at them, responded with laughter, undoing their belts with one hand while hanging onto their rifles with the other. After their trousers dropped to their ankles they sprawled on top of the women. Vincenzo and Roberto stood together, slightly apart from the German soldiers, and watched. While this was happening, the other soldiers were lining the older women and children against the walls of the houses.

Flavia's gaze focussed in on Margherita, who watched in horror; little Flavia was pressed between her and her nonna. Vincenzo reached for Margherita, yanking her away from her hysterical daughter. When Margherita spat in his face, he kicked her legs from underneath her, sending her crashing to the ground. Using her elbows to propel her, Margherita scrambled away from him. Little Flavia clung to the skirts of her nonna, screaming in terror.

As if sensing her presence, Vincenzo looked towards where Flavia was concealed. She ducked down behind the rock she was hiding behind. But, unable to tear her eyes away from the scene unfolding in front of her, she peered over the top. A smirking Vincenzo was standing over Margherita, his revolver pointed at her head as he unbuttoned his belt.

Roberto stepped between his sister and Vincenzo. He seemed to be arguing with his superior officer. Roberto turned his back on Vincenzo and leaned down towards his sister as if to help her to her feet. Calmly, Vincenzo raised his weapon and shot him in the back of the head. Roberto landed on top of Margherita. Shoving Roberto's lifeless body away with his foot, Vincenzo grabbed Margherita again, pinning her to the ground with his body. She fought him like a tigress, biting, scratching and kicking, pummelling him with her small fists. She was no match for him.

Flavia had to do something. She couldn't stay here and do nothing. She had to make the German officer see sense. Beg, if that was what it took.

She'd only gone a couple of feet when she heard gunfire.

Crouching down, she peeked through a bush. To her horror, the Germans were shooting the women they'd just raped as well as the older women and children who had been forced to watch.

White-hot rage exploded in Flavia, obliterating any thought or reason. She lurched to her feet, pulling her pistol from the waistband of her trousers. It was unlikely she could kill them all, but she might take one of them, preferably Vincenzo, before they saw her coming.

Before she could move, there were more shots – coming from above the village – and the head of the soldier next to Vincenzo exploded in a cloud of red mist. Then another soldier fell. And another.

Luca strode into Flavia's field of vision, his rifle held in front of him. He fired steadily, not even trying to hide himself.

Flavia was ready to run to him, to stand next him, to die alongside him if need be. Vincenzo looked her way again and smiled. Continuing to look in her direction, he lifted his revolver and shot Luca in the chest.

Still her husband kept going. Her screams were drowned out by more gunfire and Luca, her darling Luca, fell to his knees. He tried to get up, managed, was shot again.

Just as Flavia was about to launch herself forward, she was knocked to the ground, her face pressed into the dank earth. She couldn't cry out, could barely breathe.

'Don't move,' a voice begged. 'There is nothing that you or I can do.'

She struggled but the man was too strong, keeping her body pinned to the ground with his. The shots and screams seemed to go on forever. Flavia felt the man's body shake as he cried.

Then the sounds below stopped. The man got off from on top of her. It was Paolo, Niccolo's brother. They lay there for a very long time, both sobbing.

It was the smell of smoke that roused them. They stumbled to their knees and peered through the bush. The Germans were setting the village alight. Bodies – so many bodies – women, children and old men, including Luca, Margherita and little Flavia, were lying on the ground, unmoving. It took everything Flavia had not to run down to the village. Some of them might still be alive, could still be saved.

Flavia realised she hadn't seen Margherita's young son. 'Where's Lazzero, Paolo? Do you know? Did they take him somewhere?' Flames leapt in the sky.

'I didn't see him outside. Maybe he's hiding.'

Please God, let that be the case.

'The other men they took away, where are they?' she asked Paolo through chattering teeth.

'All dead. They led us up the hill. We thought they were taking us somewhere to work for them. But it was to execute us.'

'How did you get away?'

'I fell. Rolled down the hill. But I was lucky to have the only German with a conscience come after me. He shouted to his fellow soldiers that I was dead and told me to run.'

They waited until the German soldiers got back into their trucks and drove away. The moment they were sure they were gone, they hurried down to the village, praying to find someone alive.

But there was no one. No one to be saved. Flavia gathered Luca's broken, blood-soaked body in her arms, raining kisses on his face, whispering that she loved him, until Paolo pulled her away. Margherita, her darling friend, was lying on her back, the front of her blouse saturated with blood, her skirt still raised above her hips. Little Flavia lay next to her nonna, a bullet hole in her forehead, her eyes wide open. Flavia pulled Margherita's skirt down and closed Flavia's eyes. Then she moved the little girl's body close to her mother, wrapping Margherita's arms around her so that she could hold her daughter one last time. She felt numb, almost as if she were watching herself from a distance, and had to fight the impulse to lie down beside them, stay with them, die with them.

But she couldn't. Her unborn baby depended on her. But Lazzero – where was he? She couldn't see him among the dead.

Was his body lying somewhere else? Had he been hiding inside as Paolo suggested, discovered by the Germans in their final sweep of the houses and executed? Dead or alive, she had to find him.

Paolo kept shouting that they had to go. Not wanting to leave evidence of what they'd done, the soldiers could come back at any moment to remove any trace of the massacre.

Still the horror wasn't over. While they'd been checking for signs of life, one of the soldiers Luca had shot raised his hand off the ground and fired at Paolo, killing him instantly. The soldier looked at Flavia, pointed his weapon in her direction and squeezed the trigger. Nothing happened. Either the mechanism had jammed or he'd run out of bullets.

An icy calm washed over her. Very deliberately Flavia took the pistol from the waistband of her trousers, stood over him and, her gaze never leaving his, shot him between the eyes. She felt numb – only vaguely aware of her weapon dropping from her nerveless fingers.

She forced herself to focus. She had to leave lest the Germans returned. But not before she'd found Lazzero.

Acrid smoke stinging her eyes, she ran inside Margherita's house, one of the few not burning, calling his name. She tried not to think of all the happy hours she'd spent in this home, around this kitchen table, with people she loved. All dead now. She had to focus.

Where would a child hide? She checked under the bed in the room Margherita had shared with her family, and in the wardrobe. No one there. Then she heard it. The muffled sound of sobbing. Coming from the flour chest. She opened it to find Lazzero, his arms folded over his bent head, tremors coursing through his body.

'Lazzero,' she cried. *Thank God.*

He raised his pale, snot-covered face. 'Mama! I want my Mama!'

Flavia ached for him, but there was no time to talk to him, no time to even comfort him.

'You must come with me, Lazzero,' she said firmly, putting her own grief aside. She owed it to Margherita to save her son. There would be time to mourn later. When she lifted him out of the flour chest he grabbed onto her, wrapping his legs around her body, and his arms so tightly around her neck Flavia could barely breathe. Flavia hugged him back. After a moment she set him on the ground and gripped him by the shoulders. 'We have to go from here. You need to be a brave boy and do everything I say. Can you do that?'

Lazzero nodded mutely.

'Keep your eyes closed,' she said, lifting him back into her arms. 'No matter what happens, don't open them.'

Knowing she couldn't trust him not to, she pressed his head into her shoulder and covered his eyes with the palm of her hand. He was heavy, and she prayed she wouldn't drop him. As they passed by the bodies of his mother, sister and Luca, she clenched her jaw so she wouldn't cry out.

She couldn't bear to leave them unburied, but she hoped, in time, when it was safe, the partisans would come and take care of Luca and the rest of the villagers.

While she carried Lazzero through the forest she forced her thoughts away from what she'd just witnessed and concentrated on how to keep him safe. If Vincenzo discovered the boy had survived, he would surely hunt him down. He would never risk leaving a witness, however old, alive.

Yesterday she would never have believed that anyone would kill a child. Now she knew differently. Vincenzo wouldn't want to take the chance that Lazzero would repeat what he'd seen – not if he hoped to live in Italy when all this was over. Had Vincenzo seen her? Although she didn't think so, she couldn't be sure. He knew she was Lazzero's godmother. When he didn't find him, he might look for them both at the castello.

Where could she be certain Lazzero would be safe? It came to her in a flash. In plain sight. It had worked so far with the painting, and it could work with a child. If there was a way to get him to Julia's villa, no one would pay attention to one more little boy, especially one under a different name. When it was all over Flavia would make sure he was reunited with what remained of Margherita's family.

She couldn't risk taking him to Fiesole today. There was bound to be extra German activity on the roads and in the woods. So she would leave him at the convent in Pratovecchio and ask the nuns to care for him until she could take him to Julia's herself.

Taking care not to make any noise, she carried Lazzero through the forest, keeping an eye out for Germans. She had Luca to thank that she knew exactly how to travel without being seen. The sounds of trucks and motorbikes, as well as thick, dark plumes of smoke all along the valley, told her that Vallucciole hadn't been the only village to suffer from the Nazis' quest for revenge.

Whenever her thoughts turned to what happened, she pushed them away. She couldn't break now. Not until Lazzero was safe.

It was after midday by the time they reached the convent in Pratovecchio.

Sister Magdalena opened the door and ushered her in.

Lazzero still clung to Flavia like a limpet. He hadn't said a word since she'd found him in the flour chest. She placed him on his feet and crouched down until she was at his eye level. 'Always remember that your mama loved you very much. I promise to come back for you as soon as I can.' She hugged him tightly. 'Do what the nuns say. Be a good boy.'

A nun took Lazzero by the hand and led him away. He looked over his shoulder, staring back at Flavia with wide, shocked eyes until he disappeared from sight.

As briefly and as calmly as she could, Flavia told Sister Magdalena what had happened. The nun crossed herself, her face creasing in distress.

'I'll come back for the child later,' Flavia said. 'If for any reason I don't return by tomorrow night, please find a way to get him to the Villa Bencista.' She told the nun what name to use if she did.

The nun nodded. They'd devised numerous ways of getting fugitives to safety in these troubled times. 'And you, my dear? You'll be safer here too.'

'Thank you, Sister. I'll be back as soon as I can.' The convent would provide sanctuary for her and her baby until the horror was over. First, she needed to return to the castello one last time.

Taking the back lanes Flavia walked as swiftly as she dared without attracting attention. She forced the images of what she'd witnessed from her mind. She needed to keep focussed if she was to make it back to the convent.

To her dismay, Stia was abuzz with German soldiers checking the locals' papers before barking at them to move on. She'd never make it to the castello without the cover of darkness.

Walking confidently, but glad her hair was hidden by her hat, Flavia joined a group of women who'd just had their documents checked, and followed them into the church.

Crossing herself, she slipped into a pew. She would be safe here until night fell.

Dropping to her knees, she buried her face in her hands. How could God have allowed such evil to happen? She hoped Vincenzo and the Nazis would burn in hell for what they did. But she wanted Vincenzo to suffer on earth too. After all this was over, he had to be held to account. People needed to know his role in the massacre at Vallucciole.

She knew what she had to do to try and make sure that happened. When the villagers had agreed to hide the painting of the Annunciation in this church, she'd hidden the document she'd found between the painting and its backing paper. Waiting until the other women had left and she was alone, she retrieved the manila envelope from behind the painting and finding a pen left near the altar started writing. Tears streamed down her cheeks, splashing on her words.

When she was finished she sat for a while, thinking. Appreciating there was a chance she might be killed during the war, after she'd secreted the document she'd found behind the painting she'd put a clue in her diary, directing whoever might read it – her godmother, she imagined – to the painting.

If she didn't make it through the war, when all this was over the triptych would be returned to the church in Porciano and her account would be found then. One way or another, the truth would be told and, God willing, Vincenzo made to pay for what he'd done.

THIRTY-NINE

AMELIA

Amelia was shaking and crying as she finished Flavia's account. She wiped her face with the sleeve of her T-shirt. For Flavia to have her husband, godchild and best friend killed in front of her! The sheer horror of witnessing what she did and being unable to prevent any of it. The cold-blooded murder of children... The rape of women before they too were killed. Images like that would stay with a person forever.

She felt Flavia's shock, disbelief and grief; her anguish and anger. Amelia had experienced every one of these emotions over the last months. No wonder she'd felt such an affinity with Flavia. Was this why Flavia had led Amelia to her diaries, this church, her account? So that Amelia could be the instrument of her revenge?

Why did Amelia have to go searching for this? Didn't she have enough pain in her own life without actively seeking more? But, like it or not, she was all in now.

She dug her fingernails into the palms of her hands and forced herself to think calmly and logically.

The papers in the envelope had to be what Lucrezia asked Flavia to keep safe. Clever, resourceful, brave Flavia had hidden the diaries with the clue about the painting in case something happened to her.

Amelia was more convinced than ever that Flavia didn't kill herself. Her baby was all she had left of Luca, and she'd have done anything to protect her child. She'd also promised Lazzero she would come back for him. From what Amelia had learned about Flavia, she was certain she would have done everything in her power to keep that promise. Where was Lazzero now? How old would he be? Was he still alive? Had he made it to safety? She wanted, *needed*, to know.

She forced herself to read Flavia's account again. Vincenzo was a monster. Had he ever paid for what he'd done?

Rosina would be the obvious person to ask, but Alessandra's father-in-law had made it clear Amelia was not welcome at the farm. She must know Roberto was at Vallucciole during the massacre, but why would she think she was in any way to blame for what had happened? Did she know that at the last he'd tried to save his sister – paying with his life in the process?

Another thought crossed her mind – could Alessandra's father-in-law be Lazzero, raised by Signora Rossi, after Margherita's death?

Amelia got up from the pew feeling like an old woman. She couldn't bring Fiona back to life but maybe she could do something about what had happened to Luca, Margherita, her children and the rest of the innocent people who'd been slaughtered. Flavia had done her part, now it was time for Amelia to do hers.

All she had to do was work out how.

She could show the account to Beatrice and Alessandra's father-in-law, or Rosina herself. Leave it to them to do with it whatever they wanted. Let them decide whether Vincenzo – if he was even still alive – should be brought to justice. As far as Amelia was aware there was no statute of limitations on war crimes.

Still reeling from what she'd read, she trudged up the path back to the castello.

Flavia had every intention of making a life for herself and her child. Why, then, did she die? And when? Before or after her child had been born? It could have been months, even years later. In which case where was her baby? Was he, or she, still alive?

Before she decided what to do, Amelia needed to find out what had happened to Vincenzo. Did he have family still living who would talk to her? If not, was there anyone who might be able to tell her more about him? Perhaps he'd been made to face his crimes back in the forties, or was killed during the war. In which case what would be the point of raking up the past? Before she approached anyone closely connected to the massacre, she required more information.

Immediately she thought of Benedetto. He was a researcher and bound to know how to find out about Vincenzo. Remembering that he put his number into her mobile, she rummaged in her bag for her phone and rang his number.

He picked up straight away. 'Pronto.'

'Benedetto, it's Amelia.'

'Amelia! I was hoping you'd call. How are you getting on at the castello? Found anything interesting yet?'

She'd completely forgotten about the manila envelope and its contents, having shoved it in her bag without examining it. 'Possibly. I have no idea whether it's of value, but I think Flavia believed it might be.'

'What is it? Can't you tell me more?'

The document could wait. 'Of course. But not until I speak to Beatrice. However, that's not the reason I'm calling. You said you're a researcher for your brother.'

'I did. I am.' He sounded unusually unsure.

'I'm assuming then that you know where to find information about Italian collaborators during World War Two?'

'What sort of information?' he asked, sounding even more wary.

'I want to trace someone Beatrice's mother and her family once knew. Someone your father might have known, in fact. A Vincenzo Lambini. He was a major in Mussolini's army before siding with the Germans after the Armistice.'

There was a long pause on the other end of the line, and Amelia wondered for a moment if they'd been cut off.

'Lambini is a common surname. Is there anything else you can tell me about him? Do you have a rank? Or a photo? Or anything else that might help?'

'He was a Blackshirt.'

There was another long silence.

'It's not much to go on,' Benedetto said finally. 'Could I ask why you're interested in him?'

'I'd prefer to keep that to myself for the moment. All I can say is that it is to do with the war.'

'Are you sure it's your place to be digging into the past?' Benedetto's voice had turned as chilly as a Scottish winter.

'I only want to know what happened to him, that's all.'

'Okay. I'll do what I can. I'll call you back if I find something.'

Before she had the chance to thank him, he disconnected. Back inside the castello, Amelia took another shower and dressed in fresh clothes. She was going to see Father Michael again. By now he might have found a date of death for Flavia or a register of the birth of her baby. Lifting her bag from the kitchen table, she placed the papers inside and headed for her car.

FORTY

Amelia found Father Michael in one of the smaller buildings used for meditation. He was sitting on a cushion surrounded by a group of youngsters. When he saw her, he lifted a finger to indicate she should give him a few minutes, so she wandered back into the garden and sat on one of the benches overlooking the valley.

Two swallows swooped and dived in an aerobatic dance, and the noise in her head quietened. No wonder people flocked to Father Michael's church.

'Hello,' his soft voice came from behind her. She felt his weight settle next to her on the bench. They sat in silence while she considered what to say and how to say it.

He spoke first. 'I think, this time, you wish to talk to me. Am I correct?'

She nodded.

He smiled. 'In that case, let's have that tea.'

They walked back across the road, down a little path that took them along the side of the church and towards a house. These gardens were beautiful too. There were more benches and tables dotted around. Small groups of young people sat talking quietly, or laughing, or just reading books. They looked up, acknowledging Amelia and Father Michael as they walked past and into the house.

'You have visitors?'

'I keep my house open. Anyone who needs solace can come here. Tourists, the homeless, the needy, the distressed, they can all stay for however long they like.'

It crossed Amelia's mind he could be running a secret cult. Everyone she'd seen so far was young, and no doubt easily impressed by this good-looking, charismatic man.

'How do you afford it all?'

'The church is busy, and busy churches bring in donations. It's not as expensive as you would think. People who come to stay often bring their own food or help in the gardens where we grow vegetables.' He gestured to the trees surrounding the house. 'We have figs, plums, apples. Apricots too. All a person has to do is reach a hand out, and God provides.' His mouth twisted into a mischievous smile. 'But our guests could not survive on fruit alone, so the women from the nearby villages bring extra food and take away sheets to be washed. Some of them have family members they don't see and are happy to have these kids to care for.'

Amelia was struck by how simple he made it sound; he was hardly more than a kid himself.

Again, as if he could read her mind, Father Michael smiled. 'I'm thirty. Not too old to forget what it is like to be young, but not too young to know where the boundaries between a priest and a troubled soul should be. What else should a church be if it can't offer refuge to those who need it? For whatever reason.'

It was clear he meant every word.

It was cool inside his house. He led her into the kitchen and, as they entered, a group of youngsters sitting around the table rose silently and left.

'I don't want to chase them out,' Amelia protested.

'They know when I bring someone inside it's probably because I wish to speak to them or them to me in private. This kitchen is my most popular confessional. I have heard more secrets, absorbed more pain here than anywhere else.'

Amelia took a seat at the table while he made tea. She felt the beginning of another panic attack, and for a moment considered bolting. She dug her nails into the palms of her hands in an attempt to ward it off. She was here for a purpose and couldn't leave until she found out what she wanted to know.

As if he knew she needed time to compose herself he waited until they both had steaming mugs in front of them before he leant forward. 'I'm all ears.'

'Did you find any record of Flavia Corsi?' she plunged straight in.

'As a matter of fact I did. I wrote it down.' He flicked through a notebook until he found the right page. 'Here it is.' He looked up. 'She married a Luca Rossi in the church on seventeenth of March 1944. There is a date of death too. The thirteenth of April 1944.'

The same day as the massacre at Vallucciole. Flavia and Luca were only married three short weeks! Her blood chilled as realisation hit. Had she got it all wrong? Had Flavia taken her own life after all? Was the loss of Luca and Margherita in the end too much to bear? No. She couldn't accept that.

'I've found evidence of a crime that was committed here in the Casentino during the war,' Amelia continued. 'Stuff that might not be in the public domain.'

'What sort of evidence?' he asked, sounding perplexed.

'It's an eyewitness report of what happened at Vallucciole. Do you know that story?'

'Everyone in the Casentino knows about Vallucciole. Many people had relatives who lived there.'

'The account was written by Flavia. She witnessed the massacre. She hid it because she thought one of the perpetrators might have known she'd seen everything, and was frightened he'd find a way to silence her.' Was that what had happened? Had Flavia been killed for what she knew?

He looked intrigued. 'The Germans were very good at covering their tracks, but even they couldn't cover up something as big as Vallucciole. Everyone knows they were responsible.'

'It wasn't just German soldiers who were there.' Amelia went on to tell him everything she'd discovered, leaving nothing out, including that Margherita's son had witnessed the death of his mother and sister before being rescued by Flavia.

When she finished she saw her anguish reflected in his eyes. He stood and poured sherry into two small glasses, handing one to Amelia. 'You think Roberto told the Germans about Vallucciole's connection to the partisans?' He sat back down and regarded Amelia steadily. 'But Roberto warned Flavia, and he tried to prevent his sister being raped. It sounds as if he had no idea the Germans intended a massacre.'

Amelia nodded. 'I agree. There wasn't much love lost between the brothers, but I don't think Roberto wanted Luca dead. Roberto was only Vincenzo's driver. He might not have known the full extent of what was intended. I can't imagine he expected the Germans to murder his sister and her children, and in the end he died trying to save Margherita. Whatever role he played, at least he atoned in some way. However, there is no excuse, no mitigating factors as far as Vincenzo is concerned. He didn't like being rejected by Flavia, couldn't tolerate her disdain for him. I think he knew about her and Luca. Maybe he wanted Flavia to go to Vallucciole, knowing her presence would draw Luca. He tried to rape Margherita and shot Roberto for trying to stop him. Even if he wasn't an active participant in the rest of the murders, he stood there and watched. That makes him as guilty as the Germans, in my book.'

'This Vincenzo was a Blackshirt?'

'Yes. When Italy changed sides he remained with the German army.'

A look of revulsion, quickly suppressed, crossed Father Michael's face. 'I understand the Germans were always hunting the mountain villages for partisans. And there was the killing of the German soldiers by partisans further down the valley. The Germans would have wanted retribution.' Father Michael leant forward. 'What do you intend to do?'

A cloud passed over the sun, draining the light from the kitchen. Amelia shivered.

'I'm going to find out who Vincenzo was and make sure the whole damn world knows what he did. I also intend to find out what happened to Flavia after she left the church. She was pregnant and a practising Catholic. She was determined to live for the sake of her baby. I don't believe she committed suicide. I think she might have been murdered.'

Father Michael continued to study Amelia for a long time, and once again she had the uncomfortable feeling he could see to her very core.

'What happened in Vallucciole was a sin against humanity,' he said. 'But horrible and tragic though it was, it is not what is eating you inside, is it?'

Amelia gasped and, as she did, everything she'd been holding in burst from her like a tsunami. At times the words poured out, at others she sobbed silently. She told him what she'd been unable to share with anyone – the truth behind what happened that last day with Fiona. That she didn't even say goodbye to her child.

At the final moment Fiona had decided she'd rather stay with Amelia than go with her father. But Amelia had needed her to go so she could meet her deadline. In the end she'd fastened her furious, wailing little girl into her car seat and told Cameron to drive. She'd never even kissed her goodbye. Let alone told her she loved her.

She told Father Michael how she'd felt so guilty she believed she didn't deserve to live, hadn't wanted to anyway. How Dad had found her drunk on the edge of the cliff outside her home and dragged her away. When she didn't want to be saved. She realised now that a chunk of her anger had been directed at Dad. Not just Cameron.

A truck had smashed into the rear door of the car on the side Fiona had been sitting in her car seat. Cameron had survived but had spent a couple of days in an induced coma in ICU.

She told Father Michael how their grief had torn them apart

instead of binding them together – how after leaving hospital Cameron had retreated into his pain, leaving her to cope on her own. How a few weeks after the funeral he'd moved back to London – despite her begging him to stay with her in the home they'd lived in as a family for too short a time. How after he'd left she'd refused to speak to him – blocked his number on her phone, set up a filter on her email in case he tried to contact her that way. How bloody furious she was with him, how hurt by his failure to deal with his own pain, let alone help her with hers.

Father Michael didn't say anything. Didn't take her hand to squeeze it. He simply pushed a box of tissues towards Amelia. There were no murmured empty platitudes. Just his comforting, accepting presence.

Eventually Amelia was all cried out. Only then did he speak.

'Let me get this right. You blame yourself for your daughter's death? You think that if you hadn't had a deadline she would have stayed home with you? You also believe that because you didn't kiss Fiona goodbye she died believing you didn't love her?'

Hearing the words, spoken like that, baldly, without the skirting around she'd become used to, made her howl again. She didn't think a person's body could hold so many tears. She must have cried a well in the last ten months.

'Yes,' she whispered eventually. 'Yes, I do.'

'Listen to me, Amelia,' Father Michael knelt by her side. Now he took her hands, forcing her to look at him. 'You did not kill your child. Neither did your husband. It was a terrible accident. You wouldn't be the first mother who handed over her child, grateful to have time to yourself. I imagine you told your daughter many, many times that you loved her. And that there were many more times when you showed her how much.'

The image of Fiona's tearful face pressed up against the window was branded into her memory. But yes, a day didn't go past when Amelia didn't tell her child she loved her. Memories of her little girl spooled through her head like a video. Bedtime, baking, reading, laughing, games of hide-and-seek, Fiona squealing with delight, bath time in a cloud of bubbles, cuddles and kisses. So many cuddles and kisses – as well as laughter. Father Michael was right. Fiona had known she was loved.

'And your husband,' he pressed. 'He didn't kill your child, either.'

Amelia knew that. Of course she did, but it hadn't stopped her anger towards him. After Cameron had been brought out of his coma, it had been up to Amelia to tell him that their little girl was dead. It was the second worst moment of her life. She knew Cameron wished he'd died instead of their child and that he felt responsible for what had happened, believing he should have found a way to avoid the crash. He'd turned away from Amelia, preferring to drown his grief in the bottom of a bottle. And if Amelia were honest, although police had determined the accident had been caused by the other driver texting at the wheel, she'd blamed Cameron too. If he'd been going slower, if he'd chosen a different route, he might have been able to avoid the lorry and their daughter wouldn't have died.

In the days following Fiona's funeral, Cameron wouldn't talk to her, hold her, would barely look at her. They'd wandered the house that had once been filled with love and laughter like two strangers. Instead of comforting each other, they'd turned inwards, focussing on coping with their own grief.

He'd spent more and more time out on his boat, and when he was at home he drank himself unconscious. Her anger had built until one day she'd exploded, unleashing her pain in a vomit of cruel, accusing words.

It had rocked her to the core that their love hadn't been enough to survive their child's death.

Unable to face the daily reminders of their daughter and the life she'd once cherished, Amelia had considered ending the pain by jumping from the cliff outside her home in Cove. Only her father's unexpected arrival at her house had prevented her.

The core of anger and resentment towards him that she'd clung to for so long began to soften as it dawned on her now that

Cameron had been as broken as she was – perhaps more so. They'd loved each other so much once – was it too late for them to find a way back to each other again?

'I can't begin to imagine your pain, Amelia,' Father Michael continued. 'I can see why you might be mad at God. I can see why you thought about taking your life.'

'I thought Catholics believe suicide is a sin.'

'I don't think anyone has the right to take a life, not even their own. That doesn't mean I can't understand what drives people to it. However' – he held up his hand as if to stop her contradicting him – 'I believe it was God's wish that your father found you before you could. I think He told him you were in trouble, and He brought your father to you. I also believe He brought you here. He will have forgiven you. All that is left is for you to forgive yourself.'

She started crying again. By the time she'd regained control of her voice, her tea had cooled to the point a greasy film had formed over the top. She took a small sip to moisten her throat. 'A person can believe in some sort of afterlife without believing in God, can't they?'

This time it was his turn to give a baffled shake of his head.

'I mean,' Amelia rushed on, as if his agreement would make all the difference, 'they say that we all have atoms of Einstein and even Hitler – all the dead people inside us. It's not too far a stretch to think that the atoms of my child – just like all the other dead people – are out there clumping into something else – another person perhaps.' She didn't tell him that she thought they might also just hang around keeping the form of their human host, like the ghosts that had come to her in the castle. Even Father Michael must have his limits, and Amelia had probably shocked him enough.

He gave her a gentle smile. 'Fiona will always be part of you. I think right now, for you, that has to be enough.'

They sat in silence. The turmoil inside Amelia stilled. She didn't know how long it would last, but for now it was enough.

'It's hard to imagine what it was like during the war – the fear, the horror of it all,' she said eventually.

'Even I sometimes wonder why God allowed – *allows* – innocents to be killed.'

Amelia raised an eyebrow. 'Your faith isn't absolute then?'

He smiled wryly. 'I have my dark moments too. But ultimately my faith remains strong. I believe God takes the pure and innocent early because they are pure and innocent.'

Amelia shook her head impatiently. 'I will never believe that. If there is a God, he would rout out and punish the evil. All those people who died during the war and the wars that came after. He took away the people they were meant to be, the children they were meant to have. I feel such rage at times, I think I'll implode.' Her voice dropped to a whisper. 'I want to stop feeling like this.' Yet, she was scared if she did it would mean she'd let Fiona go. She wasn't ready to say goodbye. She was stuck like those trapped in ice in Dante's vision of hell – unable to go back and unable to go forward.

'Perhaps you should speak to a doctor.'

She squinted against the sun that once more streamed through the window. 'I did. And it didn't help.'

'Then perhaps you should speak to God. Open your heart to Him. Ask Him to take this rage and despair from you. Ask Him to take some of your burden.'

She wished she could.

'I think a lot about revenge and retribution,' she told Father Michael, who had lapsed into silence.

'Are we back to talking about what happened in Vallucciole?'

She nodded.

'This Vincenzo Lambini may still be alive,' Father Michael said gently, 'and even if he isn't, he may well have family who know nothing about his activities during the war. It's not up to you to decide who deserves to be forgiven. It is up to our Heavenly Father to decide Vincenzo's fate.' A muscle ticked in his cheek. 'The war ripped this country in two. It took a long time for Italy to heal, and some believe it still hasn't healed properly. There are many who never want to think back to those days, who wish it all to be forgotten.'

'I'm aware of that,' Amelia replied, thinking of Rosina.

'Are you really prepared to be judge and jury?'

'I wouldn't be. I'd just be telling the truth of what happened.'

'But is it yours to tell? And how can you know that it is the only truth? For most of us it falls somewhere in between. Only God knows everything with any certainty. Only He has the right to judge. Many people were executed without a trial by the partisans after the Germans retreated. Was that not murder too? In war very few people come out with their hands completely clean of blood.'

Amelia thought of Flavia killing the soldier. She couldn't believe that Flavia should be punished for it. In life or death. And as for Roberto – did he deserve forgiveness for his final act? His last desperate attempt to save his sister and her small family's lives?

Notwithstanding, she was still determined to find Vincenzo. Alive or dead. 'Is there a list of men sentenced to death and executed by the partisans? If Vincenzo's name is on that, I won't take it any further.'

'I don't know if such a list exists. You'd have to speak to someone who is a war historian. Even then I suspect he may well have changed his name. Many war criminals did.'

Outside the kitchen Amelia heard muffled voices and restless footsteps.

'I'm sorry, Amelia, but I need to let them in to make their supper. I also need to get ready for mass. Would you care to join us?'

She managed a weak smile. 'Not today. Another time perhaps?'

'Whenever you are ready.' He gave her shoulder a brief squeeze. 'Come back, Amelia. Any time you need to talk – or if you just want to be quiet.'

'Whether I do or not, thank you for listening to me.'

He stood in front of her and made the sign of the cross. 'God bless and comfort you.'

On her way home Amelia stopped at the convent in Pratovecchio. The door was opened by a nun, her face wizened with age, her tiny frame so riddled with osteoporosis she was shaped like a question mark. Bent as she was, she barely reached Amelia's shoulder.

Amelia explained she was researching the history of the Corsi family and wondered if there was anyone who might have known the family during the war. It was a long shot but worth a try.

'Sister Magdalena might know. She has lived here the longest. Let me find out if she is available.'

Amelia waited in a sitting room with faded floral wallpaper on which several prints of the Pope and the Madonna and child hung.

Eventually the door opened and a nun, even older than the one Amelia had just met, entered. Although she leant on a walking stick, she seemed to float across the room. 'I'm Sister Magdalena. Sister Maria told me you wished to speak to me?'

'Thank you for making the time,' Amelia said after they were both seated. She gave the nun the same quick explanation of why she was there. 'I understand you might have known the Corsi family.'

The nun cocked her head to the side. 'Yes I did.'

'Did you know Flavia Corsi?'

Amelia held her breath while she waited for the nun to answer.

'Ah, Flavia. Yes, I knew her.' She smiled. 'It feels like a very long time ago.'

Amelia's heart kicked against her ribs. 'I don't suppose you know how she died?'

Sister Magdalena's expression darkened, and she crossed herself. 'She took her own life. It was very sad. I must say I was very surprised. Even though I saw her that day and she was deeply distressed.' The nun gave a grimace of regret. 'She must have been more distraught than I appreciated.'

Whatever the nun said, Amelia still wasn't ready to accept that. 'The last time you saw her, was it when she brought the little boy?' she asked.

Sister Magdalena lifted an eyebrow. 'You know about that?'

Amelia nodded.

'Flavia had brought us two women before then. Many monasteries and convents across Italy helped fugitives during the war when the Germans occupied Italy. We were no different.'

Amelia leant forward. 'What happened to the child? Do you remember?'

'I remember everything about those terrible days. Flavia promised she'd come back for him – that's what made it so strange when she didn't. She also said if for any reason she didn't come, we were to send him to friends of hers.' The elderly nun's eyes were bleak. 'She didn't come back for him, so as per her wishes we sent him to her friend's villa to be with the other children.'

'Was it the villa Bencista?'

She didn't hesitate. 'Yes. It still has the same name, although it is now a small hotel. It is in the outskirts of Fiesole.'

It was the same villa Flavia wrote about in her diary. Was it possible Julia or her descendants might still live there? Amelia felt a thrill of anticipation. If so, would they be able to tell her what happened to Lazzero?

As soon as she left the convent, Amelia phoned the Villa Bencista and booked a room for the following night.

Immediately she walked through the castello's front door she knew from the way the hairs on the back of her neck rose that someone had been inside while she'd been away – and might still be there.

'Hello?' she called out in Italian, and then again, more strongly, in English.

As she looked around, she sneezed. The sound reverberated

around the room. If the intruder were still there they'd have heard her.

At first, everything seemed to be exactly how she'd left it. The mock-up boards she'd just about finished were on the floor, the empty cardboard boxes stacked against the wall. Yet, something wasn't right. The tower of boxes weren't aligned perfectly the way she'd left them and there was the faint whiff of cologne. There was other evidence of someone having been there. The pen she always left on the table, because it was the one she most liked to use, had been replaced in the pencil pot.

Amelia was filled with an all-consuming anger. She'd had enough of being frightened out of her wits – whether by ghosts or intruders. She grabbed the rusty spade from its place by the door and, brandishing it in front of her, charged up the stairs.

Holding her breath, she crept up the stairs to the next floor. No one was there and nothing, as far as she could see, had been touched.

There were still three floors to go apart from the mezzanine and the ramparts. Whoever it was could be hiding anywhere, ready to jump out at her. Perhaps she should go for help? No. Flavia wouldn't be such a wimp, and Amelia needed to show a bit of Flavia's backbone. She was fed up being frightened, and refused to be anyone's victim. Whoever was letting themselves into the castello when she wasn't there had to be stopped.

She paused at the door of the sitting room.

Her unwelcome guest had been in this room, that was certain. Her laptop was slightly out of position on the dining room table, and a vase that had been on the left of the windowsill was now on the right. Her intruder would never have been hired by MI5.

Tiptoeing into the small kitchen, she tentatively pushed open the door that led out to the Juliet balcony. Her breath came out as a whoosh as she realised it too was empty.

She sneezed again and her eyes began to itch. She recognised her usual reaction to cat hair.

The cat must have sneaked in again – knocked the boxes. But cats didn't replace pens in pots or move vases around.

Two more floors and the roof to check. She'd never seen the point of locking the door to the top ramparts. She edged it open and emerged onto the rooftop still holding the spade in front of her like a misshapen spear. There was no one there.

FORTY-ONE

The next morning, Amelia had packed an overnight bag and was about to leave for Fiesole when she noticed a missed call from Benedetto. She hurried up to the ramparts to call him back.

'Can't find anything. I'm sorry,' he said. 'As I said, Lambini isn't an uncommon name and without more information...'

He couldn't have tried very hard, given he'd spent less than half a day looking. However, this was her obsession, not his.

'What about records of court cases against the Fascists?'

'Frankly I'd be surprised if there are any. The executions of collaborators that took place during the war weren't exactly done in the most official way. The partisans were often judge, jury and executioner. Even if there were records, most likely they'll have been lost or destroyed by now. I'm afraid it's pretty much *un punto morto*.' He sighed heavily. 'Just leave it, Amelia. This is none of your business. I can't believe this is what Beatrice wanted you to do.'

But it was what *Flavia* wanted her to do. She was more and more certain of it. Not that she could tell Benedetto that.

He lowered his voice. 'If I were you I wouldn't go around telling people what you are doing. They won't like it.'

Was that a threat? It certainly sounded like it. She dismissed the thought and the unease that went with it. She was just being paranoid again.

The journey to Fiesole took just over an hour. Amelia found the villa, a little way out of the town, without too much trouble. The moment she stepped into the reception hall, she was transported back to the thirties.

The entrance hall had a chequered floor, with a grandfather clock on one side of the door and an ornate umbrella stand on the other. The walls were lined with paintings. The reception was a large wooden desk that might once have served as a dining table. It had a bell on it. Amelia rang it, and while she was waiting she peeped in the sitting room to the left of the reception. It was furnished, as Amelia imagined it had been when Flavia visited, with heavy wooden chairs, card tables, engraved bureaus and tapestried footstools.

Although Amelia was a little early for check-in, the owner's daughter, who introduced herself as Andrea Valpetti, said Amelia's room was almost ready. In the meantime, she could leave her overnight bag with her and she would arrange to have it taken to her room.

'Why don't you go onto the veranda and sit in the shade?' she suggested. 'I will bring you something to drink. What would you like?'

Amelia asked for a caffè lungo with milk, then walked through the French doors and outside. She breathed a sigh of pleasure. The veranda was covered in sweet-smelling wisteria and had uninterrupted views towards Florence. She could see right across the valley to the Duomo. Exactly the view Flavia described in her journal.

So, this was where Julia had lived, where she'd sheltered the orphaned children – including Margherita's son. Where Flavia and Natalia attended dinners and parties and stayed the night. Where they'd left for their desperate dash to safety.

Whatever had happened to Italy in the past, the villa was an oasis of peace. Flavia had been happy here. Of that Amelia was sure.

Andrea brought Amelia's coffee herself.

'Have you come far?' she asked, setting a tray with a silver pot and milk jug and a china cup and saucer on the wrought-iron table in front of Amelia.

'From the Casentino. I'm staying at the Castello di Porciano. Do you know it?'

Andrea clasped her hands together. 'Of course. My mother is still good friends with the current contessa. Their families have known each other for a very long time.'

Excitement spiralled along Amelia's spine. 'Does your mother live nearby? Could I speak to her?'

'I am sorry. She is having a holiday with my sister in Greece. She returns only next month.'

That was disappointing. 'Have you always lived here?' Amelia asked, as she poured milk into her coffee.

'My family bought it in the late fifties.'

It was not the response Amelia had hoped for. Excitement morphed into disappointment. She'd hoped Andrea was related to Julia – perhaps even her daughter.

'When was it turned into a hotel?'

'Soon after we bought it. When people started coming back to Florence. Not everyone wants to stay in the city. It's so busy, so hot. Up here it is much cooler. People can relax here but still visit the city easily. Florence is only about fifteen minutes away by bus.'

'The villa doesn't look as if it has changed very much,' Amelia said.

'We didn't think it needed to. Of course, there were things we had to do to make it into a hotel, but we kept those changes to a minimum. Although we did add a spa recently. People expect things like that now.'

'I understand children from across Italy stayed here during the war,' Amelia said, as Andrea made to turn away to tend to her other guests.

'Yes. In one of the outbuildings. It is the building we converted into the spa.' She crinkled her brow. 'How did you know that? I'm not sure that was ever public knowledge.'

'I read a little about the villa. I'm interested in its history.'

Andrea's face lit up. 'We have many photographs of how the villa used to be, if you are interested.'

'Yes, I would love to see them.'

'We hang as many as we can on the corridor walls. Guests like to see them. We have too many to display them all though.'

'May I look?'

'Of course. This way.'

The walls leading to the bedrooms were lined with photographs. There were several of people gathered around the piano, sitting in groups in wicker chairs on the verandas, playing cards or other board games in the sitting room or library. The scenes moved through time, the styles of dress changing with the decades.

To her delight, Amelia picked out Sophia straight away. She was wearing a cocktail dress with the full skirt and tight bodice fashionable in the fifties and was holding out a glass of champagne in a toasting gesture. 'That's the current contessa's mother, isn't it?' Amelia asked, pointing to Sophia.

'Yes. She was a very beautiful woman. She was a nurse during the war, I understand, but gave it up after the war ended. She spent the rest of her life between Florence and Porciano. She was well known and admired in the Casentino valley.'

Amelia scrutinised each photograph in turn but to her disappointment couldn't identify Flavia in any of them.

'Are there any photographs of Flavia Corsi? I understand she was brought up with Sophia and stayed here as a guest of the previous owners.'

To Amelia's disappointment, Andrea shook her head. 'I couldn't tell you. Before my time, I'm afraid. There may be some of her in one of the boxes. As I said earlier, there is only room to display a limited number of the photographs on the wall. I could ask Bruno if you like?'

'Bruno?' Where had Amelia heard that name before?

'He's like my grandfather. He came to live here during the war and never left. When we bought the villa, the previous owners made keeping him on part of the deal.' Andrea smiled broadly. 'He is the most charming part of the hotel.'

Amelia's heart skipped a beat. He had to be the Bruno that Flavia had mentioned in her diary. 'He's still alive?' she said stupidly.

Andrea laughed. 'Oh, he is very much alive. Perhaps a little old in body but very young in spirit. He comes down to dinner with the guests often. He likes company when he dines, particularly young company. Shall I put him at your table tonight? He won't stay long. His appetite isn't what it used to be.'

'I'd like that very much.'

'Good. That's settled then.'

A woman in her twenties with a pixie haircut appeared. 'The Signora's room is ready.'

'Thank you, Lisa. Signora Simpson is just finishing her coffee. Then I'll take her up myself. Did you put our guest in one of the rooms with a view?'

Amelia couldn't help smiling as she wondered if Andrea had seen the film of that name. She realised she'd smiled more often in the last hour than she had for months. She and Cameron had watched the film together, curled up on the sofa, large glasses of red wine in hand, rain lashing against the window and fire blazing. A wave of longing and pain washed over her. God she missed him. Was it really over between them? Was Father Michael correct? Maybe if they found a way to forgive themselves and each other they could start over – resurrect the love they'd shared?

Her hotel room was everything she could have wished for. Like the rest of the villa, it felt untouched by time. It was simply furnished with a plain wooden double bed, a large mahogany wardrobe and a matching dressing table with an old-fashioned triple mirror. She studied her reflection, assessing her appearance from the different angles.

The face staring back at her was still thin and gaunt, but the deep hollows in her cheeks had filled out slightly. The bad hair dye had faded, and her roots were beginning to show. Her eyes were still dull, almost vacant, and as she leant forward to study herself more closely she noticed lines that weren't there before. Was this how she appeared to others? She recoiled from the thought. She didn't want people to see the unbearably sad and broken woman in the mirror, however much she felt like that inside. She wanted them to see a woman who would fight to hold onto life, no matter how painful.

She gave her reflection a rueful smile and turned to the window. The shutters had been opened wide to let the breeze in. The view was at least as good as that from the castello, stretching as far as the eye could see. Terracotta-roofed villas dotted the landscape, and it was easy to imagine the stealthy figures of Flavia and escaping soldiers slipping between the olive groves under cover of night. Amelia's fingers sought out her father's pendant, and as her fingers gripped the metal she was filled with resolve and the tiniest surge of hope. If she could find a fraction of the courage of Julia and Flavia, she'd find a way to go on living.

On impulse she telephoned reception and asked for an appointment with the hairdresser at their spa. They could fit her in at five. A small step, perhaps, but one in the right direction.

She lay down on the bed, closed her eyes and, for the first time since the accident, immersed herself in happy memories untainted with guilt.

Later, downstairs before dinner, she was introduced to Bruno. He was stooped with age but his eyes, almost hidden by bushy eyebrows, were bright and curious. He shook Amelia's hand vigorously.

'I am so pleased to meet you,' she told him. 'And honoured' – the word didn't feel too quaint today – 'that you agreed to join me for dinner.'

'The pleasure is all mine. What man wouldn't be delighted to have the company of a beautiful woman while he eats?' They grinned at each other in mutual appreciation.

Amelia knew she wasn't beautiful, but she was pleased she'd made the effort to dress for dinner. For the first time in months, she'd put on make-up. Foundation, blusher and lipstick had added some colour to her pale face, and the hotel salon had returned her hair to its usual colour – a deep chestnut brown. All in all, she thought she could just about pass for normal.

Out on the veranda they were served prosecco and *aperitivi* as well as water in tall, frosted glasses garnished with a slice of lemon. Amelia took a mouthful of the fizzy wine but put it aside in favour of the icy, tart water. Along with her refreshed appearance, her taste buds appeared to have returned. The plump olives tasted of sun.

A short while later, Bruno held out his arm to take Amelia into dinner. Charmed by his old-style manners, she decided that for the rest of the night she'd pretend she'd been the Amelia she'd been before.

The dining room was down a flight of stairs in what once was, Bruno told Amelia, the old kitchen and the servants' quarters. 'There isn't enough room in the original dining room to feed as many guests as the hotel usually has,' he said, almost apologetically.

A waiter showed them to their table in front of enormous windows overlooking the manicured lawns. Bruno waited for Amelia to be seated before he took a chair himself.

'Tell me again how you know the contessa,' he said, once they had ordered.

'My father's mother – his adopted mother, to be more precise – knew the contessa's mother. Dad corresponded with the current contessa over the years, and when she was looking for someone to help her record some books and compile a brochure for her museum, I put myself forward.' There was no need for any more detail. Her ability to make small talk – never her greatest skill – was rustier than ever. 'What is your connection with the villa?'

If Bruno was surprised by the directness of the question he gave no inkling of it.

'I came here from Milan during the war. I was ten. My family were killed by a bomb in 1942.'

'I am so sorry.' Another reminder that she was far from the only person who had lost someone they loved.

'Were Julia and Giuseppe here then?' She held her breath as she waited for his answer.

'Yes, they were. How did you know?'

'I understand Julia had a small children's home here during the war.'

'That's right.' A smile spread across his face. 'She was a wonderful woman. When the war was over I had nowhere to go, no family to take me, so I remained here until I went away to work. This has been my home for most of my life – Julia was like a mother to me until she died.'

Bollocks. Despite the odds, Amelia had been hoping to find Julia alive.

'Did you ever meet a woman called Flavia?'

He thought for a moment before shaking his head. 'I was young back then, and my memory isn't what it was. I can't really say I remember anyone called Flavia. There were always many guests, even throughout the war.'

This wasn't going the way Amelia had hoped. 'What about a boy called Lazzero?'

Bruno frowned. 'I'm sorry. The name is not familiar. There were many children at that time, some stayed for months – years even – others for just a few weeks. I wish I could be more help. Was this Lazzero important to you?'

'No, but he was important to someone I care deeply about.' Amelia took a sip of water. 'I understand you might have photos of the time before the villa changed hands? Besides the ones on the wall, I mean.'

'Many were lost during the war, but yes, I'm certain I do. Julia put me in charge of looking after the photographs when I came to stay with her. I was a boy who liked to have something to do – who needed to feel useful.' Tears shimmered in his eyes. 'She knew how scared I was that I'd be sent away.'

Amelia ached for him and the other lost children. She longed to tell him she understood his pain but held back, not trusting herself not to break down. 'Would it be possible for me to have a look at the photos?'

'Of course.' He smiled in anticipation as the waiter, a large tray balanced on his shoulder, appeared with their starter of minestrone soup. 'Could it wait until tomorrow? It may take some time to find the ones that you are interested in.'

Amelia would have preferred he went off to find them there and then.

'Tomorrow will do perfectly,' she said instead.

FORTY-TWO

The next morning Amelia woke at seven. Too wired to go back to sleep and not ready for breakfast, she dressed quickly and slipped outside.

The morning was cool, the grass still wet with dew – although there was promise of the heat yet to come.

Leaving the grounds of the villa, Amelia headed up the steep road to the town of Fiesole. The archaeological ruins weren't open yet, so she decided to investigate the cathedral. Flavia was certain to have visited when she came to Fiesole.

The cathedral was unusual in that it had a lower floor, for the tombs of the rich and aristocratic, and a raised floor. She wasn't the only early visitor. A couple in their sixties wandered around, guidebook in hand, consulting it each time they stopped in front of a painting. The only other person in the church was an organist, playing classical music.

On the raised level were two side chapels, both with large, stained-glass windows. Despite the early hour, the sun streamed through them, falling on triptychs painted in gold and deep purples, reds and blues. The ceilings of the chapels were also painted in similar colours, adorned with golden stars. The beauty took Amelia's breath away.

For centuries people had lived and died, suffered and rejoiced, yet this art had remained – a promise that there would always be light even in the darkest of times. How many people had stood where she was standing and found peace, or forgiveness, or comfort? The connection with the past, she was reminded again, was a continuous one.

Whatever happened to an individual, life went on. Millions of people had lived, loved, hated, murdered and died, yet civilisation still continued. There was – despite the horror and pain – beauty. The Renaissance artists used glorious colour to bring light back into the world after the Dark Ages, and Amelia felt a glimmer pierce the darkness inside her.

She didn't know how long she remained there, but behind her the organ player started playing 'Time to Say Goodbye', and as the notes soared around the cathedral, the turmoil churning inside Amelia once more quietened down.

Her beloved child, part of her soul, was dead. As were Flavia and Margherita and her daughter, along with the rest of the villagers murdered that day and millions of others during the war. So many lives cut short. Wish as she might, she couldn't bring them back. There was no sliding door for Amelia to choose, nothing she could do that would change what happened.

It was the very possibility of her daughter that had been taken from her. Fiona, she thought, would have been a nurse or a doctor. Perhaps a ballerina. She could have been anything and Amelia would have been there to cheer her on, comfort her, support her, always, always loving her. Amelia would never hold her daughter in her arms as she wept for a lost love, never watch as she promised to marry the man she adored, never attend a graduation ceremony. Fiona would never again feel the sunshine on her face, or the wind in her hair, or breathe in the scent of freshly mown hay. She would remain frozen in time – forever young.

Something shifted deep inside Amelia. It was time to stop telling herself she had to live, and time to start doing it. She owed it to Fiona to experience what her daughter no longer could. To try and reach for happiness, and to keep reaching no matter how often she fell short. To make the most of this life with all its beauty as well as pain because Fiona could not. Not to do so would make her death a double tragedy.

She was a long, long way from saying goodbye to her child, but perhaps she could let go a little.

By the time she returned to the hotel, breakfast was almost over. She gobbled down a coffee and croissant before hurrying back to the reception to wait for Bruno.

Andrea was attending to the elderly couple Amelia had noticed in the cathedral, pointing to places on maps, printing out bus timetables and answering questions. While Amelia waited for her to be free, she re-examined photographs on the wall, trying in vain to find one of Flavia.

Having finished with the couple, Andrea informed Amelia that Bruno was waiting for her in the music room. It was similar to the sitting room but with the addition of a grand piano. Andrea whispered that she'd ensure they weren't disturbed before closing the double doors to give them privacy.

On the low table in front of Bruno's chair there had to be dozens, if not hundreds, of photographs. He looked a sadder version of the man she'd had dinner with the night before.

He waited until she was seated before speaking. 'These photographs have brought back so many memories.'

'Happy ones, I hope?'

He smiled wistfully. 'Mostly. Please. Feel free to look through them. We children were supposed to keep out of sight when the adults were entertaining, but I liked to hang around them. Julia never really minded,' he continued as Amelia scanned the photos. 'In fact, she often asked me to mix drinks for everyone. I loved doing it. It made me feel grown up and important.'

Amelia found a photo of Flavia almost immediately. She was part of a group standing in the same room they now sat in. The woman next to Flavia was, according to Bruno, Julia. She was a little shorter than Flavia but very elegant. They both looked so young. Continuing to sift through the photographs, Amelia spotted one of a group standing on the veranda. To the left, very slightly apart and wearing the uniform of a Blackshirt, was a man with a jutting jaw and small eyes. Her stomach turned over. She passed the photograph to Bruno.

'Who was he?'

He studied it for a moment. 'I think he was called Major Lambini.' Bruno's mouth bent downwards in displeasure. 'He didn't come very often. He only stayed in my mind because we were terrified of him. We had to make ourselves scarce when he was around. I think his parents were friends of Julia's parents – or perhaps the fathers worked together. Yes, that's right. I remember now. They did. In a lawyer's office. I think he was a clerk and Julia's father the boss.'

He lifted the photo closer to his face and peered at it. 'Yes. I am certain now. Vincenzo Lambini. He wasn't really part of the circle, more on the periphery. Only tolerated because he was a Blackshirt, and people were frightened of them. He was a pushy sort. I suspect he hoped to court one of the young women who visited. None of their parents would have stood for it. Even if he wasn't one of Mussolini's thugs.'

Amelia held her breath as she waited for Bruno to continue.

'Some Italian men lost their way. You can't entirely blame them. Most of the men of his age were brought up to believe that Mussolini was God.'

'Do you know what happened to Major Lambini?'

Bruno's shoulders slumped. 'As I say, I didn't know much about him.' He shrugged. 'Maybe he was killed during the war like so many young men. Come to think of it, I believe I heard years later that he'd died in a German prisoner-of-war camp. I can't be sure. It was a time of great confusion.' He leant back in his chair and closed his eyes, looking every bit his age. 'A terrible time.'

Vincenzo dead? In a prisoner-of-war camp? At least that would be some sort of justice. If she could be sure it were true.

Amelia gave Bruno a few moments to collect himself. While she waited, she shuffled through the photographs; there were no more of Vincenzo, although there were several of Sophia, Flavia, Julia and another dark-haired woman who she thought might be Natalia. Disappointingly, Bruno couldn't tell her.

He was about to toss a photograph onto the pile but something about it caught Amelia's eye. She studied it. In the photo Sophia stood next to a man Amelia didn't recognise. But she did know the couple next to him. Her heart stood still. They were her grandparents! Much younger versions of themselves than in the photos her father had of them, but still recognisable. Her head spun with the ramifications. They knew Julia. Julia took in orphaned children. Amelia's father was adopted from Italy. Was this where they'd found him?

'Did you know a little boy called Sebastian?' she asked. Her father's name. She held her breath as she waited for him to reply.

Bruno thought for a moment. To her disappointment he shook his head.

'No. I am so sorry. I don't remember a Sebastian or a Lazzero. Neither name rings a bell. There were so many children.' His expression brightened. 'But Julia kept a register of all of them – who their parents were, their home addresses, and if they were ever claimed by their parents or another relative. And, in the instances where their family was killed, who took them to live with them.'

He pushed himself out of the chair, walked over to the bookcase and took down a slim leather-bound volume. 'Remind me of those names again.'

Amelia did. He ran a finger down each page before turning to the next. His finger paused, and he looked at Amelia.

'I'm sorry. No Sebastian. Do you have a surname for Lazzero?'

'Flavia never mentioned a surname, but his date of birth was sometime in 1940 – and he would have come from Vallucciole.'

Agonising minutes passed before his finger paused again. He

peered at Amelia over half-moon reading glasses. 'There is a Niccolo. Could that be him? It's the only entry where it doesn't give the surname or note where he came from.'

Amelia's pulse leapt. If they'd wanted to keep Lazzero's whereabouts secret they wouldn't have put down his real name or where he came from and might well have renamed him after his dead father.

'Is there a date of birth?'

'Fifteenth of March, 1940.'

Weirdly, the same birthday as her father. Instinctively her hand went to the necklace he'd given her.

'There's a further note,' Bruno continued. 'No family left alive. Adopted by a couple called Quinn who took him to the UK.'

Amelia's thoughts raced as she made the connections. Lazzero was – is – *her* father! *Dad* was the little boy Flavia rescued from the burning ruins of Vallucciole. The possibility hadn't crossed her mind. But the more she thought about it the more it made sense. The Quinns had been in Italy – they must have adopted him after no one claimed him. He must have been so confused, felt so abandoned. It explained so much. Her father's emotional distance. His unhappy memories of Italy. Even if he hadn't actually witnessed the murders of his mother and sister, his grandmother, his uncle Luca – everyone he loved – he must have known something terrible was going to happen to have hidden. At the very least he would have heard the screams and the gunfire. Hardly surprising then that he'd suppressed the trauma of his family's murders, that he remembered so little about his childhood – that he'd never returned to the country where he was born.

It all fitted. Another thought struck her. If Dad *was* Lazzero, Margherita was her grandmother, Roberto and Luca her great-uncles. Alessandra's nonna – Rosina – Dad's aunt. Did *she* know her nephew had survived? She slumped back in her chair as she tried to take it all in. She'd just inherited a family along with their history – good and bad.

She became aware Bruno was looking at her strangely.

She mustered a shaky smile and stood. She needed time to absorb everything she'd learnt. 'Thank you so much for showing me these photographs and sharing your memories.'

'It was my pleasure. I don't know if what I've told you is any use to you, but I've enjoyed our little chat. The young aren't usually interested in the past. And truth be told, it's not always easy for me to return there – I was such a sad boy, but it is good to be reminded there were happy times too. I believe the more often happy memories are recalled, the more they become stronger than the sad ones.'

She desperately hoped that one day that would be the case for her.

A short while later Amelia checked out. On her way to the car, she telephoned Benedetto. The phone only rang twice before he answered.

'It's Amelia,' she said. 'I have some information that might help us find out what happened to Major Lambini.'

FORTY-THREE

Benedetto and Amelia arranged to meet at the castello at three. In the meantime, Amelia was on a mission, desperate to confirm Lazzero and her father were one and the same. So instead of taking the road leading to the castello, she took the one to Vallucciole, praying that whoever lived in that single remaining house was home and willing to talk to her.

The stars were aligning. This time her knock was answered. A very old lady with white hair, lined skin and a turned up mouth answered the door.

'I am sorry to disturb you. My name is Amelia,' she said, holding out her hand for her to shake. 'I was here the other day, but you were out. Would you mind if we had a chat?'

The woman smiled. 'I am always happy to have visitors. Please come in.'

She led Amelia through to a sitting room-cum-kitchen and gestured for her to take a seat.

'What would you like to ask me?' She looked at Amelia with bright, inquisitive eyes.

'I'm not sure where to start. I guess the beginning is as good a place as any.' She told her hostess about the job at the castello, the diaries and her obsession with finding out about Flavia. The old woman listened attentively, tears streaming down her cheeks.

'Flavia, my lovely Flavia,' she murmured when Amelia came to the end of her story.

Amelia's breath caught. 'You knew her?'

'Knew her? Mama Mia! She was like a sister to me. My dearest friend.'

'I'm afraid I don't understand. How did you know her?'

'She was married to my brother, Luca.'

'Luca?' Amelia was completely baffled.

'Yes, Luca. My dear, dear brother.' The woman's voice caught on a sob. 'My Flavia. My Luca. They were like the fireflies this village is called after. Their light didn't shine for long but while it did, it shone brighter than the sun.'

Amelia was still struggling to make sense of what the older woman was saying. 'Excuse me, but there is no other way to put this – who on earth are you?'

She looked at Amelia askance. 'I am Margherita, Flavia's friend, Luca's sister.'

Margherita! This woman could not be *Flavia*'s Margherita. 'But – you died!' Amelia blurted.

A smile crossed the old lady's face. 'Well, unless I'm a ghost, as you can see, I am very much alive.' The light left her eyes. 'There are times I wished I *had* died. I lost both my children that day, as well as both brothers and my friends.' She was quiet for a long time, looking off to the middle distance, seemingly adrift in the past. Amelia stayed quiet, instinctively knowing not to rush her. Eventually she turned back to Amelia, a frown creasing her brow. 'Is that why you are here? To ask about what happened in Vallucciole during the war?'

Amelia nodded, still too dumbfounded to speak.

Margherita stood, crossed over to the gas hob and lit a flame under a coffee pot. She turned back to Amelia, her whole body suffused with sadness. 'I was one of the few survivors of that day. Two men escaped with their lives. They were in a faraway field tending to the animals when the soldiers came. They live in Rome now. They didn't want to come back to what remained of Vallucciole and the terrible memories of that day – and who could blame them?'

'But you stayed. After all that happened? How could you bear it?'

Margherita smiled sadly. 'I had no choice. How would my son know where to find me if I didn't?'

'Your son?'

'Yes. My Lazzero. I needed to be here in case he came to find me.'

'Your son... Lazzero,' Amelia echoed. Several things hit her at once. She'd been so caught up in the realisation Lazzero was her father, it hadn't sunk in until that moment that Dad's mother, Amelia's grandmother, was alive and in the same room as her.

Amelia removed the pendant from around her neck and handed it to Margherita. 'Do you recognise this?'

Margherita paled. 'Where did you get it?' She snatched it from Amelia and held it to her lips.

'My father. He was given it as a child. He was born in Italy but adopted after the war.'

'But this is the same as mine!' Margherita's fingers scrabbled at the neck of her collar. She showed Amelia her necklace. 'Look!'

Margherita's pendant did appear very similar to Amelia's.

'It was a wedding present from my husband,' Margherita continued. 'Before he went to war. He had it cut in half and gave one to me – as a promise we would always be two parts of one soul, that he would always come back to me...' she swallowed hard, 'like the mothers of orphans left at the Hospital of Innocents – you know that story?'

Amelia nodded, recalling what she'd learned about the Ospedale degli Innocenti.

'But he couldn't keep his promise. He was killed in battle. Apart from my children, this was all I had left of him. That terrible day, I gave Niccolo's half to my son and made the same promise to him. One I couldn't keep either.' Margherita took the pendant from around her neck and matched the battered silver disc to Amelia's. 'Look – they fit exactly!'

Amelia took a deep breath. There was no longer any doubt. 'I believe my father is Lazzero. He remembers a woman giving this to him, saying it was a promise she would always come back for him.'

Margherita stared at Amelia. The hope in her eyes was painful to see. 'Your father is my Lazzero? He is alive? Can it be true?'

'Yes! Yes, he is. He is getting on, but he is still healthy.' Amelia showed Margherita the photo she kept in her purse of him as a child and another of him after he married her mother. Margherita studied the first photo before kissing it and moving onto the second. Although tears still streamed down her cheeks, her face was suffused with joy. 'He is still very handsome.'

'If he is your son, then you must be my grandmother. My nonna.' Amelia choked her own tears back.

Margherita pressed the photographs to her breast. 'I have hoped and prayed...' She swallowed hard. 'I told him to hide and not to come out until I told him it was safe. But when I came round he wasn't there. I searched far and wide for him. When I couldn't find him I thought the Germans must have found him. But when I couldn't even find his body, I prayed some good soul had found him and kept him safe. That one day he'd find his way back to me.' Margherita reached out to stroke Amelia's cheek. 'I have been waiting so long. I never gave up hope I would see him again. And now I have found you too – my grandchild.' She beamed at Amelia.

Amelia had so many questions she wasn't sure where to start. Swallowing the lump in her throat, she began with the most pressing.

'Why did Flavia think you'd died during the raid on Vallucciole?'

'I almost did. I was very badly injured, shot in the shoulder. I lost consciousness. I came round to find all the bodies around me and my little daughter Flavia in my arms. She was dead.' Her voice broke. 'My beautiful, beloved daughter.' Amelia became aware tears were running down her own cheeks. She and her grandmother shared the unbearable loss of a child. So much pain, so much heartache, continuing down the decades.

'*Everyone* was dead,' Margherita continued. 'My brother Roberto, my darling Luca, Niccolo's nonna, his mother, his brother, my friends. Almost everyone I loved.' She drew a shuddering breath. 'I needed to find Lazzero. I'd told him to hide in the flour chest, to bury down in the chestnuts we kept there during the war years. But he wasn't there. I called out for him – told him to come to me. But he didn't answer. I searched everywhere! I didn't know what to do. I couldn't stay in the village in case the Germans came back.'

She blew her nose. 'I buried little Flavia – I couldn't leave her there. It took the last of my strength. I had none left to bury the others. I bandaged my shoulder as best I could and made my way to my mother's farm in Porciano, praying Lazzero had found his way there and was safe. The journey took me hours – I had to keep hiding from the German trucks. But my son wasn't there! I could go no further. I collapsed. My mother found me there. She'd heard what had happened at Vallucciole and came looking for me. She and Rosina took care of me. It was weeks before I was well enough to continue searching.' She swiped the tears from her face with a sleeve. 'I looked everywhere for him, but no one could tell me where he was. There was so much confusion – people were still so scared of the Germans, so many people displaced. As soon as I could, I came back here, to this house. If I couldn't find him, I hoped he would find me. I've been waiting ever since.'

She turned back to Amelia and frowned. 'You said Flavia thought I was dead! Why would you say that?'

Amelia explained about finding the account Flavia had written of the massacre hidden behind the painting.

Margherita gasped, and the colour drained from her face. 'Flavia was there? No!'

'She saw it all, including Luca's death.' Amelia repeated everything she'd learnt from Flavia's diaries. 'She was too late to save you and the others, but she found Lazzero. She took him to the nuns, promised to return for him, but in case she couldn't she asked them to send him to her friend Julia's villa in Fiesole under a different name. So that's what happened. He was adopted from there by my grandparents.'

Margherita appeared to be struggling to take it all in. 'He was in Fiesole – so close – all the time I was looking for him. Why didn't they return him to me?'

'I believe Flavia kept his identity secret. She was frightened if Major Lambini discovered he'd survived and had been a witness he would have him hunted down. Remember, she intended to go back for him.'

'Lazzero never talked of me?'

'No,' Amelia admitted. 'I think he was so traumatised by what he witnessed. He must have thought you were dead. But he kept the pendant. It made him feel safe.' She swallowed hard. No wonder it had been difficult for Dad to show affection, to allow himself to care. 'My father was in his mid-forties when he married my mother,' Amelia continued. 'I'm an only child. They divorced when I was fifteen. Mum went to live in Australia with her second husband. I stayed with Dad.'

'Oh! That explains why you are so young.' She reached across and gently touched Amelia's face. 'Pretty too – though a little sad, no?'

'Do you know what really happened to Flavia? Who found her?' Amelia asked, instead of replying to the question. Now wasn't the time to share her own loss with her grandmother.

'A soldier. The Germans claimed she threw herself from the fourth floor of the castello. I never believed it,' Margherita said fiercely. 'She was carrying Luca's baby. She would have done anything to protect their child. Do you know Flavia and Luca were married? Oh, they loved each other very much.'

Amelia nodded.

'I always believed she was murdered by the Germans,' Margherita continued. 'Now I understand why they killed her.

They must have known she was a witness to the massacre. The war was coming to an end. They didn't want to leave witnesses to their atrocities. Flavia was someone known in Italian society – people would have taken her word.' She buried her face in her hands, and her shoulders heaved as she sobbed, mourning the loss of her friend all over again.

Amelia waited until her grandmother regained her composure.

'Does anyone in the valley know about Major Lambini?' Amelia asked. 'His part in the massacre? Didn't you tell them?'

Margherita shook her head and placed her trembling hands in her lap. 'I know you will find this difficult to understand but at first I was too distraught, too ill, to talk about what happened. Then later when the war was all over no one wanted to rake up the past. Everyone just wanted to forget those terrible years. The major was long gone – dead, people said.' She drew a shuddering breath. 'But it wasn't just that. My brother, Roberto, was a traitor. He was there at Vallucciole – part of everything that happened. He brought those murdering bastards to the village where his sister, his niece and nephew lived. He must have known what they were going to do. To his own family! I was so ashamed. How could I say anything without dragging my family's name through the mud? How could I hold my head up in the valley? I only stayed in case my child ever came back. I couldn't even bear to look Rosina in the eyes.' Her voice caught in a sob. 'I let everyone down. I couldn't even save my children.'

Amelia's heart broke a little more. One day her grandmother would learn that they shared the excoriating grief of losing a child, believing they could have prevented their death – *should* have prevented their death. Like Amelia, Margherita would have to find a way of forgiving herself, accept that she wasn't to blame for what had happened.

'There wasn't anything you could do.' There was something Margherita didn't know. 'It wasn't your fault. Roberto tried to save you! He told Flavia that German troops were on the way and that she had to warn you and the villagers. He stood between you and Lambini, taking the bullet meant for you.'

'He did?' Hope flared in Margherita's eyes. 'I only remember he was there.'

'I'm sure. Flavia wrote everything she witnessed down. When you are ready I will show you.'

Margherita gave a small shake of her head. 'All I care about at this moment is that my darling Lazzero is alive.' She leant forward and grasped Amelia's hands. 'That's enough of the past for the time being. Now, please. Tell me about my son. Every little thing. Then I will take you to the graveyard here in Vallucciole where Luca and Flavia are buried side by side.'

FORTY-FOUR

On the way back to Porciano, Amelia stopped in Stia and sent her father an email. She explained she'd found his mother, that she was very old, but had been waiting for him all her life. Could he come? Get the first flight to Florence? She hoped he would. She thought for a moment, drew in a deep breath and sent a second email.

Benedetto was waiting for her in the garden of the castello. Dressed as stylishly as ever in neatly pressed trousers, baby-pink shirt open at the neck, hair brushed back from his forehead. He jumped to his feet when he saw her pull up and came hurrying towards her.

Amelia was totally drained and would have preferred to meet the next day. But it would be rude to cancel now, especially since she'd been the one to ask for it.

'Have you been waiting long?' she asked as he kissed her on both cheeks. Now she was closer to him she noticed there was something off about him, his slicked-back hair over-oiled, his baby-pink shirt creased, his loafers without their usual high polish.

'Not too long. Less than half an hour.'

'Shall we go inside?' she suggested. Cloud had covered the sun, and it was getting chilly.

Benedetto followed Amelia up the floors, pausing in Dante's

Hall when he saw what she'd done. She had to admit it looked pretty good. The display cabinets holding the pottery and china remained centre stage, but in one corner Amelia had draped two items of Flavia's clothing over chairs – her evening dress and the amazing coat. Propped against the walls were mock-ups of the notices, waiting for Beatrice's approval. The boards started with the Warrior Abbess and photos of the monastery she'd founded; they continued with Dante and the evidence that he might have written some of his most famous work – including part of his *Inferno* – while a guest in the castello. She'd also drafted a short history on the wars between the Guelphs and the Ghibellines. The final poster explained how after this time the castello fell into ruins, and went on to show the renovations the contessa's grandparents had started.

The pièce de résistance – or what would be the pièce de résistance when more artistic hands than Amelia's redid it – was the cross section of the castello with sketched figures on different floors – each allocated to a different time period. Just as she'd imagined her ghostly friends.

'I'm impressed,' Benedetto said, sounding as if he meant it.

'Beatrice will need to acquire some more professional photographs to replace the ones I took with my phone, as well as the services of an artist, but that shouldn't be a problem. I have some photos of Flavia and Sophia that were taken before the war, and if Beatrice is agreeable I plan to add them.'

An expression Amelia couldn't quite identify flickered across Benedetto's face. 'What about the war stuff? Are you planning to add that?'

'It'll depend on Beatrice. She's returning in a couple of days. Did you know?' An email from her had been waiting in Amelia's inbox when she'd stopped to send her father an email. 'Shall we go into the sitting room? Are you hungry? I could make you something to eat.' Her head was still spinning from the realisation that her father's mother was alive.

He shook his head. 'Coffee or something stronger will be fine.'

Benedetto was not smiling today. He jiggled his leg nervously, looking everywhere except at her. Amelia was puzzled. Definitely not his usual urbane self.

'Do you mind if I put a fire on?' he asked, wrapping his arms around himself. 'It's so cold inside.'

'If you like.' She didn't think it was that cold, but then she was Scottish.

He busied himself with the fire while Amelia made coffee. Finding some leftover biscotti, she put them on the saucer. It wasn't much of a snack, but it would have to do.

The fire was going well by the time the coffee was ready. Benedetto was sitting back on his heels, staring into the flames, a pensive – almost anxious – look on his face. Once again Amelia was struck by the difference in him. When they'd had lunch the day they'd met, almost a month ago now, he'd been confident, self-assured and almost arrogant.

He rose to his feet to take the tray from Amelia, placing it on the coffee table. 'Tell me everything you found out.'

Amelia sat on the sofa, leaving the armchair closest to the fire for Benedetto. She poured the coffee and handed him his. 'A man who knew him vaguely seems to think he died in a prisoner-of-war camp. Even better, I found someone who was there at Vallucciole, but survived the massacre. She can place him at the scene.'

'Who is this witness?' He leant forward, staring at her intently.

'That's not important right now.' It wasn't up to her to decide what Margherita should do, or who she should tell. 'In the meantime, there must be military records. We should be able to trace Lambini through them.'

'And when – if – we do. What then?' His tone was curt, almost abrasive.

'I'm not sure it's just up to me.'

'What if I told you he's definitely dead?'

'You've discovered that already? That was quick. What happened to him?'

'He died a lonely old man. That should give you some satisfaction.'

'I'd rather he was still alive so he could answer for what he did.'

Benedetto clenched his hands together. 'Given he's dead, what would be the point?'

Confused, Amelia took the conversation back a step or two. 'How do you know he's dead?'

Benedetto leant back and crossed one leg over the other. His eyes locked on hers. 'Because Vincenzo was my father.'

It took a while for his words to sink in. *What the fuck!* She hadn't seen that coming. Prickles of unease spread across her skin. '*Your* father?' she echoed. 'But you don't have the same surname.'

'My father was no fool. He knew there might be repercussions after the war ended. He changed his name then, long before he married my mother.' Benedetto's eyes were cold, his full mouth set in a flat line. 'So many records had been lost it wasn't difficult, if one was patient, to apply for a new birth certificate under a different name. Especially if you did it under a name of a dead person with no family.'

Amelia's head was still spinning. Vincenzo was Benedetto's father. Beatrice couldn't have known. Did Benedetto know what his father had done? His participation in the murder of innocent men, women and children. His fellow Italians.

Her unease unfurled into tentacles of dread as another thought occurred to her. 'How long have you known?'

'That the Vincenzo you were looking for was my father?' He shrugged. 'All along.'

He folded his arm across his chest and gave Amelia a belligerent look. 'I didn't know my father well. My mother met him when she was on holiday in Austria in the late sixties. She was his third wife. The marriage wasn't a success. She left him when Fabian and I were still young and brought us back to Italy. Dad moved to South America.'

'So he was never a prisoner of war?'

'No. It was a rumour he put about. It was what he wanted

people to believe. It's what I believed for most of my life. He told my brother and I when we were children that he had been captured by the Germans and spent the remainder of the war as a prisoner. We had no reason to suspect he was lying.'

'Did you know he was a Blackshirt?' Amelia felt physically ill as the ramifications of what she'd learnt hit home. 'Did you know about his involvement in Vallucciole?'

'God no. At least not until my brother decided to run for office. As his researcher it was my job to make sure there was nothing in his past that could come back to bite him. I never expected to find anything, you understand. I was just being thorough.' He stood to stoke the fire. 'At first when I couldn't find any evidence of my father being a prisoner of war I wasn't too worried. As I said, thousands of records were destroyed during the war – especially at the end.

'But something kept me looking. I wanted his army records. Who knew? Perhaps there was a war medal he hadn't told us about that we could use to our advantage. I couldn't find anything where it was supposed to be. I knew he'd been an officer, but when I asked him what regiment, he became vague.'

'You found something eventually though.'

'Yes,' he said, keeping his back to Amelia. 'He asked me to visit. He was very ill by then. I think he knew he was about to die and wanted to confess to someone. He was still a practising Catholic. Perhaps he wanted absolution.'

Could anyone be absolved of a crime as heinous as his?

'He admitted his part in the massacre at Vallucciole?'

'Yes.'

'Why didn't you say something before?'

'Why do you think? Who would want something like that to become public? I hoped you wouldn't find out, but you've been like a dog with a bone. Determined to uncover secrets that were nothing to do with you.' Benedetto's voice was heavy. 'Why couldn't you have left it alone? As soon as you give Beatrice – the world – his name, who knows what will happen then? Can you imagine what it will do to my brother's election chances if it comes out that his father was a war criminal?'

'Fabian doesn't know?'

Benedetto turned around to face Amelia. 'I saw no reason to tell him. If it had come out then Fabian's campaign would have come to a halt before it was started. My brother is naive. I imagine if he does know the truth he'll go to the press himself.' He pinched the skin between his eyes with his fingers. 'They'll eat him alive.'

'No one could blame your brother for what your father did years ago!'

Benedetto gave a bark of laughter. 'In politics everything matters. They might have forgiven Fabian if he had three mistresses, but his father a member of the Fascist movement? One who sided with the Germans and committed atrocities against his own people? The things he did? No, no one would accept that.'

'Fabian will have to know now.'

'No!' Benedetto shouted, stepping towards Amelia. 'No one must. Not him. Not anyone.' His face had turned puce. 'Why should the sins of the father be visited on the children?'

'What else did your father tell you?'

He gave a heavy sigh. 'He told me he killed Flavia. He said that Flavia was at Vallucciole and saw it all. He wanted to make sure she never told anyone what she'd witnessed. I think back then he thought if he killed her, he'd be safe. As soon as he could he looked for her. The stupid woman, instead of putting as much distance between her and the Casentino, returned to the castello.'

'She wanted her wedding ring, her mementos of her husband Luca.'

'She was in a fury. Told my father she would make sure he'd stand trial for what he'd done. He couldn't let that happen. Before she died—'

'Before he pushed her out the window,' Amelia corrected through gritted teeth. 'For God's sake, she was expecting a baby!'

'Perhaps he didn't know,' he protested – as if that made his father's actions any better. 'She told him she had written an account and hidden it. He didn't know whether to believe her. When it didn't materialise over the years he assumed it never would. Perhaps she *had* been lying.' He glared at Amelia. 'When I heard you'd found a letter mentioning a discovery of some sort, I began to wonder if it did exist. Then when Kelly told me you'd found those damn diaries...' He spread his hands wide, as if inviting Amelia's understanding. 'I needed to know if her account was in her diaries. I had to find them.' He shook his head. 'If only you'd gone back to the UK the way you were meant to. You are a very stubborn woman.'

It took a few moments for his words to sink in. Thoughts tumbled through her head: the times she was sure someone had been in the castello; the fleeting image she had of a figure looking up at the ramparts; the misplaced objects.

'The person in the castello the night of the storm – that was you?'

He didn't deny it. 'I thought the diary containing the account would be easier to find than it was.'

'How did you get in?' she demanded.

'I had a spare key made by a local ironmonger. Beatrice doesn't know. I got it made months ago in case it came in useful. Then you started barring the door at night, so that was no use. During the day you were never out long enough for us to search properly.'

Amelia's sense of foreboding increased. 'Us?'

'I couldn't do it on my own. People might have wondered why I was in the castello when you weren't there. I asked Kelly to help. You almost caught her once.'

'Kelly helped you?' Somehow Amelia wasn't shocked at the revelation; a part of her had known it, even as Kelly had sworn it wasn't true. 'She told you what happened to me, didn't she?' She didn't need his nod to know Kelly had. The day Amelia found the christening gown on her pillow was the same day she'd told Kelly about the diaries and the accident. How could the American have used that against her? And to then turn round and try to convince Amelia she'd imagined it all.

A knot of anger formed behind her ribs. 'Kelly knew what I was going through, knew I was beside myself with grief, yet the pair of you tormented me, put the christening gown on my bed, moved things around. You wanted me to think I was becoming unhinged, losing my mind.' *Again*, she added silently. 'Anything to get me to leave.'

He widened his eyes in mock surprise. 'That is rather a dramatic way of putting it. All we wanted was enough time to search the castello. If we unsettled you, we thought you would go back to the UK – or at least move into a *pensione*. You turned out to be remarkably resilient.'

Several emotions vied for ascendancy. Vindication and relief that she hadn't imagined someone in the castello, hurt bafflement that Kelly – someone she'd liked and confided in – had used her pain for her own purposes. Most of all she was furious. Everything he'd done to her had been just so he could stop people knowing about his father. It didn't even seem to bother him his father had been a cold-blooded mass murderer. Only whether it damaged his brother's political career. He was an absolute arsehole.

'Why would Kelly help you? I thought you hardly knew each other.'

He took another step towards Amelia. She held her ground. 'The same reason anyone does anything,' he continued. 'For personal gain. She was certain Flavia had found something significant and had hidden it somewhere in the castello, and she wanted to be the one to find it. But never mind that now. You said you found evidence of Vincenzo's involvement. What was it? Was it in one of the diaries? Where are they?'

Before Amelia could stop herself, she glanced at her bag on the dining table.

They both lunged for it. Amelia was closer, fitter and younger. She grabbed it and clutched it to her chest. If he got hold of the diaries and chucked them and the account into the fire she'd have no proof. And she was damned if she would let him destroy a single word Flavia had written. He was between Amelia and the stairs to the floor below, so the only way was up. She bolted for the steps, appreciating again those excruciating runs she'd made herself go on. In less than a minute she reached the door leading to the ramparts. She could lock it, keep Benedetto out. Shout for help. Except for one thing. The key to the ramparts' door was the wrong side, and to her frustration when she tried to pull it out it wouldn't budge. She wasted a few precious moments trying to wriggle it free, without success. Perhaps rust had jammed it. Whatever. There was no time to fiddle with it – not when she could hear Benedetto pounding up the stairs behind her. She flung the door open and dived through, slamming it behind her. Panting, she pressed her back against it, knowing she couldn't keep Benedetto out for long.

Just as the handle turned, Amelia noticed the spade she'd left there, picked it up and stood to the side of the door. The door edged open.

'Amelia? Don't be ridiculous. Let's talk about this. I won't hurt you. I just want the diaries and whatever Flavia wrote that mentioned my father.'

Amelia said nothing. Instead, when he emerged from behind the door, she unleashed months of pent-up fury and slammed the flat part of the spade on his head. It made a satisfying thud as, almost in slow motion, he fell to his knees, then to the ground. For one petrifying moment she thought she might have killed him. She crouched next to him and checked for a pulse. It was there. *Thank God.*

His eyelids flickered, and he groaned. Amelia jumped to her feet and away from him. Slowly he turned his head in her direction. 'What did you do that for?' he mumbled, rubbing the back of his skull. 'Kelly said you were mad.'

'Then you should know I'm capable of anything.' She brandished the spade at him. Just let him try and come at her. She almost wished he would. It had felt so good to whack him, she might do it again just for the joy of it.

Benedetto lurched to his feet, grimacing.

'Stay where you are,' Amelia hissed. She took a calming breath. 'It's too late. Nothing short of you killing me will stop the truth from coming out. I will make sure everyone knows what your father did.'

Benedetto looked as if he might pass out again.

'Here's the deal,' Amelia continued. 'You come clean about your father, and your brother takes whatever consequences there might be. In addition, you admit that your father murdered Flavia.' She looked him directly in the eyes and allowed herself a smile. 'I think that is the least Flavia deserves.'

FORTY-FIVE

FLAVIA

13 April 1944

Flavia waited in the church until night fell. People had come and gone, no one paying her any attention.

She had used the time to pray to God to give her the strength for all the days, months and years to come. But now she had to try and put her grief aside so she could focus on the task ahead. Once inside the castello, she only needed a few minutes. Enough time to change her bloody clothes and collect her most precious possessions – her wedding ring and the only photo of Luca she had. While she was there, she'd retrieve the ripped-out pages of her diary. They would bolster the account of the massacre she'd hidden behind the painting.

She slipped out of the church and into the dark. Curfew had started so she had to take great care not to be observed, particularly by the German soldiers patrolling the streets.

Moving swiftly and silently along the cobbles, every sense attuned to danger, she kept to the shadows, barely breathing, only moving when she was sure there was no chance of being seen. When she made it to the hill and could leave the roads and lanes for the fields, she sighed with relief, although she knew she couldn't allow herself to drop her guard even for a second.

Several times she had cause to give thanks for the time she'd spent training with Luca. Any vestiges of the unworldly young woman she'd been when she'd first met him had gone. Her muscles were toned, her senses sharpened to filter the noises that mattered from those that didn't. That wasn't the only way she'd changed, though. Over the last few hours her heart had broken, leaving a cold stone in its place. She had killed, and would not hesitate to kill again.

When she reached Porciano, she crept between the houses, giving those occupied by the Germans a wide berth until she was crouching behind the damaged wall of the castello, her back to the woods.

The castello, once a place of laughter and love, now crouched in ominous silence atop its hill.

She waited, blowing warmth into her frozen fingers until the guard disappeared inside. The sound of laughter coming from the house used as a bar by the soldiers filled her with fury. Were they not ashamed of what had been done in their name? She forced the rage away. She had to stay focussed. Put all thoughts of everything, including the baby, out of her mind until she'd reached safety again.

She had almost given up on the castello when, finally, the guard disappeared. She knew from past experience he'd be gone for at least ten minutes.

Easing open the heavy front door, she slid inside, letting her eyes adjust to the darkness. Knowing every inch of her Casentino home, she didn't need to risk lighting a lamp. She ran up the steps, moving rapidly through the castello, stopping at the kitchen to pick up a knife, dropping it into her satchel. She'd need it to gouge out the mortar where she'd hidden the ripped out pages of the diary.

As she stepped back into the living area, she paused. Something wasn't right. As the scent of men's cologne wafted towards her, fear stole her breath.

Vincenzo was sitting in the darkness in the chair closest to the fireplace. Bringing his vile presence into her home. Fury doused the fear like a water hydrant. She'd never hated anyone as she hated this man.

'What are you doing here?' she hissed, her heart bashing painfully against her ribs. 'Get the hell out of my home.'

'You and I both know I'm going nowhere,' he said, getting to his feet. 'I guessed you'd come back.' He gave a sorrowful shake of his head. 'People like you and your lover, Liberte, are so predictable.'

'What do you mean?'

'I counted on him hearing that we were heading to Vallucciole and knew if he did nothing would keep him away. And that if you thought he or your peasant friend were in danger you would follow him like the slut you are.'

She didn't think it was possible for her blood to run colder. Had Roberto set them up? His own sister and brother?

'I would have followed my husband to the ends of the earth.'

Vincenzo gave a ghoulish smile. 'So, it's true. You married a farmer, when you could have had anyone. You could have had me!'

'Luca was a thousand times the man you will ever be.'

'A dead man is what he is. A dead fool,' he said viciously, spittle gathering at the corners of his mouth. 'What I can't understand is why you came back. I gave you a chance to get away. Didn't you know I saw you at Vallucciole?'

She'd suspected but hadn't been sure. 'I needed a change of clothes.' She glanced down at her clothes, soaked with her husband's blood. She was dizzy with rage.

'I would have enjoyed playing cat and mouse with you – I was looking forward to it. But I suppose this is simpler.' He rested his forearm on the mantelpiece, letting his other hand caress the holster of his gun. 'What happened at Vallucciole was his fault,' Vincenzo continued. It was as if he couldn't bear to say Luca's name. 'He was the one with blood on his hands. He should have given himself up. He knew he was a wanted man. He must have known that Göring would hunt him, and anyone suspected of helping him and his band, down. Italy would have been at peace by now if it hadn't been for the partisans.'

'Peace! Under the German occupiers?' she snarled. 'Never! And to murder innocent women and children! You will never be able to justify that. Your name will live in infamy. I hope they execute you.'

'Who will tell them? Not you. And if not you, who? There is no one else.' Relief washed over her. So he didn't know Lazzero had survived. She had to make sure it stayed that way. She could never let him know there was another witness.

He took a step towards her, closing the distance between them. His voice dropped to a whisper. 'No one will remember your name at all.'

She knew without a shadow of doubt he had no intention of letting her live. She didn't care about her own life, but what about her baby? Luca's baby. If she died it would die with her, and she'd promised Luca she would do anything to protect their child.

Her mind raced, looking for a way to escape, even while she knew it was hopeless. Even if she could evade him, one shout would be enough for him to bring dozens of soldiers running. She shouldn't have dropped her pistol after killing the soldier. All she had was the small kitchen knife in her satchel.

Vincenzo came towards her, unbuckling his belt. 'There are ways of making you forget your lover. It will give me pleasure to know that mine will be the last body you'll touch.'

His last step closed the distance between them. He shoved her onto the sofa, the same sofa she'd lain on with Luca. She would rather die than have Vincenzo's body violate hers.

She forced herself to wait until he was on top of her, his revolting face slack with desire, before taking the knife out of the satchel and plunging it into his back. Once. Twice. But before she could thrust it in again, he screamed in agony and rolled off her. 'You bitch! You will pay for this!' His hand yanked at his holster.

She leapt to her feet but had only taken a couple of steps when she felt a blinding flash of pain accompanied by the crunch of bone. Her legs gave way and she crumpled to the ground, dropping the knife.

He rolled her onto her back and, his face contorted with rage, smashed the butt of his weapon into her face. Her vision blurred.

'You fool. Who will love you now?'

Vincenzo grabbed her under her armpits and dragged her across the floor and towards the open window that had once led to the ladies' balcony.

She struggled, but she was dazed from the blows to her head. All she could do was dig in her heels, in an attempt to slow him down. There was no point in screaming. No one would come to her aid. There was no point in begging for her life, so she wouldn't give him the pleasure.

He forced her to her feet and spun her round, keeping her upright by gripping her shoulders. There was nothing now between her and the ground far below.

'How high would you say this is, bitch?'

Too high to survive.

She twisted and spat, pleased to see droplets of blood spray his face. 'Even after you have gone to hell, your name will live in infamy. Everyone in Italy will learn what you have done.'

'With you dead, who is left to tell them?'

'Because I have written it down. Everything that happened at Vallucciole. What you did. I have hidden it, somewhere you will never find it. But I can promise you this – your name will be cursed for generations.'

'You're lying.'

But she heard the uncertainty in his voice. His fingers tightened on her shoulders. Memories rushed through her head, tumbling over one another like a river over stones. She thought of everyone she had loved and lost, who would be waiting for her: Luca, Margherita, her parents, her baby. Her biggest regret was that she hadn't been able to protect her child. At least soon they would all be together. It had started to rain, soft drops landing on her face. She looked up at the moon, remembering the times she and Luca had lain wrapped together on the ramparts. And then she was falling through the air, the stars all around her.

FORTY-SIX

AMELIA

Amelia was in her favourite position: the roof of the castello. Beatrice was returning tomorrow, and Amelia had a lot of explaining to do. She really, really hoped that the documents in the manila envelope would turn out to be important. Beatrice might find it easier to forgive Amelia then.

From her vantage point she could see the road most of the way to Stia. There was no chance of anyone approaching without her spotting them. Dad's flight would have landed almost three hours ago. He'd insisted on taking a taxi to the castello. That had to be it, making its way up the road now.

Just as she was turning away to go and meet him, she noticed two black-clad figures, a slim woman between them, making their halting way from the direction of Alessandra's farm. Both were wearing long skirts, and patterned scarves over their heads, tied under their chins. One was taller than the other. The smaller woman waited for her companion to get her breath, then the pair set off again. There was something both familiar and very determined about the two women. When they turned away from the village of Porciano, and approached the castello, she recognised them. It was Rosina, Alessandra and Margherita.

She ran downstairs and outside. They'd made good progress and were almost at the castello. Amelia hurried towards them.

Margherita looked at Amelia with bright eyes. 'Is he here yet?'

Amelia had been back to Vallucciole to let her know Dad was coming to Porciano. She ushered her visitors into the chairs under the chestnut tree.

'Nearly. A few minutes. But I was going to bring him to you.'

'Do you think I could wait even a minute longer to see my son?' Margherita said with a click of her tongue.

Amelia turned towards the other old lady. 'Hello, Rosina. I don't know if you remember but I came to the farm twice.' Margherita and Amelia had agreed between themselves that Margherita would be the one to tell her sister about Lazzero, Amelia's father. To her surprise and Margherita's obvious hurt and bafflement, it appeared that the two women had rarely met over the years. Rosina had been the one who'd refused to keep in touch.

Rosina squinted up at Amelia and waved her stick. It wasn't a threatening gesture, more like an extension of a pointed finger. 'Of course I remember you. There is nothing wrong with my memory. Why do all young people think that just because a person is old they are feeble in their head?'

Amelia loved that these two feisty old ladies were related to her.

'I thought you would come back again, but you never did,' Nonna Rosina continued. 'Toh! The young have no gumption. If I wanted to know something I wouldn't have let anyone put me off.'

'I didn't want to upset you. And neither did your son. Or Alessandra for that matter. They told me you hadn't been very well, and the doctor had said you weren't to get overexcited.'

'Basta! What is left for an old lady like me except a little excitement? Otherwise they might as well put me in the ground now.'

Amelia was astonished. She sounded nothing like the distraught old lady she'd met on both occasions. She exchanged an amused glance with Alessandra.

'When you get older you get more emotional,' Rosina continued. 'You'll find that out for yourself one day. But why people think it's wrong to cry...' She shook her head. 'They might as well say it is wrong to laugh, to love, to be happy – are these not all emotions too? And if we are not to feel them then what is the point of living? I may as well be an empty receptacle for someone to post food into my mouth.'

Recognising the little girl who'd stubbornly followed Flavia and Margherita everywhere, Amelia laughed.

A taxi pulled up, and Dad stepped out of the passenger door. He put his bag on the ground and looked at the old lady taking tentative steps towards him. Amelia hung back to allow him and Margherita a few moments. A myriad of emotions chased across his face, as Margherita came to a stop a couple of feet away from him. Alessandra hovered nearby.

'So I decided,' Rosina continued, speaking to Amelia, 'if you wouldn't come and see me, I would come and see you.'

'I'm glad you did.' Amelia's eyes were still fixed on Margherita and Dad. She didn't know who made the first move, but suddenly Dad was holding Margherita in his arms and they were both crying. Tears stung behind her lids as she turned away to give them some privacy.

'I need to confess something. I am to blame for what happened,' Rosina said, clutching Amelia's sleeve. 'I told Roberto about Luca and Flavia when we saw him at Vallucciole during the war. Mama wasn't happy to see him there. They had a terrible argument about him being a Blackshirt, and Mama said the shame of it was why we had left the farmhouse to stay with her sister. I didn't understand why everyone was so angry with him. He was a good brother to me when I was a little girl. I bragged to him that I knew something he didn't. I'd seen Luca with Flavia the last time we'd visited. I saw his expression when he looked at her and her face when she looked at him.' Her mouth trembled as tears slid down her cheeks. 'I think Roberto told the Blackshirt major, and they came up with the plan to lure Flavia to Vallucciole – which in turn would lure Luca.' She swallowed hard. 'So you see it was my fault they burned Vallucciole to the ground – killed all those people, including my niece!' She looked over at her sister, still in the arms of her son. 'I could barely look at Margherita – let alone be the sister to her I should have been.'

Amelia's heart broke for her. How could Rosina have thought she was in any way responsible, for all these years?

'Oh, Rosina. It wasn't your fault! It was retribution for the soldiers the partisans killed.' But could there be a smidgen of truth in what she said? Would Vincenzo have killed Flavia had he not known about Luca? Was Rosina right about the plan to lure Flavia and Luca to the village? They'd never know for sure. Besides, at the last moment Roberto had tried to redeem himself. 'Roberto did ask Flavia to warn your sister. *And*, he tried to shield Margherita from Major Lambini. By doing so he likely saved her life. If he hadn't been there, she'd be dead. You are not responsible. No one is to blame for another's evil deeds.'

Whether Rosina believed her or not, Amelia hoped that one day she'd forgive herself. Like Amelia, she had to find her own way to learn how.

Amelia turned at the sound of the taxi pulling away. She sucked in a breath. In front of her, looking pale and uncharacteristically nervous, was Cameron.

As Amelia's husband stepped towards her, the world shrank until there was just the two of them.

'I came as soon as I got your email,' he said, his voice hoarse as if he hadn't used it for a long time.

He looked different to when she'd last seen him. His thick hair was clean, and he'd shaved. His once-dull eyes were bright, although Amelia could see sadness still lurked there.

'It's good to see you,' Amelia said. Her heart felt too big for her chest. 'I didn't know if you'd come.'

'Christ, Amelia, I would have walked here if it meant seeing you again.' He took another tentative step towards her. 'I know I put you through hell. I've given up alcohol, and I've been dealing with my guilt and my pain. Do you think you could forgive me? I'll wait – forever – if that what it takes.'

Amelia's throat tightened the way it always did when she was trying not to cry. 'If you can forgive me.'

She held out her hand and her husband folded her into his arms. They clung to each other as they sobbed. It would take time – and courage – but she knew they'd find their way back to each other.

That night, as everyone slept, Amelia went up to the ramparts for the last time. Once she had brought Beatrice up to date – she hoped the contessa wouldn't be too upset about Amelia poking around in her family's past – Amelia, Cameron and Dad were going to stay with Margherita in Vallucciole for a few days. Maybe longer.

The night air was balmy, the sky studded with stars, the moon a perfect orb in the inky sky.

She waited, hoping she would come one last time.

She closed her eyes until she heard the rustle of silk and her low laughter. Her perfume drifted in the still air. She was not alone. Luca was with her, and they were dancing. His chin rested on the top of her head, and Flavia's face was turned into his chest. Suddenly Flavia spun around until her back was against him. He wrapped his arms around her, his hands resting on her stomach. Flavia looked straight at Amelia, smiled and gave a small nod. Then two small figures, two little girls, appeared at their side. Flavia pulled them towards her, drawing them into the embrace so there were now four figures instead of two. Whatever people might think, Amelia wasn't crazy. She saw Flavia, Luca, Margherita's daughter, young Flavia, and Fiona as clearly as her own reflection.

Finally ready to say goodbye, she reached out to her child one last time.

EPILOGUE

One year later

Amelia stood at the window, Cameron's arms wrapped around her as they watched the storm from the sitting room of their cottage down by the harbour.

As the rain splattered on the panes, her thoughts turned to Porciano.

The document Flavia had found wasn't ultimately part of the original *Inferno*, but it was believed to have been written by Dante. It was too valuable to be kept safely at the castello, but a copy would be part of the display, and the mere fact of its existence was bound to draw more visitors to Porciano and the rest of the Casentino valley.

Benedetto's brother Fabio had publicly admitted and denounced his father's part in the massacre at Vallucciole. It had caused a bit of a stir, which had soon died down. It seemed people were happy to leave the past alone.

A wail roused her from her reverie, and she turned as Cameron crossed to the cot and picked up their baby. Little Flavia.

Holding their tiny daughter in one arm, he placed the other

around Amelia's shoulder. Amelia looked at her daughter, feeling the familiar surge of love. Flavia wasn't Fiona, would never be anyone but herself, and that was the way it should be. But if she'd inherited her namesake's courage and her dead sister's joy, Amelia would never ask for more.

A LETTER FROM THE AUTHOR

Huge thanks for reading *Valley of the Fireflies* – I hope you were hooked on Flavia and Amelia's journeys. If you want to join other readers in hearing all about my new releases and bonus content, you can sign up for my newsletter.

www.stormpublishing.co/emma-fraser

If you enjoyed this book and could spare a few moments to leave a review, that would be hugely appreciated. Even a short review can make all the difference in encouraging a reader to discover my books for the first time. Thank you so much.

I was staying in the Casentino valley, tutoring at a writing retreat, when I first visited the Castello di Porciano and met its then-owner, Martha Specht Corsi, known locally as 'the contessa', whose ancestors had been a prominent family in the valley since the eleventh century. Dante was a guest at the castello during his banishment from Florence. The whole region is steeped in history.

We got on so well, I returned as Martha's guest on several occasions. During one of those visits my hostess took me to the (almost) deserted village of Vallucciole, where I learned about the massacre. Like my character, Amelia, the village and the story haunted me – particularly when I realised that one of the houses was still occupied. Who, I wondered, could bear to live among the ruins of the homes once belonging to the Nazi's victims? And so the idea for *Valley of the Fireflies* was born.

Thanks again for being part of this amazing journey with me

and I hope you'll stay in touch – I have so many more stories and ideas to entertain you with!

Emma Fraser

ACKNOWLEDGMENTS

Thanks to the wonderful Martha Specht Corsi on whose family history much of this book relies. A gracious hostess, a fount of knowledge about Tuscany, and whose abiding love and knowledge of the land of her ancestors helped make this book possible. Thanks also to Luca Grisolini whose dissertation on the atrocities carried out by German troops in eleven villages in the Casentino, of which Vallucciole was the worst, ensured I had documented facts to reference.

The orphanage at Villa Bencista is based on Iris Origo's diary, *The War in Val d'Orcia, An Italian War Diary 1943–1944*, now a book published by Pushkin Press.

Finally, I should mention Catherine, on whom my character Kelly is based, for allowing me to cast her in the role of the villain when nothing could be further from the truth. Thanks, too, for having me and Martha over for those six o'clock gins and tonic.

Printed in Dunstable, United Kingdom

82019694R00211